RULES

A plan quickly formed as Adam remembered Raleigh's reaction to their embrace. In their kiss, he tasted passion, forgotten chemistry, and her alarm at the loss of control. He felt her tremble as he kissed her hand in the moonlight. And today, when he moved too close, he witnessed the mixture of fascination and trepidation. If insults didn't chase her away, perhaps fear of his touch would.

Adam turned from the window to find her standing a few feet away from him. "Lovers, Raleigh?" Adam took a deliberate step toward her and studied her intently. "Is that the plan?" Her eyes widened a fraction before they narrowed in suspicion. He reached out and tilted her chin, angling her face toward his own. A small smile played on the corners of his mouth as he slowly stroked the perfect oval of her face. He felt her pulse quicken and waited patiently for her reply. *Yes,* he thought, *this will work.* "Lovers?"

"Yes." Raleigh forced the words out calmly, cursing her own unwelcome reaction to his nearness, his touch. Her breath backed up in her lungs. Had he always pulled her like this?

BOOK YOUR PLACE ON OUR WEBSITE AND MAKE THE ARABESQUE ROMANCE CONNECTION!

We've created a customized website just for our very special Arabesque readers, where you can get the inside scoop on everything that's going on with Arabesque romance novels.

When you come online, you'll have the exciting opportunity to:

- View covers of upcoming books
- Learn about our future publishing schedule (listed by publication month and author)
- Find out when your favorite authors will be visiting a city near you
- Search for and order backlist books
- Check out author bios and background information
- Send e-mail to your favorite authors
- Join us in weekly chats with authors, readers and other guests
- Get writing guidelines
- AND MUCH MORE!

Visit our website at
http://www.arabesquebooks.com

RULES OF ENGAGEMENT

Selena Montgomery

BET Publications, LLC
www.bet.com
www.arabesquebooks.com

ARABESQUE BOOKS are published by

BET Publications, LLC
c/o BET BOOKS
One BET Plaza
1900 W Place NE
Washington, D.C. 20018-1211

Copyright © 2001 by Stacey Y. Abrams

All rights reserved. No part of this book may be reproduced, stored in a retrieval system, or transmitted in any form or by any means without the prior written consent of the Publisher.

If you purchased this book without a cover you should be aware that this book is stolen property. It was reported as "unsold and destroyed" to the Publisher and neither the Author nor the Publisher has received any payment for this "stripped book."

All Kensington Titles, Imprints, and Distributed Lines are available at special quantity discounts for bulk purchases for sales promotions, premiums, fund-raising, and educational or institutional use. Special book excerpts or customized printings can also be created to fit specific needs. For details, write or phone the office of the Kensington special sales manager: Kensington Publishing Corp., 850 Third Avenue, New York, NY 10022, attn: Special Sales Department, Phone: 1-800-221-2647.

BET Books is a trademark of Black Entertainment Television, Inc. ARABESQUE, the ARABESQUE logo and the BET BOOKS logo are trademarks and registered trademarks.

First Printing: May 2001
10 9 8 7 6 5 4 3 2 1

Printed in the United States of America

ACKNOWLEDGMENTS

With love and eternal gratitude to Mom and Dad, Andrea, Leslie, Richard, Walter, and Jeanine. Special thanks to Leslie, my first editor; Karen and Tomasita, my Arabesque editors; and the friends who kept my secret.

Prologue

The explosion registered a few hours later. It was only then that the blood caked to the arm of the jacket began to chip and fall to the hard, uneven ground. It was only then that the numbness, the blessed mindlessness, wore off—leaving behind searing, tearing pain. Teeth, clenched against the agony, began to knock against one another. And the memories returned with a vengeance.

Behind her tightly closed eyes, she relived the moment the ball of amber flame hurtled toward her body as she tumbled down the slope—her final act of betrayal. Minutes before, she had run from behind the empty shop stalls, the scents of jasmine and dates and horses fading with the dying sunlight, replaced by the acrid stench of gunfire. She heard the staccato report of guns, saw Cavanaugh's body fall behind a row of wine barrels left by a weary shopkeeper. Once again, the black-robed bodies in the vehicle turned their deadly weapons away from him and aimed at her. She reached for her belt, searching for the small explosive, running toward the hill's edge, to him. Her hand circled the disc of plastique, pressed the release, and pitched it under the Jeep. The driver shouted to his comrades and fired one last round. A bullet ripped through her shoulder, and she lost her balance, stumbling against an empty trough. The Jeep exploded, and shrapnel rained down on the abandoned hilltop marketplace as she dragged herself to Cavanaugh's body. Dismissing her shoulder, she crawled over him, protecting his face and wounded belly from the flying debris. With her uninjured arm, she reached for his face, turning it to hers.

"Jericho? Cavanaugh? Speak to me, please," she begged, her voice harsh, ravaged by smoke and panic.

Cavanaugh's glazed eyes stared past her. "Prax—. Merlin. Is target."

"Cavanaugh, get up. We've got to get to base camp." She looked over her shoulder at the wreckage, and seeing no movement, began to slowly shift away. Cavanaugh's hand gripped her forearm, halting her careful retreat. Blue eyes blazed into brown ones.

"No. Time. Praxis. Merlin. Sphinx gone Lazarus"—wracking coughs interrupted his labored words—"Merlin. Next."

She struggled against his hand, surprised by its strength. "Cavanaugh, we've got to get you to shelter." *Please, don't die on me. Please. Not again.*

"No time. Listen. Chimera"—Cavanaugh paused, fighting for air—"Go now. Tell Atlas. Need Merlin. Sphinx gone Lazarus. Praxis going to Scimitar. Four weeks. Go!"

"I'm not leaving you. Their reinforcements will come soon to collect the dead. I won't leave you here." *I shouldn't have left you alone. This is my fault. My fault.*

He glared at her, forcing her eyes to his own. "Go now. Tell Atlas."

"No. I can't leave you here." *He made me run away, made me let him die.* "I'll help you up." She slid her uninjured arm under his head and tried vainly to lever him to his feet.

"Damn you, go!" Cavanaugh twisted away, his face turned toward the gathering sunset. The blazing orange and dusky mauve of the fading day intensified in the glare of the incinerated Jeep and the burning stalls.

"No. Not without you." *Not again. I won't run again. Ever.* Again, she attempted to gather him in her arms, panting as pain lanced through her torn shoulder.

Cavanaugh groaned, tears streaming down his weathered face. "Go on. You can't save me."

She hushed him. "Shh. You're not going to die."

"I *am* dead. We both know it." He coughed, his body shaking. "Let it go."

"I can't. Not again. And I won't leave you behind."

"Do your job, Chimera. I taught you better." Cavanaugh stared at her, his eyes fierce. "Move!" he shouted as he contorted suddenly and shoved her down the slope. A few seconds later, a second explosion filled the air behind her as he detonated his own fatal disc.

So the explosion registered again and again, and consciousness returned in a rush. Unsure of how much time had passed, she scrambled off the rocky shelf where she'd landed after Cavanaugh pushed her. Her legs protested as the blood struggled to circulate again. She cradled her injured arm and slid down the hillside to the small cliff leading to the cave where they had stored their gear.

Disregarding her useless, painful arm, she shoved aside the green, prickly brush that hid the cave's entrance. Base camp, a cave they had discovered only six days before, was a recess on the side of one of the many hills of Jafir. No more than seven feet tall and only a few feet wider, the cave served as a hiding place for spiders and less friendly animals. She dragged herself inside, replaced the camouflaging bushes, and flicked on the portable lamp they'd suspended near the entrance. She moved to the dark packs leaning against the far wall.

She rummaged through the first pack, found the medical kit, and opened the box. Clutching a brown bottle labeled DISINFECTANT, she flipped open the lid and poured the liquid directly into the wound on her shoulder. Chimera doused the torn shoulder again, pouring liquid along first one scratched arm and then the other, to kill whatever may have come with her on her tumble down the hill.

Fighting the nausea that threatened to overtake her, she covered the flesh wound with a bandage, securing the adhesive. After probing her head for cuts and finding none, she placed the base of a syringe between her strong, white teeth, uncapped the hypodermic with her free hand, then plunged the needle into her injured arm. As the miracle mixture of hydrocodone, vitamin boosters, and antibiotics coursed through her veins, she pulled a palm-sized communicator from the second pack.

"Chimera to Atlas. Chimera to Atlas. Over."

"Atlas here. Status." A disembodied voice filled the room, urgency masked only by training.

"Jericho terminated." Chimera's voice emerged flat, unemotional.

"Repeat transmission." The voice barked out the command.

"Jericho terminated," came the quiet reply.

"Remains?"

"Self-destruction, as ordered."

"Verified?"

"Verified."

"Chimera status and E.T.A."

"Chimera temporarily down. E.T.A. six hours. Metacure." On the other end, Atlas noted that Chimera had been injured but had initiated the medical protocol. Chimera paused, fighting the drug and the guilt. "Jericho transmitted."

"Transmission imperative?"

"Imperative."

"Relay."

"Sphinx gone Lazarus. Merlin next target. Praxis alive. Four weeks."

"Copy. Rendezvous at Eagle Point in six hours."

"Roger. Chimera out." And for the second time that day, she slipped into unconsciousness.

One

The oversized, pentagon-shaped dining room rang with the sound of laughter, banter, deal-making, and soft jazz. Dozens of politicians, journalists, executives, artists, and others circled the room, moving from conversation to conversation, foraging for new information, better entertainment. The denizens of Atlanta's high society mingled with aspirants and sycophants. Near the doorway, a young man stood ready to take coats, keys, and handbags. Framed by beveled French windows along the far wall in the corner, a jazz quartet played, allowing the music to spill onto the terrace and into the adjoining ballroom. A bar lined two of the five walls, flanked by brimming buffet tables on either side. Waiters darted between knots of attendees, bearing trays and taking drink orders.

Raleigh stood on the edge of the crowd, listening with half an ear to the exploits of Judge Russell in his younger, more mobile days. She shifted again to find her quarry, unaware of the attention focused on her by men and women alike. Raleigh wore a black, raw-silk gown that skimmed rich, coffee skin. The evening dress was suspended by narrow straps at her shoulders and fell to her ankles, and the bodice was high above her breasts but plunged to her waist in the back. A slit in the side gave admirers a glimpse of a long, slender leg as she shifted to allow a lawyer to leave their party. Her toned, muscled arms were unadorned, as was the rest of her, save the diamonds that winked at her ears. She lifted her glass toward full lips tinted with sheer color, curved into a polite, almost genuine, smile.

Raleigh nodded absently to the judge, acknowledging his compliment on her gown or shoes or something, her own gaze and attention fastened on the man holding court in the center of the room. Adam Grayson was tall—six three, she knew, and well built, lean rather than bulky, his runner's body admirably filling the black tuxedo. His burnished bronze skin was taut, the handsome features chiseled and distinct, accented by sharp cheekbones and a firmly molded mouth. Broad shoulders tapered into strong, wide hands. As he angled toward Elizabeth Walton, their hostess, his head lifted and his gaze caught hers. Raleigh arrogantly thought she had prepared herself for this moment, yet she fought back a gasp as their eyes made contact.

Amber eyes dueled with midnight black for supremacy, an engagement of complicated, primal desires and instinctive, visceral resistance. Refusing to yield to the jagged need flooding her system, Raleigh returned his gaze steadily, her chin tilting in recognition of the battle. Only he noticed her fingers tightening on the glass. With a slow, almost courtly nod, he returned his attention to his entourage. Tearing her eyes away, Raleigh tried to ignore the heat that arced through her. He didn't recognize her. The stab of regret at this knowledge mortified her. She was a woman who cultivated detachment and immunity to male charms, especially this man's. If he didn't remember her, she could still salvage her mission. She could walk away right now and have a waiter deliver the message. In a few minutes, she would be on her way home, pride intact, while he dealt with the consequences.

Yet, she lingered in the room, listening with only half an ear to a playwright's anecdote. For too long, she had pretended the past was truly past. But one moment, one look, and the memories became frighteningly real.

He could lure her with a look, weaken her with a smile. She sipped from her glass and ruthlessly ignored her attraction to him, because protocol demanded it. Desire wasn't a part of tonight's mission or the master plan for her life. She knew better than most that it could lure, then maim, its most ardent followers.

Three years ago, she'd forgotten the rules, and she'd lost everything. She'd regained her freedom and learned to live without the rest. Raleigh smothered an impotent sigh. Whether he recognized her or not, Adam hated her now and would despise her even more when this was over. No matter how her heart thudded when their eyes met, she couldn't afford to forget it. Once again, she gave her attention to the judge, her peripheral gaze and sixth sense furnishing a full and constant account of his movements. She started this, and she would finish it.

The group around Raleigh and the judge thinned, leaving the two alone for a moment. "Judge, it's so wonderful to see you out and about. Liz thought you would be in that cast for weeks yet." Dragging herself fully into the present, Raleigh grinned happily at the maturing adventure-seeker who was also a justice for the Eleventh Circuit. Judge Kenneth Warner was an attractive widower in his late sixties, his chocolate brown skin showing little sign of aging. A stalwart of the Civil Rights era, his legendary victories for people of color and women as well as the poor had propelled him to the court by the age of forty and to the chief justice spot by fifty-two.

"Nothing short of amputation can keep me down." Kenneth Warner laughed his practiced, devil-may-care laugh and wondered what distracted Raleigh. One of the pleasures of Raleigh's company was her seemingly absolute absorption with whomever she was with. "Liz tells me you're in town for a few weeks this time."

He gallantly took her arm, steering Raleigh toward the crowd and the bar, hoping to catch a glimpse of whomever had captured her attention so fully, and equally intent on capturing a real drink of his own to replace the tepid Coke Liz had forced on him earlier. "We never see enough of you, dear. What with your isolation in that dismal government lab, you hardly come up for air. Overworked and underpaid, no doubt." He moved closer to the bar, a small smile growing with the thought of a gin and tonic, a forbidden pleasure these days. But tonight he felt young and able to handle the kick, despite his doctor's warnings about his blood pressure and liver.

"Casting aspersions on your employer, Judge? I'm shocked." Raleigh twisted lightly to turn them away from the throng and the bartender, well aware of the physician-prescribed moratorium on alcohol. "And I am neither overworked nor underpaid."

Judge Warner noted her maneuver and tried to

turn her again, hoping to circle around and approach the bar from behind.

Raleigh continued, enjoying their silent game of keep-away. He couldn't possibly know how good she was at it and that she never lost. "I simply harbor a deep and abiding distaste for socializing, unless I can be in your company," she flirted, then signaled a waiter. As the young woman appeared at her side, she stage-whispered her order. "Another glass of mineral water and a virgin gin and tonic for the Judge. He seems to be thirsty."

Judge Warner strangled a laugh and tried to sound gruff, knowing he had been well and truly checkmated. "Liz Walton talks too much. I'm a grown man, and I can drink what I please," he growled.

"I adore you entirely too much to let anything happen to you." She pressed a warm kiss to his cheek. "And that includes the quiches on the buffet table as well." As the Judge muttered something about busybodies and young women too big for their britches, Raleigh scanned the room again for her prey.

Adam threw his head back and laughed at A.J.'s quip about the rigors of socializing. His young cousin had cajoled him into attending Liz Walton's annual fete, and she had been holding him close since they'd entered the room, as though curbing his unspoken urge to bolt. At twenty-two, A.J. had spent yet another summer working her way steadily up the corporate ladder at GCI, ignoring his parents' attempts to install her in the upper management offices from the outset. She had joined the family at the age of nine, after the sudden death of her parents in a train accident. To Adam, she was his sister, regardless of her biological parentage, and his family felt the same way. But A.J. resisted her hereditary access to power and insisted on proving herself. Yet despite her more modest beginnings, A.J. was as much a Grayson as he was. She knew who to acknowledge and who to pamper, trained by a childhood in the public eye. She knew, as much as he, that Liz Walton's soiree was a must-attend, and she'd pulled the short straw. Liz's personal fortune and razor-sharp political sensibilities guaranteed her an excellent turnout to her soirées and the various committees she chaired throughout the city.

Adam resisted attending the dinner party for as long as possible, chafing at the thought of spending another three-hour stint listening to the gossip and innuendo surrounding life in the New South. Atlanta was his home, but he understood the city's foibles well. Hours of conversations about the next mayoral election, the demise of downtown, and the best golf courses awaited him.

Adam, however, knew duty outweighed any reticence on his part, and attendance might help him assuage the blame that haunted him daily. He owed his family for their easy acceptance of his withdrawal from the spotlight three years ago, and if this was what they wanted, they would have it, despite his reluctance. A reluctance that was quickly fading away. The woman standing with Judge Warner had been watching him surreptitiously for an hour now. Their silent exchange admitted as much, and more besides. She fascinated him as nothing had in years. Part of his interest stemmed from the odd sense that he'd seen her somewhere before. Then there was the alchemy of desire, the electric kind that scorched nerve endings and promised pleasure. Adam read promise in heavy-lidded eyes, and he would discover if she could fulfill this vow.

Bending to A.J., he murmured, "A.J., who is the woman speaking to Judge Warner? I think I've met her, but I can't recall where."

A.J. narrowed her eyes at the unusual question but answered quietly, "I don't know exactly. Liz told me she was a special guest of hers, and a friend of Alex's. Her name is Dr. Raleigh Foster, a chemist by trade. That's all the information I could milk out of Liz. Of course, her ability to keep a secret makes her the perfect city council president. She says no more than absolutely necessary, and she makes it seem as though she's spilling classified information. Why?" She cast a speculative glance at her perennially bored cousin.

"Curiosity."

"Curiosity killed the cat, Adam."

"Satisfaction brought him back, A.J." Adam kissed her smooth cheek and whispered conspiratorially, "Don't wait up."

A.J.'s speculative look went unseen as Adam made his way toward the woman. She shook her head wryly. Adam Grayson rarely made public appearances not of his own design anymore, and only at those on behalf of the family business, Grayson Conglomerate International, which owned and subsidized various holdings around the globe. From microchips to romance novels, GCI loomed as a force to be reckoned with and watched closely. And no one should be watched more closely than its billionaire leader, Adam Grayson.

Adam had assumed control of the financial empire at age thirty-one after his parents decided to move from capitalism into philanthropy. Before their surprising retirement, Adam's habit of disappearing for months at a time, without more than the briefest of warnings, had irritated and worried his friends and company insiders. For almost a decade, Adam shunned the corporate world and lived a secret life. Not even A.J. had been able to pry out the secret of those missing years. But when his parents stepped down, Adam abruptly abandoned his peripatetic lifestyle and settled into the work. Now, three years later, Adam's position as CEO remained undisputed. Even the staunchest rival admitted Adam's financial wizardry and the almost uncanny acumen with which he developed his companies.

A.J.'s eyes darkened as she thought about the way he buried himself in balance sheets and financial reports. The only explanation for Adam's retreat from the world was that his best friend, Phillip Turman, had died a mysterious death while on a Congressional fact finding mission. After Phillip's death, Adam became a recluse, refusing to share his mourning with her or anyone, only venturing out when she wheedled him into acting as her escort.

A.J. watched him approach Dr. Foster, pleased by the unusual display of interest on Adam's part. Although he'd dated frequently throughout high school and college, his relationships had been short-lived lately, killed by disquiet on his part. Besides, Adam rarely approached women because they always seemed to find him, drawn by brooding good looks and the aura of power and danger that surrounded him. A.J. observed approvingly as Adam spoke to Raleigh. With any luck, tonight she'd be able to report to her aunt and uncle that their eldest was showing new signs of life.

A.J. watched as Adam took the young woman's hand and lifted it to his lips. Raleigh inclined her head toward him, no smile touching her striking face. She accepted Adam's arm, and together they made their way toward the dance floor in the adjoining room. As they disappeared behind the door, A.J. smiled knowingly and shook her head. Adam was a big boy. He could handle himself.

Adam stared down at the woman in his arms, puzzled by a nagging sense of recognition. He couldn't recall having met her before, but she seemed oddly familiar. Sharp cheekbones led to slightly tilted, intelligent eyes. A high forehead, strong nose, and a stubborn chin completed the face, framed by a gamine cap of black curls. Each feature seemed too distinct to be placed together, yet the combination mesmerized him. Tall as well, her body brushed against him, giving him a sense of high, full breasts and a generously curved and athletically fit body. She had the build of a dancer, not of ballet but of a sensuous and intricate dance like the tango or samba. He could see her on stage, luring her partner with come-hither looks and undulating hips. His gut twisted at the vivid image, assailed by an unfamiliar need.

Certainly, he'd been attracted to women before tonight. Indeed, he harbored a healthy appreciation for and enchantment with the opposite sex, despite his sporadic dating habits. With two younger sisters and a formidable mother, he'd learned to value women and to venerate those who'd taken control of their worlds. But more essentially, he liked women, any and all. Still, this connection to the woman in his arms disturbed him as nothing had in years. Her scent, something not quite spicy, not quite floral, drifted between them, teasing him. His arms tightened as a shaft of desire shot through him. With effort, he controlled the primitive urge to haul her against him and ravage her softly painted mouth. Hell, he didn't even know what her voice sounded like. When he'd asked her to dance, she had nodded her acceptance, and neither had spoken during the first two songs. He needed to hear her voice, he realized, taken aback by the intensity of his longing to hear her speak his name.

Adam Grayson rarely ignored impulses—preferring instead to choose how those urges were satisfied. He understood intimately the balance of instinct and control. Tonight, he would indulge one and not lose the other.

Executing several graceful turns, he navigated Raleigh out of the French doors, onto the terrace, and beyond the press of the guests. Surrounded by the sultry air of a September night in Atlanta, he reluctantly released her and stepped away, his arm still lightly circling her waist.

"Allow me to introduce myself. Adam—"

"Grayson." Raleigh finished. "President and CEO of GCI, an international concern that grosses billions every year. The wealthiest African-American in the world and arguably one of the wealthiest people altogether. You are described as unorthodox, excruciatingly private, and brilliant. The son of M.G. Grayson and Carolyn Sanders Grayson, you are the first of four children—Adam, Rachel, Jonah, and A.J., your cousin. You recently returned from Tanzania and London and would rather be anywhere than here, tonight." She looked up at him with cool amber eyes. The color was clear and unusual and doing uncomfortable things to his nervous system. "How did I do?"

"Not bad." During her recitation, he had led them further away from the doors. Now he moved them into the dimly lit garden that lay just beyond the terrace. Adam flexed his hand against her waist, stopping them. "Should I be flattered?"

"Flattery is the least of my intentions," she said, her contralto voice as imperturbable as the eyes watching him, reading him. It was exactly the voice he'd hoped for, a voice he remembered or had woven in his dreams.

"Well, most women don't go through my dossier on first acquaintance. They tend to prefer the illusion of ignorance. Of course, most don't spend the greater part of the night watching me." Wary now, he studied her expression, seeking a hint of her intentions. Was she simply another social climber who wanted to latch on to him? Normally, he would assume so and move on immediately. But her connection to Elizabeth Walton and that growing sense of familiarity gave him pause. Something wasn't quite right. Adam enjoyed puzzles and savored the thought of solving this one. He would play this out at his most urbane and see where it ended.

"Ignorance is a dangerous habit." Her eyes still held his. "It can get you killed if you're not careful."

Adam tightened his grip on her waist and moved her off the garden path. His pulse quickened precipitously as his arm brushed the velvet flesh left bare at her back. He thought he felt Raleigh shiver in response, and he smiled to himself. Despite her cool recitation, she wasn't unaffected. "Advice or a warning?"

"Neither. Just an observation," she baited.

Observation? He heard the veiled threat in her husky, mellow voice. What kind of game was she playing? "You haven't introduced yourself yet." Adam flexed his hand again, testing the resilience of her waist and his own restraint. This time her shiver of response was unmistakable.

"No, I haven't." She stepped away from him, breaking his hold on her waist. "My name is Raleigh Foster." Raleigh searched his face, as though looking for a sign of recognition. Why should he know her?

"A pleasure to meet you, Dr. Foster." At her quizzical look at the use of her title, he continued. "A.J. said you were a chemist."

"So you've asked about me. And I've been wanting to meet you."

"Good, because the feeling is mutual." Adam reached for her hand and lifted it to his lips. Her slim brown fingers were bare, the nails short and rounded. Dr. Foster possessed the hands of an artist, not a scientist. "So, now what?"

"I'm here to help you." She tugged her hand from his grasp, and he decided to let her go. For now. "If you want to keep your company, that is."

His company? His voice lost the silky, charming tone, quickly replaced by thinly veiled loathing. "Is that what this is about? Blackmail? Industrial espionage? Not very original, Dr. Foster, although most of your kind are not quite so brazen. Or stupid." His hand shot out, catching her wrist. Like the rest of her, the bones were thin but not fragile. "How much do you want?"

"I don't want your money. I came to deliver a message about your company. It's very important." Coal-black eyes raked over her, and the hand around her wrist tightened. She refused to tug it away, to balk at the obvious intimidation.

"A message? About my company? Why? Do you work for me?" Raleigh saw bewilderment in his eyes, a vain attempt to place her. Distrust layered the confusion, and just beneath it lay a darker appetite, a hunger she dared not identify.

"No, I don't work for you. But I have come into information that is quite important to the health of your company." Raleigh moved her hand experimentally, testing the strength of his hold, trying to ignore the warmth of his slightly work-roughened hands on her skin. She once again felt his body brushing against her as they began dancing again, the strength of his arms wrapped around her.

"So what is it? What do you need to tell me?" His rich baritone purred over the words. "What do you want?" Adam stepped closer, until only a breath separated them. Despite his annoyance, he could feel his blood heat.

Raleigh held herself still, refusing to react to the blatant sexuality of his last question, knowing it would vanish in just a moment. She focused instead on the note of suspicion.

"I'll tell you, but I need something in return." Raleigh stared at him, measuring his reaction.

"What do you need?" Adam returned her gaze, unblinking.

"You."

He tossed his head back and laughed, the sound hard, dismissive, and erotic. "How novel, Ms. Foster. Using my company to get to me? A bit more forward than I'm used to, but I accept."

Anger yielded to arousal and he bent his head swiftly, her lush mouth captured beneath his hungry lips. Raleigh parted her mouth in a surprised gasp, and he quickly claimed the open territory. As he toyed with her bottom lip, teasing the tender flesh with his teeth, Adam thought only to punish her for seeming to be more, somehow. But the first taste of her raged through him, potent and drugging, obliterating intent, leaving only compulsion. Transfixed, he plunged into the recesses of her mouth, searching for an antidote to his craving. His hands raced up her back, gliding over silken flesh left exposed by the drape of the dress. While he pulled her closer, one hand threaded through tight curls, angling her head for his mouth's next foray. He eased up on the kiss, searching for yielding, for answers.

Compelled by exotic, alien urges, Raleigh could feel her arms moving, raising to encircle his neck, pressing her more firmly against him. She could not remember why this was wrong, only that she needed his mouth here, his hands there, now. The experience of him against her, holding her, was unbearably arousing. Unwilling to cede control to him, she molded her mouth to his, changing the slow, seductive rhythm of the kiss to fast and hungry. Only speed and energy would eradicate the possibility of thought, the need for resistance.

As Raleigh strained upward, her movements forced his hands lower, to where the dress closed just below her waist, and his hard fingers traced the new textures, igniting fires along her skin. Then his hands dropped further below. Raleigh shuddered, breath moaning past lips swollen from passion. Adam's mouth streaked across her cheek, down her throat, to the hollow where her pulse beat madly.

Her fingers burrowed into his hair, holding him against her skin, keeping reality at bay for a moment longer.

Adam nibbled along her collarbone as his hands roamed her skin, refusing to miss a single inch, a possible touch. He brushed his mouth against the perfumed flesh that rose to meet his touch. He had to touch her again, there. And taste her mouth, now. Recapturing her lips, he took them both deeper.

Raleigh inhaled sharply, speared by pleasure as his hand closed around her breast. One more moment, one more touch, and she'd forget everything, forgive anything. One more moment . . . She stiffened against him as awareness coursed through her, appalled by her behavior. Raleigh struggled against him, but Adam tightened his hold, unaware of her distress. For a moment, she surrendered, dragged under by the waves of untutored want. *One more moment,* she thought hazily as his hand covered her breast, plucking at the taut peak. He swallowed her gasp of stunned pleasure. Alarmed by the heat that suffused her body at his touch, Raleigh panicked.

"Damn!" Adam jerked his head back, his mouth covered by his hand. "You bit me!"

Fighting for breath, Raleigh muttered, "You deserved it." She stepped back quickly, out of reach. She fought to keep her hands at her sides, to keep herself from reaching for him. "I didn't mean that type of proposition." She gamely ignored her too-fast heartbeat, concentrating instead on controlling her unsteady breathing. "I meant a way to save your company."

"You were there with me every moment, Raleigh." Adam accused, his voice still thick with arousal. When she did not reply, he said, "But we'll do this your way, for now. Who are you?" Adam advanced toward her, pleased to see her retreat even further, backing into one of the magnolia trees that lined the path. "Why would I need you to save my company?"

"Because I'm the best." *Remember your role, Raleigh,* she thought, overcoming the urge to move into his arms.

"The best at what? What kind of game are you playing?"

"Mr. Grayson, I'm not playing at all. I offered you a proposition, not an invitation." Raleigh replied, confidence reasserting itself as her pulse slowed.

"Then what is your proposal? Do you have a product to offer as a panacea to an unknown ill facing GCI? If so, my cousin A.J. handles research and development for our company." Adam regained his equilibrium and brought both the anger and desire under control. To test her, to test himself, he stepped forward and plucked her hand from her side. He carried it to his lips, pressing his open mouth to the palm, mocking his earlier gesture. Adam noted with pleasure how her fingers jerked in response. "I'll tell her to expect you." With a derisive smile, he dropped her hand, sketched a bow, and turned to walk away. "Good night, Dr. Foster. It has certainly been . . . provocative."

"Adam, wait." The sound of his name halted his steps, but he did not turn around.

"Yes?"

"Mr. Grayson—" Raleigh hesitated, unsure of her next move.

At the return of his surname, he spun on his heel to face her, his look thoughtful. "Are we back to that? Adam is fine."

"Mr. Grayson," she said firmly, "I don't want your

money or your recommendation." She paused to gauge her affect. "I want you."

"My dear Dr. Foster, I believe we just covered this territory. By my recollection, it was dangerous ground." Adam lifted a hand to rest lightly on his injured lip.

Raleigh flushed but did not demur. Her eyes searched his again and she nodded, as if reaching a satisfactory conclusion. "You really don't recognize me, do you?"

"No. Should I?" His eyes narrowed on her face, not certain what he was supposed to see. Then images flashed in his mind, and he stared at her, stunned into rigidity. She was thinner than his memories, angles where curves once lay, longer hair, sharper features, and a huskier voice. In his mind, he heard a burst of gunfire, the shrill of metal torn away from its moorings. Astonishment ebbed, washed away by a surge of impotence and hatred that threatened to crush him. "Chimera?" His tone went flat over the question.

"Hello, Merlin," she responded, her voice carefully controlled. She braced for the explosion. "Long time, no see."

"What the hell are you doing here?" Adam held himself motionless, his voice the only signal of the rage and pain battering his control. And the guilt, the burning acid of guilt. "You're dead."

"Not quite." She paused, steeling herself to plunge the knife. "My partner saved me." And then the twist, the final act. "Poor Phillip."

With those words, the floodgates broke, submerging him in memories long held at bay.

Two

Phillip Turman, his best friend. The man he considered his other brother. The man who knew his secrets and his dreams. The man he left to die in Jafir. Was it only three years ago that he'd sacrificed friendship for duty? Only three years ago when he wasn't CEO but a special agent who dealt in gold, computers, and treachery?

Adam recalled first contact with the ISA, a not-so-chance meeting at Carla's, a dark, crowded restaurant where he and Phillip would consume mounds of greasy fries and plates of hot wings while pouring over international tax and corporate finance. Adam and Phillip, the only two black men in the joint degree program for law and business at Harvard, had met at orientation almost four years earlier. Loneliness and isolation bridged the distance created by backgrounds and circumstance. Adam had come late to the dean's opening address, his eyes searching the room for the other black faces. After four years at Harvard and his own acceptance to the programs, Adam had turned his attention to scoping out the newest crop. He'd charmed Elizabeth at the law school admissions office, had bribed Donna Marie in the business school, and had come into possession of the applications of the other black admits. Adam felt no compunction as he pored over each one, committing their stories to memory. It always paid to know your competition, even if they were allies at heart. He'd been most interested in learning about the other man who had decided to gain academic command of both law and money.

Phillip Turman was a Morehouse graduate from Baltimore, the only child of a single father who worked as a janitor for the city. He grew up listening to his father's tales of city turmoil and bureaucratic nightmares, tales learned from poorly discarded meeting notes and memos. His quiet manner, remarkable mind, and intense focus had made him a legend at a school renowned for producing successful men, according to his recommendations. Despite his less-than-affluent background, Phillip quickly rose through the ranks to become a leader at school and a voice in local politics. But his sights were set higher, on returning to the D.C. area and one day running the nation.

Adam had picked him out of the scattered few seated in the auditorium. Phillip sat near the front, just left of center. The dean's voice droned on, waxing philosophic about the beauty of law and the erudition of justice. Tall and ruggedly handsome with dark, mahogany skin, Phillip had the tightly packed build of a running back. As Adam watched, Phillip took notes, occasionally turning to scan the crowd, then jot something down. *He's taking notes on us,* Adam guessed, mildly amused. He settled back to observe. When his turn came, he glanced out the window, watching the undergrads cross the green. As he looked on, a plain young woman loped just under his window and glanced up. Chuckling at an impudent kiss she blew to him, he winked in response and smiled at her. The newly infatuated coed's step bounced as she continued on her way. Judging that enough time had passed, Adam turned to see how long his write-up would take. Phillip wrote for a few seconds, capped his pen, and closed the notebook.

Adam settled back into his seat, undecided about whether to be insulted or not by the brevity of Phillip's commentary about him. He chose to be flattered and resolved to seek Phillip out after the speech. That night, Phillip and Adam had ventured over to Carla's in what would become a weekly ritual. Adam learned that, rather than taking notes, Phillip had been drawing wicked caricatures of fellow students. Adam's cartoon consisted only of a dollar bill with a pair of reading glasses. Phillip explained that he couldn't see back far enough to do justice to Adam, so he'd drawn himself a reminder. Now, four years later, they sat at the same table, poring over class outlines and wondering about the future.

"You realize, Adam, that in a matter of days, we will walk away from this bastion of privilege with two of the most coveted degrees in all the world," Phillip said with an intonation reminiscent of the dean's supercilious, obnoxious tones.

"Indeed we will, my friend. Indeed we will." Adam took a swallow of beer. "The question remains, however, what the hell will we do with them?"

Phillip looked over at his friend. "What's this 'we' stuff? I've got a job. You're the one who can't seem to choose." He rested his face in his hands, a forlorn expression in his eyes, his voice pitched to falsetto. "Oh, whatever shall I do? Should I go work for Mommy and Daddy and make a million a year, or accept employment from Covington for only a few hundred thousand? Oh, I know, I'll slave away for Drexel and split the difference," Phillip concluded with an exaggerated sigh. He ducked just in time as a french fry barely grazed his head. "Now, now, no need for violence, Mr. Grayson," Phillip said, chuckling.

"This is serious, Phillip. I honestly can't decide. All I know is that I refuse to stay in Cambridge any longer than I have to." Adam shook his head, troubled by his indecisiveness.

Phillip sobered, realizing Adam was truly anxious about his decision. "What are your current options?" he asked.

"I can stay here and continue to run CompuSecure, but after eight years here, it's time to move on. Mom and Dad have agreed to buy the company from me, at market value." Adam paused to pop a fry loaded with ketchup into his mouth. Wiping his lips, he continued. "Then there's the fact that I have absolutely no interest in law. After I pass the bar in Georgia, I hope never to see another brief or motion to anything as long as I live."

"That leaves Wall Street or GCI." Phillip signaled the waitress to bring a new pitcher. "I know you don't want to stay in the Northeast, but you've never done securities work before. And New York is a whole new ballgame. Swimming pools, movie stars. Oops, that's California." Adam laughed at the small joke, appreciating Phillip's attempt at levity. "But seriously, why not GCI? It's not as though you'll be seen as the boss' son. You've worked your way up from checker in Food Magic to junior account executive at GCI International. You've done exceptional work, and you're graduating at the top of your class. No one can legitimately claim nepotism.

You've run our *own* company for goodness' sake." Phillip leaned forward, his eyes on Adam's. "But the real question is, what do you *want?*"

Adam's eyes darted away to look over Phillip's shoulder. "I don't know, man. I just don't know. I mean, you've known since day one that you were going to head back to D.C. With this job at Justice in Antitrust, you're right on track. And Lorei's finished up at Yale with her M.S.W., so you'll be able to move home after graduation and get married. I don't have the love of my life and, for the first time, I don't have a job to do." He shook some Tabasco sauce over the fries and the wings. "I am absolutely free, and it scares the hell out of me."

"Come on, Adam, don't give me that. You're not frightened, you're bored." Avoiding Adam's scowl, he pressed on. "Yeah, bored. You've got no one to take care of and no real duties. Rachel is off to college, Jonah and A.J. are doing just fine, and your parents love running GCI. Lorei and I are together, just as you planned, and your little computer security company is breaking the bank without either one of us working there anymore." Phillip stopped and tapped a finger against his lips. "You know what you need, my boy? You need adventure. And challenge. And, for heaven's sake, some fun. And maybe sex, although that's never seemed to be an issue."

"I couldn't have said it better myself." Both men turned, startled, to look at the man standing behind Adam. The squat, short man spoke over Adam's head. His face was clean-shaven except for a small mustache, liberally laced with black and gray. Surprisingly, his hair, cut close—almost militarily close—was pure black. The man was pale with a light brown complexion that showed no wrinkles or age, though Adam guessed he was around forty or so. He wore khakis and a blue denim shirt, with the sleeves rolled up, displaying muscular, sparsely haired forearms. Dark brown eyes watched both men examine him without blinking.

"And you are?" Phillip demanded, annoyed by the interruption and the obvious eavesdropping.

Ignoring the question, he said, "So you must be Mr. Turman." The man reached past Adam to grasp Phillip's hand. "Congratulations on the Justice Department appointment. I know those honors program spots are hard to come by. Glad you got one." Phillip's irritation quickly turned to suspicion.

"Have we met before, Mr.—"

"Russell, James Russell. And no, we've never met before." He continued to ignore Adam, focusing only on Phillip. "Congratulations on your upcoming nuptials. Ms. Alexander is a lovely young woman." At that, Phillip scooted his chair back, preparing to stand. "You two will make an entrancing couple. *If* you make it to the altar." His thick Texas accent slid over the words.

"If? What do you know about Lorei? If you've harmed her in any way—" He pushed the chair back against the wall and advanced on Russell. Adam shot a hand out and grabbed his arm to forestall the punch he knew was coming.

"He's just toying with you to get a response. Nothing's happened to Lorei." Adam murmured quietly. When Phillip remained stiff and angry, Adam spoke more firmly. "Sit down, Phillip. Nothing's happened to Lorei." He waited for Phillip to make eye contact with him. "Besides, Carla will kill you if you hit a customer. Sit down, Phillip." With a short nod, Phillip backed off and returned to his seat.

"CIA, Mr. Russell? Or is it FBI?" Adam asked.

"Neither. Hate the clothes. Will try not to be insulted." Russell answered, still watching Phillip. "Good guess, though."

"So who are you with?"

"Who says I'm with anyone?"

"Don't be coy, Mr. Russell. Your stealthy eavesdropping and the *'This Is Your Life'* parlor trick are way over the top. As you intended." Adam turned to look at Russell. "So what do you want with us?"

"Rather arrogant assumption, isn't it? Why you *and* Mr. Turman, and not just him?" Russell waited for the answer.

"Because if you only wanted Phillip, you wouldn't start off by antagonizing him and threatening his fiancée and do it all in front of me."

"I didn't threaten his fiancée. I complimented him." Russell grouchily corrected.

"Whatever. The point is, you made your initial remark about me, indicating that you'd also analyzed my temperament. Am I wrong?" he queried, his voice full of certainty.

"Nope. Absolutely right." Russell turned to pull a chair from a nearby table. "Mind if I join you? Good." He snagged a handful of fries and a wing. Within seconds, both were gone. "Damn good food here. Reminds me of home." Phillip continued to frown at the man, but Adam sat patiently. Russell motioned for a glass from the waitress. Taking a healthy swig of beer, he continued to chatter. "Of course, there we call 'em barbecue and it's usually ribs, not midget chickens. But I'm not one to complain about good food. Nope." He shoveled a few more wings into his mouth, spitting out the bones unceremoniously. "Who's the premier of Sadiad, Adam?"

"There is no premier. It's a constitutional monarchy. And her name is Abenwa Desiddes Bunefiqua." Adam replied, almost diffidently.

"Main export for Tunisia?" Russell quizzed.

"Primarily textiles, although they've moved into hydrocarbons due to their excellent Mediterranean location. And its official name is Al Jumhuriyah at Tunisiyah." Adam munched on a stalk of celery as Phillip looked on, amazed.

"How the hell did you know that?" Phillip demanded, indignant and impressed.

Russell snorted. "One of Mr. Grayson's 'hobbies' is the study of North Africa and the Middle East. Did you know he speaks French, Arabic, and a Berber dialect?" He smiled at Adam, as proud as any parent.

"If we're done with Trivial Pursuit, want to tell me what you want? With both of us."

Russell glanced around him quickly, his eyes missing nothing. Satisfied with their security, he spoke. "I'm with the International Security Agency. You've never heard of us and never will. If questioned, no one would acknowledge our existence." He frowned at both men to ensure they understood his message. "Essentially, we are an extra-governmental organization that monitors global situations and provides assistance when necessary. Our members include more than seventy-five nations, at last count. We operate at our own directive and without interference." He paused again, reading their reactions. Phillip leaned forward, slightly nonplussed. Adam relaxed against the chair back, nursing his beer.

"We've been observing the two of you for a little more than three years. You, Mr. Turman, are an excellent legal scholar who will one day walk the corridors of power with ease. Your understanding of the rule of law and its business and technological implications are impressive and very useful. The papers you authored are used even now by people in power to buttress their policies." Seeing no reaction from Phillip, Russell continued.

"You're an affable man, one who inspires camaraderie and devotion rather than envy. You treat your friends well and have few enemies. You plan each move carefully, always with an eye on your ultimate goal. Whether the world will ever be ready for a black president or not remains to be seen, but you are well on your way." He grinned at them both, pleased with his guesswork on Phillip's greatest, most quietly held, aspiration. "You have no shortage of patriotism, but you'd prefer a desk job to adventure any day. Luckily, because we need you, we can compromise. Rather than asking you to come to work for us full-time, Phillip, we'd like you to consider an on-call assignment. You would take your position with Justice, and we'd call on you from time to time to troubleshoot for us." He let that sink in. "So whaddya think?"

"I think the Justice Department might have a problem with this." Phillip began.

"Nope. The attorney general has notice that one of his boys will be on our payroll. Besides, we know you won't leave Lorei for very long. Any other questions?"

"Why me?"

"I just told you why."

"I'm not the only legal scholar with an interest in the rules of law and business."

"But you are the one with a electronic technology background, two degrees, and unassailable integrity. We analyzed you for three years, Mr. Turman. You're not the only one we've looked at. We know about your father and his paper collecting. And about you and the law exam you refused to take because you'd seen the answers. We know exactly who you are and who you can become. We need both men."

He looked at Adam then, gauging his thoughts. "Adam Grayson, son of billionaires and a wealthy man in his own right. You've got money, power, and position. What you want is a challenge. You're restless and ingenious and intuitive. You respect authority but rarely yield to it. You tend to trust your instincts and take charge with ease. And you hold your responsibilities very seriously, never shirking duty for personal gain. These qualities, plus your facility with languages and familiarity with the Middle East and North Africa, make you very attractive to us. We'd want you full-time, beginning the day after graduation. You'll have to sell CompuSecure to your parents, but you can keep the proceeds." He shifted to encompass both in his solemn examination. "You are not a package deal, but we'd rather take both than one." He spoke for a while longer, giving them a thumbnail sketch of the ISA, its inception after World War I, and the current mission. Then he stood, dropping his napkin onto the table.

Adam stared at Russell, searching for subterfuge or evasion. "We don't get to ask questions?"

"Not the ones you want to ask. Not until you agree. You've got seventy-two hours to decide."

"Where do we contact you?" Phillip asked.

"Call the number on the napkin by eleven P.M. on Thursday. Only one should call with both answers." Russell nodded to them and turned to leave. "Take care, gentlemen."

Adam reached for the napkin, a meditative expression on his face. It was a look that always scared Phillip. "Adam. Adam, no. You can't be serious. You and I running around like some black version of 'Rocky and Bullwinkle.' " Phillip shook his head vehemently.

"You're right. We've got to think code names. What about Cain and Abel, the original brothers, serving a vengeful God with an odd sense of humor? You, the dutiful son, planting nine months of the year and sleuthing for three." Adam smiled broadly, amused by his proposal. "And I would be Cain, the strong older brother, destined to save the world."

"You're mixing your theologies here. First of all, that's not even good Greek mythology. Secondly, Cain killed Abel if I'm not mistaken, and was forsaken by God."

"I've always thought that Cain was misunderstood. What was wrong with his offering?"

"I'm way too drunk for a dogmatic argument tonight. Or at least I plan to be." Phillip reached for the pitcher, only to have Adam slide it away.

"I want to do it, Phillip. I need to join." His voice was quiet, certain, almost desperate.

"I don't know, Adam. It's not what I had planned." The dubiety of it all disturbed Phillip in a thousand ways that he didn't understand. "And it just doesn't feel right. It's like something out of a bad B-movie. The mysterious stranger and you, playing some kind of smart-aleck recruit. Come on, Adam. Stuff like that doesn't happen in real life, especially not to guys like us."

"Why not? You and I have done everything we should. It may be odd, but, man, this is the chance of a lifetime for us. The two of us, saving the world.

Challenge, adventure, and fun. And imagine the contacts."

"He said they'd take you without me."

"Just think about it, will you?"

"Adam—"

"Just think about it."

On Thursday night, Russell replaced the receiver, a satisfied smile on his face.

So they joined the ISA, Adam full-time, Phillip assisting when Adam needed a partner he could absolutely trust. As a congressman, Phillip secured funding for the ISA and provided political cover for their projects.

When Adam got the assignment to infiltrate Scimitar, he seized the opportunity. He ascended quickly inside the organization and passed each test set. And then, those last days in Jafir, his first real encounter with the true power of Scimitar and the faithlessness of Raleigh. The day he betrayed his best friend.

For sixty weeks, he'd been living in Jafir, building on his reputation as Caine Simons, a renegade computer genius for sale to the highest bidder. Dangled in front of several terrorist organizations, the ISA's prime target had taken the bait and hired him. Now, he and Phillip had one last assignment to complete, and he would gain entrée into the secret world of Scimitar. Scimitar was known throughout the region for its complex agenda. Unlike other terrorist groups, it was not known for initiating the random violence that plagued the Middle East or for perpetuating the endless civil wars of North Africa.

Instead, Scimitar enjoyed a reputation as a protector of villages, a source of security in a volatile area. While Muslims, Jews, and Christians battled for political supremacy, Scimitar mimicked the age-old tales of Robin Hood and kept the towns alive and beholden to its generosity. But unlike Robin Hood, the leader of Scimitar was no saint. Kadifir el Zeben bore the marks of the modern-day terrorist and an ancient scholar of war. Born in Jafir and educated in European boarding schools and American universities, Zeben had assembled a band of cohorts who worshipped Christ, Allah, and Jehovah, with equal fervency, but knelt at the altar of power before all. Zeben grounded their association in something more basic than ethnic or religious rivalries.

In Scimitar, Zeben created a Middle Eastern NATO, an order dedicated to protecting the region from Western encroachment at all costs. So Scimitar stockpiled weaponry, hoarded hard currency, and courted the goodwill of the people.

The ISA spent more than five years infiltrating Scimitar from every angle. Adam and Phillip supplied one faction with unlimited capital. Adam's talent with computers and Phillip's electronic wizardry earned Adam a coveted position of trust within the cell operating outside Jafir, one of the few tiny nations to resist an alliance with Scimitar. As a final test of loyalty, Adam was ordered to divert funds for the purchase of chemical weapons newly introduced to the market. Phillip agreed to feign a congressional fact-finding mission and assist him. He'd arrived hours before, and Adam rushed him directly to their meeting.

"I've got to tell you about my moonlighting," Adam whispered to Phillip as they waited in an anteroom of Zeben's opulent mansion.

Priceless tapestries hung from walls hewn from ancient granite. Overhead, hand-carved solid beams of teak crossed one another in an intricate pattern, creating an internal canopy. The smell of incense permeated the space, mixing with the faint aroma of Cuban tobacco and French wine.

Adam and Phillip sat on a settee, plush and richly embroidered. In sharp contrast to the age of the room, a darkened window separated the men from the next chamber, Zeben's conference room. They'd been in the house for days and had finally been summoned to meet Zeben's lieutenant.

"I'm making some extra cash on the side as a baby-sitter."

"For whom?" Phillip murmured quietly, aware of the possibility of silent monitors. However, the legend of Zeben's paranoia about internal privacy gave them little cause for worry. While he would bug anyone else's quarters, Zeben refused to risk infiltration. Still, the men exercised caution by talking almost inaudibly.

"She's the one supplying the weapons we're helping Scimitar buy." Adam took another drag from the cigar in his hand. He hated the taste of tobacco, but his alter ego was known for his addiction to the things. If anyone was watching, they'd see nothing out of character. But he'd break the nasty habit next go round.

"She?"

"It's Chimera," Adam replied, his lips barely moving. Odd how he longed to know her real name. She had an alias, but even that wasn't enough. *What do her parents call her,* he wondered.

"The wunderkind?"

"One and the same." He'd teased her about her

youth only until he learned that she could curse so inventively. The memory made him smile.

Phillip saw the secret grin and wondered at its origin. Rather than ask a question he wasn't certain Adam would answer, he lifted his glass of wine and took a small sip. "What happened to Jericho? I thought she never left home without him?"

"Atlas recalled him for a special job. I've been assigned to sit on her until his return."

"I hear she's only twenty or something."

"Twenty-two," Adam corrected hastily. "Atlas recruited her when she was twenty, but she's twenty-two."

Quite vehement, Phillip thought. *Very interesting.* "So she really did graduate from a doctoral program before she was legal."

"Yes. chemistry and linguistics." Adam announced proudly. Chimera had an amazing mind, the kind that could absorb anything.

"She sounds smarter than you, Merlin."

"Let's not go overboard," Adam said mildly.

"What's she like?"

Adam's brow furrowed with concentration. "Brilliant," he said instantly. "Focused. Reserved. Hilarious. She can be an ice princess one second and silly as hell the next. She makes me think. She makes me happy."

Happy? Phillip hid his surprise at this last bit. As far as he was concerned, his best friend had just declared his undying love. Until that moment, only his family, Carla's cooking and death-defying missions had ever made Adam Grayson happy. Phillip probed a bit more, intrigued. "You've spent a lot of time with her, huh?"

"A fair amount. She's renting a warehouse on the

outskirts of town. She builds her bombs there. I head out there a few times a week to check in, keep an eye on things." Adam shrugged negligently. "No big deal." No need to mention he'd been there yesterday until dawn.

"What does she look like?"

"A twenty-two-year-old," Adam muttered. *This conversation has gone on long enough,* he thought. Phillip might get the wrong idea about him and Chimera. They were just friends. Any other feelings were simply the result of months of abstinence. An abstinence that began when he first met Chimera. "She's a woman."

"Details, man, details."

"She's pretty. And tall. She's actually very tall, almost five-eleven. But curvy, not bony." Adam smiled to himself, a picture forming in his mind. "And she has this smile that takes forever. She never laughs, and then one moment, you'll see this—this sunrise on her face."

This man's fallen hard, Phillip speculated, *and he doesn't even know it.* "But you're just baby-sitting?" he asked wryly.

Adam missed the sarcasm. "Yes. Atlas doesn't think she's ready to be completely on her own. She's been sheltered. From college to grad school to here." But her nightmares told another story, one she wouldn't or couldn't share. The screams that woke her night after night came from a darker place.

"I would hardly call the ISA *sheltered.*"

"Chimera moves from fantasy to fantasy. If she has a personal life, she never lets on. Just brushes my questions aside."

"Do you talk about your family?"

"In the abstract. But she won't even bend that

much. Says it's against company policy." *Like falling for your partner,* he reminded himself.

"It is," Phillip said. They'd had this argument at least once a mission. Adam treated the rules as suggestions to be disregarded at will, not orders to be followed without question.

"But the rules are like a drug to her," Adam offered with incredulity. "Can you believe she's actually read the *Rules of Engagement?*" His mouth twisted into a derisive smile.

"So have I," Phillip said flatly.

"I rest my case," Adam replied with a laugh. "You've always been too committed to orders, even when they make no sense."

"Patriotism isn't 'too committed.' I took an oath, and I follow it. To the letter."

Adam held up his hands in mock surrender. "I forgot, you're worse than she is."

"Envy is not an attractive quality in a man," Phillip retorted, irritation forgotten. Adam was a maverick, but he always came through. "Is Chimera difficult to work with?"

"Not really. You two are a lot alike. She's also horribly stubborn and terribly arrogant. She resents the hell out of my position as her primary. She thinks she's ready to go it alone."

"And she's not, I take it."

"Maybe after she's faced a real crisis. But not yet."

"Will she be in the meeting?"

"Yes. We re-route a few million from some unlucky soul's Swiss account, and she produces a nice selection of hand rockets and nerve gas. Chimera and I will handle the details. You can stay low. I'm sure the wonder-child and I will be okay."

* * *

Adam opened his eyes, focusing on something beyond Raleigh's head but not beyond her understanding. His face, lean and dark, lit only by moonlight and a faint glow from the garden lamps, frightened her. Stirred her. She strained against the urge to go to him, to tell him the truth. But duty and orders and vengeance held her rooted in place, her back pressed against the bark of the tree. He would have to wrestle with the regret and the helplessness and the failure. She needed all three if her mission were to succeed. She wouldn't help him, not now, not ever.

"Adam." His name came to him quietly, the voice soft, reminiscent of one used to calm wild animals.

"Go away." He turned again, intent only on leaving her and the memories behind. A hand grabbed his arm to stop his retreat. He tried to shake her off, unprepared for the strength of her grip. But he wasn't surprised. Chimera had always been stronger, smarter, and more deadly than she looked. And he would not be deceived again. Adam spun around, knocking her off balance, but she refused to release him. "Leave! I won't tell you again."

"You don't scare me, Merlin," she said purposefully using his code name. "Atlas has a job for you, and you need our help." Raleigh maintained her grip on his arm.

"I don't work for the ISA anymore. And I certainly don't need your help." His cold, flat tone spoke volumes about violence and retribution. "You've delivered your message, Chimera. Tell Atlas 'thanks but no thanks.' " He looked pointedly at the hand holding his wrist.

"It's about Praxis, Adam." She watched him absorb her words.

"Praxis is secure." His tone brooked no argument, but a cold chill crawled down his spine.

"No, it's not, and Scimitar will soon have it." Deciding that she'd made all the progress she could for the night, Raleigh dropped his wrist but did not move. "Atlas would like to see you at the office in the morning. 9:00 A.M." Adam did not respond. Without a sound, she walked around him and slipped back into the house.

Adam remained in the garden, his mind trying to wrap itself around the revelations of the past few minutes. Chimera was alive. No, he corrected himself savagely, her name was Raleigh Foster—at least tonight.

But more than her name had changed. The striking face was different, the proud cheekbones more defined, the cat eyes shades lighter. Three years, thirty pounds, and a voice darkened by smoke and chemicals later, and he hadn't even recognized the woman who had forced him to kill his best friend. He started to count the stars, their brightness unusual so late in the year. Usually, the lights from the city almost drowned out the night sky, leaving only the company of the moon and the flickering lights of planes heading toward Hartsfield Airport. But tonight, for some reason, the stars seemed brighter, different. Tonight and for every night after, his life would be different. Because, somehow, she was alive. If he met with them tomorrow, Atlas could explain what had gone wrong. Why Chimera had escaped and Phillip was gone. And who would have to pay.

Three

The rumble of conversation and music flowed unnoticed around Raleigh as she slipped inside the house. With polite nods to acquaintances, she quickly made her way to Liz Walton and pulled her aside, smiling apologetically to the woman's disappointed audience.

The contrast between the two women was startling. Whereas Raleigh's lean, black-draped frame towered over the women and many of the men in the room, Elizabeth Walton was a fluffy, diminutive five-three, resplendent in a pantsuit of blues, pinks, and yellows. Raleigh wore her dark hair in a short cap that framed her face, but Liz's gray and white dreadlocks cascaded past her shoulders. The contrasts did not end there, however.

Elizabeth Walton, a formidable woman, enjoyed parties and people and gossip, unlike her daughter's best friend. Liz thrived on knowing everything about everyone and doling out information in small doses. Yet, despite her reputation for knowing all, no one ever doubted her trustworthiness. While she might share a story or two to liven up an event or make a point, she held secrets in the strictest of confidences.

"Liz, I need to go," Raleigh whispered, her voice steady only through sheer force of will. She refused to succumb to the urge to press her fingers against lips still warm from Adam's kiss.

"Come now, dear. You've only just gotten here, and it's not yet midnight. And you still haven't spoken to Ambassador Franks or Councilwoman Gottfried." She peered up at Raleigh and smiled innocently. "And what happened to that nice young man, Adam Grayson? You two looked quite nice dancing together. You certainly don't do that enough, Raleigh." Liz absently patted the hand on her shoulder, dismissing her announcement. "A few more minutes won't kill you."

"Liz, I need to leave. Now." Her hand on Liz's shoulder tightened warningly. "This is no time to play matchmaker, Liz." She whispered even lower. "I've got to make a call."

Choosing to ignore the matchmaking remark, she replied soothingly, "Why don't you run upstairs and use the phone in Alex's old room?"

"It's not that sort of call."

"Well, what sort of— Oh." She patted the tense hand again. "In that case, run along, dear. I'll make your farewells for you. Just tell Rivers to drive you around the city." With so many people in the house, they'd arranged for Raleigh's gear to be stored in the garage. She held her smooth cheek up for a kiss. "And do be careful, darling."

"I will. Good night, Liz." Raleigh made her way through the crowd, resisting the urge to turn and look at the man she knew had reentered the room. Rather than wait for someone to retrieve Rivers, she circumvented the valets and found him herself. As the car made its way south from Buckhead, Raleigh closed her eyes and replayed the events of the night.

What had she been thinking? Her assignment was

simply to deliver a message to Adam, not to antagonize him before the mission ever began. And maybe that's what she tried to do. Make him so angry that he'd refuse to cooperate. Refuse to return. Adam was furious, but now he had a score to settle. With her, with Atlas—and now with Scimitar. Maybe he'd have ignored Atlas, but not her. Not anymore. The question was, would he put it all together? Would he figure out the last pieces of the puzzle?

Pale yellow flickered on the freeway, reflecting dully off the tinted windows of the car. She brooded out the window, her mind racing, trying to avoid the one perilous thought that threatened to destroy her carefully laid plans. He'd kissed her. Their first kiss had been all too brief. And when it finally happened again, she bit him. Despite her distress, Raleigh smiled ruefully. Not her neatest escape, but a fairly decent one. Hoarding that small victory, she decided to tackle her last project for the night.

She sat up and reached for the car phone. She pressed a series of numbers, waited for the recording, and dialed several more digits. Finally, a voice came on the line.

"Report."

"Contact made. Message delivered."

"Response?"

"None." Raleigh hesitated, trying to decide if his wrath would be better now or in the morning. After everything else, she might as well go for broke. *I won't be sleeping tonight, anyway.* "Secure channel?"

"Channel secure. Go ahead."

"Contact made." She braced herself for the explosion. "In person."

"Repeat. And you'd better say it right this time." The voice promised reprisal.

She sighed, knowing the second time would be harder. "I gave him the message myself. At the party."

"But he didn't recognize you, right?" He offered her a little wiggle room.

"Well, not at first. But later—"

"Later! Damn it, Chimera, I told you not to go near him! How long did it take him to make you?"

"An hour, give or take a few minutes." She started to sink into the seat again.

"An hour? You saw him for an entire hour? Have you lost your mind?" He stopped himself, the sound of heavy breathing puffing through the phone, his voice terrifyingly sober. "This isn't a game, Chimera. You should know that better than anyone." Disappointment shot across the phone lines, finding its mark.

"I'm sorry. I know I violated orders. There is no excuse." Raleigh straightened her spine, preparing for her dressing down.

"No excuse? Well, honey, you've got almost six hours to come up with one. Get a flight out of Atlanta. I want to see you at seven, here in D.C."

"Yes, sir." Her voice was firm and contrite.

"End transmission."

For the remainder of the ride to the Walton's home in the Cascades, Raleigh tried vainly to think of anything other than Adam Grayson and the debacle of the night. But the first step was always to review the mission and analyze the weaknesses, of both the operative and the opponent.

Her first mistake was dancing with him. How could she have forgotten the man's lethal charm? The way he could look at a woman and steal her soul, eyes the color of the heart of midnight promising forever without a word? Agile grace and excellent rhythm were as native to him as the potent smile he cast at her, asking her to join him on the floor. Pressed against his hard, sinewy body, she'd been grateful for the silence between them. With all the effort it took not to either stiffen in his arms or to wrap herself around him, she couldn't have maintained a coherent conversation.

In the end, she simply closed her eyes and swayed to the sounds of a piano and smoky vocals belting out songs about love and loss. He had held her this way the last night, but that time explosives, not music, filled the air around them. But those moments did not matter now.

She shook her head to dispel the memories, then continued her catalogue, ticking it off on her fingers. Her next slip lay in following him outside. She'd been prodded by an uncharacteristic need to provoke him, to cause trouble. She grinned to herself, acknowledging that the need to vex others was not atypical; however, she usually tamped the urge before it could take flight. This self-regulation was a remnant of a life as the daughter of a criminal and then as the adopted child in a family of politicians. In either lifetime, annoying others could lead to trouble, abandonment—or death. So Raleigh had learned to master her more impish side, saving it until Chimera could use it to accomplish her ends.

She'd forgotten the cardinal rule when he took her hand to dance, then led her into the garden. Despite her better judgment, she ignored her own instructions. She gave in to the need to face him down, to unsettle him with her knowledge of his past, to slip under the confidence he wore like a second skin. The feminine part of her also wanted to know if he remembered—the feel of her flesh, the curves of her body. The moments they'd shared before they were doomed, before he made his choice and she made hers.

And that was her third and most damning error. Why had she waited so long to stop the kiss? Raleigh's skin heated as she remembered the feel of his lips against hers, his hands against her naked skin. Raleigh couldn't control the shiver that followed in the wake of the reminiscence. Hours later, the singular flavor of skin and kiss lingered. She understood, from experience, that hours could pass before forgetfulness set in.

The final misjudgments were letting him recognize her and taunting him about Phillip. They needed his cooperation, not his animus or resentment. And Cavanaugh deserved his retribution. Vengeance that she would only find with Adam's help.

Atlas unknowingly repeated these thoughts the next morning. He prowled around the room, circling Raleigh like a hungry beast. The harsh fluorescent light bounced off the balding dome of his head, gleaming with perspiration born of rage. His shoulders hunched forward, leading him around in a remarkable imitation of a horse being guided by a rope around a show ring. Occasionally, he would stop, glare at her, reverse course, and begin again.

In signature counterpoint to his pacing and obvious ire, he spoke in a moderate tone, allowing his words, not his volume, to chastise her. He railed against her flagrant violation of his directions and denounced her foolishness in permitting Adam to identify her before the appointed hour. Months of careful planning shot to hell by her twice in as many weeks.

Raleigh flinched at the criticism, knowing many in the agency held her responsible for Cavanaugh's death. Still, she refused to respond, realizing that Atlas was probing for a reaction, any explanation for her recent spate of bizarre behavior.

Atlas stopped his pacing and thudded down behind the massive teak desk, hand-carved by his great-grandfather and willed to him by his late mother. The desk, like his ranting, illustrated the contradictions of the man. Chaos reigned in the center of the desk, with papers strewn about in no particular order.

Two forgotten cups of coffee sat next to a giant bear claw pastry and three open packages of Ding Dongs. But a look at the perimeter of the desk revealed another Atlas. Staplers, paper clips, and pencil holder were lined up with military precision on the right, in formation to salute the intricate structure of letter holders, file rings, and paper baskets that ringed the desk. Behind him on the wall, an oversized, laminated map of North Africa, the Middle East, and the Mediterranean bore the marks of frequent use.

Atlas settled into his chair and sat ramrod straight, facing Raleigh. He just didn't understand what was going on inside her head, not that he *ever* really knew. But the one thing he would have staked his reputation on was the fact that the agent they called "Chimera" never disobeyed orders. He taught her that himself. Recruited at the tender age of twenty, two days after her college graduation, he'd been lauded several times over the years for her excruciating attention to detail and her adherence to rules.

Unlike the agency's many mavericks, like Adam, a director could count on Chimera to assume her role, play her part, and deliver the goods. With nary a political incident to show for it. However, since he'd assigned Raleigh and Cavanaugh to chase down rumors of Phillip Turman's reappearance, she'd flouted instructions and taken too many risks. She secretly trailed a member of Scimitar, leaving Cavanaugh to be lured into a trap. This latest confrontation with Adam Grayson only added fuel to the speculation that her youthful fervor was outpacing her mature considerations—a dangerous race. Threads were unraveling faster than Atlas could anticipate, and pulling on the strings was the one woman who could tie them off.

He studied Raleigh a moment longer, trying to assess what she needed to hear. He could not afford to lose her now, with so much at stake.

"Your confrontation with Grayson was inexcusable. You have no right to jeopardize the lives of several men and women just because you have a separate agenda."

Raleigh listened to him, her face impassive. "Yes, sir."

"If you can't handle death, this is the wrong business to be in, young lady." Atlas searched her closed features, hoping for some clue, some hint. "And you should do all of us a favor and get out now if you can't take it." His voice hardened, and he leaned forward, his almost clear, brown eyes drilling into her own amber orbs. "So, what is it gonna be, Raleigh?"

"I apologize, sir. I should have delivered the message as instructed and not engaged the target. It will not happen again." Although her words sounded penitent and respectful, for the first time Atlas wondered if Raleigh was lying to him. And to herself.

"Good. Because if it happens again, I will take action. You need Adam to get to Phillip. And I need Phillip back here as soon as possible. Understand?"

Raleigh didn't quite meet his eyes. She had other plans for Phillip Turman, if indeed he was alive. But those were private thoughts.

"Do you understand?" Atlas repeated impatiently.

"Yes, sir."

Satisfied that he'd done all he could for now, he relaxed in his seat, a small frown knitting his brow. "How're you doing, Raleigh?" He slid a hand across the desk to reach for hers, but they remained in her lap. Hiding his hurt at the new distance between them, he withdrew his hand, bringing it to his chest. "No one understands better than I do, Raleigh, how you feel about losing Cavanaugh. Hell, he was my best operative."

Raleigh stiffened at this, her eyes clouding over with emotion. "With all due respect, sir, you have no idea how I feel." She stood, clasping her hands behind her back. "If that is all, sir, I believe I should leave before Mr. Grayson arrives." She lifted her briefcase from beside the chair and headed to the door.

Just as she reached for the knob, the door opened. Surprised, she found herself face to face with Adam. Her gaze ran over him quickly, taking in the clean lines of the navy suit, the crispness of the white shirt, the absence of a tie. The cut of the suit emphasized the rangy leanness of his body, hinting at masculine grace. When her inspection reached his face, she stepped back involuntarily, for a moment alarmed by the wrath blazing in his eyes.

"Going somewhere, Raleigh? Or perhaps the more appropriate 'Chimera'?" Adam leaned against the doorjamb, filling the space between the door and the frame. Behind him, Lewis, Atlas' assistant, stood anxiously.

"I asked him to wait while I buzzed you, sir, but—" The normally unflappable Lewis stammered.

"Don't worry, Lewis, he doesn't do decorum very well." Atlas stepped from around his desk and offered his hand to Adam. "Welcome home, Merlin."

Taking the proffered hand, Adam stepped forward to embrace his recruiter and mentor, James Russell. "It's been a long time, Atlas."

"Too long, Adam. Too long." Without turning his eyes from Adam, he spoke to Raleigh. "Well, since he's here, you might as well have a seat, Raleigh." Raleigh bristled as Atlas placed a companionable arm around Adam's shoulders and led him to the seat she had just vacated. Wasn't this always the way? Adam, the beloved son; Raleigh, the dutiful daughter? Cosset one and berate the other? Stifling her aggravation, she mentally replayed her promise to obey instructions and forced herself to move away from the door to the seat beside Adam.

Adam settled into the chair and steepled his fingers together, waiting for Atlas to make the first move. He watched Raleigh take her seat, startled by the surge of arousal sparked by the sight of sleek, elegant legs emerging from below the short hem of her indigo suit. Captivated, he followed them as she crossed and then recrossed them. He allowed himself to study all of her, taking in the small waist and striking profile. She'd certainly grown up quite a bit in the past few years; every treacherous inch of her seemed provocative and desirable. Gone was the precocious urchin who seized his heart, and in her place was a calculating siren who set his blood at a fever pitch.

When he left the ISA three years ago, he'd made it quite plain to Atlas that he had no interest in returning. And he didn't believe for a moment that Praxis was the issue here. Atlas wouldn't send one of his best operatives to deliver a message unless something else was happening. Obviously, they weren't ready to tell him, but they needed his help. And Raleigh was a part of this. He came for answers. He didn't have to wait long.

"I understand you and Raleigh were, um, reacquainted last night." Atlas began. He noted the sudden alertness in Adam's body before he relaxed again. What hadn't she told him?

"You could say that," Adam agreed, not sparing a glance for Raleigh. He could only assume that she didn't report everything to Atlas. "Our meeting was certainly—enlightening."

Atlas waited for elaboration and then continued over the lengthening silence. "Adam, what can you tell us about Praxis?"

"Praxis is still in the developmental stages, as I am sure you are aware. It is a microzeolite delivery system designed to release photochemicals into the air. The microscopic sponges actually clean the air of impurities through absorption and then deposit filter particles to continue the process. Essentially, it's an airborne ventilation and environmental management system. When complete, the Praxis system can be used by industrialized third-world nations to drastically reduce their pollution at a fraction of the current cost, and all without jeopardizing their only hope of economic progress."

Raleigh spoke for the first time. "What about security? Who has access to the data?"

"Only the team of biochemists and molecular chemists assigned to the project have access to the data or the lab. All the records are stored in programs monitored by CompuSecure. Only a handful of nations are even aware of the concept. So what's going on?"

"Well, as Raleigh told you last night, we have reason to believe that Scimitar has come into possession of the formulas and plans. Or soon will."

"Reason to believe?"

"An agent reported a transaction between Scimitar and someone who claims to have a prototype in the making. What I need to know is why they would want Praxis? We understand the potential economic gain to the company that controls the system. But Scimitar is a terrorist organization. What could they get out of this?"

Adam turned to Raleigh, "You know, don't you?"

"I have a theory," she acknowledged.

"Which is?"

"The microzeolite delivery system doesn't just release and absorb photochemicals. It could also be programmed to carry chemical weapons. Especially substances that employ the components found in industrial exhaust. In the wrong hands, Praxis could be the most destructive chemical weapon ever devised, with the capacity to target entire cities—unlike current local delivery systems." she explained.

Atlas looked to Adam for confirmation.

"She's right. That's why only four scientists have been assigned to the project." Anticipating the next question, he continued. "The Praxis scientists were thoroughly investigated. By some of your people, too."

"When?"

"We began work on the project five years ago. Darrick Josephs, the molecular chemist heading the project, was a few years ahead of Raleigh in school. He came to us straight from the academy. Leslie Davis has been with us for fifteen years. The other two, Audrey Hall and Damon Ladaris, came from Wyatt and Slater and Yin labs almost eight years ago."

Atlas nodded and stood. He moved around the desk to perch on the edge. "Adam, Praxis is out there, and somebody from your shop is selling it. We need to know who, and we need to know how. According to our sources, we've only got three weeks before Scimitar gets their hands on this thing."

"What do you want from me?"

"Your help, Adam." Atlas replied.

"Of course, I'll cooperate with the ISA." When Atlas nodded with satisfaction, he continued. "I can give you access to the labs and the team's records. Whatever you need." Adam pushed back his chair to stand. "Just let me know." He reached for Atlas' hand and clasped it firmly. "Good to see you again." Saying nothing to Raleigh, Adam headed for the door, wondering which one would stop him.

"Adam, wait." Atlas said with mild exasperation. "Sit down."

Adam remained by the door, leaning negligently. "Was there something else?"

"Do you remember who did the background check for you here?"

The reply was terse. "Phillip and Cavanaugh."

"Cavanaugh's dead, Adam." Atlas watched the news register in the narrowing of Adam's coal-black eyes. Then, as though nothing had been said, the eyes returned to their habitual cool stare.

"How?"

"An ambush in Jafir."

"I guess that means Dr. Foster was there with him," he said quietly. Adam relished the moment the barb struck home, and she lowered her lashes.

"Raleigh was at the scene, yes." Atlas moved to stand beside Raleigh, resting a hand on her tense shoulder. "Internal Review has cleared her of any connection to Scimitar, Adam. Just as they did three years ago, before we found out she'd survived the attack. But one thing is clear—you two are the only ones left." The word *alive* remained unspoken but echoed in everyone's mind. "We have to assume that you are the next target, Adam. And that your connection to Praxis is no coincidence." Atlas began to pace around the room, in his stoop-shouldered fashion.

"So someone else knows the truth and wants to use the Praxis project to lure me out. Then they can deliver me and Praxis. Two for the price of one." Adam smiled without humor. "And where do *you* fit in?" he asked Raleigh.

"They didn't try to kill me in Jafir, so I assume they either don't know about me or don't care. Either way, I know Praxis and Scimitar. And I'm the only one left, besides you, who can determine who our turncoat is."

"You believe it's someone in the organization?"

"It has to be. No one else knows the links between code names and aliases." Adam knew that she was correct about the practice at the ISA to furnish each operative with a code name for use by other agents. When sent on a mission, each operative assumed an alias for the duration of the mission. During their last mission, Raleigh had become an amoral grad student, one conversant in chemical weapons and explosives. Her partner, Cavanaugh, code named "Jericho," became Ethan Rhodes, a wealthy industrialist with a weakness for dark women and danger.

In an unusual move for the ISA, Atlas had also brought in Adam to monitor Raleigh after Cavanaugh left for another assignment. He had been Caine Simons, the playboy mercenary for hire with a flair for computers and hacking. Phillip, as always, had been his partner Stephen Frame, the quiet one who could rewire satellites and reroute information with ease, hence his code name "Sphinx."

"Any suspects?"

Raleigh did not hesitate over the lie. "No." Obsidian eyes probed amber for weakness or hidden truths. Seeing nothing beyond the measured look, Adam turned to Atlas again.

"So, I repeat, what do you want?"

"Adam, we need to find out who has compromised the organization. Even though our section is separated from the other regional oversight groups, a mole can move anywhere once it's gotten inside."

"I'm retired, Atlas. *That's* non-negotiable." Adam said without rancor.

"Even if it means we can find Phillip's killer?" Atlas asked.

"I know who she is," he replied, piercing Raleigh with a look full of accusations. "I told you that three years ago."

Trying not to wither beneath his condemnation, Raleigh returned his look with cool disdain.

Not quite so dismissive, Atlas jumped to her defense. "Raleigh had nothing to do with Phillip's death, Adam."

"The hell she didn't! She gave Scimitar the explosives they used to destroy the warehouse and the hut. She let them bomb him, even after I warned her about Phillip." The accusation rose like acid in his throat, and he fought to keep himself still. "She refused to warn him."

Shrugging off Atlas' hand, she surged to her feet. "My orders were to infiltrate and deliver. Yours were to do the same. You wanted to violate protocol and jeopardize the mission. We were explicitly told not to make radio contact. With anyone." Her tone was ripe with indignation and shame, because she had given them the weapons, even if Phillip hadn't died. Maybe that's what turned him against the ISA. "I'm sorry about—"

"Don't say his name." In two strides, Adam moved to stand over her, knocking over the chair he'd just vacated. Despite her height of five-ten, he topped her by a good six inches. "Don't you dare."

"Or what, Adam? What?" Raleigh taunted, while inwardly she trembled from a combination of regret and fear. She had almost killed Phillip, just as he said. But she had been following orders, like a good solider.

"Don't push me, Chimera." Rage ebbed, replaced by a tension born of culpability and contradictions. Knowing who she was and what she'd done, he still wanted to drag her against him and assuage the ache that had plagued him since the day he thought she'd died.

Raleigh faced him for endless seconds before turning to Atlas. "I told you this wouldn't work, Atlas."

"What won't work?" Adam forcefully turned her to face him. "What do you want?"

"Atlas wanted us to go back, to reestablish our contacts with the Scimitar faction in Jafir. To get them before they get to us. But it obviously can't work." Raleigh pushed his hand from her arm.

"We've been out for three years. And if they know who we are, it's a suicide mission."

"My cover may not have been blown," Raleigh stated.

Adam returned his attention to Atlas. "They believe she's dead."

"Yes. And we have confirmation. Cavanaugh died two weeks ago while in Jafir with Raleigh. He was back under as Ethan Rhodes and pretended to search for her."

"So why is he dead?"

"We aren't sure. He received a phone call around midday and was told to come to the marketplace at the Desira Plateau. I was out, and when I returned, I found a note from a friend and went to meet him. By the time I found him, he'd been ambushed. He lived long enough to tell me about Praxis."

"I still don't understand. If the mole knew about him, why not about you?"

Atlas answered this time. "Raleigh was never placed back on the active roster. After Cavanaugh realized she was still alive, she took a few months to recuperate and then worked with him exclusively. She's not in the system anymore."

Raleigh finished the explanation, trying to ignore the guilt of survival. "If they'd known who I was as well, they'd have sent for both of us. But I made it out alive."

"You always do," Adam sneered. If he felt a surge

of gratitude at her escape, he refused to acknowledge it.

"That's enough, Adam." Atlas decided it was time to play the next card in his hand. "Sit down, both of you." When neither moved, he glowered at both and barked, "Sit!" After Adam righted his chair and when they were seated, he continued.

"Adam, you certainly are in danger, and Raleigh might be. And you two are the only ones left who can get back inside and find out who the traitor is." Anticipating Adam's next objection, he plowed on. "Raleigh has developed a new cover, solid enough to withstand reentry. With you. She's known to be a free agent, one with a background in chemical weapons. Because Praxis depends on computer expertise as well as chemistry proficiency, her seeking you out as a partner makes perfect sense. Raleigh is their source for the chemical weapons, and you will be her source for the delivery system hardware. They'll just assume that she's been duped by you and doesn't know who you are."

"So we're colleagues?" Adam questioned, accepting the cover story with an unsettling feeling deep in his gut.

Raleigh answered this time. "No." A smile twisted her full lips, her voice throaty with scorn and disbelief. "We're lovers."

Four

A palpable silence greeted Raleigh's announcement. Adam quickly schooled his features to indifference. He and Raleigh posing as lovers? Absurd. He could barely stand to be in the same room with her, let alone make believe they shared a bed. *I learned my lesson,* he thought bitterly, *in blood.*

As he opened his mouth to protest the obscene charade, a torrid image of their embrace in the garden flashed through his mind: silken flesh wrapped against him and ripe lips mating with his own as her scent rose between them. *I didn't learn my lesson too well,* Adam mused, growing hard at the memory. He stifled a grim chuckle. As usual, Atlas knew what he was doing, although he probably had no idea how clever the ruse was. He had to hand it to the man: playing Raleigh's lover was the perfect cover. Why pretend to desire when both of them received ample proof of his attraction last night?

He wanted Raleigh Foster. And wanting Raleigh meant wanting Chimera, the woman who'd taken his best friend from him. Even now, standing in Atlas' office, he could not quite reconcile the seductive, cool mystery lady of last night with the duplicitous, stubborn child-woman he remembered as Chimera. Yet, finding out who murdered Phillip and who was after them and Praxis meant he'd need the ISA's help—and that meant her. Raleigh of the beautiful amber eyes that promised pleasure and the rigid code of conduct that guaranteed death.

"When would we leave?" Adam queried.

"In a few days. You fly into Jafir and reestablish contact with the Scimitar cell in the capital city of Desira. We've already got a couple of agents inside, setting up your cover." Atlas responded quickly, pleased by Adam's acquiescence.

"I haven't agreed yet, Atlas," warned Adam. "I've got a few more concerns."

"Okay. Ask your questions." Atlas knew better than Adam did that his first question was his agreement. But if he required the illusion of self-determination, he'd give it to him. Recovering Praxis and possibly Phillip Turman meant more than either Adam or Raleigh could fathom. And it would only happen if they did it together. He could humor them both, for a while.

"So, I become Caine Simons again. Where have I been for the past three years?"

Atlas answered. "According to the rumors we're spreading—internally as well—you double-crossed Phillip, he got killed, and you decided to lay low for a while. Now you've gotten wind of Praxis, and you're looking to broker the final stages of the deal."

"Why would Scimitar need my assistance?"

"They've managed to obtain the specs for the prototype, but they're having some trouble constructing the hardware. The computer system required, as you well know, is light-years ahead of any technology most of them have ever seen. You guys at GCI are making it mighty difficult for them."

"But not impossible."

"No, not impossible," Atlas concurred. "But Caine Simons is the best."

"And that's me."

"Yep."

"Tell me again why she has to come."

Atlas cut a warning glance at a seething Raleigh, who seemed poised to speak. With a small shake of his head, he replied, "Scimitar also needs a chemist who can tell them how to make this a weapon of mass destruction."

"Who is she?"

"Dr. Andrea DeSalle, formerly of Wyatt and Slater and currently your mistress and associate. You two are the power couple responsible for the still unsolved bombing of the American Embassy in Morocco six months ago and the recent theft of several million from an EU account in St. Gerasse."

"Do we have the job?"

"No, but you are on the short list. In one week, there will be a special caucus in Desira."

"Are we auctioning off our services?"

"Nope. Zeben has a more entertaining time planned. Day one is a tournament of chance." Atlas forestalled Adam's question with a raised hand. "I have no idea what that means. Just that you and your partner will be judged based on your performance. Then, day two commences with more practical exams like fire bombs and transceivers."

Adam could feel his adrenaline surge, its presence like an old, forgotten friend. No takeover had ever had the same kick. "Do we know the other competitors?"

"On hand will be almost every adversary you've encountered, and several we all wish were underneath a Turkish prison. We've gotten reports of some of the most unholy alliances you can imagine. One team has a psychotic computer geek from the IRA, a biochemist who does side work for the Mossad, and a weapons expert from our very own CIA."

Old-home week, Adam decided. *Feels good to be back.* But he kept his thoughts to himself. "I know only greed or fanaticism make such strange bedfellows, so what are the terms of the prize?"

"The winner gets the contract to complete Praxis and seventy-five million dollars, U.S. If the demonstration works, an additional twenty-five. Plus a free turn at the finished product for their own sacred cause." Atlas moved to stand at the map hanging behind his desk. "But if Scimitar doesn't have the hardware or the chemicals yet, why the rush?" he asked, a master testing his recalcitrant pupil.

"The anniversary of the birth of Kadifir el Zeben, Scimitar's tyrannical founder, is during that time. And the African League begins talks with the Arab Alliance then. It's hard to imagine a better captive audience than the heads of state for Morocco, Senegal, Jordan, Tunisia, and Egypt, not to mention Lebanon, Chad, and Syria. If Jafir's president can broker a strategic partnership where the United Nations and the United States failed, he finally gains access to the means to destroy Scimitar and its legitimacy on the world stage. With a debacle caused by Scimitar, however, Zeben takes control. A sign of military force equal to the other nations is an effective bargaining chip. If he successfully unleashes Praxis, Scimitar overruns Jafir, Zeben becomes ruler of the most strategic island in the Mediterranean, and every zealot in the region will promise obeisance."

"And no one else is safe from extremists," Atlas added, nodding with approval.

"They plan to deploy Praxis in Desira?"

"No. Zeben intends to start small, then offer use to the highest bidder," Atlas said soberly. "The target is the village of Sabren."

"Where Phillip died," Adam whispered. Once again, grief, guilt, and disloyal passions rose inside, threatening to choke him. Vibrating with restrained emotion, Adam jumped from his chair and stalked over to stand at the single window in Atlas' sixth-story office in DuPont Circle.

The ISA's American headquarters operated in the heart of D.C.'s other political center, removed from the political bickering of Pennsylvania Avenue and Capitol Hill. In DuPont Circle, crowded bookstores and ubiquitous restaurants served patrons from nearby foundations and think tanks. Below him, men and women clad in suits, jeans, and leather jackets scurried across the street. In true Washington fashion, masses waded through constant, schizophrenic traffic, oblivious to honking horns and the near-fatal collisions left in their wake.

Adam stared down at the people, willing himself to calm down. Holding back his fury had always been the hardest part of the job for him. He lived in a world with no room for untamed emotion. Growing up as the eldest son of the Grayson empire, he'd learned to control himself for the cameras and the never-ending stream of guests. The maelstrom swirling inside him demanded release, but he knew how to wait it out.

"Adam?" Atlas said quietly.

"Yes?" Adam answered, his voice neutral and devoid of emotion.

"Are you in?" Atlas examined the tense back of his protégé, gauging Adam's thoughts.

"I don't know." *I don't know if I can go back there, even for you, Phillip. Not if I have to be with her. It cost you your life last time.*

"What else do you need?"

"I don't know." Adam shrugged, his back to Atlas and Raleigh.

"Don't give me that crap, Adam. Either you're in or you're out. It's your company and your project. Your choice." Atlas snorted and rolled his eyes. "I never took you for a coward, Merlin."

"Reverse psychology, Atlas?" Adam sneered.

"Did it work?" As quickly as he'd grown annoyed, Atlas smiled warmly. "Just tell me what you need to make it work."

"Another partner. Not her." Adam said tersely.

"I just explained this, Adam. Without Raleigh, you don't get back in."

"I don't trust her, Atlas. You know that." *I certainly don't trust myself when I'm with her. I forget myself when I'm with her.* Isn't that why Phillip was dead—and he wasn't? "I don't think she's the right person for the job."

"Stop talking about me as though I'm not here," Raleigh commanded softly and got to her feet. She flicked a dismissive hand at Adam and advanced on Atlas, her husky voice dripping with ice. "I agreed to give him the message and to work with him if necessary. But this is my case, not his. Cavanaugh was my partner. And if this petulant, arrogant, guilt-ridden has-been agent can't work with me, we can find somebody else," she said coldly.

"Guilt-ridden has-been?" Adam spun around, incensed. "I left my best friend to die while I made out with the automaton who killed him. But to understand that, you'd need a heart where your rule book is."

Before Raleigh could speak, Atlas intervened. "Adam, I need an answer. Raleigh stays in unless she chooses otherwise. What are you going to do?"

With one last glare at Raleigh, Adam turned back to the window. Going back to Jafir wasn't simply about him and the need to save Praxis. He owed it to Phillip to find out what had gone wrong three years ago. He owed it to A.J., who deserved to know the truth about her husband's death. The accident in Jafir was about more than Raleigh's refusal to help him.

Too many pieces were missing, too many questions unanswered. How had Scimitar known where to find them? Why had he and Raleigh escaped but not Phillip? Questions like acid served to eat away at his world and separate him from his family, his friends, and himself. He knew he couldn't trust Raleigh to do it for him. Further, if he bowed out and let her do the mission with another agent, he'd never find the answers he needed. Caine Simons would live again. But this time, Chimera would not become a distraction.

"Adam?"

Raleigh's smoky voice interrupted his reverie, and his gut tightened in reaction. The resolutions of a moment ago faded swiftly, erased by the sudden tension that signaled the return of desire. His disloyalty began years ago. This wasn't simply about a kiss in a garden but a secret longing years older when he had fallen in love with a young woman sent to sell weapons to the enemy. Brilliant shards of memory cascaded through his mind, each bright piece edged with recollections of hidden passions, secret wants. Memories returned, ones of Raleigh laughing with him at night under a million stars, of her quick wit as they plotted strategy, of holding her as firebursts surrounded them. Images bordered by his care not to give in to his craving, the compulsion to touch and hold her, even then.

Then the images shifted, reminding him of why hatred had replaced affection. Again, he heard her treacherous voice, the harshness of "no," as she refused to contact Phillip and warn him, the resolve in her eyes as he pulled away to go after Phillip. Memories withered again, yet the conflicting hunger to both throttle and kiss her remained. Guilt had been much simpler when he thought she was dead.

Who was he kidding? There was no way he could pretend to be her lover without doing something stupid. Not when the sound of his name on her lips stirred him, despite his contempt. Hell, just standing in a room with her made him ache to have her. Weeks together in a hotel would undo him. And if that ever happened, he'd lose what shred of self-respect remained. No matter what Atlas said, only one option remained—he would do it himself.

But Atlas said she had to choose to quit.

"Adam? Are you still with us?" Raleigh's taunting voice filled his ears again. She was resilient, he had to give her that. Knock her down, and she came up fighting. Raleigh had always faced disaster head on, afraid of nothing. Indeed, the only time he had ever seen fear in her had been in the moments after he kissed her last night. A plan quickly formed as he remembered her reaction to their embrace. In their kiss, he tasted passion, forgotten chemistry, and her alarm at the loss of control. He felt it tremble through her fingers as he kissed her hand in the moonlight. And today, when he moved too close, he witnessed the mixture of fascination and trepidation. If insults didn't chase her away, perhaps the fear of his touch would.

Adam paused, remembering the other kiss they'd shared. That time, she'd been afraid, but not of him. He'd imagined shyness, not knowing until too late it was ruthlessness. Now he'd use any weapon at his disposal to get rid of her, whatever had been. Adam turned from the window to find her standing a few feet away from him.

"Lovers, Raleigh?" Adam took a deliberate step toward her, studied her intently. "Is that the plan?" Her eyes widened a fraction before they narrowed in suspicion. Adam reached out and tilted Raleigh's chin, angling her face toward his own. A small smile played at the corner of his mouth as he slowly stroked the perfect oval of her face. He felt her pulse quicken and waited patiently for her reply. *Yes,* he thought, *this will work.* "Lovers?"

"Yes." Raleigh forced the words out calmly, cursing her own unwelcome reaction to his nearness, his touch. Her breath backed up in her lungs. Had he always pulled her like this? *Stop it,* she ordered sternly. She was no longer an anxious twenty-two-year-old with no experience. She was a grown woman, one who'd survived more than her share of dangerous situations. Not the least of which had been his desertion on that hilltop.

She owed him for ever making her believe in them. Desire, like everything else between them, had always been mutual. So, if she felt her knees trembling, he'd feel his quivering, too. With studied nonchalance, Raleigh lifted her hand to cup his cheek, her thumb toying with his bottom lip. Should a man's lips be so hard, so inviting? "Lovers. Is that a problem?"

"Not for me," Adam murmured as he traced the shell of her ear. Was her skin this warm every where? "Not at all." His hand slid to her nape and began to slowly massage. "You?" *Now.* The word swirled through his brain. *I want her now.*

As though she'd read his mind, she breathed, "I'm game if you are." *For anything,* she thought distractedly. Raleigh leaned forward, just as Adam started to bend to her, his other hand lifting to her waist.

"Ahem." At Atlas' loud cough, the two guiltily sprang apart. "So pretending to like each other won't be a problem for you two."

Raleigh took a quick step back, then stopped. She would not retreat from Adam Grayson—or anyone. No matter how her skin tingled. "If Adam is ready to discuss the mission, we can begin."

"Oh, I'm ready. But I will not work with her." Obstinacy hardened his eyes.

"I completely agree," Raleigh concurred with a mutinous tone.

Raleigh's last comment caught Adam off guard. "You agree we can't do this together?"

"Absolutely. You don't seem to have mastered the basics of hormone control yet. I certainly wouldn't put the fate of the region in your hands." Raleigh turned to Atlas, her chin jutting forward in preparation for battle. "I'll do this with Dobson or Behr—your choice. Either one can do the hardware."

Fully indignant, Adam countered, "If anyone is off the case, it's you. I'm the one who knows Praxis and the computer security program, as well as the delivery system. And I didn't notice you pulling away from my raging hormones."

"With all due respect, if you knew so much about computer security, this wouldn't be a problem, would it?" Raleigh sniped.

"This leak is not the result of a breach in my security system." Adam replied coldly.

"Either someone broke into your precious system or one of your scientists sold us out. Take your pick. It seems you either can't choose good help or design a solid security protocol," Raleigh said derisively.

"And how do we know that *you* aren't the mole? Hmm?" Adam accused. "Mighty convenient that you seem to always come out alive, while good men die in your stead."

Hot shrapnel and thick smoke. Dark back rooms and foul-smelling flesh. The report of a gun and the click of a switchblade. Adam was right. She did leave good men in her wake. Maybe Phillip was alive, but he, too, could have been her fault. Adam saved her life once, and if he discovered the truth about Phillip, hcr dcbt was over.

Raleigh searched for a way to give Adam what he wanted and to retaliate for Cavanaugh's murder. She'd let Adam locate Phillip, and she'd be there to get answers of her own. She had the skills and the cover, and no one would jeopardize their mission to expose her. Adam could have a new partner. Raleigh Foster would go in. Alone. And if she died in the attempt, Praxis would still be safe. And Adam, too.

Atlas and Adam watched in silent disbelief as Raleigh turned away to pick up her briefcase and then walked to the door. As her hand grasped the cold, suddenly slippery knob, she looked over her shoulder at Atlas. "He's right. Good men do die in my place." When Atlas moved to go to her, she held up a hand to stop him. "No. Let him have it. Leighton or Sims can go in."

"Raleigh—"

"No, Atlas. I can't do it again. I won't be responsible for another death."

"Cavanaugh wasn't your fault, Raleigh. And neither was Chance." Atlas crossed the room to her.

Chance? Adam watched quietly as Atlas reached to embrace Raleigh, and she recoiled into the door. Refusing to be rebuffed, Atlas clasped Raleigh's shoulder and shook her gently. Raleigh, the firebrand who'd been so remote and mysterious last night and so blatantly seductive only moments before, this woman had her head bowed in what could only be shame. Adam knew he'd won, but he wasn't certain that he was pleased with his victory. Somehow, this was no longer about Jafir and Scimitar, but a story he didn't know. Atlas' next words confirmed his suspicions.

"Raleigh, he wasn't your fault. You know that."

"No, I don't. And you don't, either." She finally brought her eyes to Atlas and continued, "But it's not only about him. I've been making mistakes lately, boss. We both know this one is too important to lose. Let Adam have it." Raleigh lifted her hand to cover Atlas' and squeezed, then removed his hand.

"No." Adam's calm statement stopped Raleigh for a moment, then she turned the knob again and opened the door. "If she's out, I won't do it, Atlas."

"What?" Atlas spun around to confront Adam and pushed the door closed without looking at Raleigh. "What is going on here? First you accuse her of murdering your best friend, then you refuse to work with her, and when she quits, you change your mind," he accused Adam, then impaled Raleigh with a livid stare.

"And you play the martyr and slink away because of incidents that are completely irrelevant, and you almost let this jerk scare you off." Raleigh combed through her short hair and twisted her head away, staring into space.

"Unless you were planning to go to Jafir, anyway?" Atlas concluded, tipped off by her telltale gesture. Raleigh as the maverick and Adam as the peace-maker. What the hell was going on here? "Would someone like to tell me what happened last night?" he demanded.

"This isn't about Adam or last night," Raleigh began.

"This is about Raleigh, not last night," Adam said simultaneously.

"Enough!" Atlas bellowed, and he moved to stand behind the desk once more. He leaned forward and raked his gaze over Adam near the window and Raleigh at the door. Stunned by the uncharacteristic shout, neither dared move. "Since I'm the boss, I'll tell you how this is gonna work. Raleigh, you are to head home and not leave your apartment. You will not think about Cavanaugh or Phillip or Adam. At all. And discard any scheme to go into Jafir alone." Realizing his guess had been correct, Atlas glared at Raleigh for a moment longer, reproof evident.

He then turned to Adam. "Adam, I'll give you the current files, and you'll get back on your jet and return to Atlanta. On the way home, you'll remember who's in charge here and that stopping the sale of Praxis means more than either of you."

Atlas sat down in the leather executive chair and shifted to encompass both in his sight. "The two of you are going to meet tomorrow at GCI headquarters in Atlanta and see if you can figure out if this is an internal leak from GCI or if we do indeed have a mole. Either way, you will both be on a plane to Jafir on Wednesday morning. Is that understood?"

"Yes," Adam muttered.

"Yes," Raleigh grumbled.

"Now get out of here before you both make me angry."

Raleigh opened the door, only to stumble into an eavesdropping Lewis. "I heard yelling," he explained. Raleigh rolled her eyes at Lewis and shoved past him to the exit. Adam started to follow.

"Adam, wait." Atlas commanded.

"More dressing down, Atlas?"

"No. Have a seat."

Adam settled into the chair he'd righted earlier. "If you plan to tell me to leave Raleigh alone—"

"No, Raleigh can take care of herself on that score."

"Why didn't you tell me she survived?" Adam demanded.

"You quit, Adam. You walked away, not me."

"One phone call, Atlas. One. Instead, you let me believe that I lost two people that night. Didn't you owe me the truth?"

Atlas hesitated, unsure of his next words. He was the one who'd discovered Adam, trained him and Phillip, tried to comfort him after the accident. Now he would use the man he thought of as a son. Use him to possibly betray the man Adam considered his brother.

"You knew the rules, Adam," Atlas said.

The rules. Always the rules. Suddenly furious, Adam slammed his hands on the desktop, the sound echoing through the office. "You and Raleigh and these damned rules! Do you ever think about anything else? Anyone else?"

"What about you?" Atlas countered. He lifted a pen and studied it, running it through his hands. "You won't let up on her."

Adam shrugged, hoping to dislodge the uneasiness settling between his shoulder blades. It felt like guilt. "Why should I? She can handle it," he muttered. Restless, he stood and wandered to the window, propping himself against the window frame. He'd done nothing he shouldn't have.

Adam always was an easy mark, Atlas thought, shaking his head. Push the right buttons, and he'd defend anyone. "As strong as Raleigh is, she's young. Because of her mind and her attitude, it's easy to forget she's only twenty-five. And very naive in many ways. She went from high school to college in a year, then finished grad school while other women were dancing at parties and falling in love. Cavanaugh was one of her best friends, and she watched him die. She needs to find his killers, and I need her to recover Praxis. You need her get back inside and uncover your answers, too. But you seem intent on hurting her."

Adam chafed at the charge. "I've said nothing she hasn't deserved."

Flipping the pen onto the desk, Atlas fixed Adam with a steely look. "Raleigh was not responsible for Phillip's death. Scimitar was."

Adam turned from the window to confront Atlas. "But she could have colluded with them. Two men down, Atlas, and you haven't considered the possibility?"

"No. She did not consort with anyone."

"That first explosion in the warehouse was a warning. It wasn't meant to kill us."

"I don't have the answers. That's why I need you."

"I can't trust her, Atlas. She let a man die, for no reason."

"Raleigh acted properly. She was following orders."

"Don't defend her to me, Atlas. I was there; you weren't." Adam strode to the door, then spun to face Atlas, the wound raw and exposed. "She knew about Phillip, and she did nothing. Whether she consorted with Scimitar or not, she was a part of his death. I may have to work with her, but I will not forgive her. And don't ask me to."

"With any luck, I won't have to ask. You'll learn the truth for yourself." Seeing Adam's quizzical expression at his cryptic remark, Atlas changed gears. "Just don't hurt her. She can't take much more. And from your reaction to her, neither can you."

"Then she needs to grow up or get out of the game."

"Like you, Adam?"

Adam pulled the door open and spared Atlas one last glance, "Yes, like me."

Five

The elevator doors slid shut behind her and Raleigh wearily fumbled for her key. Before she inserted it into the apartment lock, she scanned the exterior for the microfiber she had pasted over the hole. Raleigh realized, as did most of her colleagues, that a proficient intruder could override an alarm or short circuit a perimeter defense. Older tricks of the trade suited her.

Satisfied to see that it had not been moved, she removed the fiber, entered the apartment, and deactivated the silent alarm. She slid her suit jacket from tired shoulders, tossed it onto the sofa, and glanced at the answering machine resting on antique maple end table. Ten messages? Not right now. She was in no mood to talk to anyone about anything.

What beckoned at the moment was the huge, black recliner tucked into a corner of the room, a house warming gift from the Walton's. Raleigh sank gratefully into the chair, leaned her head back into the plump cushions, and emitted a deep sigh. The unshuttered bay window, the centerpiece of her apartment, streamed sunlight into the living room, mocking her displeasure.

Closing her eyes, she contemplated the ball of

tension playing behind her forehead and the dull ache of want knotting her stomach. Both appeared on her drive back from ISA headquarters. And they were both his fault. The insufferable, heavy-handed, maddening Adam Grayson.

"I can't do this," she muttered to herself, "not with him." She was angry, strung-out from her early flight, and her feet hurt. Unwilling to let go of the anger, and too wired for sleep, she puzzled over how to ease the discomfort now snaking through her feet. Moving her arms was out of the question. One shoulder was still sore from an assassin's bullet, aggravated by her brief tussles with Adam. Yet another ache to blame him for. Besides, the tension in her head had taken up residence along her shoulders and back, and the thought of bending to take off her shoes almost made her teary. Contorting her body, Raleigh managed to pry first one shoe off then the other with her toes and brought a cramped foot to her lap.

"There has to be a way out of this," Raleigh reasoned. As she rubbed a sore arch, she shook her head in consternation. "I can't make it through three weeks with Adam Grayson. One of us won't come out alive." Changing feet, she continued to complain to the empty room. "And I won't even have my sanity to fall back on. The man has me talking to myself."

All her life, she'd made a point of maintaining her distance from others, of preserving her private space. The Raleigh Foster she created from that child depended on no one, needed nothing. She had a few friends, a few in college and grad school. Then she met Alex Walton during her first year with the ISA. They moved in together at Atlas' suggestion. Liz Walton's government ties made Alex a safe friend. She had quickly become her closest friend too. But not even Alex knew the whole story about the death of her father, Chance Foster. After she'd lost him, she was determined to be the best—and she'd done it. Top of her class, spotless record with the ISA, and no scars on her heart. Except Adam Grayson.

He was the first man, the only man. For him, she dropped her guard. With him, she found a haven in the chaos of her chosen life. Because of him, she'd almost loved. But Phillip's betrayal had utterly destroyed that small bit of happiness and left her with nothing.

In those days, she and Adam had collaborated on the Jafir project, a mission designed to help him infiltrate Scimitar. Adam would furnish the funds, and she, the ammunition. In the beginning, she and Cavanaugh operated in one area of the city, with Adam and Phillip in another. At the last minute, however, Cavanaugh had to leave the country. She'd never run a case alone. After a bitter fight about removing her, Atlas grudgingly decided she could remain behind and finish the mission alone, but she would report to Adam on her progress.

Although she only knew him as Merlin and as Caine Simons, she resented his assignment as babysitter. And they worked in concert, using the unusual parameters of their universe to flirt, though neither would ever admit it. But it was flirtation, pure and simple. With Adam's aid, Raleigh found a stash of plutonium in an Iranian mine waiting for a buyer. Her present to him was a miniature transmitter to destroy a Moroccan tycoon's safe and steal millions in gold bullion, all without leaving a shred of evidence behind.

With him, she laughed and learned to be silly. She forgot to be self-conscious about her abilities or her youth. With Adam, she became a different woman, one who was strong, sure, independent. He helped her discover that security, and much more she hadn't known. Until it was too late to share it with him.

Adam Grayson had been an enigma to her. A man who could be cold and ruthless with a contact, and gentle with a child in the marketplace the next. On long nights in the desert, patrolling their worksite, he serenaded her with music from the well-worn flute he carried with him. He understood the world beyond their guarded borders. They argued about literature and music, commiserated about sports and politics. And he would stay with her when the nightmares came, hold her as she fell back to sleep.

To conceal their connection to each other, they rented a vacant warehouse on the outskirts of town where Raleigh worked and slept. The owner, a greedy, nasty young woman hiding profits from her aging husband, agreed to the clandestine deal. They were almost finished, the order complete.

But, despite their closeness, neither spoke of the time before they came to Jafir. There was no room in their line of work for family histories or shared secrets. They knew their time together was limited, and accordingly, each held parts of themselves separate, inviolate. Time would soon run out, and they would go their separate ways. But even she, with her developed defenses, could not prevent her heart from racing when he entered the room. Accidental touches set off fireworks. The sight of him made her flush with pleasure. Because their time was short, however, she never told him so. And she vowed that she wouldn't. Admissions left the door open for expectations, she knew, and she learned a long time ago to expect nothing. From anyone.

She'd been thinking about her decision to hold her peace the night their world erupted. They'd been sitting in the dank warehouse, a space lit by oil lamps and a decrepit generator. Merlin's laptop whirred companionably as she clipped wires for the ignition of a two-chamber explosive. He'd shown up unexpectedly, a couple of days before they were to complete the final phase of their mission. The warehouse held most of her equipment and some of his.

Merlin worked out of the satellite hut with Sphinx, his partner. He would come and check on her, but his base was there. In fact, he'd been scheduled to help Sphinx do the final wire transfer tonight. With that last portion of funds, Merlin would become a part of the Scimitar inner circle and Scimitar could afford her last batch of explosives.

Raleigh looked around the room at her handiwork. Near the front door, a supply of chips, remote receivers, and computer paraphernalia leaned drunkenly against the doorjamb. Barrels of oil and fertilizer and vials of hazardous chemicals lined the perimeter of the warehouse. The Scimitar's order called for three additional Catatonia Surprise bombs, the double-barreled masterpiece that could destroy ten city blocks in a matter of seconds.

Adam passed Raleigh a canteen of tepid water. She took a swig from the nearly empty container and tossed the remaining contents back to him. Barely glancing up, he snapped the canteen out of the air. He possessed razor-sharp reflexes, obviously honed by years of practice. *What else can those hands do quickly,* she'd wondered, then blushed at the thought. These weeks with Adam had revealed a sensuality she'd never realized, a brazenness that disconcerted her. With every passing day, it became harder to hide her feelings.

Thoughtfully, she considered him, this man who stirred up desires she'd never imagined she'd feel. In the dusky light from the lamps, the most jaded observer could explain why his alter ego was a successful playboy instead of some other cover story. Eyes as black as coal radiated cunning and determination and a banked sexuality. Coiled muscles rippled beneath the thin cotton T-shirt he wore in deference to the humidity of the island. As it had too often, of late, her heart thundered in her ears. How many times had she imagined sliding her hands under that T-shirt and over the smooth skin she was certain lay beneath? She was contemplating how best to find out when he spoke.

"Is there a problem, Chimera?" Adam studied her with concern. "You have an odd look on your face."

"Nothing's wrong. I'm fine," she managed without giggling at her own outrageous thoughts.

"Are you sure?" He seemed unconvinced by her response. Instead, he walked over and crouched in front of her. The T-shirt, as dark as his eyes, stretched enticingly as he reached up to feel her forehead.

Raleigh reared back to avoid his touch. The chair teetered, then righted itself. Embarrassed by her reaction, she stared at the floor, refusing to meet eyes she was certain could read her mind.

Adam tilted her head up by the chin. With a reassuring nod, he explained "I was just checking for fever. You don't have to be afraid of me."

"I'm not afraid of you," she said as she pulled her chin from his light touch. Pleasure flickered where his skin met hers, scattering her thoughts.

Adam gave her a long look, then lifted her hand from her lap. His fingers closed around her wrist, the thumb drawing circles on her palm. "Your pulse is racing," he noted without inflection. "Are you sick?"

"No," she protested as she tried to pull her hand away. *This is all I need,* she thought with dismay, *to lose control two days before the end.* "I'm just jumpy," she explained while she looked at her feet.

"You're not the jumpy sort, Chimera. After three months, I can say that with certainty. But you *are* being evasive."

Her head shot up at that last comment. "Evasive? What do you mean?"

Adam smiled, the slow, sexy smile that never failed to send her system into overdrive. "We've danced around this for quite a while, Chimera." He turned her hand over and linked their fingers.

"I don't know what you're talking about." She tensed, tempted to acknowledge what could not be said.

"I'm talking about whatever is between us. The way I think about you at the oddest moments. The way I can't wait to get to this warehouse to see you. I'm talking about the fact that you feel the same way."

"No," she disagreed as her heart skittered. This would be foolish, wrong.

"Yes," he argued as he drew her to her feet. "Now you're just lying."

"About what?" she challenged. When evasion failed, counterattacks were the next best thing.

"About this." As though time ceased to exist, he lowered his mouth to hers.

And a firestorm struck. His mouth roamed across hers, igniting small fires with one kiss, soothing them with another, only to light more flames. Hard, demanding fingers traced the curve of her breasts, the length of her waist. He pulled her deeper into his embrace, his entire body meshed with her own. In untutored response, her hands trembled as she reached up to hold him, to caress the nape of his neck, measure the breadth of his shoulders. She experimented, churned by need and want and passion. Denials, evasions dissipated, burned away by their embrace. In the torrid silence of the moment, only the rumbling of their hearts could be heard.

But then the rumbling increased, reached a deafening crescendo. It was a thunder Raleigh recognized as the signature sound of ammonium nitrate aided by her special ingredients. The next explosion ripped the rear of the warehouse from the frame. Debris and rotting wooden planks missiled through the space, clubbing Raleigh to the dusty floor. A second falling board caught her in the stomach and forced the air from her lungs.

Fire lit the night sky, which poured in from the gaping hole in the now-open roof. Raleigh greedily sucked in large gasps of air. Surrounded by fallen lamps and highly explosive material, she managed to struggle to her knees. The smoke blinded her, but she managed to grab her backpack.

"Merlin!" she coughed out desperately. "Merlin!" Where was he?

Rising above her suddenly, Adam scooped her under his strongly corded arm, supporting her as if she were weightless. They ran from the building, Adam half carrying her, half dragging her to safety.

Singed fingers clenched her knapsack. Collapsing together on the rocky ground, Adam ran trembling hands over her body, searching for broken bones, cracked ribs. When he found nothing, he clasped her to him. Raleigh pushed away and frantically checked him for injuries.

Caught between the smoldering building and the dark expanse of night, he held her sooty face between his torn hands. And softly pressed his mouth to hers.

"I almost lost you in there," Adam breathed.

He's so beautiful, she thought wonderingly. "You didn't. You can't." Dazed, she covered his cheek with her palm.

Adam pressed his mouth to her open hand, then pulled her to her feet. "This was no accident," Adam said.

"They knew we were inside."

The warmth in his onyx eyes vanished. "Yes."

"But, you weren't supposed to be here."

"Yes. I told Sphinx I'd meet him back at the satellite hut." As he spoke, Raleigh saw realization dawn. "The satellite hut! That will be their next target!" He reached for the knapsack and the communicator Raleigh always carried with her.

"We can't contact him, Merlin." Raleigh shook her head sadly.

"Of course we can. He's gotta get out of there." Adam grabbed for the sack again, and Raleigh shoved it behind her.

"No, you can't! Think, Merlin! We're under radio blackout for a reason. They may have broken our code. If we make contact, they can complete their decryption."

"So?"

"If we use this, they'll also be able to locate us for sure. And every other communicator on this frequency."

"I don't care!"

"There are at least fifteen more people here, Merlin. I can't justify sacrificing their lives and years of work for one man."

"That 'one man' is my best friend."

"He understood the risks."

Without warning, Adam lunged at Raleigh. She rolled away, scissoring her legs to catapult to a fighting stance. Braced on the balls of her feet, she faced him.

"Don't do this, Merlin."

He circled her menacingly, eyes locked. "Then give me the radio." Shooting a leg out, he knocked Raleigh to the dirt. Kicking out, she swept him to the ground in front of her. They wrestled for a few more minutes, neither gaining ascendancy.

"Time's running out, Merlin. If you plan to save him, you need to go now," she pleaded, her chest heaving. The satellite hut lay less than two miles from their position. "Maybe they haven't hit it yet."

"Give me the damned radio, Chimera!" He pinned her to the baked earth.

"No!" She bucked underneath him and hurled the satchel into the flames. Both heard the crack as it connected with a barrel, and the flames consumed it.

Surging to his feet, Adam loomed over her, violence barely restrained. "You will pay for this, Chimera."

Concern fled. "Try me."

"If he dies, it's on your head."

"I've done nothing wrong."

"You just destroyed his one shot at survival! And you gave Scimitar the weapons. That's enough."

"Don't blame me for that! You were about to give them the money to finish paying for it."

"But you chose to offer them a preview."

"My orders were to give them a sample."

"Yes," he scoffed, "your damned orders. I hope they keep you company when you're alone again, Chimera. You'll need them."

Battered by the malevolence emanating from him, she tried to reason with him. Raleigh got to unsteady feet and reached for his shoulder. "Merlin?"

Adam slapped her hand away with a growl of impotent rage. "And to think I thought I cared about you. That I left Sphinx alone to come and tell you that I love you."

Raleigh recoiled as though struck. "You don't mean that."

He stared at her, then nodded in bitter agreement. "You're right. I don't mean it."

Then he left, at a dead run, heading for the hut. Only cinder and ash remained, and Phillip's body was never recovered. She stayed behind, trying to salvage her conscience. But in the aftermath of the explosions, the Scimitar soldiers captured her.

She finally escaped, with Cavanaugh's help, but not before the ISA had presumed her dead. Months in the government hospital left her thinner, harsher, different. Cavanaugh stayed by her side, coaxing her back to health. She owed her life to him, her sanity. She owed Cavanaugh peace.

Adam had to trust her and her abilities. Without his cooperation, she'd lose her only chance to find out who was after them and who killed Cavanaugh. Atlas had an agenda, as did Adam. As did she. To locate Phillip and Praxis. And neither Atlas nor Adam would stop her from avenging Cavanaugh's death. She hadn't been able to do it before, when her father had died in her place. But she'd do this last act for Cavanaugh. With Adam's help.

Beside the recliner, the phone rang, startling her. Each staccato burst ratcheted her headache up a notch. Soon, mercifully, the answering machine's perfunctory greeting announced, "I'm not in, please leave a message." *Beep.*

"Raleigh? Raleigh? Raleigh, it's Alex. Pick up the phone. Mom said you flew home last night. Pick up the phone. I'm just gonna keep talking until you do. And you know I will. Besides, your machine won't cut me off until you run out of tape, so this may take some time. While I'm waiting, I'll tell you about my latest plot idea. Allegra, the heroine, is a sleuth. Don't you love the word *sleuth?* It's so much more elegant than *detective. Sleuth.* Visions of Easy Rawlins and Jane Marple, combing through clues and—"

Raleigh acknowledged defeat and snatched the phone from its base. "Hello, Alex." She cradled the receiver against her shoulder, turning her attention to her calf. "I suppose asking you to go away for a while would do me no good?" she questioned, without much hope.

Alex replied cheerfully, "None whatsoever."

With a resigned sigh, Raleigh looked longingly at her bookcase with its silent books, then closed her eyes again. Alex was her best friend, or at least a friendly voice, and today she certainly needed one. "When did you get back to D.C.?"

"Yesterday morning. I got your message about going to Atlanta. How's Judge Warner?"

"The judge is fine. He asked about you."

"What'd you tell him?"

"I said you were as big a pain as ever."

"But twice as cute, right?"

Raleigh chuckled wearily. "Right."

"So what are you doing back so soon? I thought you were gone for a few weeks."

"Then why were you talking to my machine?"

"Like I said, Mom told me you were back. Oh, and the need for human contact. I've been starved for affection." Alex's dramatic tones drew another smile from Raleigh.

"Alex, sweetheart, it's a machine."

"You take what you can get."

"I thought you had Michael or Matthew or whatever his name is."

"Old news. He thought Proust was a wine and *Cleopatra Jones* was a porno flick. Philistine," Alex grumbled. "Nope, now it's just me and your machine. And I don't appreciate you interrupting our tryst."

"Then I'll let you get back to it. Bye, Alex."

Knowing Raleigh just might hang up the phone, Alex called out, "Wait! Raleigh? Don't you dare!"

"Make up your mind. It's either me or the machine."

"Not much of a choice, you know."

"Adding insult to annoyance, Alex?" Raleigh asked warningly.

"You know I've always loved you more. I choose you."

"I always lose at this game."

"If you weren't due back until Monday, why are you home?"

"Finished my job."

"Why not stay in Atlanta for the weekend?"

"I had a meeting."

Alex recognized the familiar pattern of short answers that usually accompanied discussions of Raleigh's employers. "Sounds like fun."

"Yes. Loads."

Alex heard the obvious sarcasm and the underlying weariness twisting through her words. "You sound grumpier than usual. Wanna talk about it?"

"Nope."

"Good. I'll be there in half an hour. Bye!"

Raleigh began to tell her not to come and instead found herself listening to the dead air of the telephone. Given that Alex had to travel from Adams Morgan to DuPont Circle by Metro, she estimated that her promised thirty minutes would likely be closer to forty-five. Alex was notoriously absentminded and would return home at least four times before making it to Raleigh's door. Despite the fact that Alex owned a perfectly good car, her cause this year was air pollution, so she refused to drive during the day except in emergencies. Forty-five minutes. Just enough time to sulk for a while longer.

Forty minutes later, Alex sailed through the door and into the living room. Giving the room a long, arrogant look, she said critically, "Raleigh, you know there are laws against such Spartan surroundings. And in case you hadn't noticed, color is in this millennium."

She wandered into the room, eyeing it critically. As was her custom, she stopped at the window. On the window seat sat a group of photographs. One held a picture of Raleigh with Alex. A larger frame displayed a portrait of the Walton family with Raleigh. The third photo, a small, color snapshot, bore the picture of a young man in his early twenties. The oddly colored eyes, the sharp chin, and the high forehead were identical to Raleigh's own face and belonged to her father, Chance Foster.

As always, Alex was drawn to the picture of the man who'd raised Raleigh for the first eleven years of her life. On the rare occasions when Raleigh spoke of her father, there were shades of affection and remorse. But the stories always ended abruptly, never explaining how Chance Foster died.

Alex knew more than others, that a social worker found her in a hospital room waiting to be interviewed by police following the death of her father in a backroom brawl. After that, Raleigh had been raised in a series of foster homes until she'd gone to college. Alex suspected more than others that whatever killed Chance Foster had scarred Raleigh more than she would ever admit. She'd learned, in the early days of their friendship, that despite the nightmares that woke her, Chance Foster and his death were off-limits. Even now.

"Redecorating in your mind, again?" Raleigh asked wryly.

"One can only hope." Alex turned to face Raleigh, her chocolate-brown eyes concerned. She saw the pallor under Raleigh's skin, the banked tempest in her eyes. "You want to tell me what's going on?"

"I told you. Everything's fine." Raleigh moved past Alex and headed for the kitchen. "Want a drink?"

"A Coke if you've got it," Alex called out.

"You know I've installed a drip in case you start to take the stuff intravenously."

"Raleigh, it's not fair to tease me like that," Alex replied with mock seriousness as she entered the kitchen. The room repeated the spare lines of the living room but had a bit more color, pleasing her artistic sensibilities. Of course, Alex had picked out the mosaic tiles personally.

"Then don't ask dumb questions." Raleigh poured a glass of Coke and unscrewed the top on a bottle of water. She carried them to the table.

"Like what's wrong?"

"I said—"

"You lied." Alex struggled to control her hurt. "I am your friend, Raleigh, whether you like it or not. When will you start to trust me, even a little bit?"

"It's not that I don't trust you—" Raleigh began.

"But it's secret or private or otherwise off-limits. I know the drill." Setting the glass on the table with a thud, Alex stiffly rose from the chair. "I'll talk to you later."

Raleigh rubbed a hand against a throbbing temple. Remorse intensified the pounding. Alex was right. She always hid behind work or history or silence. "Alex?"

"Yes?" Her body ramrod straight, Alex paused in the doorway.

"Look, it's been a long day," Raleigh explained contritely.

"Shutting me out isn't a new event, Raleigh." Alex turned to confront Raleigh, and fury replaced resignation. "I guess I'm finally fed up, though." Advancing on her, Alex ran a slim hand through waves of ebony hair. She halted in front of Raleigh, building up steam. "For weeks now, you've wandered around this apartment like you've just lost your best friend. Since I'm not dead, I'll have to assume it's someone else. But who?" Alex tossed her hands up and rolled her eyes heavenward. "How should I know? You don't tell me anything. You disappear for months at a time, doing work for some covert organization no one else has ever heard of. I don't ask about the bruises and casts and bullet wounds, because I know you won't answer," she railed, her gaze moving to Raleigh's shoulder.

Raleigh resisted the impulse to cover her hidden wound.

"But it's been different lately, Raleigh. *You've* been different. And I don't think you have anyone else to turn to. You won't talk to me, and by my calculation, that leaves no one," Alex concluded. "You look awful, Raleigh. Much more, and you're gonna break."

Raleigh walked over to Alex, eyes dark with emotion. She *was* different. Alex was right. She did need to tell someone. Everything else was changing, why not her? Taking a deep breath, she spoke. "Is it that obvious?"

"Only to someone who has known you most of your life." Alex steered Raleigh to the kitchen table. "I promise not to divulge any trade secrets or engage in counterespionage." As they sat, Alex sipped her Coke, waiting for the story.

Raleigh took a deep breath and confessed. "It's a man."

Alex could not disguise her shock. "A real man?"

"Yes, a real man." Raleigh was momentarily distracted from her angst by annoyance. "What kind of question is that?"

"The obvious kind, given your rather solitary lifestyle, my dear. So who is he, and when do I get to meet him?"

"Can't tell you, and never."

Alex understood the parameters of conversation with Raleigh, even in the privacy of her home. Despite daily sweeps and numerous anti-listening devices, the possibility of uninvited listeners loomed too close for carelessness. "Oh."

Raleigh contemplated Alex for a moment, the habit of privacy and self-sufficiency warring with the need for companionship and solace. A bit of both won. She began slowly. "I've known him for a while. Before, it was never an issue. I was mildly infatuated with him."

"Mildly infatuated?"

"That's all."

Staring at the floor, Raleigh never noticed the flash of pain on Alex's face. Raleigh was her best friend. She had been in love with someone and never told her. But she doubted that Raleigh knew she's been in love. "What happened?"

"Nothing came of it."

"Why not?"

"It was inappropriate," Raleigh hedged. *Plus, I killed his best friend,* she thought.

"Did you tell him how you felt?"

"Of course not."

"And now?"

"Now I have to work very closely with him, and my feelings are complicated."

"Complicated how?"

"I don't really know him. And I'm not sure I trust him. He certainly doesn't trust me."

"And you can't avoid him?"

"No."

"Is he attracted to you at all?"

"I wouldn't think so . . ." Raleigh trailed off, bracing herself for her next revelation. "Except that he kissed me."

"What?"

"He kissed me."

"What happened?"

"I bit him." Her voice was sheepish. "He deserved it," she said defensively.

"Oh, Raleigh."

To avoid the lecture certain to follow, Raleigh rushed on. "Anyway, I've got to work closely with him and manage these, um, feelings. And I don't know how."

"What are 'these, um, feelings' exactly?"

"Lust. Attraction." Raleigh closed her eyes and pictured Adam, framed by the sun on the Desira Plateau and by the magnolias in Liz's garden. "Alex, he's got these intense black eyes that seem to see everything and still look right through you. And he has a voice like liquid sex."

"How would you know? Or is this another secret you have yet to share?"

"Shut up." Raleigh squelched down the urge to stop her confessional and continued her litany. "He's brilliant and beautiful and my sworn enemy. With a mouth like sin." She covered her giggle with her hand.

"Raleigh Foster giggling over a man? What is the world coming to?"

Raleigh stiffened, embarrassed by the outburst. Alex caught the movement, and quickly moved to forestall the return of the serious Raleigh. "Don't run away from me, Raleigh. Take it like a woman. You've spent years making fun of my penchant for falling in love with unsuitable men, so you can't begrudge me."

With a sad half smile, Raleigh returned to her seat. "I don't know what to do. He hates me, and he has every reason to. And I have every right to hate him." She dropped her face into her hands and sighed. "But I don't. And I'm feeling so many things right now."

"So what's wrong with that?"

"I'm losing control." She, the one who never disobeyed, had defied Atlas' directives twice. Once by sneaking away from Cavanaugh, and then again last night. "I don't know who I am any more."

"Raleigh, what's wrong with that?" Alex repeated. "Everyone has to change, even you."

"I don't want to be someone else." Raleigh pounded a fist on the blond pine. "I spend my life playing parts. I know who Raleigh Foster is. And I don't want to change her."

Alex grabbed her hands and cupped them in her own. "You do know who you are, Raleigh. But maybe it's time you became someone more. You grew up early, honey, but there's no law against finding more. You've earned the right to test your limits."

"What if I lose myself, Alex? What if I just fly apart? When I'm with him, I can feel it happening. I get lost in him. And I've made promises that I can't break." She took a deep breath. "And I can't have both."

"Why not? What will stop you?" Alex waited until Raleigh looked at her. "You've always done the impossible, kiddo. What's to stop you from having it all?"

Raleigh's face slowly settled into lines of determination. "Fate. But I can work with that." She could work with Adam and find out if Phillip was Cavanaugh's killer. She would remember that he was Phillip's best friend. But maybe, she could have both. Adam's love and Cavanaugh's revenge. At least she could try.

Six

"You can break the encryption code, can't you?" Raleigh asked sarcastically as she leaned forward to peer over Adam's shoulder. Once again, he shifted to the right, obstructing her view of the blue computer screen. For the umpteenth time that morning, she was treated to a close-up of the back of his head, and she fought to control her need to do him physical harm.

"Can you stop standing over me?" Adam snapped back, twisting to glare at her. His long fingers drummed an impatient tattoo on the desk.

"Yes, if you would stop blocking the screen." Grasping the arm of the chair, she managed to roll it a few precious inches. "Perhaps in your years as the titan of corporate America, you've forgotten about teamwork?"

Adam slid the chair back into place, then rolled forward a few inches more. "And perhaps in your years of play-acting, you've forgotten that you don't know the first thing about decoding files."

"I know enough," Raleigh retorted coolly. The scent of his cologne, a strong woodsy fragrance uniquely him, reached her nose as she leaned over him again. She battled not to inhale. Deeply. *He's driving me crazy.* "Of course, I don't make a habit of sneaking into government files."

"No, you blow up their buildings instead," Adam smirked.

They'd been bickering since early morning, and lunchtime was quickly approaching. Their search of GCI's files revealed nothing worthwhile. The reports submitted by Phillip and Cavanaugh offered only what they'd always known, and their investigation of the scientists' private documents yielded little new information.

After an argument with Raleigh and brief consultation with Atlas, Adam had decided to hack into the files of other ISA sections. Although all were part of the agency family, each section hid secrets from the others, as spies often did. The code of honor in the ISA demanded allegiance—with necessary caveats, as Atlas reminded them. They could break into the separate division files, but they were forbidden to hack into the primary organizational files.

Adam spoke again. "Is there a reason you've been such a brat today?"

"A brat?" she repeated with a tone that Adam knew spelled danger. But he found he couldn't resist.

"Yes, a bad-tempered, ill-mannered brat," he said.

"Could it possibly be three days of red-eye travel back and forth to baby-sit you?" Raleigh asked with falsely dulcet tones.

Adam bristled at the insult. "If anyone's doing the baby-sitting, sweetheart—"

"I had to take you to D.C. and fly back here to watch you not find anything useful in your own files. Perhaps 'baby-sitting' is a bit of an overstatement." Raleigh leaned in to smile at him. "And 'baby' may be a bit presumptuous." At the moment, he looked the part of the casual intellectual, complete with wire-rimmed reading glasses. Combined with fallen-angel looks and a whipcord-lean body, he seemed entirely too appealing. Besides, she'd always had a weakness for the sexy, intelligentsia look.

"Is this banter designed to distract me from my earlier question?"

"You had a real question?" Raleigh asked snidely.

"What is wrong with you? You've done nothing but pout and whine since you got here."

"I've neither pouted nor whined," she corrected. "If I'm slightly perturbed, it's because you've been a royal pain in—"

"Tut, tut, Dr. Foster. Watch your language."

Stifling the retort hanging on her tongue, Raleigh reigned in her temper. *Don't think about it, Foster. He's just trying to bait you.* She decided to change the subject. "If you insist on weaseling into their files, we might want to discuss what we're looking for."

"Seems obvious to me. I'm looking for any mention of Praxis."

"What about the background checks?"

"GCI files indicate that the guys did them."

"We need to confirm if Cavanaugh and Phillip actually conducted the background checks or if they passed them off to another department."

"Why would they shunt them off to someone else?"

"You all knew our division was not supposed to interfere with domestic issues. I don't understand why they'd run the checks, even for you."

"Phillip knew I needed the information, and Cavanaugh monitored domestic industrial espionage before he transferred to Atlas' unit. My company had to have the information, so I turned to the best."

"Still—" she began.

"Friendship, Raleigh," Adam interrupted. "A concept I doubt you understand."

Again she saw Alex's hurt expression from yesterday and heard a hollow note of truth in his denouncement. "I understand duty and responsibility," she said defensively.

"Ever the Girl Scout," Adam scoffed.

Bending forward, she replied sharply, "Excuse me?" Noting her angry position, Raleigh forcibly relaxed in her seat, folding her arms across her chest. *I will not let him bait me,* she recited silently.

Adam snorted inelegantly and continued to type in commands. "Not everyone sees the world in terms of the 'Rules of Engagement', Miss Retentive. Occasionally, we mortals actually help one another, with or without authorization." The computer beeped, signaling the breach of another security wall.

"The rules exist for a reason, Mister Cavalier," she retorted, stung by his assessment.

Adam laughed, a short, bitter sound. "Yes. To give people like you an excuse to not feel."

"You know nothing about me."

"I know enough."

Defensiveness fled, chased away by pride. She'd be damned if she would spend the next three weeks justifying her actions or being blamed for a crime that may not have happened. This constant barrage of recriminations had to end. Today.

"For the last time, I *was not* and *am not* responsible for what happened to Phillip," Raleigh declared.

"And, for the last time, I don't care to hear your

excuses. I was there, remember?" Cold and steel underscored his words, filled his midnight eyes.

Raleigh barely repressed a shiver. "Obviously, you only remember what you want to recall."

"I remember saving you from a burning building, while you let my partner die in an inferno on the other side of town," he grated.

"That's not how it happened," she protested. She felt compelled to explain her choices. "Adam, I am sorry about Phillip. I didn't intend for him to—"

"To die," he finished softly. "You killed him. You live with it."

"There's nothing to live with—" she began angrily. Then she was halted by a steady hum from the computer. "What is it?" she asked.

"An intercepted communiqué from Jafir. But what's it doing in Domestic Espionage?"

"The text?"

" 'Diamond acquired. Move to next phase'," Adam read aloud. "The mole is inside Domestic Espionage."

"Or that's what we're *supposed* to think," Raleigh suggested. "Can you trace the recipient?"

Adam typed in several commands, to no avail. "They've covered their tracks too well. I can't trace it."

"Well, at least we've found something."

"Not much."

"It's a start. Speaking of which"—Raleigh said, rising to her feet—"we can't spend the next few weeks at each other's throats."

"Why not?" Adam retorted.

"You really can't keep up with me, Grayson."

"Don't get cocky, Foster." He stood as well, intrigued by her offer. "What'd you have in mind?"

"A truce. A temporary cease-fire. No more mention of three years ago. I can't change it, and we can't agree on it."

Adam sat silent for a moment, then spoke. "And you, what do you do?"

"What do you want?" As soon as she said the words, she wanted to snatch them back. Stifling a blush, she waited for his answer. The knowing look in his eyes did not bode well, particularly in light of their last conversation about needs.

With a faintly amused smile, as though he'd read her mind, he replied, "I want you to acknowledge that the rules don't all apply this time. I can't go under with a partner who will dispute me at every turn."

"If you expect me to become an adoring sycophant, you will be sadly disappointed," Raleigh said warily.

"No abject adulation. Just a little bend. And a few rules broken," Adam coaxed, his smile at once fascinating and alarming. Brilliant white teeth gleamed against darkly stained lips in a feral, masculine smile. The mischievous grin was the antithesis of his gaze, for his inky black eyes remained shadowed and aloof.

"Within reason."

"Same here."

With an uneasy truce in place, the next few hours flew by. Adam printed out reams of information, and Raleigh searched for mentions of Praxis, GCI, or the diamond. They ordered in food from the company restaurant. Adam sifted through another stack of papers. Raleigh sat next to him, reading reports on the secretary's table, her lithe legs propped against the drawers of the desk. They seemed to stretch for miles, beginning someplace just below her shoulders.

"Break time." Raleigh bolted up in the chair, placing both feet back on the floor.

Grateful for the distraction, he mocked, "The child needs a nap?"

Her chin came up, a sure signal of an impending battle. He remembered the gesture, the impertinent tilt revealing the elegant line of her throat. And the sensitive, sensual place just below her ear, where the skin was soft and fragrant. Where a man's lips could linger, revel. The blood thudded through his veins, heavy and dark. Abruptly, he tore his attention away from the all-too-appealing column to focus on her words.

"Ten minutes," Raleigh said. "And 'this woman' has been flying cross-country for two days now," she reminded him.

"As have I," he replied without sympathy.

Raleigh smirked at him. "Sans private jet?"

"Touché."

Raleigh rose from the chair, stretching sinuously, a feline movement. She stretched her arms overhead, and the fine jersey of her dress strained across taut, rounded breasts. Oblivious to Adam's attention, Raleigh rolled her shoulders, dropped her head forward, and arched her back. The short skirt of her jade-green dress climbed up her thighs and clung lovingly to each firm curve. Her satiny skin glowed against the rich hue of the dress, beckoning for a touch, a caress. His touch. His caress.

"Raleigh—" he began, his voice hoarse with arousal.

"Yes?" Raleigh slowly uncurled her body and faced him.

"Is your break over?" Adam coughed to clear his ragged throat.

"I thought I had ten minutes." Raleigh tugged at her hiked hem, smoothing her skirt into place. Adam followed the movement with grave disappointment.

"Sorry to interrupt." *I've got to get out of here before I drag her to the floor and do something foolish.* "I'll be right back." Escaping the suddenly stifling room, Adam went to the outer office. He skirted the secretary's desk and strode out the exterior door. As it closed behind him with a whisper of sound, he paused. "Get a hold of yourself, Grayson," he muttered. "Remember who you are."

The discreet platinum plate beside the door read ADAM GRAYSON, CHIEF EXECUTIVE OFFICER. Fate and heredity had given him the title, but skill and dedication made it true. Late nights, dramatic acquisitions, and healthy profits established him as the legitimate heir to his parents' legacy. Critics who once derided his selection now turned to him for advice. GCI was now his life, as surely as the ISA had once been.

The world he created for himself lay before him, garbed in steel and glass, fueled by money and power. Offices where busy minds developed methods to constantly fill the coffers ringed the high-rise in midtown Atlanta. Twenty-seven stories, each level filled with GCI administration and company subsidiaries. People who depended on him, believed in him. He craved that sense of responsibility as much as he'd once hungered for adventure. At GCI, the edge of danger had been smoothed, civilized, almost vanquished.

Rather than contend with mercenaries and high-tech thugs, he spent his hours engaged in skirmishes of capitalism with Italian-suited privateers and Ivy-League educated marauders.

If he longed for the days of hidden identities and layered secrets, he refused to acknowledge it. He had buried the past along with Phillip. And his feelings.

Until Raleigh returned from the dead.

Then the man he'd convinced himself he'd become vanished in one careless moment. In less than a week, he had come back to the life he'd abandoned in disgust. But now the disgust resembled leashed anticipation. Already, he could feel Merlin steal into his mind, reminding him of how it felt to be alive. Decoding files, chasing phantoms—these were the actions of the man he'd once been. The man he was fast becoming again. And Adam felt helpless to withstand its lure, knowing it was too powerful to turn away a second time.

With the return of his alter ego came other hidden desires. Desires he believed had been incinerated in a haze of flame swirled through his veins, heating his blood. Answering its summons, he'd agreed to partner with his enemy and even to abide by a truce. Dormant longing leaped to life full-blown, clouding his mind with visions of Raleigh. The smoke of her voice, the grace of her walk, the curve of her body. Memory tangled with the present, and passion wrestled with bleak, harsh instincts.

He no longer knew what would win. Should win. The puzzle of Raleigh seemed beyond his reach.

But solving the riddle of Praxis was within his ability.

On the seventeenth floor, his brainchild, Compu-

Secure, occupied a suite of rooms. For the last few hours, he and Raleigh had combed division reports searching for any clue to the identity of the GCI or ISA mole and found nothing. But the main ISA files, off-limits and protected by impenetrable security systems, held the key. Impenetrable security systems. Based on CompuSecure software.

Returning to his office, Adam pulled Raleigh from the couch and headed for the door.

"Excuse me, where are we going," Raleigh protested.

Ignoring her disgruntled noises, he placed his palm against the security panel and keyed in the seventeenth floor. Bypassing the security codes, they entered CompuSecure. A marked departure from typical office décor, the room sported a set of randomly sized worktables, cubist desks, and florid colors on the walls and floors. Bright green, vivid blue, and muted tangerine vied for prominence. The original interior walls had been demolished, creating a completely open workspace. The curiously shaped desks and their futuristic computers were scattered throughout the area.

A mainframe computer towered over the other furnishings. Upon closer inspection, Raleigh saw that the mainframe actually opened to reveal a sliding console that held a smaller computer, steadily whirring away.

"Adam, what are we doing here?" Raleigh asked cautiously. She was afraid she already knew the answer. But Adam confirmed it.

"We're going inside the ISA. All the way," he answered defiantly.

The old Raleigh would have protested the break in protocol, the direct violation of orders. Instead, she replied, "What can I do?"

Hiding his surprise at her easy acquiescence, Adam said simply, "Just watch for now." Drawing up a chair, Adam began entering commands into the computer, his fingers flying over the keys. Raleigh assumed her post, peering over his shoulder, seated in a chair she filched from a nearby desk. Intrigued by one display, she stood to get a closer look. She swiftly read the file, leaning forward to double-check a document's wording.

Her breasts brushed against Adam's back, then pressed against him as she leaned forward even further. Shivers of excitement coursed through her, tightening her breasts, pooling in her stomach.

Refusing to show concern for her awkward position, Raleigh decided to ease away—and quickly recognized her error. The unhurried pace heightened her awareness of his sleekly muscled back, the fabric between them only intensifying the sensations.

Finally, she was able to stand and step away from him.

"Must you hover?" Adam grumbled tightly.

"Must you take so long?" she retorted huskily.

"If you insist on hovering."

"I'm not 'hovering.' I'm researching."

"Can't you wait until I print it out?"

"Obviously not."

"Well, you'll have to wait." Adam rolled the chair forward, completely obscuring her view of the monitor.

Incensed, Raleigh hooked a foot underneath the swivel-bottom and jerked it backward. Reacting quickly, Adam grabbed her arm and pulled her down on top of him. The chair spun wildly, spurred by the force of her fall. Drunkenly, they careened into the far wall. Adam quickly wrapped his arms around Raleigh, holding her in his lap to prevent her spill. At the same moment, Raleigh clutched at his shoulders. Jarred by their collision with the wall, Raleigh found her mouth next to Adam's.

In an instant, antagonism slid into an edgier, needier emotion. She silently studied the dark, sensual, unsmiling mouth and recalled with stunning clarity its feel against her own. *Run,* she thought distantly.

She lifted her hand, reaching for his taut cheek.

Tracing the line of his jaw, Raleigh brushed her fingers along dark caramel skin, amazed by its smoothness. Its heat. Unable to break away, she stroked his cheek with the palm of her hand, slid her fingers into his hair. Hard. Soft.

Questions jumbled her mind. Hard. Soft. Could both be true?

If she kissed him again, would the aching end?

Raleigh lowered her head and pressed her lips against the corner of his mouth. Delightful.

Raleigh feathered a kiss across hard, masculine lips, searching for answers. Awareness burst across her skin, flooded her system. Captured by the sensations, she bent to kiss him again, to taste him more fully.

At the last moment, Adam turned his head a fraction to meet her.

Raleigh jerked away and leaped from his lap. She stumbled. Adam reached out to steady her, but she stepped away. Mortification washed through her.

"I'm sorry. Uh, thank you. For holding me. I mean, for catching me," Raleigh stammered.

They couldn't do this. She couldn't do this. He wasn't Merlin anymore. The man she loved was gone. It would be suicide to pretend otherwise. She couldn't afford to misunderstand their encounter in the garden, his overture in the office. Calmed, she reminded herself of a fundamental rule of war—a truce did not mean forgiveness. The moment at the party had been a trick of moonlight and mystery. The episode in Atlas' office was nothing more than an attempt at intimidation. He was Adam Grayson. Too dangerous, too attractive, too bitter to want her again. Forgetting this lesson would be more perilous than Scimitar could ever be.

"I am sorry," she repeated, her voice stronger this time.

"No problem," Adam replied quietly.

Silently, Raleigh returned to the workstation.

Adam remained in the seat and watched her walk away. *She bewitches me,* he mused. *Drawing me in, only to turn away at the last moment, leaving me ready and rejected.* But his discomfort had less to do with her forwardness than with his reaction. How could something so simple as the brush of lips feel so elemental? When he held her against him, the temptation, the want stunned him. Her lean yet remarkably lush body teased him. Then her eyes, at once starkly innocent and thoroughly mature, beckoned him. Suddenly, he couldn't look away. Not when she lowered her lips. Not when her mouth almost met his.

Then he saw himself plunging inside those dark recesses, tasting her again. Adam understood the wanting. Just as he understood what would follow. He'd forget—again. Forget his mission, forget his distrust. His slick grasp on control would slip away completely. But there was no place in his world for her brand of treachery. Staring at her mouth, he wanted to savor it. He had to resist. However, before she'd discovered his weakness, she turned away.

Adam pushed the chair back to the console. Raleigh said nothing and continued to read the screen. She had her head bowed low over the computer, not lifting it at the sound of his return. Adam pulled up a file and continued his search. Silence stretched between them until Adam spoke again.

"I think I've found a clue." He waited for Raleigh to look at him. "In the Domestic Espionage files, I located a notation about a project named 'Momentum.' "

" 'Praxis' is Greek for action," she said.

"Exactly."

"Is there a separate file or simply a mention?"

"Just a note, but I'm sure there must be a file."

"Can you access it?"

"Not yet."

"What's the date on that report?"

"Last year."

"If Espionage has a file on Praxis *and* the communiqué, they could know who our mole is."

"Then why wouldn't they tell Atlas? Autonomy aside, none of the groups would intentionally put another agent's life in jeopardy."

"But a single agent might, if he's the traitor. It's not as though either file was easy to get into."

"An agent from Domestic Espionage working with one of my scientists and with Scimitar," Adam concluded.

Raleigh concurred. "It makes sense."

"Well, then let's find out who our culprit is." Adam printed out a list of files and handed them to Raleigh. "Use one of those computers to cross-reference each name on this list with GCI personnel files."

The list of files contained the names of the agents in the Domestic Espionage group. Raleigh entered the command codes Adam gave her and started digging.

A few hours later, she found a match.

"Darrick Josephs," Raleigh announced wearily.

"What?" Adam stalked over to the computer and scowled.

"He's been with Domestic Espionage since graduation."

"That was before Cavanaugh left the group."

The implication was obvious. "And while Phillip was on loan to them," Raleigh said, spinning the chair to face him.

Taking a step forward, Adam replied angrily, "Phillip wouldn't betray me."

"And Cavanaugh would betray me?"

"The files prove that Cavanaugh helped the ISA put Darrick Josephs into my company. It proves that Josephs has had access to Praxis and to internal ISA information. No one knew more about the agency than Cavanaugh."

"He wasn't a traitor!" Her golden eyes flashed with vehemence. "How do you explain Phillip's role then? You said both ran the check." She pointed an accusatory finger at the damning name. "Phillip knew much more about computers than Cavanaugh did. He could have encrypted the files," Raleigh challenged.

Cold fury filled Adam's eyes. "Phillip would not betray me," he repeated stonily.

"But Cavanaugh would betray me? I nearly died in Jafir."

"Who got you out?"

"Cavanaugh. But—"

"No." Adam cut across her response, his voice icy with rage. "Cavanaugh set us up and decided to come back and get you, probably in an attack of conscience. And he let Phillip die."

"Or maybe Phillip set us all up. We never found his body. And how about why? And how? Praxis was in its early stages then," she reasoned. "Who could have known enough about its potential to stage such an elaborate scheme? Put a mole in the ISA and in GCI so that you can use him one day to sell the blueprints. Since Phillip wasn't working for you anymore, he wouldn't have had access himself."

"Phillip would never do that. But Cavanaugh would. Maybe he was getting tired of the ISA. And he knew more than enough about Scimitar. He's the one who got me in there. Why not put a traitor on the payroll to help pad his retirement? You said he was ambushed in Jafir. Maybe he was double-crossed. And I'll prove it." It was an oath.

Raleigh corrected him, her voice full of promise. "You're wrong, Adam. But *we'll* find out. Together." As though she would let him do anything alone. *I trust him as far as I can throw him,* she fumed. Accusing Cavanaugh when she knew Phillip was behind it. And now she had proof.

"Together," he repeated solemnly. As if he would let her out of his sight. Cavanaugh was part of this, but of course, she refused to consider the possibility. She'd always been blindly loyal to the old man. Naiveté and loyalty were a dangerous combination, especially in an agent. Still, Cavanaugh had been a good friend to him. Part of Adam hoped both he and Raleigh were wrong.

"Maybe we're missing another piece of the puzzle," Adam said as he reached out and tapped her arm thoughtfully. A tiny furrow appeared between his brows.

"What are you saying?" Raleigh asked with suspicion.

"Think about it." Adam absently stroked his finger back and forth along her shoulder. "Phillip and Cavanaugh both knew about Praxis. And they both had access to these files."

Surprised by his unexpected touch and the sudden change in tone, Raleigh tried to ignore the sensations shimmering up her arms. "Why would either one—"

"Leave such an obvious trail?" Adam finished, his thumb tracing small circles. "I don't know."

Butterflies fluttered inside her stomach. She would not be distracted, or would she? "Hiding in plain sight." Raleigh answered confidently, sliding her hand away.

"Hold on." Adam drew his hand up and rested his chin on his fist. "Perhaps it's intended to be obvious."

"As I said, we'd never suspect the obvious, so it could be a ruse to throw us off track." Raleigh replied.

Adam leaned forward and captured her shoulders. "No. Not hiding in plain sight but as a plant. If it is a plant, then Cavanaugh or Phillip is the culprit and we look no further." He slowly massaged her tensed muscles, a habit developed during their time in Jafir.

Her skin warmed beneath his touch. "The real mole escapes detection. And if it isn't a plant?" Raleigh breathed.

Adam's hands tightened briefly, then released her. "If it isn't a plant, then Cavanaugh is the culprit—and he betrayed us both."

"You forgot the third option," Raleigh insisted.

"And that would be?"

"Phillip was the turncoat, and that's why he died."

"Phillip would not turn on me!" Adam thundered.

"And Cavanaugh would deceive me?" Raleigh countered.

"Cavanaugh is the more likely suspect," he grated. "I say we concentrate on him."

She raised a brow at the ring of command in his voice. "Who put you in charge? This is *my* mission," she said mildly.

"*Your* mission, hell. Praxis is my technology. And Scimitar was my case."

"You deserted us, remember?" she taunted. "I'm responsible now." He'd have to get used to working for her now.

"We'll see about that."

Seven

Incensed, Adam stalked to the phone and punched in a series of numbers. *We'll settle this once and for all,* he thought with irritation. He might have to be her partner. He might have to curb his tongue when it came to Phillip. But hell would freeze over before he took orders from a novice. *Particularly this one,* he seethed. Calling Raleigh obnoxious would not begin to describe her demeanor when she thought she was right. Add authority to the mix, and she'd be insufferable.

Settling on the corner of the desk, he caught a glimpse of her from the corner of his eye. Raleigh remained in her seat, her expression a study in mild amusement and defiance. It would please him to no end to wipe that smug look from her face.

Her re-entry into his life carried with it nothing but aggravation. Like the weapons she created, she'd burst into his world, shattering the fortress he'd painfully constructed. Banked desires, repressed guilt, and torn loyalties battered him from all sides. Indeed, he had felt little else since their eyes locked two nights ago.

Assailed by emotions he could scarcely contain, he'd forgotten the rules of engagement. Remember the objective. Protect the battlements. Allow no infiltration. Crush the enemy.

He lost the first skirmish because he'd been taken by surprise. Although his mind did not recognize Raleigh, his body did. She'd shed the lingering adolescent plumpness, revealing a sleek, stunning form. The pleasant alto deepened to a magnificent contralto that purred over insults and slid under challenges. More than just the physical attraction, however, was the basic connection between them that spanned distance, time, and betrayal. It retained the power to erase lucid thought, necessary intention. So he submitted to a partnership, despite his plans to the contrary. And he acquiesced to a truce, violating his promise of intolerance.

But all was not lost. He would exonerate Phillip from this latest charge. Once they'd recovered Praxis and found Zeben, he would settle his vendetta against Scimitar, in spite of Atlas' instructions. Maybe he could also win on the personal front, forcing Raleigh to concede defeat on the field of pleasure.

I may yet lose the war, Adam mused fatalistically, *but every battle counts.*

Cradling the receiver, he listened for the nearly inaudible click that would signal his connection to the ISA office exchange. Because the organization did not officially exist, a caller had to be routed through several existing agency lines before ISA personnel would acknowledge the call.

As the call was routed through cabinet offices and Senate subcommittee phone lines, Adam continued to fume. Atlas trusted her, but surely he understood that Adam was the better choice. Otherwise, why bring him out of retirement? Certainly not to add insult to grievous injury by granting this child dominion over his movements?

With her pertinacious sense of fair play, Raleigh would insist on turning Zeben over to the authorities. Adam didn't intend to let them have him. If he indeed ordered the hit on the satellite hut, Zeben would die at his hands.

When dead air greeted his first attempt, he depressed the hook and dialed a second time. After the third attempt, he realized the protocol had changed and he no longer had access. Not without assistance. From her. Plus, the indigo display on the CompuSecure wall clock read five after midnight. Atlas was at home now, presumably fast asleep in bed. They'd have to contact Atlas on his private line. A number he no longer knew. Add another insult to the growing litany of injuries. He grunted unintelligibly and shoved the receiver at Raleigh.

Barely suppressing a smirk, Raleigh took the phone and contacted Atlas on his secured line. Adam lifted the companion receiver and listened in.

"Chimera reporting."

"This couldn't wait until morning?" Atlas barked, his voice gruff from sleep.

"Merlin decided it was imperative." *I'm not taking the fall for this,* her look said.

"Report."

"Partial target acquired. Dubious origin," Raleigh said. Explanations would have to wait until later, when Adam wasn't around to dispute her facts. Finding the correlation between Josephs and Phillip only increased the likelihood that Phillip wasn't a captive but a willing participant in the Scimitar theft. The information belied Atlas' theory of coercion or memory loss, pointing instead to a plan at least half a decade old.

"What next, then?"

"Will proceed as planned." First a flight to New York, then to Geneva. Switching planes, they'd head to Crete, then hop a private jet to Jafir, courtesy of Caine Simons.

"Confirmed. Anything else?" The impatience was audible.

"Inquiry." She waved an insolent hand at Adam, inviting him to speak.

"Identify primary," Adam requested with clipped tones.

"What?"

Surveying Adam impudently, Raleigh repeated the question. "Identify primary. Some confusion exists for your less-than-bright team members."

Adam glowered at the jibe. "I'm not the one who's confused."

Atlas intervened, his accent thickening dangerously as he drawled his warning. "I will not spend the next few weeks mediating your private Romper Room."

"Then identify primary," Adam demanded. He glared at Raleigh.

Raleigh noted the steady tap of his fingers on the glass top with satisfaction. It was Adam's telltale gesture of annoyance and irascibility.

After a short, deafening silence, Atlas spoke. "Chimera will be primary."

Adam's dissent was instantaneous. "Come on, Atlas! You can't be serious. I've been here before. What if she chokes again? Will I be the next one to die while she waits for instructions?"

"Chimera has most recent information and contact."

"It's my—" Adam began.

"Duty to work with your primary," Atlas finished. "End of discussion."

"Thank you," Raleigh chirped, openly relishing Atlas' defense of her. *So much for our truce,* she thought almost sadly. At least now she knew to keep her defenses in place. That impulsive kiss earlier grew from a weakening toward him. For a moment, she remembered the man who had once been her friend, her true partner. She couldn't afford to disregard the facts. Adam was Phillip's best friend and, by extension, her foe. Residual attraction—and that's all it was—could not interfere with her goals. Besides, the kiss had been an accident, and, at worst, an experiment. Alex told her to test herself, to see what she could handle. Her jittery reaction proved one thing. To finish this with her heart intact, distance was required. A great deal of distance. A difficult commodity for lovers, even in name only.

Salvation lay in focusing solely on the mission. Finding Phillip, proving his guilt, and avenging Cavanaugh took effort, concentration, and space. As primary, she could come and go as she pleased, without accounting for each second. She'd be the one to secure their supplies and to take meetings with contacts. She'd be free to search for Phillip and prove Cavanaugh's innocence.

Atlas broke into her reverie. "Any other questions?"

"No, sir." Complacent, Raleigh answered without hesitation.

"No, sir," was Adam's surly reply.

"Good. Next report should be after touchdown. Good night."

"Was that really necessary?" Adam fumed when they'd disconnected.

"You started it, Adam, remember?" Amber eyes glowed with satisfaction. Mocking his earlier dig, she explained, "As I recall, your natural inclination is to issue commands. I don't take orders from you." She grinned up at him, amused by his anger. "But you do have to listen to me." She waited for the eruption.

She didn't wait long.

"Look, little girl, I will never need instructions from you. I've forgotten more about Scimitar than you'll ever *learn,*" he shot at her.

Raleigh bristled and fired back, "First of all, I'm not a child. You seem a bit confused about this. Secondly, I've been at this as long as you have. Probably longer."

Adam snorted skeptically. "Dream on. I was there when you joined."

Raleigh continued as though she hadn't heard him. "And finally, you will take orders from me, beginning the day after tomorrow when we reach Jafir," she goaded.

Frustration, as molten as rage, flowed through him. "Atlas named you as primary, not commandant. I may have been out of the game for a while, but I do remember the difference," he grated.

"There is no difference," she taunted. Raleigh cocked her hip, planting her fists on either side. Enjoying his outrage, she decided to spell it out for him. She was in charge this time. "I speak, you listen. I dictate, you follow. Are you beginning to understand?"

Too much, Adam thought dimly as Raleigh continued her litany. She'd learn that she couldn't bait him without retribution. Adam closed the distance between them and took her shoulders between his large, hard hands. "I understand more than you, obviously." He bent his head to hers, his warm breath heating her lips. "You see, Raleigh, there is a difference."

Raleigh stiffened her shoulders. He wouldn't scare her away this time. So what if her heart beat faster when he touched her? She stood up to him yesterday; she'd do it now. "What difference?" she asked with bravado, raising her hands to push him away.

"The same difference that exists between flirtation and seduction." Adam moved closer, murmuring quietly.

"I don't see the connection," she muttered faintly.

"Being primary simply means you can suggest. Like flirting. The brush of lips you tried earlier, the teasing yesterday, that's flirtation. Playing at arousal, playing with desire." He captured her ear between his teeth, testing the captive flesh. Kisses whispered along her cheek, her forehead, her closed eyes. Everywhere but her mouth.

Raleigh's breathing quickened, and her hands lifted to his strong, masculine chest. She could feel herself sinking into him, swept away by the tide of now-familiar passion. Ridges of muscle gave little as she pressed her hands to him, and he fit into her palms perfectly, as though made for her touch. Since that night in the garden, everything had changed. But nothing had changed. *Step away,* she ordered herself dimly as she scraped her nails against the corded muscles of his neck.

Sensing her retreat, Adam shifted, pulling her

closer to stand between his braced legs. She gasped as she felt him press against her. He drew her impossibly close, until only cloth separated them.

From a thousand miles away, his voice drifted toward her. "But commandant. That's true power. Like seduction. Seduction is command." The words scorched her skin, a susurration of sound. "It's taking what you want, not trifling with 'what-ifs.' It's purely sexual, purely heat." He nibbled at her throat, her jawline. "Flirting seeks agreement." He drew a damp line around her waiting mouth. "Seduction demands surrender."

Raleigh groaned, searching for his elusive lips. Surrender was inevitable, but it was not hers alone. "Then kiss me," she commanded softly, pulling him into her.

Mouths met, merged by urgency. His tongue plundered her mouth, wiping her mind clean. She kissed him back, tasting her own surrender. Should capitulation fill her with such power? She clutched his shoulders, ran frantic fingers into his hair. Raw passion drenched her, sensitizing each nerve, amplifying each touch. The glide of his hands down her back. The tug of his teeth on her flesh.

Slim fingers scrambled to open the buttons of his shirt. She rubbed an open mouth along his bare skin, testing the strength of his surrender. He moaned, a low rumbling of sound. Hard hands grasped her bottom, kneading the firm flesh. Of their own volition, her hips thrust forward, seeking a more intimate union. His body echoed her movements.

Adam backed up until his hip bumped into a table. He turned quickly, lifting Raleigh and propping her on the edge. What had he said about seduction?

About giving in? He'd waited to touch her for years. Time refused to banish his cravings. Why not resign himself to the inevitable?

As her nails grazed the nape of his neck, he arched against her, fitting himself to her, impossibly close. He crushed her mouth, savoring her pants of pleasure. Sensation pulsed through him, demanding more.

He cupped her breasts, plucked at their turgid peaks through the thin fabric. Her touch burned through him, ravaging his control. Inchoate need flooded through him, submerging rational thought. Driven by primal instinct, he skated one hand along the sheer stocking encasing her slender calf. Frenzied, he toyed with the edge of the skirt riding up above her knees.

Keen pleasure cascaded across her skin as his tongue dueled with hers. From a distance, she heard her choked moan, the sound abandoned and wild. What was she doing, sprawled across a table with this man, her enemy?

"Adam. Stop." Her words lacked command, and he pulled her to him again.

"You don't mean that," he whispered.

Panicked, she pushed him away, smoothing down her dress with shaking hands. "Stop."

Stepping back, Adam marshaled the needs that drove him to conquer her resistance. He turned away, bringing himself under control. He'd all but devoured her. And this most recent foray only served to whet his appetite.

The fog of desire clouding his mind cleared. Abruptly, he remembered where they were. What had begun as a demonstration ended with her braced against a desk. Shame erased the lingering rapacity.

Showing her a few home truths didn't include taking her on a desk in the middle of the night. Yes, he needed her to be ready, able to maintain the pretense of lovers. If he were honest with himself, however, he'd admit that he wanted her to the point of madness. But she deserved more than this.

He asked gently, "You okay?"

Raleigh clutched a hand to her chest. "Yes," she replied tremulously.

"You sure?"

Clearing her throat, she repeated more strongly, "Yes."

"Then understand this." Adam's voice hardened suddenly. "When the question is protocol, you're in charge. But when it comes to our cover, you follow my lead."

Struggling to regain her dignity, Raleigh scrambled off the desktop. "Is that what this demonstration was all about?" she rasped, anger replacing desire.

Knowing the truth, Adam opted for any excuse she offered. "What else? You seemed to need a lesson." Calmly, Adam began to re-button his shirt, his cold gaze never leaving hers.

Raleigh ruthlessly quashed her regret at the rapidly disappearing flesh. With false insouciance, she retorted, "I don't need you to teach me anything."

Adam took a deliberate step forward, and Raleigh quickly retreated. "From where I stand, you have a lot to learn."

"Such as?"

"You can take the game only so far, then you bolt."

"That's not true."

"Of course it is," he replied silkily. "We're supposed to be lovers, Raleigh." He crossed to her and snaked an arm around her waist, pulling her to him. "Yet, when I touch you, you jump like a frightened animal."

"No, I don't!" she objected, squirming away from him.

"First, you bit me. Then you leaped out of my lap. Just now you pushed me away." He controlled her movements by wrapping his other arm around her. "Pretending to be lovers is not a matter of a few kisses and some hand-holding. They will be monitoring our every move."

"I know that," she muttered.

"Every move, in and out of the bedroom," he supplied firmly. "Scimitar doesn't trust me, and it's an easy thing to bug our room."

That last bit caught her attention. "I will *not* make love to you for a case."

"We won't have sex, but we'll come close. We're sharing a bed, Raleigh, not a room. And if you skitter away every time I get too close, no one will believe we're lovers."

Vainly pushing at his hands, she replied resentfully, "When we're in Jafir, I'll play my part. But until then, don't you touch me again."

"Don't forget who started this."

"I didn't start anything."

"Who crawled into my lap this afternoon?"

"I fell."

"And took quite a while to get up."

"I didn't hear *you* protesting."

Adam shrugged negligently. "Why interfere? I knew you'd run away at the first sign of interest. You always were evasive."

At that, Raleigh broke away completely and

marched over to grab her briefcase. As she reached the door, she realized that once again she was the one retreating.

Adam noticed the same thing. "Running again?"

"No. This time I'm walking away."

"Believe what you will," he mocked.

"Believe this." Looking over her shoulder, she pierced him with a baleful glare. "I will pretend to be your lover. I will also pretend to enjoy it. But I learn my lessons quickly, and this is one I won't soon forget." With a toss of her head, Raleigh left the office, letting the door close quietly behind her.

Outside, Raleigh leaned her forehead against the wall. Adam was right. In Jafir, she wouldn't have the luxury of fear, of skittishness. A million eyes would watch their every move. If she fled whenever he touched her, they'd lose credibility before they began.

Behind her, the door opened and Adam stepped into the hallway. She decided that the tiny stutter in her pulse was neither fear nor fascination. Ill-prepared for another argument, she waited for him to speak.

"I'm sorry," he said quietly.

The simple apology stunned her. "What?"

"You've had a long day, and I've done everything in my power to make it worse. I'm sorry."

With a half smile, she peered over his shoulder, as though searching for something. "What did you do with Adam Grayson?"

Relieved by her easy response, he gave her an answering laugh. "I've hidden him in a dark closet, at least for the moment." He rubbed his hands together in sinister glee.

"Then who are you?" she asked, playing along. If he was willing to play nice, then so was she.

He tucked her hand into the crook of his arm. "I am the man who wants to take you home."

"I just covered that ground with Mr. Grayson, and the answer was no," she said primly. "But you could be another matter altogether," she finished in a sultry drawl.

With a grin, he started for the entrance, with Raleigh in tow. He'd forgotten how she could accept foibles as quickly as she'd praise virtue. *I pushed too hard,* he thought wryly. But she'd accepted his apology without putting him through the wringer. He'd always admired her resilience, her ability to forgive with lightning speed. "This man would like to feed you dinner."

In step, Raleigh let her briefcase bang softly against her leg. A truce with food. How unexpected. The virile, threatening man of a few minutes ago had vanished, replaced by the rueful man she remembered from before. With her hand tucked into the crook of his arm, it felt like those better times, when only names were hidden. She didn't want to think of what lay ahead, certainly not her plans for the future. Raleigh nudged his shoulder and quickened her step. "What did you have in mind?"

Pleased by her acquiescence, he listed his menu. "An omelet. Maybe a salad. A cup of peppermint tea." Her favorite. She'd kept a thermos in the warehouse and a spare packet in her satchel. Odd that he remembered that, as much as he did her betrayal. But those were thoughts for another time. Now, he would feed her and put her to bed. Their three-day journey began soon, and she needed to be fresh and alert. He could give that to her, if she'd let him.

* * *

Adam parked the car at his house and turned to Raleigh. In the glare of the overhead lights, he could see the dark circles beneath her eyes, darkening the flesh. Tension radiated from her, belying their truce. She was poised for him to strike, to say something caustic.

"You have every reason not to get out of this car, Raleigh," he said as he wiped vainly at her delicate, shadowed skin. "And if you want, I will take you back to your hotel. But I promise that I just intend to make us dinner and head straight to bed." At her lifted brow, he corrected, "Separate beds."

"I'm game if you are." *And I mean it,* she realized. She didn't have the energy to fight him any more tonight. "I'd enjoy the break from our usual sparring."

"I do have one ulterior motive, however." He smothered a grimace as she shuttered her eyes in record time. She still didn't trust him, and he certainly didn't trust her.

"What?" she asked cautiously.

He held up his hands to demonstrate his good intentions. "I'd like to talk a little bit about what's happened to you in the past three years. I've been away from the agency too long to remember how to pretend to be your lover when I know nothing about who you are now."

It occurred to her that she knew only what she'd read in his dossier. Knowing what had happened in those intervening years might make her job easier. At the very least, she would understand him better. And perhaps, her reaction to him. "Will you talk to me, too?"

"Quid pro quo. Deal?" He held out a hand to her to seal their agreement.

"Deal," she answered and they shook, both cautious yet curious.

As he held her hand clasped in his, sensations he'd forgotten zinged along neglected nerve endings. But he restrained himself from pulling her into his arms or from turning away. For tonight, he'd let himself believe that he hadn't imagined their time together as friends and almost lovers. His recollections of Jafir would not all be tainted by those last horrible hours when "I love you" became a curse and he'd lost everything in one stroke. Tonight, at least, there would be peace.

Adam opened the broad mahogany doors and guided her inside with a hand at the small of her back. He led her through to the living room, took her briefcase, and set it beside a carved Hepplewhite table. "Have a seat."

Raleigh looked around the room. A portrait of what she assumed to be his family hung over a wrought-iron fireplace. The sofa was a deep brown, with cream and blue cushions. Incongruously, a misshapen mass of clay leaned drunkenly against a wall.

Following her gaze, Adam smiled. "My sister Rachel's idea of art. She was trying to be a sculptor that time, I think."

Raleigh asked cautiously, "What does she do now?"

Adam grinned, "She's an attorney. And she's promised not to harm any more helpless clay."

Wandering closer to the sculpture, she pointed to the portrait. "Which one is she?"

"The older one, with the big eyes. The younger one is my cousin, A.J."

"She was at the party with you." *The skinny girl in*

the portrait has blossomed into a lovely young woman, she thought, as jealousy she'd been unaware of slid away.

"Yep. And the boy who's not quite as handsome as me is my brother, Jonah."

Raleigh shifted back to look at the portrait again. She shook her head. "Your family is stunning. You're all beautiful." She turned and wandered to the piano. "Do you play?"

Still off-kilter from her pronouncement, Adam murmured, "Not as much as I used to."

"Do you still play the flute?" He'd always carried one with him in Jafir.

The answer this time was short. "Yes. Let's head into the kitchen."

Adam quickly installed her in a seat at the center island. He poured her a glass of apple juice and then set out the ingredients for the omelet. They sat in silence for a long moment. With remarkable efficiency, he diced onions and green peppers and sliced mushrooms, then set them aside. "Talk to me, Raleigh."

Raleigh took a sip from her glass. "What do you want to know?"

"Tell me about your childhood," Adam prompted as he cracked an egg into a mixing bowl.

Raleigh shrugged. "Not much to tell. My mom died when I was born, my father when I was eleven. I lived in foster homes until I went to college." She lifted an egg and cracked it. "Not much more to tell," she added, ignoring the tension creeping between her shoulders. She didn't talk about her childhood. *Ever.*

Patiently, Adam grated cheese into the eggs. "There must be more than that, Raleigh. What was your favorite game as a child?"

Raleigh reached for another egg, but his hand stilled her movement. "Blackjack," she muttered, annoyed. "What was yours?"

"Monopoly." Adam continued to hold her hand quiet beneath his own. "And Clue."

The laugh escaped before she could stop it. "Figures. What does the rest of your family do?"

"Jonah's in med school, and A.J. is finishing up her Ph.D. and working for GCI. But you know all of this." He remembered her recitation of his family history in the garden. "We're allowed to talk about ourselves now, Raleigh. The 'rules of engagement' don't apply here."

"I don't like talking about it, okay?" She slid her hand from his, but he quickly interlaced their fingers. "What are you doing?" she asked as her blood heated at the contact.

"Stopping the flight. Of course, I find it difficult to cook with one hand, so this might put a damper on our meal," Adam answered mildly. "Your choice." With his free hand, he whisked the eggs together.

For an answer, Raleigh lifted the onions and dumped them into the bowl. "I never noticed before that you were crazy," she announced. When he lifted a brow and added a crooked smile, she felt her heart slide closer to the precipice. If she had any sense at all, she'd pull her hand away and call a cab. She could be at the Waltons' home in a matter of minutes.

Adam poured in the peppers and mushrooms, alternately dumping and stirring with his free hand. "You'll have to come around here so I can reach the stove." He squeezed fingers gently and guided her around the block. "Beside your right knee, there's an omelet pan in the cabinet."

She stooped to retrieve the pan while he lit the

burner. Raleigh put the pan on the stove and tried to ignore their joined hands.

"The spatula is in the drawer," Adam instructed. When she placed it on the counter, he shifted her behind his back. "I'm left-handed, you're not," he explained. Together, they prepared dinner in a companionable silence, neither one willing to break the moment. Occasionally, Adam would ask for an item, but their hands never parted.

They carried their meals to the island and as they ate, they talked. Raleigh told Adam about her first day in college and her first real crush—on her chemistry professor. She laughed as he recounted his childhood with three younger siblings with fertile minds. It was almost dawn when he walked her to the guest room and gently pressed his lips to hers. Then he brushed gentle kisses across her forehead and her knuckles. "Good night, sweetheart," he murmured. And Raleigh fell asleep, pleasure curving her lips.

Adam lay in bed, sorting through a whirl of thoughts. He'd wanted to let her hand go over dinner, but the command never made it from his mind to his muscles. Even now, he could still feel her on his skin, on his lips. It had been years since they'd spoken, since he'd been able to sit with a woman in silence or in conversation. It had been since the day he lost Raleigh. Now she was back. Everything had changed. And nothing had.

She was different. Gorgeous and confident and bristling with hostility.

He was different. Wary and angry and suspicious.

But in many ways, they remained the same. Raleigh, unwilling or afraid to trust him with her story. Adam, too eager to know everything about her.

He'd built a new life, without Raleigh. Without her scent and her smile and her soul. He didn't need her, and he certainly didn't love her. And if that felt like a lie, so be it. He would make it the truth. He had to.

Reclining in his bed, states away in D.C., Atlas lit a cigar and listened to the quiet snores of his wife of twenty years. Smoke curled above his head before he remembered why the quiet seemed so loud. He'd almost lost her to carelessness years earlier. Neglect could not be dismissed with excuses and great crusades. But she loved him and accepted him, and she'd made a few rules he could never break. One was that he be completely honest with her, even if he couldn't give her details. That had saved his sanity and their marriage. He wanted to wake her and tell her of his latest mission, to hear her tell him what he'd done was for the best. But he let her sleep.

For Atlas, Jafir meant corroborating Cavanaugh's last report and his own suspicions of treason. As he had concluded before, the attack on the satellite hut and the warehouse had been too well timed to be an accident. It had proven what Atlas long suspected. A leak existed inside the ISA, and it had to be plugged. He would use every tool at his disposal to see to it, even if that meant lies and subterfuge. Their mission was larger than any of them.

So he put the ball in motion. The infiltration of Scimitar required pitting friend against friend. Loyalty against deceit. He needed them to do their jobs. Raleigh's signature combination of innocence and implacability had lured an unconscionable number to their demise. As long as she believed that Phillip held a role in Cavanaugh's death, she would pursue him relentlessly. Her demons would not allow her to do any less, regardless of the stakes. Or the consequences.

With Adam as her opponent and her partner, Atlas could be sure that no one would escape investigation. Adam, despite his recent sojourn to the private sector, was an operative at heart. Icy purpose would ensure his dedication. Lethal intellect would secure his success.

Atlas played the game with finesse, throwing Adam and Raleigh together, keeping Phillip and Cavanaugh as the motivation. The other loose ends would be snipped by the mole himself.

Puffing heavily on his dying cigar, Atlas grimaced into the darkness of the bedroom. Raleigh and Adam made the ultimate team. In Adam, Atlas had the perfect antidote to Raleigh's refusal to risk. With Raleigh, he had the key to holding Adam in check. Together, they could recover Praxis and unmask the traitor—and maybe find something left over for themselves.

Eight

Prayer calls rang out, the voices of the *imams* rising in unison to blanket the mosques and the center city. Men, robes snapping in the balmy wind, knelt reverently to pay homage to Allah, obeying the pillar of Salat. In awkward concert, cathedral bells pealed the hour, their ancient clanging an invitation to the churches whose spires pierced the cloudless sky. Adjacent to the Islamic worship centers and churches, synagogues rounded the trio of religious domains, bearing silent witness to the harmony of Jafir.

Raleigh stepped out of the jet and onto the tiny private airstrip, her body tense with anticipation, her stomach churning with regret. A warm autumn breeze blowing in from the sea fluttered the collar of her cream silk blouse and ruffled her loose slacks. She'd chosen the elegant, cosmopolitan outfit almost a day ago, somewhere over Scotland. The jeans and T-shirts she'd sported before had no place in Andrea DeSalle's world. *This is it,* she brooded. *The hour of reckoning has come.* It was right, she supposed, that her life and her livelihood might end here on these shores. A study of contradictions and opposing cultures—Jafir was the perfect place.

On its shores, she would eviscerate her beliefs, her principles, with an act of murder. To do so, she would violate the orders of her superior, the one who entrusted her with a secret duty. She would commit the one sin her father believed unpardonable. And to find her target, she would use and deceive the only man she'd ever cared for.

She wrapped chilled arms around her waist and inhaled deeply, absorbing the native scents. In a trick of nature, the complex odors became the simple smell of sandalwood and spices. *Adam.*

Stop it, she commanded, exhaling abruptly. *You're letting him come too close. It can't happen again, not with Phillip between us. Besides, there's no reason to believe his feelings survived.* Although their dinner had been a blessed hiatus, it solved nothing. She had to use him to find and kill Phillip.

The coldness of her thoughts stopped her for a moment. *But I have no choice,* she reminded herself. Cavanaugh must be avenged, and Phillip would have to pay the price. Adam would just have to stay out of the cross fire.

Unless she could somehow convince him to forgive her. Yes, he loved Phillip, but he cared about her, too—once. If she explained it to him, perhaps he would see why she'd done it. And forgive her.

Shoving balled fists into the pockets in the navy slacks, she shook her head to dispel these fanciful thoughts. *Grow up, Raleigh,* she admonished. It would never happen. Assuming that her crime of lying to him didn't convict her, murder—no matter how justified—certainly would. If she'd learned anything while working with Adam, it was that betrayal was the one sin he could not pardon, even in himself.

If he discovered she'd used him to return to Jafir, he'd accuse her of blindly following directions. Add to manipulation the fact she hid that Phillip was alive, and his mistrust and contempt would be the least of her worries. He might not try to kill her himself, but she wouldn't bet on it.

She had to face reality. When she did what she knew to be the only righteous act, the fragile peace between them would die, whether he knew the truth or not. If he figured out she was responsible, she would never be safe. Desolation settled around her like a cloak. The only recourse was to make the most of these days together and abide by their accord as long as it lasted.

Tears welled as she thought about his final moments beside her. She would stop Phillip from building Praxis, and she would vindicate Cavanaugh. She owed him that, at least.

Adam joined her at the base of the steps, aloof and pensive. Then, he looked at her. Misery etched lines into her brow, pursed her lips. Those magnificent amber eyes were filled with unshed tears. Knowing that she was remembering her last trip here, he resisted taking her into his arms and soothing the sorrow.

How could he offer comfort when he'd found none for himself?

Solace would come, soon. When he left Jafir in two weeks, he would leave the island with a measure of absolution. And if he could make their truce endure, maybe some peace.

The hum of a motor drifted toward them.

"The car is coming," Adam announced, clasping her elbow.

Gathering herself, Raleigh told the attendant to bring the bags. Showtime had arrived.

"Atlas said that Zeben sent a private car for each of the players," Raleigh murmured.

Following her line of thought instantly, Adam concurred. "He'll probably be listening in."

The black limousine halted in front of them, and a suited chauffeur, looking barely older than seventeen, scurried around to open the door. Thick black hair and dark skin complimented a swarthy, pirate-like face. *He'll be gorgeous in ten years,* Raleigh thought. Delicately helping Raleigh into the car, he apologized for the delay in rapid, lilting French.

"Ça n'a pas d'importance. Merci bien." Her beaming smile blinded the love-struck teen, and he nodded several times as he backed out. Barely acknowledging Adam, he continued to gaze raptly until Adam reached out and slammed the door.

She didn't have to speak French to the guy. *He understands English,* Adam fumed. Aloud, he muttered tightly, "Another admirer, darling?"

"Jealous, sweetheart?" She flashed a smile at him, brighter than the one she'd given the driver.

Jealous? Of some overgrown, teenage Lothario? Not likely. He started to respond when he caught the edge of her smirk. "No, simply curious," he replied blandly.

Raleigh stifled a laugh and watched the road as they headed to the hotel. Peddlers sold wares along the main thoroughfare, hawking commodities as varied as handwoven baskets and cellular phones. Multistoried buildings held international corporations, including a subsidiary of GCI.

In marked contrast to other countries in the area, no beggars approached the cars at the stoplights. Although poverty existed, Jafir settled on more humane methods of treating its ills, a progressive idea for a second-world country.

To her, it was unthinkable that an island whose expanse was slightly less than that of Sicily harbored a peril as grave as Scimitar. From the car, with the sun perched high above the Desira Plateau, Jafir's highest point, she could scarcely imagine the carnage and death she'd been party to on its soil. Still, Jafir struggled to maintain its pristine existence, the historical epicenter of peace and prosperity in a traditionally unstable region.

Positioned between Africa, Europe, and the Middle East in the Mediterranean, the nation of Jafir straddled faiths, ideologies, and economies. According to legend, the beloved daughter of the Bantu fell in love with the true son of the Yoruba. Unable to choose a homeland, the couple traveled to the edge of the world. Setting sail, guided by love, their vessel washed up onto the shores of a land human eyes had never seen. Soon, other couples arrived, the Wolof and Serer tribes, the Moors and the Arabs.

Blessed by temperate weather, plentiful game, and fertile valleys, the families grew in number. Trading with other people, the monarchy of Jafir established a reputation as a center of commerce, supplying its neighbors with ships, iron ore, and food. A multilingual business community—speaking Berber, Cush, French, Arabic, English, and the numerous dialects of the African continent—breached language barriers.

In modern times, the republic of Jafir boasted a booming economy and a healthy relationship with its neighbors. Resisting colonization and conquest, Jafir embraced refugees, establishing a hybrid of socialism and free-market systems. Yet, its location left it susceptible to the vagaries of power as other countries sought to ally themselves with Jafir or to generate unrest. The government brokered deals and signed treaties, nullifying its risk to other nations. Only one menace remained to guarantee dissension. A successful African-Arab Alliance would neutralize the Scimitar threat and assure a continued peace.

The car pulled in front of the hotel, a magnificent building of imperial proportions. Stretching for almost a city block, the Hotel Jafir melded together the architecture of diverse cultures, its arches and minarets rising from the clean, classic lines of the main building. Crowned by a cut-stone dome, the imposing structure promised luxury. Uniformed valets waited on the wide, curving, alabaster drive, opening doors and efficiently unloading luggage. Hundreds of patrons passed through its doors daily, drawn by the ambience as well as the main attraction—the Hotel Jafir boasted the only casino in the region. Despite Muslim taboos and Christian sentiments, the prospect of gaming drew in streams of tourists and citizens and filled government coffers with tax revenues.

Brushing the chauffeur aside, Adam helped Raleigh alight from the car. Pressing a discreet handful of notes into the driver's waiting palm, Adam thanked him and escorted Raleigh inside.

The interior, like the exterior, successfully blended many designs of ages and cultures. Opulent and lavish, silks hung from high-beamed ceilings, framing crystal chandeliers. Well-appointed sofas and chairs were scattered throughout the lobby, which was divided into two levels. Adam and Raleigh quickly climbed the shallow steps and approached the concierge.

"Monsieur Simons," the woman gasped with pleasure, her doe-brown eyes surveying him with undisguised interest. *"Salut!"* She stepped from behind the desk to take his hand between her own. "Although your name appeared on the guest list, I did not dare hope you would arrive," she purred in accented tones. Petite and buxom, the uniform she wore displayed her assets well. The magenta scoop-necked top complemented her rich mahogany skin and clung to every ripe curve. The barely decent black skirt displayed her legs to an advantage.

"Marie." Adam brought her hand to his lips, kissing it lightly. "It has been an age since I have seen you. Too long to stay away from such beauty."

"Then do not stay away so long," she flirted, maintaining her hold.

Deciding she'd had enough, Raleigh stepped forward and cast a meaningful, possessive look at Adam. "Darling, I am tired," she pouted. "Will this take long?"

Amused, Adam lingered over Marie's hand. "One moment, my love."

Marie smirked at Raleigh and sidled forward, hips swinging provocatively. "I will ensure that you are well taken care of, Monsieur Simons." Her feline smile offered very personal service.

"I would greatly appreciate your attention, Marie." Releasing her hand slowly, he reached for Raleigh, who shifted just beyond his grasp. "Our room, Marie?"

"I will place you in the penthouse, your favorite suite, *oui?*" Marie turned the register for his approval.

"I am flattered you remember."

I am flattered you remember, Raleigh mocked silently, rolling her eyes.

"I remember everything about your—needs," Marie breathed and bent forward to provide a better view.

Laughing delightedly, Adam signed the register, and Marie pressed two plastic keys into his palm. She reached beneath the desk and handed Adam a golden box.

"Compliments of Monsieur Zeben. You are aware that your room is also with his compliments?"

"Monsieur Zeben is quite gracious," Raleigh murmured.

Speaking directly to her for the first time, Marie agreed enthusiastically. "Monsieur Zeben is the owner of the casino. He is much beloved by the citizens."

Placing the box under his arm, Adam curled the other around Raleigh's waist. "My manners. Marie, allow me to introduce my companion, Ms. Andrea DeSalle."

"Madame DeSalle." The one who'd destroyed an entire village simply to test a theory. According to Zeben, hundreds had died painful, tortured deaths. Alarmed now, Marie favored her with a short smile. "If I can be of service, please do not hesitate to contact the desk."

"I am sure I will have everything I need in our room," she responded, stressing the word *our.*

Hearing the veiled threat, Marie decided to retreat. Caine Simons was dashing but certainly not worth death—or worse. "I do hope so." With a look of regret, Marie gestured for assistance and said good-bye.

A bellboy led them to their suite, opened the door, and ushered them inside. After placing their bags in the room, he returned to the living room. Entranced by Raleigh, he stammered over his standard lines and bumped into the door on his way out.

"You enjoy doing that to boys?" Adam asked rudely, securing the locks.

As they'd discussed on the plane, Raleigh began a sweep of the room. "As much as you relish the adoration of fawning maids."

So, jealousy is a two-way street, he thought with amusement, filing away the information for future reference. "She is the concierge, not the maid." Adam removed a miniature transmitter from the base of the telephone.

Raleigh shrugged, "Whatever." She pried two more bugs from the base of a vase and the underside of a coffee table.

"Jealousy does not become you, my dear." Rcmoving a print from its frame, he removed another bug from the corner of the canvas.

"But it does add quite a glow to my skin, sweetheart." Balancing on a chair, Raleigh reached for the overhead lights. Adam rushed over to her and caught her legs as she began to teeter. With silent instructions, he told her to climb onto his shoulders. She complied reluctantly, her heart threatening to burst from her chest. Unable to grip her pants securely, Adam slid his hands beneath the slippery lining and grabbed her naked calves.

"Only for you," he rasped out as he braced himself beneath the light. He flexed his hands, resetting his grip unnecessarily.

"I . . ." Raleigh could scarcely concentrate as ribbons of sensation ran up her legs to her center. "I appreciate it." She unscrewed the fixture, using a miniature tool set she'd designed herself, and removed three more microphones. To signal her completion, she squeezed her thighs together gently.

Adam's hands fumbled on her legs, and he squatted to let her down. Clambering onto the chair, then down to the thick, cream carpet, Raleigh took a few moments to close her tool case and reattach it to her belt.

For the next few minutes, they combed the suite, removing bugs from the bathroom, the coffeemaker, the bedroom, and the sitting room. Satisfied that they'd removed all of them, they returned to the sitting room.

Together, they unpacked a smaller set of transmitters, ones that would scramble their voices at an electronic command from a central base in the suite. Adam fixed transmitters to the phone and a few other locations, where they'd removed some earlier. Under the ceiling light, he hesitated for a minute and then decided against a repeat performance. Hoisting Raleigh onto his shoulders again would carry a world of danger neither of them was prepared to handle.

Raleigh set up and turned on the scrambler, choosing a nook in the sitting room. The scanner's range included the two main rooms but not the bathroom or bedroom. While on the plane, they'd decided against putting receivers in either room. Destroying all the bugs was not an option, but only amateurs would leave bugs in the bedroom. They would remove the transmitters in those areas, but the presence of maids and hotel staff would ensure that Zeben remained apprised of their private activities.

"All done," Raleigh announced as she entered the bedroom to join Adam—and stopped short. *Sumptuous. A pretentious word,* Raleigh thought, *but completely apt.* The lake of a bed was drowned in silk sheets of the richest hues. Solid gold layered cerulean blue, the color scheme repeated in the plump pillows and the matching wing chairs. Unable to stop herself, she lifted the corner of a sheet and rubbed the fabric against her cheek. *Heaven,* she thought with a sigh.

Her tiny moan of pleasure tightened Adam's loins in a rush. He watched in happy agony as she bathed her skin in the textures of the silk, oblivious to his attention. *To have her luxuriate in me that way would surely make everything else bearable,* he thought. Rising from the floor where he crouched to conceal their equipment, he moved to her on silent feet.

"Raleigh." Her name emerged, a rough sound of need.

The spell broken, Raleigh turned to face Adam. Raw hunger stared back at her, and she hastily dropped the sheets.

"Do that again, and I will not be responsible for my actions," he warned dully.

With a short nod, Raleigh took a step back and circled around him, heading for safer space and distance from the bed. Taking refuge in one of the chairs, she found her voice and asked, "So, now what?"

Getting himself under control, Adam replied, "Tonight is the casino bash. The gold box contained our chips for the festivities."

"Is this his normal procedure?" Raleigh fiddled absently with the brocade cord that embellished the chair.

"Yes. Zeben enjoys displaying his wealth and power through staged acts of generosity." While speaking, Adam retrieved the box and opened it. Three rows of gold, blue, and magenta coins lay nestled in black velvet. "This is almost a quarter of a million dollars."

"Then our first test is gambling acumen?"

"No. He likes to set the stage, introduce the players. Tonight is about observation. Now that he has all of the cover stories, he'll be searching for holes. And animosity."

"The list of attendees reads like an ISA wish list."

"I've worked with or against most of the tech people."

"And I have a handle on the scientists. It constantly amazes me how academia provides such a steady stream of criminals," Raleigh said caustically.

"It certainly raises the level of intellectual discourse," Adam quipped.

"Indeed." Feeling safe from Adam's predatory gaze, Raleigh picked up her cases and started to unpack. "What's Marie's connection to Zeben?"

"She's one of his many associates. In addition to her service as concierge, she also helps him count his money."

"Among other things."

"Of course."

Hoping to sound nonchalant, Raleigh asked breezily, "Did she ever help you . . . count your money?" She crossed the room to hang up her clothes, leaving an evening gown on the bed.

Adam began to unpack as well. Crisp, white shirts, dark Italian suits, muted solid ties. "No. I tend to select my own bankers. Marie is a beauty, but a bit obvious." He unzipped the bag containing his tuxedo and laid it on the bed next to her dress.

"Oh." Arms overflowing, Raleigh filled one of the two dressers with clothes and undergarments. On her second trip, a teddy fell to the floor.

With an economy of motion, Adam retrieved the garment from the floor. Hooking his fingers under the straps, he studied the simple, chocolate-brown piece. High-cut thighs and a modest bodice with none of the lace he expected. *How like her,* he mused. "Yes, I prefer a more restrained type. One not quite so willing to barter."

All but snatching the garment from his hands, Raleigh ducked her head in embarrassment and swiftly folded the scrap of material, shoving it into the drawer. "Glad to hear it," she muttered.

Adam stifled a laugh and removed his flute from its case. Raleigh saw it and started to speak. But the look in his eyes stopped her. The flute on the bed was new. The one he'd carried with him in Jafir had been destroyed in the blast. She'd looked for it, before the soldiers came. Their eyes locked for an eternity, then Adam turned away.

After unpacking their bags in tense silence, Adam suggested they order in lunch. The waiter quickly arrived with a tray laden with food, courtesy of Zeben.

Munching on a crusty roll, Raleigh said, "We meet with our supplier in two days. In the shops on the Desira Plateau."

Amazed by the speed of her consumption, Adam mumbled his acknowledgement. He'd forgotten just how quickly she could eat. In a matter of minutes, she scarfed down a bowl of French onion soup, a generous salad, and a healthy sized entrée. He glanced down at the salad fork in his hand and the half-eaten salad.

Unaware of his scrutiny and relaxed by the meal, Raleigh continued speaking. "The tournament should be over in a couple of days. Then we find Praxis."

"I'll talk to Marie, see if she can point me in the right direction. I'd send you, but she seems afraid of you."

"That's unusual. I rarely strike fear into women's hearts."

While she spoke, Adam brushed a crumb from her chin, then another from her lips. What he'd intended as a casual gesture quickly became more. Her lips were unbearably soft, smooth velvet. *And so ready,* he thought as her breath shuddered over his thumb. He could kiss her now, and she'd welcome it. But now was not the time. Reluctantly, he returned to his meal. "You were saying?"

Her mind went blank for a second as his touch lingered on her skin. *What was I saying?* she thought desperately. *Something about Marie? Oh yes, Marie.* "I must say," she began a trifle brightly, hoping to mask her reaction. "I enjoyed Marie's reaction to my introduction as Andrea DeSalle. I've never been the femme fatale before."

"No doubt about it, your resumé disturbed her. But, your ice-queen stare frightened her more," Adam agreed, cutting into his fish.

Her breathing returned to normal, and she threw her head back imperiously. "Frightened? Darling, she was terrified."

Adam laughed at her, and another thought struck him. "What do you mean, you've never been the femme fatale? That's how I met you."

"No." She corrected, taking a swallow of water. "That time, I was the brilliant grad student with the lecherous older man. He used me for my brain, not my body. As you well remember."

Adam leered at her jokingly. "I don't remember your body being all that bad."

"Damned by faint praise," she muttered, not totally serious.

"I didn't mean it that way." Adam had the grace to look chagrined. "I only meant you were quite appealing."

"Lugging around ten pounds of baby fat and at least twenty more from college? I don't think so. My metabolism didn't kick in for some time. I was built on rather generous lines then, sir."

"Lushly rounded, as I recall. You had some very interesting curves." Adam examined her again with satisfied recollection.

Uncomfortable with his perusal, Raleigh wandered into the bathroom and pressed her forehead to the mirror. "Lushly rounded"? Indeed.

"Of course, I am not objecting to the current state of things," he called out. "You've grown into a beautiful woman, Raleigh," he said from behind her.

Raleigh looked up and caught his reflection in the mirror. "Thank you for the compliment, Adam—but beautiful, I'm not."

Adam snorted. "I don't like you enough to feed your vanity. It wasn't a compliment. It was a statement of fact."

Disbelief and longing warred within her, the battle plain in her eyes. Adam read the yearning and felt compelled to respond. Did she really have no clue about her beauty? Could she be so blind? In addition to her eating speed, he'd forgotten about the hidden pockets of insecurity she disguised so well. But he wasn't here to build her self-esteem, he decided. He'd tell her the truth only because it would make her cover more plausible if she believed it herself. This wasn't for her, it was for the case. The case.

Catching her shoulders, he shook her lightly. "Shall I tell you what I see?"

Raleigh shook her head mutely.

Ignoring her demurral, he continued. "I see flawless skin, a shade caught between chocolate and coffee. I see a proud nose, a pair of perfect lips, and maddening cheekbones. You have the most remarkable eyes, like fire trapped in amber. I wish I'd noticed them three years ago." Reaching around her, he nudged her chin, forcing her to look into the mirror, to meet his eyes. "Did you know that you have the slowest, sexiest smile? It takes a million years to light your eyes, but it makes my heart race just to see it. And you smell like the sun and some flower I don't know the name of."

He slid his hands down her arms, his original intent forgotten. "Did you know that your skin is so soft at the crease in your elbow, I could lose myself just touching you there? That you can sit so still and quiet, thinking through every angle of a problem, that looking at you is like watching a miracle? Yes, you are stunningly brilliant. But you are funny and wonderful and beautiful."

Raleigh shook her head.

"No, don't deny it. You are so incredibly lovely."

He smoothed his hands down her tense arms to capture her wrists. "And don't get me started on your body. We've got to be downstairs in a couple of hours, and I don't have the time," he finished, not quite jovially. Stroking his hands up and down her arms, he pressed a quick, tender kiss to the top of her head. "I need to wrangle some information out of Marie, then I'll meet you up here for our entrance."

Speechless, Raleigh nodded her understanding,

and Adam strode out of the room. When she heard the door close behind him, Raleigh bent her head and started to shake.

She collapsed to the floor and hugged her knees to her chest. Adam Grayson thought she was beautiful. The most stunning man she'd ever seen told her she was charming and graceful and lovely.

No man had ever told her that, not before or since her transformation. Mildly pretty, yes. Even the ambiguous "striking." But no man had ever said she was beautiful. And, heaven help her, she wanted to believe him.

Rising from the floor, she looked into the mirror. "Well, Ms. DeSalle," she said resolutely, "it's time to get gorgeous."

Raleigh finished unpacking, including her special travel kit that contained her lock picks, various vials, and other tools. Cavanaugh used to call it her "MacGyver pack."

Cavanaugh. The name brought her up short. How could she forget, even for a second? She clutched the tool kit to her, ashamed of her disloyalty. When Adam had spoken to her, her mission slipped just beyond her consciousness. The weight of guilt and resignation had shifted for a moment, replaced by wonder and happiness. She had not been carefree for so long. But being carefree was a luxury she could not afford.

Chastened, Raleigh mechanically went through her toilette, slipped into her dress, and fastened on earrings and necklace. Dully, she used the makeup tricks Alex taught her to widen her eyes, play up the natural arch of her brow. As she painted a deep red onto her lips, Adam's voice played in her head. A perfect mouth, he'd said.

Over and over, his description played in her head, drowning out the guilt. A strange energy suffused her body, a feeling of freedom. Tonight, she'd believe him. Tonight, she'd let go of vendettas and lies and subterfuge and concentrate on fun. Tonight, she would become Andrea DeSalle, corrupt scientist and femme fatale. And she'd wring every drop of pleasure from the experience. Soon enough, the midnight hour would strike, ending the peace and almost-friendship she and Adam had shared today. But tonight was hers. And she'd live it.

Nine

"Give me a minute to change clothes, and we'll head down," Adam announced as he entered the suite. Hopefully, his hasty departure had allowed her enough time to dress. Maintaining his distance got harder and harder. It would have been a hopeless endeavor if he'd remained one more second. Temptation clawed at his gut, demanding relief. Standing in front of the mirror, eyes locked, he'd nearly submitted to the lure of unexpected vulnerability. The hint of fragility.

That fragility appealed to him, confused him. He certainly had not planned his spontaneous pronouncement. He'd assumed her remarkable self-possession was impenetrable. She'd flirted with the bewitched chauffeur, accepted the nervous adulation of the bellhop as her due. Even at the party, she was strong, assured, coolly sexual. Yet the combination of shock and—dare he say—*hope* at his offhand comment about her beauty had compelled him to say more. Confronted by her constantly imperturbable facade, it was easy to mistake reservation for confidence. He didn't intend to make that mistake again.

When he left the room, he'd wandered through the hotel, reacquainting himself with the staff and pondering the latest wrinkle in a plan that grew more complex every second.

Their embraces had to end. Despite her response and their cover, she probably couldn't handle it. But, being Raleigh, she'd never admit defeat. She would match him, measure for measure, without regard for its emotional toll.

He was a grown man, fully capable of controlling his baser urges. But that glimpse of her, soft and susceptible to something as innocuous as a compliment, had convinced him. The ruse would play only in public, but in here, she would find sanctuary. He could give her that if nothing else.

"Andrea?" Maybe she decided to beg off tonight's party. He wouldn't blame her.

"I'm almost ready." Raleigh crossed to Adam, her head bowed as she wrestled with the zipper of her dress. "If I could get this zipper done. I think a piece of material is in the way." Coming to a halt in front of him, she presented her back to him. "Help."

Adam nearly swallowed his tongue. Creamy brown skin, bare except for a thin strip of material angling across her sleek back, beckoned him. With shaky hands, he grasped the zipper and removed the offending section of cloth. Fingertips grazed soft, fragrant flesh as he pulled the fastener into place. "Done."

Raleigh sauntered a few steps away, then executed a quick pirouette. "So, Monsieur Simons, how do I look?"

Devastating, he thought, dazedly. The dress—if he could call it such—was a fluid tube of crimson that clung to every voluptuous line. The band of cloth posing as a strap cut diagonally from shoulder to chest, leaving both arms naked—and an enticing expanse of flesh in between. The angular top fit snugly, emphasizing the curves of her breasts. A dangerously short skirt exposed miles of slender leg. She'd darkened her lids with smoky gray and slicked her lips with a rich red. Diamonds dripped from her earlobes and neck, catching the light with every movement. No woman would see her and not envy. No man would see her and not ache.

"Caine?" she questioned softly, seductively. Fully in character, Raleigh performed a quick shimmy. Running slow, certain hands over satin-clad hips, she pursed her lips. "I assume this will be appropriate." She edged closer to him, her perfume teasing him. "But if you see something you don't like, I can change."

"You look dazzling." Adam declared quietly.

His solemn words stole Raleigh's breath, but Andrea took them as her due. "It's not too short?" she vamped.

"Yes. And every man will see you tonight and thank heaven it is."

"Good," she purred as she crossed to the wet bar. "Something to drink?"

Drink? He could barely breathe. In the blink of an eye, the vulnerable woman-child disappeared, replaced by a fascinating siren. "No, thank you," he managed. Adam removed his jacket, loosened his tie. Escaping to the bedroom, he said, "I'll only be a moment."

Adam showered, shaved, and dressed. He pulled on a white dress shirt, the requisite tuxedo, and tie. He was still fumbling with his sleeves when he walked into the living room.

Giving a low whistle, Raleigh plucked at his undone sleeve and fastened the gold cuff links he dropped into her hand.

Playing to their invisible guests, testing her powers, she asked coquettishly, "Are you sure we have to go downstairs?"

She circled his neck with arms perfumed by lotion and scent. Stretching up to bring her eyes almost level with his, she sighed in a stage whisper, "I'm certain I could entertain us quite well, right here." Then she caught his earlobe between her teeth, raking the captive flesh.

Adam growled softly and closed his arms, bands of heated steel around her.

Raleigh scored the nape of his neck with ruby-red nails. She moistened suddenly dry lips. His obsidian eyes followed the movement hungrily. Emboldened by the tension emanating from him, she raised her mouth to his. Need fisted in her stomach, churned in her blood. Adam's arms contracted in visceral response, pulling her into the cradle of his thighs.

Heady with desire, with newfound power, she slanted her mouth across his lips, seeking entry. Her eyes slowly closed, the lids too heavy to remain open. When his lips remained sealed against her forays, she sank her hands into his hair, tugging gently. Daring him to resist, she traced the shape of his mouth, tasting him. Roles forgotten, she thought only about the flavor of his skin, the texture of his kiss. Almost savagely, she nipped at his bottom lip, instantly soothing the wound with her tongue. He would open to her, let her inside.

With a deep moan, Adam relented, devoured her mouth, his tongue sweeping inside. Pressure built inside his heart, inside his loins. How could he deny them both what seemed so right, so necessary? Only having her would assuage the tension, bring relief. "I want you. How could I have imagined I wouldn't?"

In mute response, Raleigh strained closer, rapacious, ravenous, wanting only to crawl into him. Strong, firm hands cupped her breasts, swept her hips, and kneaded her bottom, spreading fire with every touch.

Eager fingers fumbled with the buttons of his shirt, reaching for the taut, muscled flesh beneath. She sighed, a sound of liquid pleasure, as she felt his heart thud underneath her palms. Under her touch, his skin burned, a raging furnace.

It was this, this heat, which she craved. It was Adam, his intensity, which she needed. Standing in his arms, she had both.

She felt something break apart inside her. The ice, the reticence that crowded her senses, governed her, cracked, melted. With his torrid caress, his fervent kisses, her heart warmed. Helpless to prevent her descent into madness, into love, she moaned, a wanton, wary sound.

Hearing it, hearing her, Adam deepened the kiss, smoothing her dress around her hips. "Raleigh?" he whispered, for her ears alone.

Raleigh. Not Andrea. No safe pretense here, no place to hide. If Andrea DeSalle began the erotic venture, Raleigh Foster was here now, fully engaged, fully aroused. Whatever she said or did now would be attributable to her. Only.

Retreat, her mind screamed, apprehensive about the revelation. The hand in his hair slid away, skimming down his throat to caress his cheek. "Caine."

He heard the withdrawal, the return of logic and propriety. But his body rebelled, refused to concede defeat. He skimmed over her breasts, drawing tight peaks. Smiling at the gasp of excitement, he continued his loving assault, gliding his hands down to her midriff. Then lower.

"Enough," Raleigh whimpered. She gathered her fortitude. "We've got to stop." Framing his starkly beautiful face, she pulled away. "We're running late," she admonished, her words not quite steady.

"Yes, we are." His mild tone belied the passion smoldering in his eyes, the harshness of his voice. Drawing his thumb along her cheek, he pierced her with a gaze that promised retribution. "We'll save this for later. I'm eager to meet our competition." He tucked her hand into the crook of his arm and whispered conspiratorially, "Remember where we were."

Housed in a separate wing of the hotel, the sounds of excited chatter and noisy machines guided them to the casino. Inside the vast space, gaming tables jockeyed with slot machines for attention. The dimly lit interior gave the impression of constant dusk, offering no hint of sun or moon. Like American casinos, the patrons wore shorts and blue jeans with the same frequency as beaded gowns and sharply creased suits. Muted music flowed through the area, barely audible above the din. An occasional shout of victory or groan of despair punctuated the noise, adding to the frenzy.

Taking her hand, Adam skirted the main entrance and headed for a second, smaller room. A uniformed guard standing watch eyed them silently as they approached. Whipping out a black plastic card, Adam presented it to the unsmiling man.

"Caine Simons and Andrea DeSalle."

With an abrupt nod, the guard turned away and

passed the card through a narrow white scanner. When the scanner flashed a green light, he returned the card and reached for Raleigh's black satin evening bag. He flipped through the contents quickly, unscrewing a tube of lipstick, removing the case of chips for inspection. He quickly frisked Adam. Satisfied, he entered a code on a nearby panel and waved them into the room.

In a marked contrast to the main casino, elegance and ambience dictated the fashions. Gaming tables were scattered throughout the floor, with roulette, poker, baccarat, and other games of chance, but no pedestrian slot machines. Whereas the main casino's stations posted discreet signs listing minimum bids, no similar plaques were evident. This was obviously the domain of high rollers.

Twenty or thirty men and women milled about, perched on velvet stools or talking to one another, exchanging little information. They were felons and financiers, each hoping for the opportunity to score probably the biggest prize of a lifetime. But the prospect of winning a few hands did not appeal to the occupants, not when millions of dollars lay within reach. This night was about sizing up the competition, judging who was a player and who only thought he was. The stakes were fabulously high—life and death wagered on a whim.

Absorbing the atmosphere, Raleigh felt the familiar rush of anticipation surge through her veins. Danger and intrigue, as much as her passion for justice, were why she'd joined the ISA. She had been born for this, bred to play these roles. With minimal effort, she could transform herself into any one of the people in this room. She silently thanked her father for the gift.

Before his death, Chance had traveled the country with Raleigh, never staying in one place for very long. Sometimes, Chance Foster was a bookie, other times a gambler, and sometimes a salesman. The legitimate jobs never lasted long, and soon he and his genius daughter were off for better climes and longer odds. During those years, Raleigh learned to count cards and pick locks, to balance secret books and imitate anyone she met. Along the way, Chance fed his precocious daughter works on math and languages and any subject that interested her, which was almost everything.

She'd selected science—chemistry—as her con of choice. With the elements at her command, she could shape and control her universe. When Cavanaugh offered her the chance to return to the life she remembered, but on a grander scale, she'd had no choice but to join. This time, she'd live on the side of right, if not always on the right side of the law.

Now, excitement pulsed through her, though only faint boredom showed on her face. "Caine, be a dear. A glass of Evian, please."

Adam signaled for a waiter, and one materialized beside him to take his order.

"Zeben has yet to make an appearance, I see," he murmured.

"I suppose he's watching the developments."

"Yes, I would assume so." Both noted the frosted glass window hanging high above the crowd. From his vantage point, Zeben could monitor the evening without interruption.

"Shall we play or mingle?" Raleigh asked.

"Why not both?" Tucking her hand in his, he led her to the roulette table. The croupier acknowledged their arrival and gestured for them to place their bid. Raleigh set a gold chip on the green felt.

"Lady bets eleven." The wheel spun dizzily, and the tiny black ball bounced past numbers, clicking against the wooden chamber. "Eleven wins," he stated, pushing a stack of chips to Raleigh.

Raleigh motioned to continue play.

"A high roller, I see," Adam commented. The waiter reappeared beside them and handed Adam the drinks. He sipped his Scotch and soda and passed Raleigh her water. "I would never have pegged you as the gambling type."

Raleigh shrugged as she raked in more chips. "You'd be amazed by my skills, Mr. Simons." She flashed him a quick, sultry grin.

He'd never seen her wear lipstick. Her slick, red lips ignited responses he was sure she never intended. Or maybe she had, given their embrace in the room. He continued to underestimate her, and she kept surprising him. "I'm certain I would, Ms. DeSalle. Would you care to share your list with me?"

She loved the way his sophisticated baritone slid over the words. Even the most innocent conversation could sound indecent with that voice. "In public? I think not. But you do know where I live."

"Indeed."

"Eleven wins again," the croupier announced. The stack of chips grew larger. From behind her, Adam slid his arms around her, just under her breasts.

Raleigh choked back a groan of response at the tiny punishment. Only the knowledge that their every move was observed forestalled her shifting away.

He bent over her shoulder and said, "I see some old friends," punctuating the statement with a nip at her jaw.

Two can play at this, she thought mischievously. Raleigh leaned her head against his shoulder and curled an arm around his neck, tilting her head toward his. With a sultry smile, she pressed an intimate kiss to his surprised mouth. "Come back soon," she said, then languidly wiped away a smear of lipstick, lingering over the process.

The arm under her breasts tightened involuntarily, and his eyes flashed black lightning. "Have fun," he said and straightened. As soon as he departed, a tall, dark man moved to take the seat beside her. The nape of her neck prickled a warning.

"You play well, *signora,*" he commented, his voice cultured and urbane, the accent unusual.

Raleigh noted the appellation. *He speaks Italian,* she thought. Ethiopia or Eritrea.

"Thank you, but it is only a game of chance. No true skill is required," she demurred, keeping her attention on the turn of the wheel. She won again.

"They are all games of chance, *davvero?* The skill comes in knowing when to walk away." Flashing a capped-tooth smile, he instructed the croupier to include his chips on her number.

When they won, Raleigh gave him an amused smile. "Skill also comes from choosing the right partner, I see."

With a shrug, he replied, "I see no harm in allowing others to win for me. It is important to ally one's self with winners."

"Of course."

"Allow me to introduce myself." He clasped her hand between both of his. "I am Brooks Civelli."

The hardware man. He sold millions in stolen computer property each year. "Andrea DeSalle." They'd met in London, a year before her accident. An exchange with him would be an excellent opportunity to test the strength of her cover. Although the ISA had painstakingly developed her cover, a chance of discovery always lurked in the most unexpected places.

"I believed so." Rubbing a thumb over her captured knuckles, he smiled at her. "Your reputation has preceded you, Ms. DeSalle. But not the tales of your beauty. You have been a mystery to us all."

"I am flattered."

"They say you are, um, quite adept. Very inventive."

"Grazie." Where is this headed, she wondered? From what she remembered of Civelli, the conceited man rarely paid compliments to anyone other than himself. He preferred snide remarks and petulant complaints. "I do try."

"And yet you have associated yourself with an American pig," he continued, anger edging his words. "I would warn you. Caine Simons is not to be trusted." His hands tightened, the grip unrelenting.

"You speak with authority," she replied mildly, tugging her hand away.

"As you are new to our community of, shall we say, entrepreneurs, I feel obliged to caution you about your partner." Undaunted, he drew a fingertip along her arm.

The come-on left a slimy feel on her skin. Suppressing a shudder, Raleigh continued to place her bets. "Do tell."

"He does not abide by agreements. Any alliance forged with him is doomed to fail. If he does not cheat you, he will kill you."

"He deceived you?"

"*Si.* I escaped death, but others have not been quite so fortunate."

"Spreading lies again, Civelli?" Adam said from behind them.

Civelli jumped, knocking the stool over in the process. Regaining his footing, he confronted Adam, who topped him by several inches.

"I simply told your lovely companion the truth. That you cannot be trusted," he declared. He flailed a nervous hand, scattering Raleigh's chips.

Raleigh declined another bet and smiled apologetically to the croupier and the table's other customers. She gathered her chips into her evening bag and spun on her stool to watch the action.

"Insulting a man's reputation can be hazardous." Adam examined his fingernails, boredom plain. Brooks Civelli was a shrewd man, a professional troublemaker who preyed on the talents of others. He survived by sowing dissension and latching onto the victor like a parasite. Adam managed to avoid an association with him, despite their parallel paths.

He seemed to be the only person present without a partner. Obviously smelling profit, Civelli decided that Raleigh would make a good mark. And bed companion. Women found him attractive, but he'd never understood why—nor had he cared. Adam declined to examine the punch of jealousy he'd felt when he saw the worm take the stool he vacated after Raleigh's steamy kiss. The insect would not move in on his woman. His woman? He'd think about that later. Civelli was the problem right now.

Extending a hand to Raleigh, Adam brought her to his side until she nestled against him. He felt the subtle contours of her body, felt himself harden in response.

Following his lead, Raleigh curled her fingers into his sleeve, then slid her hand down to intertwine their fingers. The casual gesture spoke of established intimacy and restrained sensuality. He flexed his hand, meshing his calloused palm with her silken skin, intensifying the sensation of heat radiating through him. Raleigh's hand stirred restlessly, then relaxed.

Adam smiled approvingly down at Raleigh, then brushed his free hand along her cheek. "Insulting me can be suicidal," he said, without looking up.

"It is no insult if it is true," Civelli retorted, his voice growing louder. Sensing a fight, people gathered around and play stopped at the other tables.

"I assume you have proof." Of course he had none because Adam refused to work with him. But without Phillip, it was his word against Civelli's.

"Of your treachery? I need no proof. Everyone knows why you disappeared for so long."

"Do tell." The rumors Atlas put out about him had done their job, only too well. He'd have to weather the storm without an actual defense.

"You murdered your partner and stole the proceeds. Now you are without funds, and you hope to steal this, too," Civelli stated, encouraged by his audience. "And you will surely dispatch this young woman as you did her predecessor."

"Caine deceive me?" Raleigh questioned. She released his hand and pressed an open palm to his chest, caressing it. She expelled a throaty laugh. "Absurd."

"Not so absurd. He has stolen before," Civelli accused wildly.

"That's what I do, Civelli. I steal." His laconic response drew a laugh from the gathered crowd. "Would you care to be more specific?"

Flustered, Civelli said, "You owe me. I brokered your last debacle, and you did not pay me. So I will unmask you for the fraud and liar you are."

"I owe you nothing," Adam said coldly.

"You owe me three-hundred-thousand dollars," Civelli blustered.

"Prove it."

"How can I when my corroborator is dead?" Civelli turned to address the crowd. "I demand that he be disqualified from the competition. He is not to be trusted." Grumbles of agreement started to sweep the room, mostly from those who'd been bested by Caine Simons before.

If Zeben were indeed observing, they had to salvage this quickly. Raleigh decided to defuse the situation.

"You are grousing about a pittance?" she mocked, stepping between Civelli and Adam.

"It is a matter of principle."

"And if you had your money?"

"Hah! As if he would pay."

"I certainly won't," Adam agreed with a flinty expression. "I don't owe you anything."

"He lies! And I do not believe he should be included in the competition. I will not stay if he participates." Running his gaze over her, Civelli said silkily, "But I would be happy to replace him, as your cohort."

Closing the distance between them, Raleigh ran a light finger down the center of his chest. "How can I be certain you are worth the risk?"

A third man's deep voice intervened, "You cannot. And that is the lure of the gamble. To court uncer-

An important message from the ARABESQUE Editor

Dear Arabesque Reader,

Because you've chosen to read one of our Arabesque romance novels, we'd like to say "thank you"! And, as a special way to thank you, we've selected four more of the books you love so well to send you for FREE!

Please enjoy them with our compliments, and thank you for continuing to enjoy Arabesque...the soul of romance.

Karen Thomas
Senior Editor,
Arabesque Romance Novels

Check out our website at www.arabesquebooks.com

3 QUICK STEPS
TO RECEIVE YOUR "THANK YOU" GIFT
FROM THE EDITOR

Send this card back and you'll receive 4 FREE Arabesque novels! The introductory shipment of 4 Arabesque novels – a $23.96 value – is yours absolutely FREE!

There's no catch. You're under no obligation to buy anything. You'll receive your introductory shipment of 4 Arabesque novels absolutely FREE (plus $1.50 to offset the costs of shipping & handling). And you don't have to make any minimum number of purchases—not even one!

We hope that after receiving your books you'll want to remain an Arabesque subscriber. But the choice is yours to continue or cancel, anytime at all! So why not take us up on our invitation to receive 4 Arabesque Romance Novels, with no risk of any kind. You'll be glad you did!

Call us
TOLL-FREE
at 1-888-345-BOOK

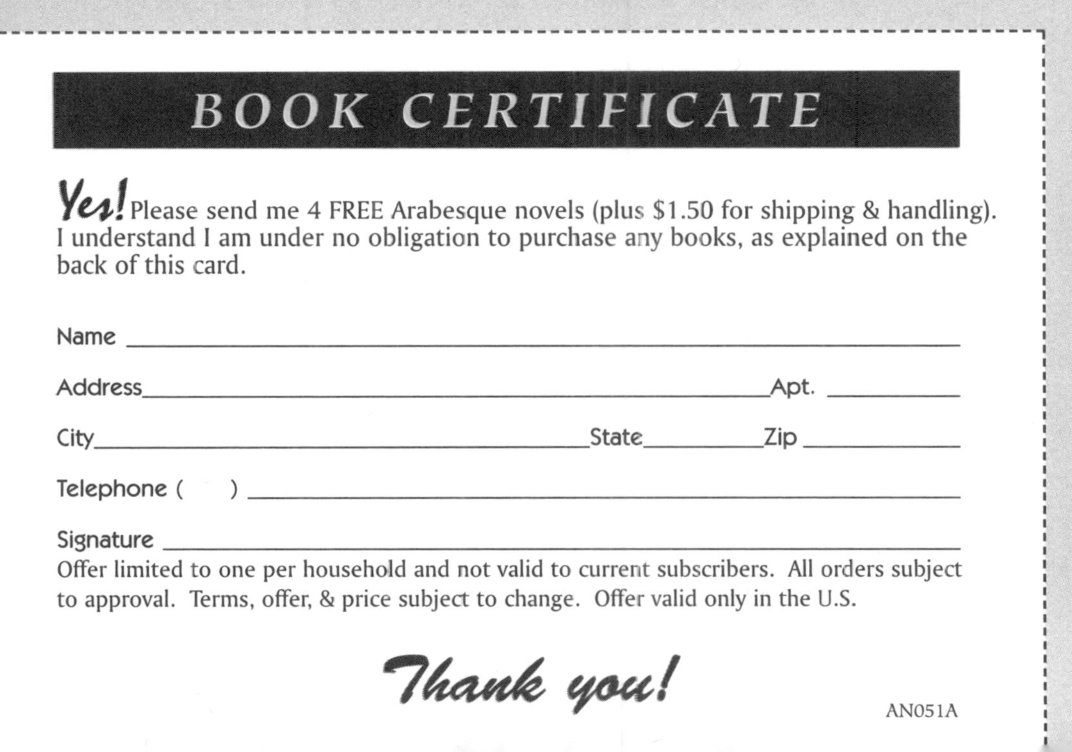

BOOK CERTIFICATE

Yes! Please send me 4 FREE Arabesque novels (plus $1.50 for shipping & handling). I understand I am under no obligation to purchase any books, as explained on the back of this card.

Name ____________________

Address ____________________ Apt. ______

City ____________ State ______ Zip ______

Telephone (   ) ____________________

Signature ____________________

Offer limited to one per household and not valid to current subscribers. All orders subject to approval. Terms, offer, & price subject to change. Offer valid only in the U.S.

Thank you!

AN051A

THE EDITOR'S "THANK YOU" GIFT INCLUDES:

- 4 books absolutely FREE (plus $1.50 for shipping and handling)
- A FREE newsletter, *Arabesque Romance News*, filled with author interviews, book previews, special offers, and more!
- No risks or obligations. You're free to cancel whenever you wish... with no questions asked.

Accepting the four introductory books for FREE (plus $1.50 to offset the cost of shipping & handling) places you under no obligation to buy anything. You may keep the books and return the shipping statement marked "cancelled". If you do not cancel, about a month later we will send 4 additional Arabesque novels, and you will be billed the preferred subscriber's price of just $4.00 per title. That's $16.00 for all 4 books for a savings of 33% off the cover price (Plus $1.50 for shipping and handling). You may cancel at any time, but if you choose to continue, every month we'll send you 4 more books, which you may either purchase at the preferred discount price. . . or return to us and cancel your subscription.

THE ARABESQUE ROMANCE CLUB: HERE'S HOW IT WORKS

PLACE
STAMP
HERE

ARABESQUE ROMANCE BOOK CLUB
P.O. Box 5214
Clifton NJ 07015-5214

tainty." Tall, gaunt, with sunken cheeks, the man who'd spoken seemed to have an aura of despotic power. His unlined skin and a polished, intelligent voice marked him as ageless, but she knew he was almost seventy.

Raleigh recovered first. "Kadifir el Zeben, I presume."

"Yes. And you are the enigmatic Ms. DeSalle."

Raleigh performed an abbreviated curtsy. "At your service, I hope."

"We shall see." With a regal inclination of his head, he mounted a small stage set up beneath the window. "Welcome, my friends. I am heartened to see so many of you have survived to accept my invitation. Tonight we begin the selection process, to determine who will assist me in my glorious undertaking. The project I have commissioned will require skill, talent, and resources. It shall also require the beneficence of the fates. Tonight we shall see whom luck will favor and whom she will spite." He held up a gold case. "All of you have received a stake of two-hundred-fifty-thousand dollars. You will gamble among yourselves for the remainder of the night. The teams with the most fulfilling challenges and the most entertaining balances will continue on. The losers will not. Defeat shall not be measured in coins but in spirit."

"How many proceed?" Civelli asked.

Zeben raised a lordly brow. "Time and the fates will tell. You have until midnight. I will announce the victors in the morning. *Bon chance, mes amis.*"

Giving an imperious nod, he disappeared behind the stage.

"Then I will make you a wager." Civelli captured Raleigh's hand in his own, pressing it to the front of his shirt. "The game of your choosing. If I win, you will join me." Civelli could already see her in his bed.

And his employer would reward him handsomely for humiliating Caine Simons.

"And if I win?"

"Name your terms."

"If I win, you apologize to Caine."

"High stakes." Would the American let him keep the woman, or would she be used for other purposes? He'd definitely have to ask for a few hours of her company.

"For some."

"Then choose your game."

"Poker," she offered.

"Agreed." He spun on his heel and went to secure a table. The crowd followed him, intent on watching the rest of the drama unfold.

Adam grabbed Raleigh's arm to detain her. "What are you doing?" he rasped, his mouth at her ear. From a distance, it would appear as though they were locked in an embrace. "Civelli moonlights as a card shark. And he doesn't want you as just a business partner," he warned.

Raleigh pressed her mouth to his cheek as she replied haughtily, "Do you see an alternative? You heard Zeben's instructions."

"I could have handled it," he said flatly. He raised his hands to cradle her head. "You didn't have to accept his challenge."

"But I did. Now, if you'll excuse me, I have a bet to win." She patted his arm and pulled away.

"Do you even know how to play poker?" he muttered darkly.

"We'll see."

Joining Civelli, Raleigh settled into the proffered chair. Deliberately, she hiked her skirt a few more inches, then lazily crossed silk-clad legs. As expected,

Civelli stared, mouth slightly agape. With noticeable effort, he turned his attention to the game.

"New deck," the croupier announced. "The gentleman chooses."

"Seven card stud, nothing wild," Civelli said arrogantly. "Minimum bet, five thousand." He cut the deck. "This should not take too long."

Raleigh said nothing. Adam moved to stand behind her and gently massaged her shoulders. She shivered slightly. His touch distracted her. Pleased by this knowledge, Adam stepped away a few paces to watch.

Civelli flipped his ante into the center of the table. Raleigh added her chip. With deft movements, the dealer snapped two cards in front of each of them, facedown. She turned Civelli's third card first. Ten of hearts. Raleigh drew a queen. Without checking her hole cards, she bet ten thousand dollars. Civelli peaked at his hole cards and called. Three of diamonds to him. Ten of clubs for her. With a pair showing for Civelli and only a queen in front of her, Civelli raised the stakes. The pot stood at sixty thousand.

The croupier paused, then dealt the final cards. Raleigh lifted the edge of her hole cards. Civelli's brows knit together as he drew his last card.

"Twenty thousand," he wagered.

"Call."

"Pair of tens and a pair of sevens."

"Nice," Raleigh agreed, turning all of her cards face down.

Civelli reached for the pot. Raleigh placed a restraining hand on his. "A bit premature. I haven't shown you mine." With a flourish, she used her first card to turn the rest in a domino effect.

"Inside straight," the dealer said, raking the pot

to Raleigh. "Winner takes one-hundred-thousand dollars."

Her seat faced the glass window that overlooked the room. A light flashed against the pane briefly, illuminating a man's figure, who was speaking into a walkie-talkie. Civelli folded on the next round and lost a third, smaller hand. He was down to his three five-thousand-dollar chips.

"It seems you lose, Civelli," Adam noted with relief.

"But I have money remaining."

"Barely enough to ante up with," Adam derided.

"Would you care to make our wager more interesting, Ms. DeSalle?" he said, a trifle desperately. He'd been instructed to beat them. His employer was rumored quite ruthless when it came to failures.

"My interest is sufficiently peaked as it stands now, Mr. Civelli." Raleigh fiddled with the chips, stacking them in neat rows. "But give it your best shot."

"The entire five-hundred-thousand dollars on one last hand."

"It's already mine," she reminded him. "What else can you offer?"

"If I win, you become my partner—in and out of the bedroom."

"And for me?"

"If you win, I leave Jafir."

"Agreed." Raleigh raked in her chips to prepare for the final hand.

"Hold on," Adam protested.

"Excuse me for a moment, please," she apologized, then dragged Adam to an empty corner.

"What are you doing?" he railed. "This isn't the time for brinkmanship. I can see that you're good, if not just lucky. Clean him out, and let's go."

"I will."

"How can you be so sure?"

"You were right, we are being observed. I don't think Civelli ever stood a chance of winning. He's simply a convenient pawn. He wants you gone. But it's not a fair game."

"He's losing. What's wrong with that?"

"I'm getting some help. From someone in the booth."

"How do you know?"

"The dealer gave me that ace for the straight and the seven for the full house."

"You saw her?"

"Yes. I'm sure the person in the booth told her to help me." She muttered under her breath, "I'd have won on my own, though."

Adam patted her shoulder reassuringly. "I'm certain you would have."

Raleigh shrugged off his hand, displeased by the condescension. "You'll see," she warned. "Anyway, I think Zeben wants us to eliminate Civelli."

"Or he's testing you," Adam mused. "He knows me, even if he doesn't trust me. Zeben is infamous for his morality tests."

"Then let's pass." Raleigh made her way back to the table and lifted a stack of chips. "These belong to you, Civelli."

"What for?"

"I've received unsolicited assistance tonight. The game was rigged."

Ten

Civelli inhaled sharply, then rose, irate. "She's cheating," he charged. "Get Zeben. The whore and her miscreant partner are cheating! She just admitted it!"

Raleigh restrained Adam as he coiled himself to attack Civelli. "Let me handle this," she hissed tightly. She confronted a livid Civelli. "I didn't say I cheated. I said I received unsolicited help."

"A matter of semantics, no doubt. You have dishonored the game."

"Prove it," she said softly, repeating Adam's earlier challenge. *One more game,* she prayed.

"You know I cannot."

"Then, you will learn not to say what you cannot support." *Challenge me to another match, idiot.*

"I—I," he stammered.

I'll do it myself, she thought disgustedly. Raleigh cut him off, her tone condescending. "Because I did not deceive you, I deserve an opportunity to wager, and our time is running short. So I recommend that we play one more match. New dealer of your choosing. And you select the game."

Her suggestion pleased him. Reassuming his arrogant posture, he ordered, "We will play an American game. Gin rummy."

Excellent. But don't seem too eager, she cautioned herself. "That's not a casino game."

"You will renege?"

Injecting a note of skepticism, she disagreed, waving her hand. "I didn't say that."

"Then you will play. We will deal for ourselves. Winner take all."

"Agreed."

They returned to the table, and a dealer brought them a fresh deck. Civelli broke the seal. Raleigh shuffled with practiced ease. After he cut the cards, she dealt two stacks of fifteen cards.

Winners and losers, finished with their contests, crowded around the players. Adam watched from a distance, impassive.

Raleigh played steadily, discarding and laying down cards without a noticeable pattern. Recklessly, Civelli drew cards, almost doubling the size of his hand.

A single card remained in the draw pile. Civelli chuckled to himself, pleased that it would be his draw. He lifted the card from the table and scowled.

The croupier stacked the discard pile, shuffled, and placed it facedown. Raleigh reached for the pile and plucked a jack of hearts from the deck. "I believe this is what you were looking for, Civelli." She spread her cards on the table, the order running from the three to the jack. "Gin."

Enraged, Civelli shoved the table at her and yelled. "Cheating harlot!" he exclaimed and jumped at her.

This time, before she could stop him, Adam slammed his fist into Civelli's jaw. Civelli dropped like a stone to the floor and did not move. Two guards rushed over and lifted him to his feet. When he refused to stand, they dragged him from the room.

The dealer handed Raleigh two golden cases, smiling broadly. "Well done, Madame. Well done."

"Well done, indeed." Zeben said, acknowledging their victory with a reptilian half smile that bared sharp, pointed teeth. Guards stood discreetly behind him, uniformed in coats and ties. People clustered in knots throughout the room and spoke to Zeben's lieutenants. Zeben decided to speak with them personally. "Civelli did not expect such a rout."

A thin, almost skeletal hand reached for Raleigh's. The skin was a dull brown parchment stretched tight over bones and spare flesh. When his fingers closed around her own, Raleigh bit back a gasp of disgust. The crisp, paper-thin hand boasted a cold and damp palm, soft as a baby's. It felt like touching death.

He's the one, she thought, *the destroyer.* Pure evil emanated from him, filled the room with its stench. Fear and loathing bubbled inside her. She took a secret, calming breath and concentrated on the task at hand. Act two had begun, and she had little choice but to play along. Raleigh submitted gracefully, accepting it as her due. " 'Rout' is a bit strong. I simply bested him at his game," she demurred. *And I will beat you, too.*

"Why did you tell him of my service to you? You won handily. I only aided you with a few cards."

"Caine and I decided that if we were to win, it should be with honor."

"Ah, the Americans and their honor among thieves. A quaint, fatal notion."

"May I pose a question?"

"Certainly."

"Why assist us? Why not Civelli?"

"Civelli is a necessary annoyance. He provides my organization with trifles now and then, but he is not designed for grand play. I intended for him to challenge Mr. Simons. He would have dispatched Civelli easily enough."

"Are you disappointed that I intervened?"

"Not at all."

"I spoiled your plans, did I not?"

He signaled a waiter with a finger, and the young man scurried forward with a tray of champagne. Zeben toasted Raleigh, "But you did so with style, a quality I greatly admire in my, shall we say, employees." He greeted Adam with the same half smile. "Mr. Simons. So good of you to join my little tournament. I feared you would not attend."

Adam took a sip from the glass. "I gathered as much from Marie. However, as I told her, I would not dare miss it. Although, I must hope our liaison will prove more profitable." Adam extended a hand to Raleigh, and she closed the distance between them. Her fingers trembled slightly, then stilled. "With such a lovely partner, success seems inevitable."

"You have made a strong showing thus far," Zeben agreed. He snapped twice, and a guard approached with a velvet case the size of an encyclopedia. "Ms. DeSalle has ensured your advancement to the next round. It will begin in the morning at nine A.M. Your instructions are inside." Beady eyes gleamed with intelligence and a hint of madness. "I am anxious to begin construction."

"We are eager to assist," Raleigh said, fighting the fury that threatened to swamp her. *Stay focused.*

"I must admit to one concern, however, Ms. DeSalle."

"Andrea, please. Yes?"

"I understand the motives of the other competitors. Religious zealotry, primitive hatred for the new, an affection for death. Why are you here?"

Raleigh curled berry-stained lips in an erotic parody of a smile. "Money is its own seduction, Mr. Zeben. When it comes with the opportunity to handle such power, if only for a moment, I cannot resist."

"Then we shall hope you will not have to exercise restraint." Zeben snapped again, and a guard approached. "Please escort Ms. DeSalle and Mr. Simons to their suite."

Raleigh and Adam followed the man to the door. Then, Zeben's oily voice stopped them. "Out of courtesy, I will not re-outfit your room with my monitors. But do not make the mistake of defying me again. Once, is noblc. Twicc, is imbecilic. Good night."

The guard keyed in the elevator code, and the doors slid shut soundlessly. When they opened, Adam and Raleigh left the elevator and crossed the mirrored hallway.

"Where'd you learn to count cards?" Adam asked as they approached the penthouse.

Flush with victory, agitated by memories, Raleigh jerked the key from her purse. "My father taught me." *My father,* she thought wildly, *the first one to pay for my sins.* Then, she killed Cavanaugh with her arrogance. *How many more,* she thought numbly, *will pay for my mistakes? I must get inside, get away from the memories.*

She checked the door for signs of uninvited guests, poring over each crevice with intense focus, then she opened the lock. Adam looked askance at the overly thorough investigation, but she ignored him.

Keep it together, Raleigh. For a few more hours. She

tossed her bag on the table and slipped out of her shoes. Adam crossed the room to engage the scrambler. "How'd you guess I counted the cards?"

"You agreed to gin and dealt too many. You had to know what he was holding, so you played until you'd seen the deck." Admiration tinged his words, much to his chagrin. But he certainly didn't have to tell her that. He watched her sharp, jerky movements. It was probably jet lag and adrenaline. He understood. Energy pumped through him as well, the aftermath of an adrenal rush. He felt volatile, on the edge.

Deliberately provocative, Raleigh sank into the overstuffed, blue velvet sofa and drew her legs up. "It worked," she announced arrogantly.

"You're lucky it did." Adam frowned at her. "Taking on Civelli was a risk. The stakes are too high for you to suddenly go renegade on me." Did she have to sit like that? His temper rose, and he pushed it back.

"Going renegade? That's your department," she grumbled snidely under her breath. *Where did that come from,* she wondered.

"Excuse me?" Adam perched on the arm of the couch. "Would you care to repeat that?"

She said, "It worked." When the scowl did not soften, she added cheekily, "And I am the primary." She shrugged. "I pick."

"We're partners. *We* pick." He poured himself a drink at the bar to curb his tongue. Soon enough, Raleigh would understand that she was primary in name only. Jafir was his turf. "Pull a stunt like that again, and I walk."

"We should all stick with what we're good at." *I am spoiling for a fight,* she thought. She had to burn off this anguish, the images. *He'll give me what I want,* she decided.

Adam tossed back his brandy with one fierce gulp and fixed her with a pointed stare. "Are you trying to goad me?" Intrigued by this possibility and its cause, Adam poured another finger into the glass and examined her.

She'd curled up into the cushions of the sofa, her impossibly long legs tucked beneath her. Prisms of light danced above her, casting an ethereal glow around her. The pulse in the base of her throat thudded against her fine skin. Her hands moved restlessly in her lap, plucking at the hem of the wisp of a dress.

Fight me, she thought. "No, just agreeing with your assessment. You're the master at walking away when you lose."

Stung, he retaliated. "If we're discussing habits, I guess that means I should watch my back. Your forte seems to be survival of the fittest," he retorted.

Molten anger and resentment flowed through her. Why did she have to be the one? To feel, to know, to survive. "You should know." She almost vibrated with antagonism.

Adam could read the emotions, and he didn't understand the cause. But he knew the cure. "What the hell is this all about, Raleigh?" he asked in a voice threaded with rage and excitement.

"I don't know what you're talking about." She rose from the couch and strolled to the bar. "You do seem a bit touchy." Raleigh filled her glass with water and sipped the contents.

Adam caught her shoulder, spun her to face him. "I'm not the one acting like a bad-tempered brat."

"Can't stand the truth?" Raleigh set her glass on

the counter. Her temper mounted, and she continued to push. "Take your hands off me."

In response, he grabbed her other shoulder. "All right."

"Let me go," she commanded in a deadly quiet voice, and she angled her head.

"I will," he promised as his mouth captured hers. She fought, pushing at his shoulders, pulling his head against her. Hard male lips dominated hers. Each foray siphoned off her reaction, replaced the tumult with unadulterated passion. Tongues fought for supremacy, and he quelled her struggle with firm hands.

This was what she needed, this release. She gripped his hair, daring him to move, to take this away from her. She twisted closer, demanding more, more. He possessed her, body and soul, forcing the memories to yield. Dark, dangerous hands shoved her clothing aside, seeking flesh. She poured herself into their kiss, into his keeping.

His taste was primal, untamed, as rich as the champagne that still exploded on her tongue. Adam stroked her breasts, freeing them from the silken confines. At the first touch of his flesh to her own, she moaned, a savage sound of greed.

"Now," she panted. "I want you now."

In response, Adam dragged her down to the floor. "You. I will have you." Fevered, he drew one peaked nipple into the heated cavern of his mouth. She arched beneath him, racked by pleasure. Strong, rough fingers massaged her thighs, parted them for his touch.

Raleigh gripped wide, uncompromising shoulders. She fumbled with—then ignored—his tie and tore at his shirt. His mouth lapped at her breasts. *Sweet,* he thought dimly, *so sweet.*

When tiny teeth grazed his chest, he groaned heavily. "Again," he gasped, breathless. They rolled on the carpet, and she rose above him, nipping at his flesh. "Now," she repeated, reaching for his buckle.

"Yes."

Brrinng! Brrinngg! The cellular phone in Raleigh's evening bag demanded attention.

"Ignore it," Adam rasped as she released his zipper. "Please ignore it." The plea was punctuated by a mind-blowing kiss.

When he freed her mouth, Raleigh sighed and looked guiltily at the bag, which continued to ring impatiently. "It must be Atlas," she implored. "It could be important."

"More important than this?" Adam challenged, pressing her into the carpet. "More important than us?"

"No, of course not. But . . ."

Disgusted with her equivocation, the mood broken, Adam rolled away. "Answer the damned phone, Chimera."

Torn between the need to finish what she'd started with Adam and the potential information Atlas might have, Raleigh reached for the bag. She flipped the phone open and drew her dress up around her exposed breasts. Adam got to his feet and began rebuttoning his shirt.

"Chimera," she managed breathlessly.

"Atlas. Debrief."

"Contact made. Team advanced."

"Contact?"

"Zeben."

"Merlin?"

"Right here." Without looking at him, she passed him the phone. Rising from the carpet, she tugged at her dress.

"Contact me on the communicator." Adam disconnected the phone, then brought out his laptop. He plugged the modem into Raleigh's phone and dialed up headquarters.

"Secured channel," he said when Atlas' face and voice came on line.

"Tell me how it went," Atlas demanded.

"Just as you thought. Zeben had us betting against one another. He selected us to continue on to the next round."

Raleigh picked up the velvet case and opened it. "It says we're to meet in the lobby in the morning. A second test has been prepared to judge our acumen. There's nothing else."

"Are you feeling well, Chimera? You seem a bit peaked."

Adam shot a warning glance at Raleigh. "I'm fine," she replied evenly. "It's jet lag." *Concentrate on the debriefing,* she told herself. *Don't think about what almost happened.*

Atlas spoke again. "So Zeben has already picked his favorites. Why the elaborate setup?"

"Zeben has a big ego. He craves attention as much as he lusts after power. With Praxis, he gets both. If he just handed the contract over, he'd miss the spectacle of grown men and women playing puppets to his Geppetto," Adam replied.

They talked for a few more minutes, and then Atlas signed off.

Eager to avoid any discussion of their embrace, Raleigh spoke first. "You never met him, uh, last time?" Raleigh asked.

After a brief delay, he responded. "No. I thought we would the day Phillip came, but he sent a lieutenant instead. Then the ambush, and it was all over."

"I didn't think he'd show up tonight."

"Neither did I. But is he ever the showman." Adam went into the bedroom.

Scooping up her jewelry and bag, Raleigh followed. Adam stood at the dresser, undoing his cuff links.

As she entered the room, the tension returned with a vengeance. The enormous blue-and-gold bed dominated the room, daring her to ignore it. Raleigh found that she couldn't, especially with Adam standing just beyond its edge. Her throat dried, and she moistened her lips. Her vamp act and his threat hung over the bed like the sword of Damocles. Would he expect her to finish what had started in the living room?

Time for a preemptive strike, she thought. "We haven't discussed sleeping arrangements," she began in a businesslike tone.

Adam stopped loosening his tie. She wouldn't renege on him now. And he owed her for earlier. "I thought we agreed. Even with the scrambler and the blind cameras, a maid could tip them off if I slept on the couch." *I don't intend to be far away from you,* he finished silently.

"I didn't mean that." She gestured to the bed impatiently. "Which side do you want?"

"Which side?" he asked dumbly.

"Left or right. I prefer the right side." Raleigh kept her gun near her at all times.

Reading her mind, Adam concurred. "Good. I'm left-handed. And since the bed faces the door, we're fine."

"Okay." Raleigh opened the bureau she'd chosen and pulled out a pair of flannel pajamas.

"You're *not* sleeping in those," Adam said flatly, snatching the garments from her.

"And why not?" she demanded as she tugged on them.

His hold did not relax. "Caine Simons would never bed a woman who owned flannel, let alone wore it," he explained dismissively, then he released the pajamas as though they offended him.

Embarrassed, Raleigh let the pajamas dangle from her hands. "Caine Simons won't be bedding me," she suggested coolly.

"You know what I meant."

With a raised brow, she replied, "Explain it to me."

Sensing a trap, he skirted the issue of Caine's prowess. The current conversation posed enough of a danger without raising the specter of sex. *Yet.* "Andrea DeSalle would sleep in silk, if anything at all."

She couldn't argue with him, although the "anything at all" was definitely out of the question. With an imperious nod, she folded the pajamas and removed the teddy. Allowing it to dangle from one thin strap, she sauntered into the bathroom in full character.

When she shut the door, she released the breath that she hadn't realized she'd been holding. The tension of the evening swamped her, overloading her senses. What the hell had she been thinking with Civelli? Her initial motive had been to show Adam who was in charge. Then, as the game progressed, she thought about Civelli's accusations and the dull look of regret in Adam's eyes. Truth gnawed at her when Civelli taunted Adam about Phillip's death, while the other patrons concurred with Civelli's assessment. Although she knew it was a part of the rumors she had helped to spread, this was different.

Separating fact from fiction would only grow more difficult. Especially if she had to share a bed with him. Her stomach fluttered at the thought of returning to the bedroom. The bravura performance buttressed her flagging spirits but left her on shaky ground. If he pushed her to follow through on the act, she wasn't sure how she'd respond. She was too tired to think about it now. The stress of lying to Adam, lying to Atlas—and sometimes even lying to herself—constricted her muscles, leaving her tense and exhausted.

She climbed into bed and closed her eyes, listening to the sound of Adam's shower. In her mind's eye, she imagined tiny droplets clinging to his powerful chest, running down his athletic body. Raleigh stirred, trying to think of something else. Anything else.

When Adam emerged from the bathroom, he could hear her deep, even breathing. Too deep. Too even. She was feigning sleep. Willing to accommodate her, he fiddled with his clothes, checked the locks, and secured the windows. He opened the bedside table to store his gun and saw a glint of silver. Pulling the drawer open more fully, he stared in disbelief at the foil packets. Just what he needed to see right now. He'd nearly grabbed her when she came out of the bathroom in that teddy. Sleek expanses of skin were displayed by the scant bottom and the simple top. Framed by clouds of fragrant steam, she'd glided into the room and crawled between the silken sheets. How could one man want one woman so badly? The discomfort in his loins mocked him, as did the packets in the drawer. With a sigh of defeat, he climbed into bed, leaving a wide space between them. *Eventually,* he mused, *sleep will have to come.*

Dark crowded hallways. The pungent scent of unwashed, perfumed flesh. Voices rising in harsh laughter, despairing tones filling the cracks in the walls. Wind whistling in the damp, cold spaces, shrieking warnings. The click, click *of dice. The* snap, snap *of cards. Then the gunshot, the loud, eternal sound of death. Chance? Chance? Wake up!*

He pushes her away, yells at her to go. Before the cops come and take her. But the police don't come. The soldiers do, pulling her with them to the prison. Iron bars, iron shackles. Around her hands. Her feet.

Rocky broken terrain. The acrid smell of gunpowder. Motors humming before they burst into flame, the screams of dying men. Falling, falling. His blood on her hands. Cavanaugh? Cavanaugh? Get up!

He pushes her away, yells at her to go. Before the soldiers come and take her. But the soldiers don't come. Adam does, pulling her with him to the prison. Iron bars, iron shackles. Around her heart. Her soul.

And another voice, begging her to save him. Don't leave me! Don't leave me here! Phillip? Phillip? I can't help you. No one can. You must pay. We must pay. The gun fires, throwing her into the wall. She lifts her hands. Blood. Blood. Everywhere. Always.

"Raleigh?" Adam murmured soothingly, trying not to startle her. He reset the safety on the gun and placed it under his pillow. He didn't want to frighten her when she opened her eyes.

"No more blood on my hands. No more," she whimpered, trapped in the nightmare.

"Raleigh? Wake up, sweetheart." He gathered her

against his naked chest, chafing warmth back into frozen hands.

"Don't touch my hands!" She jerked from his arms, crouching on the bed, still caught between nightmare and reality. "Can't you see the blood? It's everywhere. It won't come off. I try and I try, but it won't come off."

"Raleigh! Wake up! Now!" Adam held her by the shoulders, willing her to see him and not the specters in her dreams.

"Adam?" Slowly her eyes focused on his bare chest, panic receding. Instantly, she understood what had happened, but the dregs of her nightmare had not yet disappeared. As it had every time, Adam's presence both reassured and embarrassed her. She had to escape, to get away from everything that threatened to crush her—including Adam. Shaky fingers fumbled for her robe, and she climbed out of bed.

Adam watched her handle the robe clumsily and then drop it, and he wondered what she was running from or to. "Where are you going?" he asked gently.

"Um, I don't know." Humiliation gleamed in eyes bright with crystalline tears. "To the bathroom. Or the terrace. I need to get out of here."

"Come back to bed, Raleigh." Adam leaned forward, preparing to get out of the bed.

Raleigh retreated, bumping into the doorjamb. "Not now. I can't." She shook her head desperately, warding him off.

"Come back to bed," he said firmly. "There's nothing to be afraid of."

Only you, she thought numbly. *And orders and obligations and memories.* She took a deep breath and circled to her side of the bed. "I apologize. I didn't mean to wake you." The clock on the bedside table read four A.M.

"Don't insult me, Raleigh." He cuddled her against him, offering comfort.

She snuggled against his heat, reveling in the feel of vibrant life. "I didn't mean to."

Adam stroked her hair, the short curls tickling his palm. "Is it the same nightmare?"

"Almost." They'd come then, too, stealing into her mind as she napped in the warehouse, waking her in a rush. Her body's reaction to stress, the Internal Review doctor told her. The nightmares dissipated over time, replaced by daydreams about Adam.

"What was it this time?" Adam didn't expect an answer. She'd never provided a complete one before. In the past, he would cradle her to him until the shaking passed. This time, however, he wanted answers.

"Nothing."

"Don't lie to me, Raleigh."

She rubbed her forehead wearily. Before, she'd shared portions of the dreams with him. "It's the same dark hallway. The gunshots and death."

Adam eased her deeper into his embrace, trying to share his warmth with her. Her skin, clammy and cold, seemed determined to reject the heat. "You screamed about shackles. You've never dreamed about those before."

"They're from the prison." Raleigh burrowed closer, unable to see Adam's expression. Comfort, a rare commodity in their world, had to be seized. She knew, with a soul-deep understanding, that his generosity would disappear soon enough. But for tonight, she would take and wallow in his compassion.

Adam held her closer. "The prison?" What had

they done to her when he abandoned her to the night? Would his sins never end?

Surrounded by darkness and the steel bonds of his arms, she felt safe. Safe enough to share a piece of the truth. "Where Zeben's soldiers took me after the explosion at the warehouse."

"How did they capture you?" Adam frowned into the darkness, afraid of her response. "When I left, you were alone. They couldn't have come so quickly." *I wouldn't have left you to them, if I'd known.* But defending himself now was unthinkable.

"I got sidetracked," she said simply. She reached for the covers and dragged the sheets up around her shoulders.

"By what?" His scowl deepened, a hundred unhappy possibilities crowding his conscience. "The warehouse was all but destroyed."

"I had to retrieve something."

"There was nothing in there, Raleigh." Hope and self-loathing filled him. Hope that she'd tried to help Phillip. Loathing that he'd left her by herself in a war zone. "What did you go back for?"

"Nothing." Her voice frayed over the lie.

"Tell me, Raleigh. Give us this much, at least."

Broken by his appeal, she confessed. "The radio," she whispered. "I tried to find the radio."

"Why?" His world narrowed to that one question, a single answer.

"I don't know."

"You tried to save him. You turned your back on what you believed in, all to save my friend."

"No." She tried to shift away from him, but he wouldn't let her go.

"Yes," he corrected, his lips pressing soft kisses into her hair. "Yes, you did. I called you heartless, but you sacrificed your freedom to try and save Phillip." Adam took a deep breath. He opened his mouth again, but the words didn't come, submerged by guilt and hope and a feeling he didn't quite recognize. He tried again, with the only words he knew. "Thank you, Raleigh."

Don't be grateful, she begged silently. *I didn't save him then, and I will not spare him now. Don't make this harder.* Aloud, she entreated, "It doesn't matter now. Just let it go."

Adam couldn't let it go. He had to know the whole story. What other horrible things was he responsible for, would he need to beg her forgiveness for? "Then Scimitar apprehended you? How long were you held?"

"Only a few days. Cavanaugh searched for me and helped me escape."

"Raleigh. You must believe me." He shifted her in his arms to face him, to see his shame. "They told me you were dead." Adam said bleakly. He deserved nothing from her, but perhaps she would offer it anyway. "I would have come for you, if I'd known."

She cupped his face. "I know."

"Whose blood is on your hands, Raleigh?"

"Doesn't matter," she repeated.

"Share it, and it can't torment you."

Raleigh smiled, a desolate, lonely twist of her lips. "It will always torment me, Adam. It's who I am."

"Whose blood, Raleigh?"

The darkness invited confessions, welcomed them. "Chance. Cavanaugh. It won't come off. No matter what I do, it won't come off."

Chance. The man Atlas mentioned when they'd fought about her leaving the team. "Who was Chance, Raleigh? What happened to him?"

She countered his question with a question of her own. "Why do you care? It doesn't mean anything now."

"If talking about it will make you better, then I want to hear about it. I need to hear about him," he whispered. "I need to help you."

Raleigh watched him with quiet, sad eyes. "Why?"

Adam bent and brushed a tender kiss onto her forehead. He finally understood the distance, the aloofness. Raleigh had lost so much, and he'd heaped more guilt onto shoulders too fragile to bear the burden. Hadn't Atlas warned him? Hadn't his heart warned him? He sipped delicately at lips drawn into their customary stubborn line of resistance. "Why? Because I owe you something for doubting you, even for a moment. Let me give it to you."

Raleigh dropped her eyes, shaken by his words. "You owe me nothing, Adam. You had no reason to trust me then, no reason to believe me now."

Adam eased Raleigh deeper into his embrace. Her warm breath bathed his naked chest. He spoke above her head, wonder filling every word. "But I do trust you, Raleigh. With my life."

Wanting to flee, unwilling to move away, Raleigh pleaded, "Don't depend on me, Adam. I'll disappoint you."

She was too churned up to talk now, Adam decided, watching her hands move restlessly. He gently cupped them in his own and sank down into the bed, still holding Raleigh against him. "Go to sleep, Raleigh. We'll talk more in the morning."

"But—"

"Sleep, sweetheart. I'm here."

Eleven

"A treasure hunt?" Adam pulled the compass from his backpack. "He's left us in the forest to scavenge for supplies?"

A macaw chirped in the distance, answered by its mate. Wind moaned softly, rustling the leaves that canopied the bright, clear sky. Trees, towering ancient evergreens, locked limbs, shading them from the direct beams of the sun. Despite the dusky half light, flowers bloomed in profuse color. Plants Raleigh had never seen, could not begin to identify, blanketed the ground. Native animals scurried across their path to forage for food. Attracted by human sweat, mosquitoes circled lazily in the heavy, humid air.

"Certainly innovative," Raleigh suggested dryly as she fanned herself.

"A global positioning system is innovative. This is stupid."

"Unfortunately, I can't help but agree." The thin, black tank top she wore stuck to her skin, although they'd only been in the forest for twenty minutes. Khaki shorts left her legs ripe for attack by the rabid insects. She took perverse pleasure in the knowledge that Adam would fare no better. The tight, black T-shirt molded thickly muscled arms. Arms developed in active sport, not in the male refuge of an overpriced weight room. Khaki slacks covered his powerful legs and protected him from the insects. But the sticky, wet, tropical heat would plaster them to him and drive him insane within the hour.

"What's the first clue?" Adam asked shortly. He swatted a gnat. "Let's get moving. We can't let another team reach the finish first."

Raleigh opened the scroll Zeben handed to the three participating teams after providing his instructions. "It says 'Sweet nectar of time will fill your basket full,' " she translated from Arabic.

" 'Sweet nectar of time?' " Adam repeated.

"Dates," they exclaimed together, both chuckling at the simple absurdity of the clue.

"Do dates grow in the forest?" Raleigh wondered aloud.

"They are tropical palm trees, but given Jafir's variable climate, I wouldn't doubt it."

"Then dates typically grow near the shore."

"We'll head south."

With Adam in the lead, they hurried through the forest. Roots from mahogany and kola trees covered the forest floor, and passage was difficult. Raleigh noted that Adam effortlessly navigated the rough terrain, as though he hunted in rainforests every day. In spite of her considerable height, his stride outpaced hers. Occasionally, he looked back to check on her, but he never offered to stop. *Not that I would,* she thought. She could go as long as he could. Even if he did leap over vines like a panther.

As if reading her thoughts, he grinned at her, a mocking yet companionable smirk. There was an ease about him, a relaxation she hadn't seen before. Her early-morning revelations hung between them, but neither seemed in the mood to discuss them. She never intended to tell him about that, about crawling through the rubble searching for the destroyed radio. About almost disregarding her duty—not for Phillip, but for him. At least she'd drawn the line at telling him about Chance. That was one story that would remain her secret.

Her candidness shook her. It was happening again, the collapse of defenses, of barriers, when he touched her. When he cradled her so tenderly in his arms, she chose not to lie. Not because he had changed—and neither had she—but because it felt so right. Guilt, innocence, and vengeance no longer mattered in those moonlit moments before dawn. Resting in the harbor of his embrace, she felt safe. His unique blend of strength and compassion tenderly destroyed the barriers she tried to keep between them. But the price of letting him inside was too high to pay a third time.

What could she do? Because dawn inevitably came, bringing with it promises and vows. She would track down Phillip. He would furnish the answers Atlas sought, and she would do her job. Then she would do her duty. And stand by mutely as Adam turned from her, his contempt real and permanent. Why confess to a love doomed to fail? *No, not love,* Raleigh corrected immediately. *I can't—won't—fall in love with him.*

"Andrea," Adam said quietly, breaking into her panicked thoughts. He stretched an arm out to stop her headlong progress. A few inches away, an adder slithered across their path. Raleigh could see the head and the top of the body, but the middle disappeared from view in the foliage. She knew from experience that the snake could grow to be almost six feet long and fat. Many people died because they underestimated the reptile. The adder could strike with lethal accuracy, its venom inducing internal bleeding and eventually death.

With slow, measured steps, they edged away from the snake to give it a wide berth.

"Nice and easy," Adam said.

"Shh!" Raleigh hissed.

"I was trying to help." He shrugged his shoulders at her look of disbelief.

"They attack vibrations, including those from speech," she explained as though he were a dim-witted child.

"Like yours?" he smirked.

"Shh!"

Three or four feet separated them from the reptile. Then, a loud crack sounded behind them. Adam whirled around to find the source of the noise. In that instant, the adder struck out, coiling its tail around Raleigh's leg.

"Adam!" she yelled as the beast knocked her off balance. It reared a flat head to aim at its victim.

Adam dove for the head, and he grabbed the snake just under its powerful jaws. Raleigh sat up and clawed at the tail. She removed the coils and grabbed a stout limb lying nearby.

"Move!"

Adam released the snake and rolled, just as Raleigh stunned the animal with a sharp blow to the head. They ran through the forest, until Raleigh tugged on his arm to halt them.

"Why are we still running?" she gasped.

"The noise that scared the snake."

"Huh?"

"It was a gunshot." As though to punctuate his

explanation, another shot rang out. The bullet split the bark of a tree just above their heads.

"Oh!" Saving conversation for later, they sprinted deeper into the woods, heading for denser cover. The shots grew fainter and finally vanished altogether.

Exhausted, Adam finally dropped to the ground. "He didn't say we'd be hunted by scavengers," he complained as he tried to drag air into his lungs. He ran four miles a day in the damp Atlanta air. Late summer Jafir made Atlanta's muggy weather seem arid.

"Are you sure it was our competition?" Raleigh sucked in air, only slightly less winded than Adam.

"No, but I'm not sure it wasn't." Adam screwed the cap off of the canteen and tossed it to Raleigh, who drank her fill. She passed it back to him and he took a deep swallow.

"There's no mention of snipers in the scroll."

"Nothing about adders, either, I bet."

Raleigh slid her pack off and opened the pouch Zeben's men had given them that morning. "Three clues. Sweet nectar. Rocks of life. Myths about reincarnation. No word about gunmen."

Adam scooted over to read the scroll. "We didn't read this." He pointed to the border.

Raleigh brought the scroll closer, reading the border. "It's not Arabic."

"It's Shilha."

"Shilha? You read Shilha? Fewer than three million people speak this language."

"Three million and one. You didn't think you were the only one with a facility for languages, did you?"

Raleigh stuck her tongue out at him, although she

was very impressed. Adam continually surprised her. "Can you translate?"

"Yes. 'Beware the hunters, by four legs and two. Beware gifts and stolen bounty,' " Adam read.

"An all-purpose curse, but no mention of serpents. I guess we can safely assume the snake wasn't his doing." Raleigh returned the scroll to its pouch and strapped on her backpack.

Adam stood and pulled her to her feet. "And the gunmen are after all of us."

Raleigh dusted leaves from her bottom. She unhooked a canteen from her belt and drank heavily. She offered it to Adam, who took a healthy swig. "Which evens the odds. Assuming he's not cheating like he did last night."

"Not an assumption I'm willing to make. If he knows who we are, this trek in the forest could be the perfect setup. Lure us over here to complete Praxis, then kill us off."

"Or lure us over here, and kill us before we can touch Praxis."

"Either way, he wins."

"Unless he truly doesn't know who we are."

"No time like the present to find out." Setting the compass, they set out for the southern shore.

Raleigh trudged behind Adam. The closer they got to the shore, the thicker the swarm of bugs. Welts the size of her little finger swelled along her bare legs. Soon, she was scratching more than she walked. After another pause to rub at her legs, Adam called to her.

"Ahead!" From her upside-down position, she could make out a line of fronds on the horizon. Date palms. They raced to the trees and began searching for the prize. Raleigh took the stand of trees to the left, Adam the ones to the right.

She examined the bases of the trees, then climbed up into their palms. A mesh sack hung suspended between a clump of dates from the seventh tree. "I got it!" Raleigh yelled triumphantly as she shimmied down the trunk.

Adam opened the sack and removed a rectangular box. Inside were the updated blueprints for Praxis. "Good work. What's next?"

Raleigh consulted the scroll. " 'The rocks of life seek the gods, they bear witness in silver flame.' Sounds like a volcano to me, but there are no volcanoes in Jafir."

"Not active ones, no. But a few miles from here, there is an old monument to the last eruption two hundred years ago. Geologists believe a volcanic eruption of the Great Rift Valley created Jafir centuries before settlement."

"Which way?"

"Northeast." Adam put the chips in his pack, adjusted the compass, and started walking. He'd waited for hours to hear Raleigh complain, but she had said nothing. Not even when the snake attacked her. She'd never whined before; however, people did change. He was certainly evidence of that phenomenon. The woman who'd been his nemesis only days before now invited his respect. A woman who could weather an attack by a snake and gunmen possessed the innate sense of humor that he remembered. He'd been afraid that it, like the innocence he'd once known, had died three years ago. But Raleigh had yet to display any temper he could fault her for. And two hours in the rainforest would fray anyone's temper, especially given the evening she'd had.

Her screams during the night had wrenched him from a fiery, restless sleep and into full alertness. In his dreams, Atlas did not interrupt them. Slick skin slid against slick skin, mouth to mouth, hip to hip. Locked in sexual combat, they'd driven each other to the brink of madness. Then her frantic cries pierced the layers of his consciousness, and he woke to find her fighting invisible demons. At least he *thought* they were invisible. But he understood how real nightmares could be, especially when the demons had faces. Names. She'd cried out names—his, Cavanaugh's, Phillip's. And a man named Chance.

Raleigh refused to tell him the whole story, but he could figure it out. Chance, the man she'd abandoned, had obviously broken her heart. Perhaps he was from her first mission, maybe he was her first lover. Whomever he was, he'd scarred her. Chance seemed to be the explanation for the aloofness, the cool demeanor. And her physical retreat.

But what overwhelmed him had been the truth about her disappearance. When he'd reached the hut and found no sign of Phillip's body, he returned to the ruined warehouse. A final explosion destroyed the very foundations of the building. The ISA could not account for her whereabouts, and a full-scale search uncovered nothing. With his best friend and the woman he loved dead, he'd turned away from the life he'd chosen.

Now he knew that she'd stayed, tried to save his friend. She'd been held captive by animals determined to ferret out her secrets. She'd been captured because he left her there, alone. Her torture was his fault. Like Phillip's death. He convinced Phillip to join, and the work killed him. Atlas made him responsible for Raleigh's welfare, and he walked away from her. During the night, listening to her story and all the words she left unsaid, he'd heard the truth. The blame, the fault, the guilt was his. Only his. He didn't tell her last night, but he would. He had to.

After Phillip's death, he'd sworn never to return. The penance for his betrayal, he decided, would be living with the knowledge that he'd deserted his best friend. He accepted his sentence and walked away from the life that meant the most to him. *Liar,* he derided himself, *leaving the ISA was not your punishment.*

As he walked beside her, the pungent scent of the forest filling his nostrils, he accepted his lie. Penance lay not in living with guilt but in living without Raleigh. They'd stood on a hilltop, and she had condemned his best friend to death—and still he wanted her. He wanted her unflappable, noble confidence as he ran to the hut, digging through rubble, searching for any sign of life. He wanted her quiet, calm compassion as he found Phillip's pocketwatch, a gift from Phillip's father that he always carried with him. He wanted her soft, perfect embrace as he faced life without Phillip and with his torment.

The charade of hatred crumbled, shattered by burgeoning reality. In spite of everything, he wanted her. All of her. Wasn't that why he'd fought her for the radio, needing her to give in? Wasn't that why he'd been so adamant about not returning with her? Wasn't that why he found any excuse to touch her, to fill his hands with her?

And there was more. The need to soothe the shy insecurity from her eyes as they stood before the mirror. The pride when she'd bested Civelli, not once but twice. His relief when she'd turned to him in her darkest nightmares. He trusted this woman, Raleigh Foster, as much as he had adored Chimera. Wants, needs, trust. With him, for him, that meant love. *Love.* Staggered by this realization, he faced her, unsure of the answers.

"Adam?" Raleigh scanned the area surrounding them. "Is there something wrong?"

Adam shook his head. "No. Nothing's wrong. I, uh, just had a thought. It was nothing." *I'm in love with Raleigh. Again.* He wanted to shout the truth to her. He wanted to run away from her.

Raleigh stared at him, worried by his odd look. "Are you sure?"

"Yes," he answered after a brief silence. He'd process this later, after they'd recovered the other items. "Yes, I'm fine. Did you have a question?"

Unconvinced, Raleigh nevertheless gestured to the fork between the trees. "Which way to the monument?" Down one path, kola trees dropped huge nuts to the moist earth. Occasionally, a woodland creature would scamper out to collect the fruit. Mahogany had been planted in groves down the other path, young trees threaded with rope. They'd reached the edge of the forest.

"Follow the kola trees." He pointed toward a small mound in the distance. "That's the monument."

At the base of the monument, four small, black, metal boxes sat on a rock shelf, wedged between two massive stones. One space was empty. Someone had been here before them. Adam squatted down to pry one box loose, and Raleigh wandered behind the monument to take a look at the petrified lava pit.

"Wait!" Raleigh shouted, horrified by what she saw. "Don't touch it." She saw remains inside the pit of one of the teams on the scavenger hunt with them. The leader, an older white man she recognized as IRA, had worn bright green that morning to their rendezvous. They'd been shot.

But the sight that made her stop Adam was the wire attached to an oblong capsule with a timer. "It's rigged. There's a bomb."

Adam raised his hand and began to inch away. "Can you defuse it?"

"I hope so."

Raleigh crouched in front of the monument, looking for anything that would tell her how the bomb could be detonated. The capsule may be either the bomb or simply the incendiary device. Then she spotted a slim piece of wire running from the monument's plaque and down to the boxes. "I believe the explosive is time delayed. If you dislodge it from the trip wire, the countdown begins."

"How long?"

"The box is wedged in such a way that you have to remove the box to open the lid. I don't know how much time we'd have. The bomb could be in any one of the boxes. I'd have to guess."

"Then forget it." Adam reached down to pull her to her feet. "Let's go."

She slapped his hands away, irritated by his lack of trust in her abilities. She could figure this out. She had to. "We can't forget it. Without the box, we lose the game. We don't advance."

"You try to dislodge the wrong box, it explodes," he argued. His gut clenched as he imagined the possibility. They'd just have to find another way to get to Praxis.

"Then so be it. I have to try." Raleigh turned back to the monument.

Furious and annoyed by her resistance, Adam

railed at her. "Don't be a fool! This isn't a game. You could die if you're wrong."

"And we could win if I'm right," she countered with deadly calm. "It's my choice."

Helpless rage bubbled up inside him. How could she be so cavalier about her life? He wouldn't have it. "The scavenger hunt isn't worth your life! The ISA will find another way to get us inside. They'd have to anyway if we lost." Considering the matter settled, Adam grabbed his pack and started to leave.

Raleigh stood her ground. "But we haven't lost," she said coolly. "And I must get inside Scimitar. With or without you."

Adam whirled around. "Why is infiltrating Scimitar so important that it's worth your life?"

Raleigh countered with a question of her own. "Doesn't getting inside mean anything to you? Or don't you care to know why Phillip died?"

The barb struck its mark, but the pain didn't register. Not until after he responded. "Not enough to lose you again! I can't do that a second time. You're mine!" he bellowed.

Raleigh stared at him, stunned. "What? What did you say?"

Adam caught her shoulders. Desperation compelled him, a race against the demons that haunted him. "I said you're mine. And I will not let you die a second time! Not for this!"

His. Someone he wanted, cared about. Her heartbeat stopped, then thundered loudly in her ears. "You don't mean that." Alarm swamped her. She could fight her own needs, but not him. Not if he cared about her. Really cared about her. "Take it back," she demanded absurdly.

In that instant, and with her plaintive request, he

had his answers. Love filled him, flooded him. Full, brimming, seductive love. "What if you're my life?" he demanded as he pulled her closer to him. Her arms were wooden, as though she'd been struck dumb. If her reaction hurt, he'd deal with that later, too. Now, the truth was the most important thing. "What if I told you that I love you?"

Raleigh recoiled as though she'd been struck. "Don't say that. Don't you *dare* say that to me." Hysteria edged her voice.

Adam was bewildered. Fear made sense, but Raleigh was beyond fear. "Why not? Why can't I tell you how I feel?"

Raleigh paced, furious with him for bringing them to this place where she had no answers. Love wasn't part of the deal. She had too much to lose without losing the one thing she might miss the most. So she'd convince him that he didn't mean it. "What you feel is sorry. For me, for yourself." But a tendril of hope sprouted in defiance.

Outraged and deeply hurt by her dismissal of his feelings, he struck back. "Don't tell me how I feel! What would you know about love? You, the consummate ice princess. The one who only feels in her dreams."

The accusation killed the budding expectation. He didn't know her at all. How could he love a woman he misunderstood so badly? "Did you love me last night?" she asked. "Before I told you about the warehouse?"

Adam ground his teeth. "I don't know," he gritted. "I honestly don't know."

"I know. You didn't love me last night. You couldn't. Because I am the type of woman who would let your best friend die just to achieve her objective. Maybe I would even kill him myself if the cause were just," she warned. *Hear me, Adam,* she begged, *spare us both.*

He heard a plea in her low, husky voice. For reassurance? For absolution? "You couldn't deliberately take a life, Raleigh. I know that now." If he could hold her, surely she'd sense his declaration was genuine. Adam reached for her.

Raleigh evaded the touch that would surely sap her resolve and leave her floundering in a morass of untutored feelings, hopeless longings. *Better you end it now,* she thought, *before you start to believe him.* "No, you don't know that. You have no clue what I may have become in the past three years."

He dismissed her protest as nonsense. "I've spent time with you," he began. "Talking. Listening—"

She interrupted. "Fighting. Bickering."

"Kissing. Loving," he countered.

"Sex *isn't* love, Adam." she derided.

"I didn't say *sex,* Raleigh." He smiled at her, an erotic, appealing grin that weakened her. "I would remember sex."

"I'm not joking." Panic rose inside like bile. She couldn't do this, listen to this, and do her job. Indignation hadn't worked. Perhaps pity would. "Take it back. Please."

"I will not take it back." Adam smiled at her, his anger dissipated in the face of such terror. She wasn't fighting him. She was fighting herself.

"You don't love me. You can't."

"Maybe you're right," he conceded, willing to give her space for the battle. "Maybe I don't love you now. But I could tonight. And tomorrow. And the next day."

"I won't give you the opportunity to find out."

"I will unravel your secrets, Raleigh. Each and every one. I will strip you bare, body and soul. And when I've revealed you to my eyes and yours, I will stand before you. I will take your hands and tell you again how much I love you."

"Adam—"

"And you will be free to tell me how much you love me."

"It won't happen, Adam. It can't." Raleigh already mourned the day he discovered her greatest betrayal. "Because I don't love you," she lied.

The pain was deeper than he expected. But he ignored the sharp stab that followed her easy words of rejection. Instead, he crossed to her then, summoned by the sad yearning in her voice, her eyes. "I will make you forget it all, Raleigh."

Maybe he could. Maybe he did love her. Love conquered all, they said. Perhaps it could bridge the chasm between duty and treachery. "Adam?" she whispered. Possibilities clouded her heart.

"You will forget it all, sweetheart. Cavanaugh. Phillip. Even Chance."

"Chance? What about Chance?"

"I understand he's the one who hurt you. The man who made you doubt yourself. Who made you doubt love."

The fanciful haze dissipated. There was no hope, no future for them. It perished in a warehouse fire three years ago and would never be reborn. "Chance is none of your business. Do not speak his name. Ever," Raleigh instructed harshly, a perfect echo of Adam. "Now, move out of my way so I can get to work."

Rummaging through her backpack, Raleigh searched for her tool kit. Tiny scissors lined up next to a pair of miniature pliers and a device that resembled a stethoscope. She brushed past Adam and knelt in front of the metal box. Adam's shadow blocked the light. "I can't see."

He did not budge. If logic didn't work, he'd simply make it impossible for her to see the wires.

With a muttered oath, Raleigh kicked her leg out and flipped him onto his back. "Stay out of my way."

Adam lay flat, winded by his fall. Undiscouraged, he got to his feet and took his position. This time, the blow connected at his shin and forced him to his knees.

"Leave me alone, Adam."

"No."

"Either get out of my way, or I blow us both to hell."

"Damn it, Chimera. This isn't a game."

"Then stop playing with me and get out of my light." She snapped latex gloves into place, their material as thin as actual skin, which would heighten her sensitivity, if she had to diffuse the bomb by touch alone. In addition, the gloves protected against perspiration or outside elements corrupting the circuitry.

Raleigh reexamined the trip wire. It looped around each box, with separate wires running inside. The hinges on the exterior side facing them were soldered shut, eliminating a back-door approach.

"I'll have to run a shunt circuit from the main wire to the other boxes," she concluded. "It will keep this box from exploding."

"What will that do to the other containers?"

"Double their chances of exploding on contact,"

she answered grimly. "But I don't see a way around that."

Disturbed by her blasé response, Adam narrowed his eyes. "We can at least leave a sign, warning them."

"Be my guest," Raleigh said.

Raleigh extracted a length of wire from her tool kit. Snipping it in half, she proceeded to fashion her shunt circuit. A portable blowtorch fused the wires. She then started to carefully disconnect and reconnect wires, forming an alternate circuit path.

Sweat gathered on her face and streamed down her body, aided by the natural humidity and the heat of the torch. After a vain attempt to wipe her wet nose with a latex-covered hand, Adam relented enough to blot her face with a handkerchief.

He would *carry a handkerchief in his jeans,* she thought humorlessly. "Pass me thc plicrs, please." She was loathe to make the request, but her right hand held two wires together and she couldn't disturb them by reaching across her own body.

Adam pressed the pliers into her waiting palm, as neatly as a surgical nurse. When she said as much, he replied absently, "My brother Jonah is a surgical resident. We played operation as children and wanted to imitate Hawkeye Pierce and Major Houlihan exactly."

She twisted the end of a wire into a knot. "I thought you were the oldest."

"I am, but I still had to play 'Hot Lips.' "

"Not exactly fair." Raleigh reached for the kit with her free left hand, but couldn't quite get it.

Adam saw her struggle and lifted the kit toward her. "Jonah never got to be the banker in Monopoly."

The blue clamp she held reminded him of the

head of a jumper cable, but smaller. With deft motions, she fixed the clamp to the new maze of wires. "Adam, will you go and grab a couple of kola nuts for me? I'll use them as a counterbalance."

He walked off to the stand of trees. A premonition told him to turn around. Behind him, Raleigh took a lever and pried the box from the stones.

"Wait!" he yelled, running to her.

Raleigh leaned on the lever more forcefully. Just as Adam skidded to a stop in front of her, the box popped free and flew through the air. Raleigh landed on her back and covered her ears. Adam dove for the flying case, catching it just before it crashed to the ground.

A deafening silence fell over the two people lying on the forest floor.

Raleigh started to laugh. "It worked! My God, it worked."

Adam gingerly set the box on the ground. "What worked?"

"I thought about what you said, so I created a circuit breaker. Now, anyone else can get the boxes." She rolled onto her stomach and propped her head up on her gloved fists.

She lifted the latch on the front of the case. The interior of the box was empty. "I don't understand," Raleigh muttered.

Adam agreed. "Didn't the clue say that 'they bear witness in flame'?"

"Yes. I assumed the flame was the explosion." She thought silently for a second. "Maybe the item is in another case."

"Is it safe to check?"

"I rerouted the delay. If one of the other boxes contains the bomb, we'll have time to defuse it." *I hope*. But she was not in the mood for an argument, so she kept her concerns to herself.

Raleigh and Adam lifted the remaining boxes from their places on the monument. "On the count of three," she instructed. "One. Two. Three."

Raleigh's case was empty as well.

"Raleigh, come here."

Unsure of what to expect, Raleigh crawled toward him slowly. Then looked inside.

"Oh." Inside lay the largest, most spectacular gem Raleigh had ever seen. Easily the width of her palm, the diamond had been cut, but not faceted. The Kholari diamond.

"Flame. Fire."

"Beautiful."

"A king's ransom," he mused aloud. "Or a nation's."

"A jewel and the blueprints. Do you see a connection?"

"No. He said we were to use the clues to locate our supplies. The blueprints, I get. But a rock the size of your fist?"

"Will the delivery system need diamond chips? I never noticed that in the specs."

"Even if diamond chips were necessary, we'd never cut a stone like this. We've used synthetic chips in our industries for years."

"Then maybe it's our payoff?"

"Perhaps. Let's solve the last clue and get back to Desira to find out."

Raleigh lifted the stone and held it up to the light. The refracted rays bounced off the metal of the other open cases. Then she noticed a dark silver disc. "I think this was the actual clue."

Adam recognized the disc from his office instantly.

The special metallic coating was a GCI Security Measure. "It's the DVD that details how to consolidate the parts of the Praxis system. But it's encrypted. So, Atlas wasn't wrong. This is a skills test. We've gotten the blueprints, circumvented a weapons system, and if we can decode this, he's got the all the pieces—except the microzeolites."

"I assume the third clue will tell us where to get our supply."

"Probably." Adam put the DVD back in the box with the diamond and tucked both in his pack. "Let's go."

Raleigh shook her head, not paying attention any longer. "There was only one bomb," she said under her breath.

"What?"

"Only one bomb. I didn't have to create the circuit breaker."

"Was it that dangerous?" he asked.

Raleigh shrugged good-naturedly. "If I wanted to survive, yes." She stripped off the gloves and began to put the tools back into the kit. "But no harm done."

"What were the kola nuts for, Raleigh?"

"Huh?"

"The kola nuts."

The diversion. "Oh, um, for counterbalance." Isn't that what she'd said? Her greatest concern had been getting him out of range.

"Of what?"

"Your temper," she ventured. It was slightly amusing, in hindsight.

He didn't get the joke. "That's the third time you've made a unilateral decision. Primary does not mean 'irresponsible,' Chimera."

"I was not irresponsible. If the circuit breaker hadn't worked, the entire monument would have exploded. Why risk both of us?"

"It wasn't your decision to make!"

"Then whose was it?"

"Ours. Yours and mine. I deserve at least a degree of courtesy from you, I would think."

"I've been neither irresponsible nor discourteous."

"You've been that and more. Stubborn, violent, and fractious. And while we're on the subject, what was that little temper tantrum you threw last night?"

"Temper tantrum? Since when is an accurate analysis of character flaws a temper tantrum? And, for the record, you kissed me."

"You didn't seem to mind. I even lost a button."

Raleigh flushed at the memory. "Shut up, Adam."

"What? Too close? Not enough detachment?" Adam said caustically. "I suppose retreat is in order, lest we discuss messy emotions like lust and passion."

Or love. The word hung in the air between them. "We've got to find the last article."

Twelve

Suddenly, Raleigh put the pieces together. The help last night and the diamond today. Phillip was alive! And he was setting them up, wanting it to look like Cavanaugh was the culprit. Beneath lowered lids, Raleigh studied Adam's expression. There was no reason he should make the connection between Cavanaugh and the Kholari diamond. But she'd bet Phillip knew. Every second spent out in the open meant an opportunity for Phillip to pick them off, if that was his intention.

She opened her mouth to tell Adam about Cavanaugh's failed assignment to retrieve the diamond, then decided against it. Adam wanted to believe the worst of Cavanaugh. If she told him about the diamond, he'd inevitably leap to the wrong conclusions—that Cavanaugh had been the mole. That he, not Phillip, fed Scimitar the stolen blueprints and the ISA list, and then they'd killed him. Then he'd turn on her, unless she told him about Phillip. And that wasn't an option.

Finally, Adam spoke. "I still don't get the diamond."

"We have the blueprints. If there's only one diamond, the third clue must be a ruse."

"If the clues were in no particular order, the other

teams may be hunting for the remaining item right now. We need all three to declare victory."

"Maybe not. Like I said, the third clue could be a ruse. The warning told us to beware of hunters, gifts, and stolen bounty," Raleigh reminded him. "That might be the real message."

"The gunshots may have come from the hunters."

"Maybe the blueprints are a gift."

"And the stolen bounty?"

The Kholari diamond. She could share a grain of truth with him, enough to convince him to quit. "I doubt Zeben came by this honestly. It's at least three hundred carats uncut," she said.

"Of course it's stolen. It's the diamond from the communiqué." Adam stared at Raleigh, a question forming in his mind.

Before he could ask, Raleigh noticed movement in the grove of kola trees. "Adam," she said softly, "we've got company. In the stand of trees, one hundred yards to your left."

"One of the teams?"

"I think so." The noon sun glinted off the barrel of a rifle. "He's aiming at your head," she whispered harshly.

"Get ready to run." Adam bent to grab his pack and said, "Now!"

In unison, they dove behind the monument as the first shot cracked into the plaque. A man's voice shouted in Arabic.

"We've got to move," Raleigh said. "They plan to circle in from either side." She shuffled through her backpack and removed a small disc of plastic.

"Do you always carry homemade explosives with you?"

"Do you carry a gun?" she countered.

Adam closed his mouth.

Raleigh continued with her instructions. "We'll have a ten-second head start before this goes."

"Ready to run?" Adam asked.

"On your mark." She removed the safety cover.

"Go!" Adam shouted.

Raleigh pressed the release and threw the disc over the top of the monument. Adam latched on to her free arm and aimed for the mahogany trees. Bullets careened past them. A sapling splintered as they sprinted past. Behind them, the bomb detonated and rained their assailants with shattered chunks of rock. A scream echoed throughout the woods.

"Don't look," Adam admonished Raleigh when she turned at the noise.

She hadn't intended to hurt them. The blast should have delayed their pursuit, nothing more. "I—"

"Keep running." They headed deeper into the forest. The gunfire ceased. "Don't stop. We haven't lost them yet."

Adam brought his satchel forward and grabbed his compass. He dropped down behind a bush and dragged her to his side. "The rendezvous point is in the other direction. Did you get a good look at the men?"

"I saw two Arab men. And Civelli. I guess those three have agreed to work together." Raleigh shooed away a spider crawling along a fallen leaf. She watched, horribly fascinated, as a bird swooped down and gobbled it up.

Adam saw it too. "Civelli is a weasel. I suspect they convinced Zeben to let him join. He'll help them out until they finish the deal. Then they'll murder one another. They probably killed the other team."

As Zeben had alluded, honor among thieves was a myth at best.

"In the meantime, they're after us."

"Well, we can't camp out here. If they made it to the other sites, they'll know we have the loot. Knowing Civelli, they've been tracking us to avoid the heavy work."

Raleigh agreed. They slowly made their way through the trees, listening for the crunch of footsteps, the report of a gun.

Raleigh mused aloud, "If they're tracking us, won't they be looking for the last clue?"

"What did it say?"

"It said, 'To transform the lies into truth, seek the riddle of your youth.' It doesn't make sense."

"What riddle of youth?" Adam frowned, puzzled.

Riddle. Sphinx. Another hint from Phillip. She was running out of time. They had to get back to the hotel. This cat-and-mouse game proved everything she suspected. Phillip had allied himself with Scimitar and used his inside information to entrap them. He duped Cavanaugh into a secret meeting and led him to his death.

Adam, tortured by guilt, grieved for a murderer and a traitor. *I should tell him the bitter facts,* she thought. *Relieve the pain with the merciless pill of reality.* But two things stopped her. For one, Atlas forbade her from disclosing the truth. Although she didn't—couldn't—fathom Adam as a part of the plot, she wouldn't disobey the order. More important, however, was her own conscience.

If Adam figured out her ulterior motive—to mete out her personal brand of justice to Cavanaugh's murderer—he'd interfere. Despite his reputation as a rebel, Adam possessed a core of honor that she envied. That night on the hilltop, he could have taken the radio from her and saved his friend. Their fight proved he would be willing to sacrifice the lives of the others. But she remembered a moment when he'd pinned her to the ground, the communicator within his grasp, and he had hesitated. She had seized the opening and thrown him off, pitching the radio into the flames.

True honor would never condone murder, but she could. When she found him, Phillip would die at her hands. A chill shuddered through her, despite the heat of midday. She would lose Adam as surely as she had the first time, but this time his charges would be true. She *would* be the offender.

He need never know, she thought. But she would. And that knowledge would haunt her. His integrity could not excuse cold-blooded murder. Although both had taken lives before, they were not assassins. That fine distinction separated them from the men and women they hunted. Her act crossed the line and rendered her unworthy of his respect. And of the love he imagined he felt for her.

For now, however, she would concentrate on more immediate matters. Like making it out of the forest alive.

"Let's forget about the third clue," Raleigh suggested. She needed to get him back to the hotel and as far away from Phillip as possible. She couldn't have him, couldn't love him. But she would protect him. From everyone, including herself.

"All right. I don't think the third clue is that important." With his long stride and lithe gait, Adam easily outpaced Raleigh. She didn't mind. She had work to do. The less attention he paid, the better. "A scavenger hunt with three clues. We happen to find two of the three items, and one of our competitors dies in the process." He ducked his head under a low-hanging branch.

"Maybe we're that good," Raleigh joked.

"Don't insult me, Chimera," Adam smiled. "We've got an inside track a six-year-old could follow."

"Okay. So someone wants us to win. Why?" While they walked, Raleigh removed a small vial of neon-yellow liquid from her pack. She stuck the vial in her front pocket. Adam continued to speak, oblivious.

"I don't know, unless it's a trap.

"Or Zeben wants us to have the contract but make it look good." Raleigh then pulled out a small weapon shaped like a semiautomatic handgun. Unlike a real gun, the barrel was ten inches long and was the width of a child's finger. Raleigh tucked the gun under her arm and extracted a clip.

Adam hiked ahead of her. "Civelli and his new friends are still out here."

Pushing the gun into her pocket, she pried open the thin side of the clip. A shallow channel extended the length of the clip. "Do you think they'll come after us again?" Raleigh unscrewed the vial with her teeth and proceeded to fill the channel with the fluid.

"Probably. Civelli hates both of us now. He's like a vulture. He'll kill us and take the loot back to Zeben."

She closed the side opening and jammed the ammunition into place with a muffled click. "Unless we get back first. But Zeben must have known this would happen."

"Of course he did. The old man is using Praxis

as a magnet to inveigle old rivals and as a tool to annihilate potential enemies."

She lifted the gun and checked the sight. Satisfied, Raleigh asked, "What kind of vendetta would Zeben have against Caster and Ripley?" The team that died near the monument operated almost exclusively in Europe, rarely venturing across the Mediterranean.

"Maybe he wanted to expand his reach, and they're an example."

"Doesn't work. Zeben hates the West and has little interest in Europe."

"Not true," Adam argued. "Zeben wants power, absolute power. Jafir is so valuable to him because it offers him a seat from which to threaten and rule. But you are right. Caster and Ripley's deaths don't fit. What are we missing?"

A man who has turned his back on you and the ISA. A man who sold his soul to the enemy, she thought.

"And why did we get both items? Like we said, our clue wasn't exactly difficult to decipher."

"What if they have an alternate set of clues?"

"An alternate set? Our secret pal sends them on a wild goose chase while we collect the goods."

"He wants us to win."

"So, we win," Raleigh said simply.

Her voice was firm, purposeful. Adam halted mid-stride. He looked at Raleigh; she held a weapon he'd never seen before. "What in the hell is that thing?"

"I haven't named it yet," she answered with a bland smile.

She appeared capable. Strong. Slim, fine-boned hands held the gun with confidence. Hands that the night before gathered and shuffled cards like a seasoned gamester. Hands that later raced over his naked skin, tormenting and pleasing him. Hands as complex as the woman they belonged to. "I didn't realize you used guns. Of any sort."

"I don't. This isn't a gun." She held it out for inspection.

He handled the weapon carefully. "What does it do?"

"Fires missiles."

"What?" He examined the gun, intrigued. The barrel was longer than a traditional one, but the entire weapon almost fit into the palm of his hand. "Missiles?"

"They're more like darts, actually," she explained. "But I fill them with a chemical that ignites upon contact with oxygen."

"Something you concocted?"

"Yes."

"Oh." Her mind. Her sexy, lethal, mind. Nothing fascinated, attracted him more than a sharp intellect, especially when paired with legs that stretched for the odd mile or two. Raleigh devoured information with a voracious appetite. She traveled with what she called her tool kit and dog-eared copies of classics. How often had they argued over Achebe, debated Faulkner?

Raleigh misinterpreted his comment to be censure. "Come on. I'm not some mad scientist, Adam. I'm a weapons expert who specializes in explosives and chemical weapons."

"I remember." He thrust the gun at her, handle first. With comic haste, he stepped away, recalling another experiment in weaponry. "Here."

Raleigh chuckled as she holstered the weapon in a special pouch suspended from her shoulder. She remembered the mishap too. "This isn't like that handheld smoke bomb I designed."

"I was unconscious for three hours," Adam accused with mock outrage.

"Thirty minutes. And I didn't realize you were there," she defended. "You shouldn't have been spying on me."

"I wasn't spying. I was silently observing," he said piously, but he softened the remark with a smile.

"Don't worry. I've tested it in the lab. It will only ignite under certain conditions. The dart must reach a specific velocity and pressure point before air has a combustible effect."

"Is it fatal?"

"Only if the chemical makes direct contact with bodily fluids. According to my design, the dart explodes midair and releases a noxious gas. The vapors will induce nausea and fainting in a one-hundred-and-eighty-pound man."

"How soon after the discharge?"

"Ten, fifteen seconds, tops."

"Faster than chloroform?"

"Yep."

"You must have to be within close range of the target."

"One hundred feet," she answered proudly. "Give or take a few yards."

"What about the shooter? How does he avoid the fumes?"

"*She* doesn't need to be very near the target. The force from the chamber is immense. Plus, it won't burst before it has flown at least one hundred and fifty feet. That's how long it will take to reach optimal velocity."

"Fifty feet? A slim margin of error," he noted.

"But reasonable." Raleigh noticed the sunlight

wasn't quite as harsh as before. "How much longer to the meeting place?"

Because he'd been distracted, he had not been paying attention to their location. The trees were thick, and the bushes provided adequate cover. *But we should get moving,* he thought. *The longer we tarry in the forest, the smaller our odds of survival.* "It's a mile-and-a-half more," Adam estimated.

Raleigh secured her pack and rechecked the gun. "I'm ready."

Adam led them on, reorienting the compass a couple of times. The whole affair disturbed him. Too many pieces were out of place. Or just missing. Particularly the diamond. Why pay them with a gem few would be willing to fence? The contract specified seventy-five million in U.S. dollars. Whether or not the diamond would fetch such a price, fencing stolen diamonds in Africa was dangerous business, even for a criminal. Jewelry heists weren't his forte, but he'd bet the diamond had a famous past. A rock that big, uncut? It didn't jibe.

Adam wondered what Raleigh's take on the situation was. She hadn't said much about her impressions, but she typically kept her own counsel. Stubborn and arrogant, she'd rather solve a problem herself and amaze you with the answer.

A rustle sounded in the bushes behind them. Alert, Adam spun around, pushing Raleigh behind him. With a polished motion, Raleigh drew her missile launcher, prepared to fire.

"False alarm," Adam grumbled as he holstered his own gun. "A bird."

"The bird almost bought it," Raleigh muttered.

"Ah yes, death to the swallow. That's what we're trained for."

"It's a career option for those of us not to the manor born."

"All the gambling jobs gone? I understand Hollywood is always searching for fresh talent. Especially someone who can provide her own special effects."

"Ah, Caine Simons, the inveterate comedian."

"At your service." He turned to bow and saw a flash of color near a copse of oaks. Bent at the waist, he said softly, "Here's your chance to test your newest toy under actual conditions. Sixty yards and closing." Adam straightened. "How much distance do you need?"

"A few more feet," she answered as she checked the clip. "When I give the signal, head for that clump of bushes. I have an idea."

Adam readied his gun. In case the missile launcher went the way of the smoke bomb, he should be prepared. "Okay."

"Now!" Raleigh rotated on her heel and sighted the barrel. A swift yank loaded a projectile in the chamber. She squeezed the trigger and dove for cover. Seconds later, the screams of men echoed throughout the forest.

"Are you sure the poison isn't fatal?"

"Yes. It is rather painful, however."

"And you're sure they're going to faint?"

"You heard them scream. What do you think?"

"I think we need to figure out what's going on. I'd love to interrogate those men. And we should read their scroll."

"How long till the fumes dissipate?"

"A few minutes."

"I wish we had—"

"A gas mask?" she finished for him.

He smiled approvingly. "Exactly."

"That's the plan. I have one in my bag." She extricated a flexible contraption that resembled an oxygen mask from an airplane. Handing the bag and mask to Adam, she reached inside the satchel a second time, pulling out a canister the size and shape of a soup can.

"Let me guess. Portable oxygen tank?"

Raleigh unscrewed the cap on the canister. "Got it all in one." She attached the hose from the mask to the hole and folded a ring of plastic around the area to seal it.

"I notice you only have one of these."

"It's a prototype," she explained, "for use with the missile launcher."

"Who made it?" he asked dubiously.

Raleigh crossed her arms in mock offense. "Does it matter?"

"Of course not. So you go first?"

"Uh-uh," she said as she passed the canister to him. "I defused the bomb. And got bitten by the snake," Raleigh volunteered.

"They shot at me first. And you were *almost* bitten," Adam rebutted.

Raleigh decided to add pity to her case. "I hate feeling nauseous."

"And I like it?"

She pressed the mask into limp hands. Undeterred, she folded his fingers around the mask. "Hurry up, Adam. They'll wake up soon." She shot him a snide look. "Besides, you need me to revive you if I'm wrong."

Adam mumbled an expletive but fitted the mask to his face. "Five minutes—or come and get me."

"Better make it four. The fainting spells don't last long."

With another imprecation, Adam dashed over to the prone bodies. Raleigh was correct. Civelli had wormed his way onto the other team. He lay sprawled on his stomach, his face in the dirt. The second man, whom Adam recognized as an Egyptian terrorist, clutched a pack similar to his own. Adam peeled the man's hand open and slid the strap over his head. After committing the third man's face to memory, he heard Civelli stir.

Adam dragged the man upright and shook him roughly. "Wake up, Civelli. You and I need to have a little talk." Civelli was a few feet away from the other two, as though he'd tried to run from the gas. *Figures,* Adam thought, *the little coward.*

"What—I don't feel—" Civelli mumbled as the forest spun around him.

"You've got ten seconds to tell me what the hell is going on here. One. Two." Adam reached for the gun in his pocket. "Three. Four." He cocked the small pistol and held the barrel to the man's head. "Five. Six. Nine." Images of Civelli touching Raleigh flashed in his mind and the grip on the gun tightened.

"Wait. Wait. You skipped seven and eight."

"No, I didn't. You must have passed out again. Ten."

"Stop!" Civelli squealed. "I wasn't paid enough to die," he protested.

"Who paid you?" Adam demanded as he traced a cold circle on Civelli's temple. "And why?" Who would go through the trouble to help them win—only to try and eliminate them?

"The contract was to kill you and take the woman. That's all I know."

"Who ordered the contract, Civelli?" Adam closed

one hand around Civelli's throat. *The little weasel had a lot to answer for,* Adam thought mildly. *He thinks he can just take Raleigh and not answer for it?*

"I don't know," Civelli whined. No woman, not even Ms. DeSalle, was worth dying for.

Adam pressed the gun tight to the circle he'd traced. "I don't believe you." He didn't know but perhaps fear would loosen some other important fact.

"I swear. The contract came through an intermediary. Someone in Zeben's organization. But I don't think it was Zeben. I was supposed to beat you last night, and when that didn't work, I was supposed to kill you today."

So maybe there are two people to worry about. One who wants us to win and another who wants me eliminated and Raleigh with him. Why? "What about the other men? The ones by the monument?"

"A mistake," Civelli shrugged. "Mistakes *do* happen."

"Two white men, Civelli? Not even *you* are that stupid."

"I thought to eliminate more of the competition. That is all."

"I hope so," Adam said, then he slammed the butt of the gun into Civelli's head. Civelli fell to the ground, unconscious again.

Quickly, he rejoined Raleigh and showed her the other team's scroll.

"Any problems with the mask?"

"No. But Civelli came to. He was starting to desert the others when your missile exploded."

"Figures. What did he say?"

"There are two men. One working for us and one who wants me dead."

"You? What about me?"

"Civelli said you were supposed to be kidnapped but not harmed."

"Two? And neither one is Zeben?"

"Civelli didn't know." Adam glanced at his watch. "We should head for the hotel. We can read the scroll when we get there."

"What about Zeben?"

"What about him? I presume he's waiting for us at the rendezvous point. I'm no longer in the mood to meet with him. He can't be the only one to change the rules of the game. And with the diamond and the blueprints, we have the upper hand."

"For the moment," Raleigh cautioned. Zeben and Phillip were playing a game with them. With her. But they'd miscalculated. A third man was trying to help them. Raleigh and Adam had to know why. "We'll allow him to come to us."

"He won't be pleased," Adam said with a feral gleam in his fathomless black eyes.

"I'm counting on it."

"How much of a head start will we have before they are in the mood to pursue?"

"They should wake up pretty soon. The drug will make them queasy for at least an hour. They can chase us, but not without several pit stops."

On the last leg of the journey, Raleigh remained in front of Adam. The sun began to dip behind the trees, and the forest animals started their nightly ritual.

"I've never been particularly adept with time, but we've been out here a while. Are you lost?" Raleigh asked pointedly.

"No," came the short reply.

"Then why have we been walking for hours?"

"We haven't been walking for hours." At her scathing look of incredulity, he corrected himself. "Two and a half. Tops."

"Why? You said we were a mile-and-a-half away. That's not two hours."

"The rendezvous spot was a mile. The hotel is a bit farther."

Raleigh halted her steps. "How much farther?"

"Maybe an hour."

"And you kept this to yourself because?"

"I enjoy watching you walk," he cajoled. "Especially in those shorts. You have amazing legs."

"Cut it out, Adam."

Her note of embarrassment delighted him. "You asked for an explanation." He knew she wasn't immune to him. And her most authentic reactions came when he caught her unaware with compliments or declarations. Praxis was important, and he wouldn't neglect his responsibilities. He couldn't. He'd authorized the project and set up the security system. The lives of thousands depended on the success of this mission. But he realized, with every step, that his future happiness rested in Raleigh's hands.

She challenged him, baffled him, and enraged him. And she could seduce him so thoroughly, with only a look or a word or a caress. Maybe she was right. He didn't know this new woman she'd become well enough now to declare love. But he had loved the younger woman, undeniably. The new Raleigh was an enigma, but not unsolvable. Love was inevitable; of that he was certain. It was positively conceited to proclaim his intentions so baldly. Yet, she couldn't deny that the fates had drawn them together a second time, in the same place, for a reason. For salvation.

He could offer her a safe harbor from the monsters in her past and a refuge to be herself. Free to relax and trust and care without consequence. And his love was selfish. For he understood, with soul-deep conviction, that she could make him whole. In her arms, in her heart, he'd find the strength to forgive himself for Phillip's death. With love, they could forge a new life. Together.

Lobby attendants paid scant attention as Raleigh and Adam entered the hotel, bedraggled and sweaty. The concierge on duty, a squat, rotund man, intercepted them at the elevators.

"May I be of assistance?" His pug nose wrinkled in vague distaste.

Raleigh bristled, tired and irascible. The return trip took longer than the sworn hour. Dusk had settled around the island, and they'd still been tramping through the forest. Adam decided to take a circuitous route, to avoid Zeben or his men if they chose to search for them.

Long treks and despicable conditions rarely fazed her. She was in excellent shape and understood the rigors of the work. But her temper had been sorely tested. Adam's revelation and Phillip's tricks had frayed her equanimity to ragged scraps. Unlike last night's pent-up aggression, she felt weary, embattled. There was so much to sort through, decisions to make. Adam would assemble the pieces soon, and she couldn't let that happen. But she was too fatigued to operate yet.

A bath, in a steamy, fragrant tub, would soothe the turmoil. If this man would get out of her way. She plastered on a fake smile. "No, thank you."

Adam circled her waist, pulling her against him despite her damp top. "We'll just retire to our suite." He gave the man an imperious nod as the doors opened. "A shower should serve us well," he added. "However, please send a message to our generous host."

The concierge held the doors ajar. "Sir?"

"Ms. DeSalle and I would love to have him join us for a drink in an hour."

"Yes, sir."

Adam guided Raleigh into the rear of the elevator as the doors closed firmly. "You okay?"

"I'm fine," she snapped. Raleigh removed his arm. "Why? Think I can't do this?"

He held his hands up in mock surrender. "It was a question, not an accusation."

"This is my job. I can keep up." Raleigh stared into the corner of the elevator.

"I never doubted that. But you seem a bit tense."

"So?"

Adam nudged her gently, bumping his body against her stiff form. "So, that got us into trouble last night. Not that I'd resist a repeat performance, but we'll have company soon." With a lightning move, he dragged her against him. "And the first time we make love, it will take much longer than an hour."

Adam keyed the penthouse open, and they entered the suite. Raleigh methodically swept the room for newly planted bugs and Adam engaged the scrambler.

"Shower first or scroll?" he asked.

"Shower. Give me ten minutes."

She returned in five. By then, Adam had placed an order for room service and had the contents of the other team's bag strewn across the living-room floor.

"Your turn. See what you can make of the scroll. I've translated it, and it seems we're being helped along again." Adam dragged his stained, wet T-shirt over his head as he exited the room.

Raleigh's ravenous eyes followed the play of sculpted muscle and glistening skin. "All right," she managed with a sigh. She squatted on the floor and lifted the scroll. The dry parchment crinkled as she spread it out, weighing it with a flask and a jar from the bag. It held three lines of text. The scroll instructed them to solve Yoruban mythology and locate snakes. The scroll confirmed their theory. Someone was on the inside, trying to assist them. And Phillip had taken out a contract on their lives.

The scroll would lead Adam to similar conclusions, but with a mammoth hole in his analysis. He didn't know the killer was his best friend. Phillip would kill off Adam, probably for revenge and because he knew enough about computers to handle that part himself. With her as his captive, he'd get the chemical weapons expert he needed. Raleigh shook her head sadly, distressed by this conclusion. When Phillip finally showed up, Raleigh would have to ensure that Adam was out of harm's way.

Raleigh heard the shower stop. Her stomach somersaulted, and her breath rushed out on a sigh. For a brief moment, she allowed her mind to think about her relationship with Adam.

"Adam said he loved me," she said aloud. Frissons of awareness crept down her spine. But Adam didn't love her, she decided with logical precision and not a small amount of fear. He cared for her. He wanted her. However, love required—demanded—knowledge and time. They had neither. The fledgling affection of what seemed an eon ago could not sustain them for a few hours, let alone a lifetime.

Love wouldn't stop her from killing his best friend, she admitted. So, she didn't truly love him. Maybe she had watched him for years, through infrequent news articles and internal ISA documents. Perhaps she kept tabs on his romantic life through Liz, waiting out relationships with bated breath. And if memories reminded her of who he had been, it meant nothing. Who cared if he was strong, intelligent, and funny? Even if their recent time together proved him loyal, tender, and sensitive, it wasn't nearly enough for love. And if her heart skidded at the sight of him, at the sound of her name on his lips, the evidence proved only attraction.

It didn't matter that he always read her mind. From the most obvious point to the most obscure hypothesis, they'd always been in sync. Inside her mind. Her intellectual soul mate. *None of this matters,* she thought a trifle desperately. Despite her earlier musings about rekindled devotion, love simply could not be. And she'd tell him exactly that, if he dared raise the topic once more.

How easy it would be to simply accept his word. She could hold the lies inside, apart from their lives together, couldn't she? He'd never know the grim truth unless she told him—and she never would.

The lies would be worth it, if it meant Adam as her mate and lover. He understood the choices she had to make, the secrets she had to keep. The distance she'd place between them would be attributed to the Agency, the business. He wouldn't ask for explanations he knew she wasn't free to impart. And he would be there in the night, to comfort her when the nightmares burst beyond the limits of her control.

Raleigh closed her eyes in defeat. She could barely stomach contemplating her sworn task. To sustain the lie, day after day, would prove intolerable. Leaving her with one option—to keep him at bay until her job was complete. Then she would vanish from his life forever.

Thirteen

A knock sounded, and Raleigh opened the door for their room service. While she retrieved a tip for the waiter, Adam strode in, the buttons of the white shirt half done. The waiter shuffled from foot to foot, his attention rapt on Raleigh's behind. His snub-nosed, broad face seemed vaguely familiar. *One of Zeben's lieutenants,* Adam realized. A man in his position wasn't sent to deliver room service. He'd come to deliver a message. *Considering the past two days, it would be too much to hope that the message is benign,* Adam mused with resignation. Better to warn Raleigh and have a bit of fun in the process. Adam stepped up behind her and teasingly squeezed her upturned backside. The waiter's eyes bulged with envy and amusement as he gave Adam a conspiratorial, masculine grin.

Raleigh yelped and turned to confront the overly amorous waiter, a wad of bills in one hand, the other fisted, ready to punch. "If you don't—" she began.

"I was doing it," Adam returned silkily, "but you interrupted me." He caught her by the waist and pulled her to him. Raleigh's hands came up to push him away. He ignored the protest and nuzzled her cheek. "We have an audience, dear," he warned, caressing her hips with firm, knowing hands. "Don't make a scene."

"Then let me go," she retorted quietly. It wasn't fair that he could touch her and make her feel so wanton. No man's touch should evaporate her control so easily. "Now, Caine," she murmured.

"Can't." Adam nipped at the mutinous line of her lips. Her mouth parted slightly, and he swept his tongue inside for one brief, stolen taste. "He was at the casino last night. Guarding Zeben." His words carried no farther than her ears.

With the waiter watching, Raleigh played along, eager to feel him. Sliding her fingers into the open shirt, she sought and found his flat nipple. "What's going on?" she asked, thumbing the taut flesh.

"Don't know," he whispered as he pinned her against his chest, quelling her industrious hands. When she touched him, he could scarcely concentrate. "But be ready." He kissed her again.

"Andrea, darling," he said as he separated their bodies, "I just couldn't resist. But we do have company."

Slowly, lingeringly, Raleigh began to slide her hand from inside his shirt, her nails scraping his flesh. "Later," she promised throatily, only partially acting.

She turned to the waiter and pressed the tip into his sweaty palm. "Thank you," she said.

"De rien, mademoiselle." He stuffed the money in his pocket. Then he stood, subservience gone. "Also, Zeben will be along shortly. You are to disengage your antilistening devices within the next five minutes."

"Why?" Raleigh asked.

"His partner will be unable to join you, and he

would like to monitor your discussions," the man supplied.

Adam said quizzically, "His partner? I didn't realize Zeben shared his power with anyone."

"Zeben is his own master. However, there are others who share his vision," the man replied loyally.

"Does this partner have a name?" Adam pressed for more information. Who was this mysterious second man, and why wouldn't he come to meet the appointed ones, chosen to build his weapon?

Raleigh stiffened as she waited for his reply. It could all end now, in this moment.

The man shook his head slightly. "His name is not mine to share. Zeben will arrive momentarily." The man bowed and exited the room.

As soon as the door shut, Adam spoke. "A second man? That's certainly a new development. Zeben is famous for his narcissism. He'd never willingly share his dominion with another. What do you think?"

Raleigh's mind spun, searching for a response. She didn't want to lie, but the truth was impossible. "I think we'd better talk about this later." To hide her guilty expression, she went to scoop up the scroll and materials lying on the carpet. "Right now, you should disengage the scrambler."

"Before I do, let's discuss what we're planning to say to him. I personally want to know why we've been shot at and chased and almost blown up, if we're the heirs apparent." Violence swelled within him as he remembered the scene by the monument. She could have died there. It didn't matter any longer that this was their job. Zeben had threatened the life of his woman, and he would pay for it.

"Why let on that we know? And I don't think we should ask about his partner," Raleigh hedged. She didn't want Zeben to accidentally reveal that Phillip was alive.

"Why not?" Adam argued, surprised by her demurral. "We need all the information we can get."

"I don't think we should show too much curiosity. As far as Zeben is concerned, we're here to build a weapon of mass destruction, not unravel the secrets of Scimitar. Too many unrelated questions, and we may play right into his hands."

"You don't believe he already knows exactly who we are?"

"No," she said. "I'm not certain, but I don't think he knows. Think about it. He's had a number of opportunities to trap us, but he hasn't. His partner knows, I believe. But Zeben is still in the dark."

"He needs us to build Praxis," Adam countered. "He can't afford to kill us yet."

Don't fight me on this, Adam, she thought. "Possibly. But why risk it? Even if he knows who we are, he doesn't know that *we* know he knows." She smiled at the tongue-tying rationale.

"Easy for you to say." Adam laughed at her explanation. "Fine, I won't ask," he conceded. He moved to the hutch and disengaged the scrambler. Seconds later, Zeben arrived.

"I trust you had a productive day," he said after greeting Raleigh with a farce of a kiss. Dry, arid lips brushed hers in an overly familiar welcome.

Knowing her role, Raleigh did not break away, though her stomach roiled. Her hands itched to wipe his kiss from her mouth, to pull out of his spindly arms. But she remained motionless, a brittle smile etched on her face.

After he released her, Zeben took a seat on the sofa, and Adam took the chair opposite him. Raleigh sat beside Adam on the cushioned arm. Adam casually linked their hands. Zeben noticed the display of intimate affection and spoke, his tone abrupt. "We worried when you did not return to the meeting place."

Deliberately, Adam raised their joined hands and rubbed her hand against his lips, his eyes never leaving Zeben's. "We were, uh, detained." He drew her forefinger into the recesses of his mouth and sucked gently, the message obvious. *She is mine*, the gesture shouted. Reluctantly, he released her finger and continued. "Then we got lost. I thought it wiser to meet you in the hotel."

Zeben inclined his head. "So be it." He patted the seat beside him, indicating that Raleigh should sit next to him. "Please, be comfortable, Andrea." He hesitated over her name for the briefest second—or did she imagine it? "The sofa has ample space."

She had to obey the silent command, but Zeben would know that Andrea and Caine were lovers. To show him, Raleigh brought their hands to her mouth. Like a cat, she slowly licked at Adam's knuckles, tracing the ridges of bone and muscle. His hand clenched briefly, then released. Satisfied to see his pupils dilated, she left Adam's side.

"Thank you," she murmured as she sat beside Zeben. He'd taken a seat in the center of the couch, leaving her no room to avoid him. Zeben inched closer, his thigh pressing against her flesh. He stretched his arm along the back of the couch and stroked a finger along her shoulder. The sleeveless top she wore left her skin bare to his touch. She shivered in disgust, but Zeben mistook the reaction to be excitement.

"You are a rare woman, Andrea," Zeben said,

looking at Adam. "To be gifted in so many areas. I do admire your talents."

Zeben wanted to bait him, Adam realized. He hadn't yet forgiven Caine's imagined dalliance with Marie. It was obvious he thought he would retaliate by seducing Raleigh. "I am lucky to have her," Adam replied with an appreciative leer at her legs. "We make a formidable team. Everywhere."

"I can imagine," Zeben said.

Exasperated by the conversation, Raleigh narrowed her eyes at Adam. She turned to Zeben. "I appreciate the compliment, Mr. Zeben."

"Please, call me Kadifir," he said, his finger burrowing under the shirt's strap.

Disgust rose in her throat at his prolonged contact with her flesh. "A drink, Kadifir?" she asked graciously as she stood in an attempt to evade him.

"White wine, please." Zeben folded his hands in his lap and watched her move to the bar.

Raleigh opened the bar's refrigerator and grabbed a bottle. Checking the label, she asked, "Caine?"

"Scotch. Neat," he replied.

Raleigh poured the drinks at the bar, taking time to collect herself. The thinly disguised war Zeben waged against Adam to claim her as his trophy exasperated her, but she understood Adam's reaction. It was the complete absence of human heat in Zeben's touch that had forced her to leave the sofa. She couldn't forget, however, that Zeben was simply a man, despite the aura of depravity that surrounded him. He wanted to frighten her, but she refused to give him the satisfaction of seeing her shaken. No man, particularly the skeletal remains of one, would terrify her. Fortified by her gathered pride, she set the glasses on a tray and carried the drinks to the men. She took a sip from her glass of water, then took her seat again.

Forcing herself to touch him, she placed her hand over his on the couch. Raleigh repressed a surge of revulsion at the contact. "Kadifir? Caine and I are anxious to know how the scavenger hunt turned out."

His snake eyes glinted, black and shiny. "It is unfortunate that you did not return to the site. You would have been able to claim your victory."

"You are certain we won?" Adam asked blandly. He lifted his glass to his lips and drank. There was a strong likelihood that Zeben wanted to test them. It was possible that he didn't know who'd recovered the diamond and the blueprints. "How did you decide?"

"My men discovered one of the teams dead." He delivered the news with what sounded like an undertone of gratification. "The second team recovered one item." Zeben sipped his wine and reclined into the cushions.

As the silence grew, Adam posed the question, as Zeben intended. "And the third team?"

"They allege that they did indeed recover the missing two items, but that you two had stolen them." He finished the wine and set the glass on the table. When Raleigh stood to bring him more, he waved her back to her seat. He fixed Adam with a searching look. "Your friend Civelli made the accusation."

Adam returned his look with a steady gaze. "I don't understand why Civelli remains in Jafir." He rolled the tumbler between his hands, his eyes never leaving Zeben's. "Andrea defeated him last night, and the wager included his withdrawal from the competition."

Zeben shrugged apologetically. "Because of the valiant declaration Ms. DeSalle made regarding her, um, additional support at the poker table, Civelli asked that the wager be stricken from the competition—"

Raleigh interjected, "And you agreed?"

"Civelli is best contained when kept where one can see him, is he not?" Zeben replied, looking at Adam. "Otherwise, he becomes more difficult."

"Do you believe him?"

"No," was Zeben's flat reply. "The man is a parasite, not a contender. His affiliation with Fasad and Roberts offends me. I do not trust their judgment. Fasad and Roberts are useful, except for their tendency to choose poor company. In addition, none of the men could describe the missing articles." He trailed a finger along Raleigh's jaw. "Can you?"

"Of course. And we can show them to you." At Adam's nod, Raleigh escaped to retrieve the bag from the sitting room.

Zeben accepted the bag and reached inside. Bypassing the blueprints, he removed the metal case. He opened it and exhaled audibly. "Ah, the Kholari diamond!"

Nonplussed by Zeben's reaction, Adam asked. "You didn't know the case held the diamond?"

"My partner designed the scavenger hunt. I did not have access to the specifications for Praxis or for the diamond before now."

"Your partner hid them from you?" Zeben's reply confused him even more. "Why?" he questioned harshly. Another piece had just been added to the puzzle, yet he felt as though he was on the brink of something important. "Why wouldn't he give them to you?"

Zeben's expression grew stark and enraged. "He does not trust my zeal. However, he does enjoy my resources." He visibly schooled his expression to one of mild amusement. "He is American, like yourselves, and wont to mistrust."

"An American?"

Zeben lifted the diamond, admiring the refraction of light through the luminescent stone. "Yes," he answered absently.

Raleigh could see Adam's mind whirring, trying to fit the pieces together. Zeben seemed eager to share the information, distracted by his newest acquisition. Any minute now, and he'd reveal Phillip's name! She spoke before Adam formed his next question. "The third item. What was it?"

"I do not know."

"You give your partner much control."

"He has not failed me. And neither should you." Zeben focused on Adam. "It is no concern of yours," he admonished. He stood and walked to the door, his weight oddly balanced. One emaciated hand held the diamond, the other the blueprints. He dropped the blueprints on the table near the door and clutched the diamond case to his chest. "You have won the contract. Construction begins in one day. You have twenty-four hours to assemble your materials. I will send someone to fetch you then." He smiled at Raleigh. "Good evening," he hissed as he left the suite.

Raleigh held up a hand, anticipating Adam's comment. She pointed to the scrambler, and Adam immediately turned it on.

"The mole is an American," Adam said as he crossed to the bar to refill his glass. "And he's not simply feeding Zeben information, he's doing the plotting himself." He tossed the liquor back, welcoming the burn as it scorched his throat.

"You knew that," Raleigh began, uncertain of his mood. In the space of a few moments, she saw wrath, regret, and disappointment. "Why are you so angry?"

"The traitor is one of mine, damn it!" He slammed the glass to the countertop and pounded his fist on the gleaming surface. "Those blueprints were approved by me a few weeks ago. Darrick Josephs collaborated with an ISA agent and stole the plans."

"This isn't news," she repeated, bewildered by the reaction. "We learned that at your office."

"We guessed. We didn't know."

"And now?"

"I know. I know that a friend, a man I trusted, sold out his people for money. For money!" Adam strode over to the blueprints and unrolled them. He held them up to the light, staring blindly at the engineering schematics. "Do you understand what Praxis can do?" he said softly, almost to himself. "Do you really understand?"

"It cleans the exterior environment with small chemical and electronic agents that are released into the air and systematically filter out impurities," responded Raleigh quietly. "Praxis launches pods that release the chemicals and recaptures the used filters. It reverses environmental damage and deposits new filters to continually clean the air."

Adam shook the blueprints in the air. "Praxis does more than correct environmental damage. For the heavily industrialized second and third worlds, this technological advancement is invaluable. The environmental degradation caused by the Western Allies through colonialism and post–World War Two ecocide could be reversed by Praxis, making Africa and South America and the Middle East viable, healthy continents and nations once more. No pollution. No childhood asthma. Lower cancer rates and arrested global warming. Praxis can do all of that."

"When we began work on the project five years ago, the NATO governments were anxious. They feared it would be used to poison civilians because it employs both electrical and biological agents. Certain Western nations lobbied Congress to cut our funding so that the system would never be developed."

"What happened?"

"Phillip organized a caucus, and they were able to save our money. But we had to have the background checks run to ensure the safety of the project. Each employee was handpicked based on his or her politics and social affiliations. I've worked alongside them, every step of the way."

"Except when you came here."

"Yes. When I returned to GCI, I was distracted, unfocused. Then my parents retired, and I was overwhelmed with work. I put Darrick in charge, to monitor the project. He understood the stakes; they all did. He betrayed us anyway." Bitter pain shone in his eyes, a stark look of disillusionment.

Without thinking, Raleigh moved to embrace Adam. "I'm sorry, Adam." She clasped his shoulders and leaned back to look at him. "But you know this isn't your fault."

Adam stared at her for a long moment, his expression inscrutable. "You're right." He shoved her hands from his shoulders, pushing her away. Raleigh stumbled, off balance, and Adam caught her. Cold black eyes focused on her face, as though searching for something. She saw the comprehension seconds before the eruption. "I know whose fault this is, Raleigh. Cavanaugh did this!"

"Cavanaugh?" exclaimed Raleigh, her mind hunting for a plausible explanation to the questions she knew would soon follow.

His fingers closed like a vise around her upper arm. Distaste and loathing twisted his lips into a foul sneer. "And you knew it. You saw that diamond by the monument, and you knew the truth," he berated, the agony of treason fresh, excruciating. She had lied to him, without compunction. "The Kholari diamond. The reason Cavanaugh left you behind that first time. I'd forgotten the name, but you hadn't. And you wouldn't have said anything, would you?"

Raleigh couldn't control the chagrin that flashed across her face. "Adam, let me explain—"

"Explain what? I can see it in your eyes!" Rage filled him, fueled by the bitter pain of deception. "When were you going to tell me, Raleigh? When?" Livid fury and regret stabbed at his heart. *Not now,* he thought dully. He would put the impotent personal feelings aside for later, when his mind was clear. Right now, the fight was about Praxis.

She saw the resignation sweep into his eyes, shuttering his heart from her gaze. His baleful glare saw Chimera, the deceiver. Tears pressed against the back of her eyes, demanding release. Anger rode her, demanding its due. Raleigh capitulated, surrendered to outrage, the pressure of holding the stories separate, of watching her dreams die again became too much. The men in her life would tear at her, demand her obeisance without ever understanding her needs. Her desires. Even he, the man who claimed to love her, would have her divide herself.

Well, no more. She would salvage her mission, do her duty by Cavanaugh, and protect Adam from the truth. Then she would be done, and never again would anyone have such a hold on her heart.

"When was I going to tell you?" she repeated, her head cocked to the side, her expression forbidding, remote. "I had no intention of telling you."

Adam's hand clamped down harder, runners of sensation scrambling along her skin. Banked violence and a multitude of questions blazed down when he glared at her. "Why not?"

Raleigh jerked away, breaking his hold on her arm. *I can't breathe when he touches me,* she thought with desolation. *I forget the words, the reasons.* Desperate, she quickly put the couch between them. Steadied by the barrier, she retorted coldly, "You were assigned to recover Praxis. The diamond is none of your business."

"None of my business? The diamond is a part of the Scimitar scheme. It has everything to do with Praxis. And Praxis is mine, damn you! You had no right to hide anything from me!" he spat.

Anguish settled into her cold heart. Her words, when she spoke, were calm, measured. "Right? You have no rights here, Adam." She waved at the blueprints, the dimly lit suite. "This is my mission. This is my job. When you deserted the ISA, you lost any claim to rights. You know what you need to know," she said coolly.

"What about Cavanaugh? Did you know he was the traitor the whole time?"

"Cavanaugh is dead." She ignored the blow of aching loss as she spoke the words aloud.

"The same way you were dead?" He scoffed at her explanation. "Cavanaugh is probably listening in as we speak. You could have easily sabotaged the scramblers. Maybe you planned this together. Jericho and Chimera. To steal the diamond and Praxis."

"Cavanaugh did not steal the Kholari."

"I remember his report. He claimed he couldn't find it. The ISA's best agent couldn't find the diamond that Zeben will use to buy Praxis. Rather convenient." Adam waited for an explanation he could believe. Anything to prove his suspicions wrong.

"I had nothing to do with Praxis, Adam. Neither did Cavanaugh." When he sneered at her, she snapped her teeth together and shored up her defenses. *Can it hurt this much to lose something that was never really mine?* she wondered fatalistically.

Adam cast his features into a mask of repulsion. "Does Atlas know? Is he a part of this conspiracy? Did he help Cavanaugh fake his death?" The questions rained down relentlessly.

"The Kholari is a coincidence, Adam." She held her hands up in a mute plea. "You know me, you knew Cavanaugh. These accusations are ludicrous."

"I don't know you. I doubt I ever did." Emotionless, he bore down on her.

The thin tether on her temper snapped. She raged at Adam, her voice broken and distraught. "There is no conspiracy! Cavanaugh is dead! I saw him die!" she shouted as the trembling began.

"Are you sure?"

Tension vibrated through her slender frame. Raleigh folded protective arms around her waist as though to prevent shattering into a million fragments. Fragments she would never be able to piece together. Her low, husky voice strangled over the shame. "That last morning, I disobeyed orders. I went off on my own to investigate a clue about

Praxis. While I was out, Cavanaugh got a message. Scimitar ambushed him. I found his body after they'd shot him, were still shooting. I tried to drag him to safety, but there was none. We argued. He shoved me over the cliff to protect me, and he killed himself. I heard the explosion while I tumbled down the side of the plateau." Amber eyes looked blindly past Adam, imagining the gruesome scene with stunning, visceral clarity. Her eyes refocused, burning into Adam's somber orbs. "He died paying for my mistake! Is that enough proof for you?"

"So you betrayed him, and he died," Adam said mercilessly. "Is that why Chance left you? Did you betray him, too? Did you lie to him? Or was he smarter than Cavanaugh or me? Did your lover unravel the lies and decide you weren't worth it? Did you kill his love, too?"

Her response, when it came, froze Adam's soul. Her tone was devoid of the slightest warmth. It begged no quarter, offered none.

"Chance wasn't my lover. I've never had one. Chance was my father." She stared out the window, into the heart of the night. There was nothing in the room for her anymore. "And no, he didn't leave me. I killed him."

Raleigh spoke slowly, the images unfolding before her, the nightmare made real once again. "My mother abandoned us when I was born. It was just Chance and me. He got his name from one of the bookies he'd worked for as a kid. I never called him anything else."

Adam remained still. Part of him wanted to go to her, to pull her into his arms. But he needed to know the truth.

Raleigh continued to speak. "Chance loved me,

but he was too young to have a child. He was twenty-two and a gambler. But he wanted to keep us together. So we traveled around the South, and he'd pick up jobs as a runner or bookie. I never enrolled in school because we never stayed anyplace for too long. Chance tried to teach me himself, or he gave me books once I learned to read. When he realized I was pretty smart, I started making numbers with him. He'd gamble—sometimes he'd win and we'd live in a fancy hotel for a while. Or he'd lose, and we'd skip town. We were a team. I took care of him, and he took care of me."

Adam listened, beginning to understand her need for rules, for structure. She'd had so little of it before.

"When I was eleven, we moved to Atlanta. Chance joined a gambling and prostitution ring. The head of the ring, Jack Danton, gave him a steady paycheck. He even let me do some numbers for him. Then, one night, Danton came into the back room where I was reading. Chance told me to always stay in our room when he was gone. But the back room had better lights, and I liked the quiet." Although it seemed impossible, Raleigh's voice lost the last semblance of emotion.

Dark suspicions whirled in Adam's head as he read her resolve. He was afraid of what she would say next. "I was tall for my age, almost five-six by then. I didn't hear him come in, not until he said my name. Danton had a gun with him. He closed the door behind him and told me not to scream. I did anyway. But no one came to help. Danton grabbed me, pushed me to the floor."

"No." Adam's voice choked over the word.

Raleigh ignored the interruption. "I couldn't get him off me. I tried, but I couldn't. I thought he'd win. But then Chance broke into the room and pulled him off me. He tried to stab Danton, but while they were fighting, Danton stabbed him instead. Danton had dropped his gun, so I picked it up and shot him in the heart. As my father bled to death, he told me to leave, before the police came. And I did. I ran. Just like with Cavanaugh. I disobeyed his orders, and I left him to die." She crumpled against the couch, exhausted and ashen.

Shaken, full of horror, full of sympathy, Adam gathered her against him. "You were a child, honey. You didn't know. And you didn't run away, Raleigh. Not before. You were a child. He was your father. It was his job to protect you."

"I ran away."

"You survived. That's not the same thing." He dragged her eyes to his. "It's not the same thing." Adam held her close as her tears poured down his shirt. He murmured nonsense into her hair, his hands stroking her back. Finally, the tears stopped, and she moved out of his arms.

"I'm sorry for the outburst," she apologized stiffly. "I don't know what came over me."

"Shut up, Raleigh. Just shut up." He reached for her again.

Raleigh backed away. "Don't touch me. What I've told you changes nothing."

"It changes everything," Adam fumed as he felt the anger return with a vengeance. She wasn't going to run away from him now. Not when they were just beginning to get somewhere.

"This is pointless, Merlin. We'll discuss the diamond in the morning when you're in a better mood." She wondered if she could make it to the bedroom door without collapsing. Carefully, she began to walk out of the room, praying she wouldn't shatter with each new step. *Almost there,* she repeated in an endless chant. *One more step and the pain is over.*

But Adam wouldn't let her go. "You didn't run away from your father or Cavanaugh, Raleigh," he said hoarsely. "But you're running away from me."

Raleigh gathered herself and stood erect, determined to finish this. She didn't have the strength to fight him, but she knew this was a battle she couldn't afford to lose. "You have something else to say?" she asked politely.

Adam circled the sofa to confront her. The diamond forgotten, he focused only on her. Raleigh faced him, her exquisite eyes shimmering with unshed tears, defiant nonetheless. She'd never been more beautiful. Anger dissipated, burned away by a shocking, immediate hunger. "Do you love me, Raleigh?"

At his question, panic gleamed in her eyes. Anticipating her attempt to dash past him, he caught her by the waist. He crushed her to the high back of the sofa, his legs spread wide to entrap her.

She twisted frantically to escape him. "Let me go!"

"Tell me the truth, Raleigh. How do you feel about me?"

Raleigh pummeled him with balled fists, but he didn't move. He only pressed himself tighter. "I don't have to tell you anything!"

Fourteen

"You *will* tell me." Adam shifted his hands to cup her face. "I told you I would strip away your secrets, Raleigh. One by one." One hand pinned her flailing arms between their bodies. Raleigh opened her mouth, prepared to explode, and he swooped down to take her angry lips. He thrust inside the sweet, moist cavern, hunger inciting him to pillage, to plunder. The ripe taste of her, hotter, sweeter than anything he'd ever imagined, filled his senses. Adam angled his mouth, struggling to consume all of her in one torrid rush. He'd never known such a consuming passion to occupy every corner of a woman's being. But tonight, he could imagine nothing less. He would have her, tonight—mind, body, and soul.

"Mine," he growled in thick tones as he released her lips to sample her fragrant, satiny skin. He toyed with her bottom lip, traced the whorls of her ear. The sleekness of her shoulders invited him to taste the firm muscles. His tongue sketched the angles of her collarbone, the stubborn line of her chin.

Caught up, overwhelmed, Raleigh skated her open mouth along his jaw. Sorrow, panic, and anger receded, leaving only desire. With her body, if not her words, she would tell him how she felt. She nuzzled against that spot where his jaw and throat met.

"Mine," she echoed fiercely, fighting to free her hands. When he would not release her, she demanded almost painfully, the desire clawing at her, "Let me touch you."

Adam ignored her plea, stilling her captured hands.

She arched into him, meshing her hips against the steel of his thighs. She could feel the pulse beating there, intimate, savage. His heart thudded against her trapped hands, and she longed to touch him. "Please, Adam," she begged proudly. "Please."

Still, Adam refused to comply, racing his free hand down her back to fit her more snugly into the cradle of his hips. Tonight, he would have Raleigh, as he'd always dreamed, though he hadn't known she was his fantasy. But reason and responsibility chased hunger, nipping at its heels. Her first. Her only. He could undo the horror of that night. He could give her new memories, new sensations. For her—with her—they could create something miraculous.

With a hoarse groan, Adam scooped her into his arms and strode into the bedroom. He kicked the door closed and set her gently on her feet. For an infinite moment, he stood there, tracing the lines of her body with his eyes. Then he spoke, the words a dark promise. "No more waiting, Raleigh. It ends here."

Raleigh shook her head, her body filled with a power she'd never known before. "No more waiting, Adam. It begins here," she vowed. Wisps of fear, not of him but of the unknown, crept into her mind. He would be her first, her only. Bravely, she lifted her arms to encircle his neck.

Greed ripped through him. He bent to her mouth, ready to plunge into her again. But behind the strength in Raleigh's eyes, he saw the trepidation. The combination stopped him cold. How could he forget her innocence? How could he blindly plunder what needed to be pleasured?

Fingertips stroked the arch of her brow, the plane of her cheekbone. Gentle, marauding touches enflamed the column of her throat, the lips he'd kissed earlier. He would taste, touch, worship every bit of her, and she would be with him. Completely.

How could she have survived without his hands? Raleigh writhed against him as he followed his hands with anointing, indulgent kisses, soothing laves of his tongue. What would her life become without his perfect mouth to assuage the ache? She shivered uncontrollably when the strings securing her shirt fell away, revealing her naked breasts to his avid gaze. "Beautiful," he murmured, and she believed him. Strong, slightly roughened hands shaped the swollen globes, his thumbs rasping against the sensitive tips. Frenzied charges of arousal pulsed through her, centered her entire universe on his next kiss, his next touch. She strained against his mouth, holding her to him. Craving roared in her head, throbbed in her tight, tense center. Need, want, lust gathered there, demanding attention, relief.

Her frantic moan burned away the fringes of his self-control, but he held on with effort. So many flavors, like rich red wine here, thick, sweet honey there. He would relish every morsel of skin, discover every scented hollow. But he would not hurry, he thought as he knelt before her, as he sampled the piquant flavor of her flat, taut belly. He smiled when she shuddered in his arms, pleased. This would be gentle, right. He whispered it to her, against her lean, muscled thigh as he slid her hose away.

But Raleigh had other ideas. She tugged on his broad shoulders, forcing him to stand. Wild now, she gripped his shirt, rashly undoing buttons, ripping fabric. As she bared his chest to her admiring gaze, she splayed her fingers wide, intent on ravishment. She explored the textures of his uniquely male body. Questing lips relished the salty sweet tang of his flesh. Hungry hands smoothed mounds of muscles, caressed the hard planes of his heavily ridged stomach. Not quite gently, she finished pushing his shirt away, baring all of him. Small teeth bit at his biceps, soothing the tiny wounds with wet, hot kisses. She teased him, tracing a line around his center to press her lips to his back.

On fire, he reached behind him to grasp her bottom, pressing her hips against him. *She will kill me,* he thought. With every sinuous movement, every steamy caress, she stole his heart. Pleasure—acute, singular pleasure—raced along the edges of his skin, sank claws into his soul.

Raleigh licked along the column of his spine, enjoying his labored breathing. She'd waited for him her whole life, it seemed. Tonight, she would see, taste, know heaven. When she ran her palms across his chest, Adam spun around to pull her back into his waiting arms. Speed and haste outdistanced slow and careful. Together, they fell to the bed, a jumble of legs and arms. He reached into the bedside table and placed the protection on the table surface.

Hotter. Faster. Wetter. His mouth devoured hers, deep, impossibly deep. Her hips chased his, setting a primal rhythm, echoing the motions of their mating tongues. Limbs tangled, mouths dashed to seek new flavors, uncover hidden territory. He suckled a rigid nipple, drawing the crown impossibly tighter.

She planted a chain of kisses along his hard male waist, forcing a husky groan.

His fevered hands pushed away fabric, revealing soft, humid heat. Her impatient fingers plucked at buttons, freeing hard, ready flesh. Pliant, she arched into his waiting arms, fitting herself to his strength. Consumed, he rose above her, desperate to be inside her.

"Please," he whispered against her mouth, the need tearing at him, as his fingers tore open the foil wrapper.

"Now," she welcomed, opening herself to him.

Softly, insistently, he pressed against the barrier, urgent to enter, careful to pleasure. When he broke through, she tensed, unprepared for the pain. Gently, he plucked at her center, rebuilding her arousal while he let her adjust to his presence. When she writhed against him, ready once more, he strained against time and consequence, then sank deep, nestled in her honeyed warmth. Raleigh shifted impatiently, and he frantically stilled her movements with hungry hands, afraid if she moved, it would end too soon. With long, slow strokes, he readied her. When she relaxed, he tested himself, her, measuring his length inside her perfect sheath. She arched against him, meshing them even closer.

Surrendering to his needs, to hers, he took her mouth again, seeking, finding the rhythm of their kiss. She joined him eagerly, matching him motion for motion, fighting to contain the knot of tension building inside her.

Harder. Deeper. More. Moans met murmurs, groans danced with gasps of inconceivable delight. Whispered names, quiet declarations rose into the eternal night. Each fought the battle for release, daring the other to concede, to prolong. Each struggled against release, wanting the rapture to last for eternity.

Higher. Higher. Higher. The pressure built, the tautness of flesh clamoring for relief. He framed her face, forcing her eyes to his. She grasped his neck, pulling him into her kiss. Hotter. Wetter. Deeper. Harder. Higher. They chased the want together, each refusing to leave the other behind. Infinite passion, carnal pleasure, boundless devotion gathered into an endless moment. Then their world shattered, exploded, drowning them in ecstasy. In forever.

"Oh, my," Raleigh sighed languidly as she opened heavy-lidded eyes to hunt for a sheet to drape over her cool, damp body. But movement seemed a Herculean task, only slightly less daunting than the prospect of coherent thought. Taxed by the ribbons of response still rippling along sated flesh, she closed her eyes in defeat. Disappointed, she murmured softly, "Cold."

"Oh my, indeed," Adam responded with an indulgent grin. With one arm, he curled Raleigh into his body, savoring the sleek feel of her skin against his own. His other hand drew a tangled blanket up and over their bodies.

Raleigh snuggled deep into the warmth of Adam and the blanket. She was exhausted, replete, satisfied. Why had she waited so long for something so glorious? Her mind searched vainly for an answer and was sidetracked by the thought of sleep. *If I rest,* she mused dreamily, *we can do this again.* She muttered as much to Adam.

Tucking her head under his chin, he replied softly, "As many times as you'd like."

"Good," Raleigh said, drifting off.

Adam remained awake, alert, his mind chaotic with random thoughts. Uppermost was the paradox of the woman lying cuddled against him. At the age of thirty-four, he'd never lived the life of a monk. The women he'd dated had been uniformly intelligent, attractive, and experienced. Each woman filled a mutual need for pleasure or companionship. But none had filled his being so completely. Raleigh frustrated him, infuriated him. With her obdurate refusal to share responsibility and her infernal belief that she always knew what was right, she could drive him to insanity.

Yet, he'd never known a woman more loyal or forthright or valiant. He chuckled softly. Loyal. Forthright. Valiant. Arcane terms from another age, but they suited her. And she suited him.

Cool and reserved or hot and passionate, she was everything he'd envisioned his soul mate to be. And that's what she was, his soul mate. As soon as she woke up, she would retreat from him, he knew. She'd conjure a million reasons why this shouldn't have happened. He'd give her space and time to process. Five minutes should be enough, he decided with a grin. Then he'd seduce her and make her so utterly his, she'd never disentangle them. Adam folded his arms behind his head and began to dream of the thousand and one things they would do to burn down the night.

Raleigh sighed and twisted restively. He tucked her head more firmly beneath his chin, stroking her forehead with a soothing touch. When she awoke, they would also talk about Chance Foster and

Cavanaugh and the other secrets she'd concealed. But for now, he'd simply hold her. For now, she belonged to him.

"Damn." Raleigh repeated the oath as she inched away from Adam's sleeping form. She wrapped a discarded sheet around her naked body and headed for the bathroom. Once inside, she closed the door gently and leaned her back against the door and slid to the heated tiles of the floor.

"Okay, Raleigh," she whispered, "what have you done?" Raleigh took a deep, cleansing breath. When confronted by a baffling situation, do an assessment. "First of all, it was an encounter. Nothing more." If she didn't quite believe the bland description, she ignored it. "An unfortunate encounter with both physical and emotional side effects."

As though she were debriefing a stranger, she commanded, "Start with your physical status." For the time, she noticed that her body ached in the most gratifying way. Echoes of pleasure would pulse through her at odd moments, a reminder of her avid participation.

Raleigh could not control her smile as she recalled Adam's strained words of encouragement. *If I ache, so does he,* she mused happily as she gnawed on her bottom lip. She'd given as good as she got. Or so she hoped.

Uncertain, her mind drifted off to replay the night's activities. Perhaps she hadn't done it right. Maybe, because she was new at sex, he'd simply humored her. She was mortified. In the aftermath, he'd said nothing, nothing at all. What if . . . , her thoughts trailed off as she imagined what she could have done wrong. Caught up in her dark musings, she forgot where she was for a moment until she heard Adam cough in the other room. That snapped her back to attention.

"Focus, Raleigh," she said, her voice stern. "Whether you were good or not is irrelevant. Stick with the matter at hand." Raleigh got to her feet and winced at a small pain. "Physical status not compromised," she noted to herself, "but should be monitored for changes." *Like an unmanageable desire to repeat the performance,* she thought dryly.

"Now for emotional damage control." Raleigh briefly shut her eyes as she remembered the bitter scene that led to their encounter. "Okay, so I told him about Chance and Cavanaugh. Not an intentional revelation, but it's done. I doubt he'll have occasion to divulge my personal history to anyone else."

But why take the chance, she thought, a troubled frown marring the line of her brow. "I wouldn't have told him if I hadn't been furious." *But there is more to it than that,* she acknowledged.

"I wouldn't have said anything, no matter how angry I was," she spoke slowly, unsure of her words. "If I didn't trust him. If I didn't love him." Raleigh covered her mouth, shocked by her revelation.

A flush burned her cheeks. "This is insane. I can't love him. I don't love anyone."

Obviously, you do, her heart countered. *You love Adam Grayson.*

"Do not," Raleigh retorted. "I care about him."

You love him, her heart insisted.

"I find him attractive," she countered. "That's not love."

Raleigh loves Adam, her heart taunted.

"Cut it out! I might be very fond of him. And . . . and . . . I do love him. So much." Panic and jubilation fought for supremacy. Despite her careful plans, she'd fallen in love with him. Hadn't she admitted as much by telling him about her past?

How could she have imagined he wasn't the one? The one she hid from and looked for. The one who held her and heard her and made her more alive, more in love, than she'd realized. The one who taught her how to trust in and lean on and sink into another person. The one who argued and angered, who stood firm and held tight, who kissed her and touched her and made her see the stars. Adam Grayson was the man she could depend on, could trust. Could love.

Her confirmation brought panic and dismay. Nothing had changed. She still couldn't tell him about Phillip.

To sleep with Adam once had been a mistake. To do so again would be reckless.

"Course of action?" She'd take a shower, march into the bedroom, and tell him so. She would remind him that they were colleagues and that emotional involvement had no place in their relationship. Their encounter would remain simply that—an unexpected encounter, with no ties and no consequences.

Satisfied with her plan, Raleigh loosened the sheet and turned on the shower's faucet. While she waited for the water to heat, she studied her nude form in the mirror. What she saw startled her.

Eyes she didn't recognize as her own peered back at her, full of secrets and knowledge. She raised a wondering hand to her lips, touched their tender softness. Her body seemed foreign, yet uniquely her own. Lassitude stole through her, winding through her limbs, her heart, a sensation that felt dangerously like contentment. Disturbed by the thought, Raleigh broke her gaze from the wanton stranger in the mirror and climbed into the steamy stall.

Raleigh forced her mind to go blank and concentrated on shampooing her hair. For endless moments, she only heard the rush of the water as it pounded against her. The sound of Adam's voice shattered the silence.

"Your five minutes are up, Raleigh." Adam declared as he forced the shower door open.

"What?" she gasped in surprise, hastily covering her body with a useless hand towel. Her gaze was riveted on his body. *Goodness,* she thought distractedly, *he's breathtaking.*

Adam stepped into the shower, naked and fully aroused, impatience evident in the set of his jaw, the force with which he shut the shower door. With a distinctly casual gesture, he plucked the towel from her nervously clenched fist and dropped it to the floor. The loss of the towel left her open to his admiring gaze.

Raleigh's first instinct was to dive for the towel, but she could barely see the floor through the steam. Furthermore, she refused to scrounge around on the floor and search for a hand towel with Adam watching her every move. Instead, she tried to cover herself with her hands, to no avail. "Five minutes?" she managed throatily.

Adam took a moment to regret her decision not to go after the cloth. He'd have enjoyed the view. But he would have everything he wanted in a moment. Or almost everything. "When you skulked out of bed, I decided you'd have five minutes to enumerate your regrets and analyze our encounter. You did decide to call it an *encounter*, didn't you? Or did you call it an *incident?*" He smirked as he saw her unwilling acknowledgement.

"Skulked? I don't skulk." Amber eyes narrowed, insulted and embarrassed. She was tired of his laughter at her expense and his boundless amusement at her personal protocol. The time for modesty had passed, and she planted her fists on her hips, revealing herself to his eyes. The current situation called for bravado, not retreat. If her knees quivered at the sight of her first utterly naked man, it was no one's business but her own. She was gratified to see him swallow with difficulty as steam curled about her body. Raleigh cocked a hip and asked coolly, "And if I did decide that it was only an encounter, what of it? Can you think of a better term?" she drawled haughtily, despite the butterflies swarming in her gut.

"I can imagine several terms, as a matter of fact." Adam lifted the soap from the tray and lathered his hands with a determined sense of leisure. "Having sex," he commented as he massaged the froth of bubbles into her shoulders.

Raleigh barely repressed a moan. This was not going to happen again. Hadn't she decided that it was for the best if she kept her distance?

Slightly calloused hands covered her sensitive breasts and slathered soap onto the swollen globes. "But I don't think sex quite covers it. I prefer making love, personally."

"You think—" Raleigh's voice broke as his slippery hands made their way down her torso. "Making love is not—" she gasped uncontrollably when he caressed the shape of her thighs. "Not what we did," she finished on a moan.

"What would you call it, sweetheart?" Adam bent and focused his attentions on the curve of her calf, the arch of her foot. *She has lovely feet,* he decided and lingered there for a moment. "I was in bed with you, darling, and I've done this before, which gives me a bit of an advantage." He rose and turned Raleigh to face the spray as he soaped her back. "We made love, I assure you."

"I don't love you," she countered desperately as he continued the sweet torture of her slick, wet skin. "We can't make love if I don't love you." The words seemed logical, even if punctuated by uncontrollable shivers of reaction.

"You're lying again, Raleigh." Adam pulled her back into his arms and he directed the spray of water to rinse them both. "You do love me." He caressed her softly, possessively. "Believe what you will for now. Heaven knows you have reason to deny your feelings." His hands manacled her wrists, then he spun her suddenly.

Desire and intent blazed in deep black eyes. "But know this. One day, I'm going to grow tired of your evasions. You're running out of time, and I'm running out patience," Adam threatened.

"I won't love you if I choose not to," Raleigh retorted. She sank her fingers into his hair and fit his mouth to hers. "I choose what I want." The kiss they shared staggered her as she strained to absorb him, his strength, his certainty.

Steam clouded around them, enveloped them in a private, sensual world. Moans and sighs pierced the vapors, names whispered, shouted in triumph.

As Adam carried Raleigh back into the bedroom, he could see only her, think only her. An irresistible craving, she'd wound herself so tightly inside him, he would never be free. Her heart, her soul had somehow become breath and bone to him. Empowered by the knowledge, shaken by the responsibility, he answered her challenge simply, honestly. "Choose. But you will choose me, Raleigh. Only me."

The intrusive sound of the communicator beeping roused Raleigh from a peaceful slumber. She woke in a rush, alert and ready. During the night, she and Adam had switched sides, which forced her to crawl over him to reach the radio. The friction of naked skin, the accidental contact awakened Adam. He shook his head to clear it just as Raleigh engaged the communicator.

"Chimera here, over." Raleigh fumbled for a sheet, anything to cover herself.

"Report," barked Atlas, his Texas twang filling the room.

Amused by Raleigh's predicament, Adam rose from the bed and tossed his discarded shirt to her. Raleigh shrugged into the shirt with undue haste and poked her tongue at Adam, all the while avoiding a full examination of his body. Adam walked to the dresser and pulled out a pair of slacks.

Atlas' impatient voice boomed over the radio. "Chimera, report."

"Secure channel. Engage special encryption." Raleigh's request for extra security signaled Atlas to terminate any outside monitoring of the call. Only he and Raleigh and Adam would hear the conversation.

A minute later, Atlas responded, "Channel secured."

"Zeben has the Kholari diamond," Raleigh said

without preamble. "And he has the most recent blueprints."

Atlas bit off an oath. "Did you verify them, Merlin?"

Adam took a seat beside Raleigh and spoke just above a whisper, loud enough for his voice to reach the microphone. "Yes. They are the most recent specs, not older than two or three weeks."

"It's an inside job, then. Your man from GCI sold you out."

Without looking at Raleigh, Adam countered, "Maybe not quite. The blueprints are from GCI. But the diamond is an ISA thing."

"What are you suggesting?"

"That they killed Cavanaugh in a double-cross. Perhaps he recovered the diamond three years ago and hid it. Then he comes to Jafir to complete his deal with Zeben. Yet, something goes wrong, and Zeben decides to take the diamond and eliminate Cavanaugh."

"Cavanaugh wasn't a traitor," Atlas contradicted.

"Look, Atlas. The pieces fit. A missing diamond worth enough money to fund Scimitar's most ambitious project. Cavanaugh leaves his protégé behind to solve the case, but comes back empty-handed." Adam glanced at Raleigh, and she met his look with a stony glare. Turning away, he continued, "He's one of two ISA men who knew about Praxis, and conveniently, he's assigned to return to Jafir to track down rumors of its theft." Adam stood and crossed to the mirror. "This isn't rocket science, Atlas," he finished curtly.

"It doesn't feel a bit too pat to you, Merlin?"

"No."

"Chimera? Any alternative theories?"

"I don't believe Cavanaugh did this," she answered. "I know he didn't."

"I agree with Chimera, Merlin."

Adam exploded, "What? Cavanaugh is guilty as sin, Atlas. Don't you think you're letting loyalty blind you?" he asked tartly.

"I'm not the blind one here, Merlin," replied Atlas, his tone a veiled warning. "Pick another suspect."

Refusing to retreat from his instinct, Adam persisted. "Like who, Atlas? There were four of us. Phillip is dead. Cavanaugh is dead. I didn't do it." He paused. "And I know it wasn't Chimera."

Raleigh released a breath she hadn't been aware of holding. Despite the evidence to the contrary, he trusted her. She had not realized how much that meant until he spoke the words aloud. "There could be someone else," she volunteered.

"Like whom?" Adam and Atlas said together.

She heard Atlas' note of caution. "Josephs could have found another person inside the department. Or they could have tracked him down. We did."

Adam shot her suggestion down. "I made it inside the files because I know both systems. I designed them."

"You are not the only computer whiz out there, Merlin."

"But I am the only one who understands my protocols."

"The only one? No one else worked on them with you?"

"Phillip."

Atlas broke into the conversation, eager to divert them both. "We're not getting anywhere. The important objective is assessing how far Zeben has gotten with his assembly of Praxis. How much time do you have?"

"Twenty-four hours."

"All right. Chimera, I want you to make contact with Sashu in the village. He should have a lead on where construction is taking place. Merlin, you should start gathering the hardware. Use your sources from before. They're expecting your call."

"We'll wait for you to make next contact," said Raleigh. "I'd advise a forty-eight-hour hold. Now that we're on board, whoever the mastermind is, he'll be even more vigilant."

"Agreed. But contact me if you need to."

"Confirmed," Adam responded.

Atlas terminated the connection. Raleigh looked at Adam, her eyes guarded and wary. Her body stirred, remembering the hours before she slept. She'd never have guessed she could be so lascivious, so aggressive. Adam had been correct. At some point, her world had centered solely on him, on becoming his. But the interlude was over, and reality demanded secrets.

Raleigh spoke before Adam could say anything. "I'll get dressed and head into town. Sashu lives near the marketplace."

"I'll go with you," replied Adam as he grabbed a blue cotton shirt and a pair of khakis from the closet.

Raleigh selected a pair of black slacks and a copper silk blouse. "There's no need." She headed for the bathroom, her eyes averted as she brushed past him.

Adam stopped her with a firm hand on her shoulder. "There's every need. Number one, I have to go into town myself. Number two, we need to maintain the pretense. If we go into Desira together, we get better exposure." He turned her to face him. "And number three," he said with quiet sincerity, "I want to be with you."

"Adam," she sighed.

"Yes?" he answered as he pulled her into his arms. It amazed him anew how perfectly she fit. He'd never realized before how sexy someone who was tall and lithe could feel, when all of her curves meshed with all the right spaces. Unable, unwilling to resist the temptation of her mouth, he kissed her.

"Adam," she said huskily, when he finally released her lips to nuzzle at her neck. "I need to shower."

"We can do that." He bent to lift her into his arms, but she backed away, wriggling out of his grasp.

"This time, I need to actually bathe," she said primly.

Suitably chastened and aroused by the memory of their earlier interlude, Adam conceded without a fight. "Fine. But hurry up."

"I never take too long in the shower," protested Raleigh.

"No, you don't. But I can't vouch for how long I'll be willing to wait out here while you're in there." Adam warned, half serious, half joking. "Proceed at your own risk."

Fifteen

Raleigh lifted a length of vibrantly colored material from the middle-aged Jafirian man's fabric stall. She held the fabric in the morning sunlight, studied its intricate pattern, and waited for the guilt and remorse to crash into her.

It was to be expected that in this place she would face Cavanaugh's ghost. She would confront him and accept his condemnation. She would offer no defense for her actions, for sneaking away and leaving him to stand alone against an attack. There was nothing she could do to atone for her desertion, for his sacrifice. But, if his ghost came to her, she'd tell him of her plans to try. Where he lost his life because of her, she would bring him some small measure of peace.

She waited for Sashu to finish with his customer and come to her. When he caught sight of her, Sashu grinned a wide, bright smile, one he reserved for her. On that first day in Jafir, Cavanaugh had brought her to Sashu's cart and taught her to bargain for goods. For what seemed like hours, they'd haggled over a few pennies for a wide band of cloth she'd likely never wear. Cavanaugh had laughed at her selection and chastised her for paying Sashu an extravagant amount for the lamba she purchased.

Sashu had remembered her generosity and, in turn, had become her eyes and ears in the shadows of Jafir. It was Sashu who'd sent her to the marketplace when he learned of Cavanaugh's ambush. And today, if the fates were kind, he would tell her where she could find his killer.

"Ah, my friend has returned," Sashu greeted her gaily as his eyes searched the crowd for familiar faces too interested in their conversation.

Raleigh returned his careful smile with one of her own. "I told you I would not be long in returning."

"It is tragic that you come to my stall alone. He will be sadly missed." Sashu bent over her unsteady hand in a gesture of respect. "If I can do anything to lessen your grief."

"My sorrow would be diminished if I could find the one responsible," Raleigh said quietly.

Sashu nodded and pressed a square of paper and a car key into her palm. "May the gods protect those who seek justice."

Raleigh closed her fingers around the note, her fist clenched tight. "Justice will be done."

"Are you almost ready to go?" Adam asked from behind her.

Raleigh jumped and turned, startled by his sudden appearance. She recovered quickly. On instinct, she reached up on tiptoe to kiss his cheek, she said, "Caine, I thought you would be a while longer at the carpentry stall." She rested one hand on his shoulder for balance and slipped the paper into her pants pocket.

Pleasantly surprised by her spontaneous, affectionate greeting, Adam noticed the lingering impression of her lips on his skin. "We finished up sooner than I expected." As she drew away, he laid his hand on the small of her back and lowered his head to kiss her again. The complex flavors of her seeped into his skin, into his bones. He forgot where they were and lost himself in her. Only a man's amused cough broke them apart.

Raleigh pressed the back of her hand to her mouth. "Oh," she said weakly as the mist clouding her eyes started to clear.

"I missed you." Adam lifted a length of cloth from Sashu's table. It was handmade, a golden brown the exact shade of Raleigh's eyes. The material was simple, elegant, with a complex pattern in the very weft. It had been woven into a shawl. It had been made for Raleigh.

Sashu noticed the interchange and Adam's attention to the shawl. This man in love would buy his friend Chimera a gift this day. "It is as though it were made for her eyes alone," he commented as he plucked at an end of the cloth. In full salesman mode, he began his pitch. "The cotton threads are from the finest in Egypt, grown by my own cousins," he intoned. "My wife and daughters, they weave day and night until fabric as light as the air itself takes shape."

Adam interrupted his pitch. "How much?"

"Caine? What are you doing?"

"Buying you a gift. Do you object?" He folded the fabric and pulled out his wallet.

"You don't need to—"

"Good," Adam cut off her protest. *If I want to buy this woman a gift, she'll just have to take it,* he thought gruffly. "Sashu, what is your price?"

Sashu put on his negotiator's expression, a combination of cajolery and angst. "For you, fifty American dollars."

"Sashu, that is robbery!" Raleigh exclaimed sternly.

"I'll take it," Adam said without argument, and he passed a fifty-dollar bill to Sashu's outstretched palm.

After he tucked the money into a side pouch, Sashu produced a plastic bag from beneath the table and placed the material inside. "Excellent choice."

Adam and Raleigh said their goodbyes and headed toward the other stalls. He drew her under an empty canopy and removed the shawl. "Please, don't argue with me." With exquisite care, he draped the material around her shoulders. The morning sun blazed down on the marketplace, and shoppers milled around searching out clothes for growing children, dinner for hungry families. The noise, the heat, the scents receded, leaving them alone under the awning of the cart. He pulled the ends together, just under her chin. "I want you to have it. It makes me happy to give something so beautiful to someone as lovely as you."

"Oh, Adam," she said softly, her heart sliding firmly out of her control. "You undo me." She sounded not quite pleased with the revelation, and her lips pressed together in a slight frown.

"You sound annoyed," he said, dipping his head to tease her with a kiss. But the light press of lips he envisioned grew into a potent mating of mouths, from which neither wanted to be the first to break away.

With concerted effort, Raleigh placed an uncooperative hand on his chest and broke the contact. "We've got work to do," she reminded him, evening out her breath.

Adam straightened and lightly caressed her shoulders before sticking his hands into his pockets. "Did Sashu have any information for you?"

"No, but he said he'd be in touch." The paper crumpled in her pocket burned against her thigh. "And you?"

"I've got a meeting with our suppliers in thirty minutes. Do you want to join us?"

"I'd rather return to the hotel, if you don't mind," she began hesitantly.

Instantly, Adam was filled with remorse. He hadn't given a thought to how she would feel physically after last night. "Are you—that is—do you feel all right?"

Raleigh looked at him quizzically. "Yes, I'm fine. Do I look ill?"

"Not ill, but we *were* rather active last night," Adam explained with embarrassment.

She seized on the excuse with remorse. "I am a bit tired, I think."

"Do you need me to walk back to the hotel with you? Or we can get a foot cab." Adam took her arm gently, treating her as though she were an invalid.

Compunction would not allow her to press the charade any farther. "I can walk, really. But I'd rather go back. I'll catch up with you later."

"I'll be gone for at least a couple of hours. You just rest. Drink some tea and take a hot bath," Adam advised anxiously.

Moved by his concern, she reassured him, "I'm not sick. I just need a few hours of rest, and I'll be fine."

"If you're sure."

"I'm sure. Now go," she said lightly. He turned to walk away when she stopped him by grabbing his wrist. "Thank you for the shawl. It is lovely."

Adam's radiant smile broke over her in waves of light and heat. "My pleasure, darling. My pleasure."

He headed for the carpentry stalls, and Raleigh walked toward the hotel, folding the shawl and stuffing it into her bag. As soon as she was out of Adam's eyesight, she pulled the note from her pocket.

Baren Warehouse. Phillip was at the old warehouse, with Praxis. Her body lurched, and her feigned illness became frighteningly real. In a few minutes, she would confront the man who had condemned Cavanaugh to death. The man Adam loved like a brother.

Raleigh returned to the marketplace and found the old Pinto Sashu had arranged for her parked beyond the marketplace. She put it into gear and headed for the warehouse. Parking the car, she checked her satchel for her tool kit. Instead, her searching fingers encountered the amber shawl. The surge of love disconcerted her. *It doesn't change anything,* she told herself curtly. *Love doesn't change anything.*

She made her way up the hillside and saw the first row of fences. Her miniature blowtorch carved through the fence as if it were butter. She repeated the process at the second row. For a moment, she was astonished by her ease of entry. But this was supposed to be a deserted warehouse, not a weapons factory. Too many guards or obvious security systems would alert the government.

The warehouse was a vast, two-story building, with an upper tier overlooking the ground floor. As she recalled from her previous visit with Cavanaugh, the building contained three offices and then the main floor. There was a security booth and a wrap-around landing on the upper level. The windows were almost ten feet above the ground, preventing anyone on foot from spying on an activity. In the rear of the building, however, a metal fire-escape ladder led up to the second-floor landing.

Raleigh nimbly scaled the ladder and, seeing no one, pried open the window. She dropped lightly to the floor and crouched into a defensive position. Behind her, she heard the sound of heavy footsteps. Timing the steps, she lashed out and caught the man in his solar plexus. He doubled over and fell to the floor, gasping for air. She waved a vial of chloroform under his nose, rendering him unconscious.

A quick look over the railing revealed three men on the bottom floor. One stood guard at the entryway. The second blocked her entrance to the main warehouse. The third man sat at a work table, making notations on a blueprint.

Crawling along the grated floor, she was careful to move silently toward the door leading to the first level. She eased the door open and made her way down the stairs. At the second doorway, she loaded a dart into her pistol. Without the space she needed, the dart would explode upon contact with the opposite wall. The fumes would knock out everyone in the main room and keep the man upstairs unconscious for a few minutes longer. Raleigh covered her nose and mouth with the gas mask. Silently counting to three, she jerked the door open and fired. Seconds later, the men began to cough and wheeze. The guard at the entryway fell to his knees, clutching his roiling stomach. She stepped over the sentry at her door and made her way to the man at the worktable. He had collapsed over a sheaf of papers, his head lolling to one side.

Not quite gently, Raleigh pushed at the back of his head, turning him toward her. The solidly hewn, ruggedly attractive face was slack from the drug.

Thick, luxurious lashes closed over eyes she knew to be a vivid chocolate brown. Built along powerful lines, he was quite tall, even slumped over the table. She could tell, just by looking, that he outweighed her by at least one hundred pounds. Unfortunately, the weight was pure muscle. He was the kind of man you wanted at your back to protect you or in front to lead the charge.

Although they'd only met a few times, she had no doubt about his identity. Phillip Turman. As she leaned over the inanimate man, she pressed Adam's gun to his temple. She'd stolen the gun while he'd showered. *Now,* she thought, *before he wakes up.* She released the safety.

I trust you.

I love you.

You've done nothing wrong.

She shook her head from side to side to dispel Adam's voice. She had to do this. For weeks, she'd thought only of killing Phillip, of taking from him what he'd stolen from Cavanaugh. Now, Adam's words echoed in her mind, making her doubt her mission.

"Murder is wrong, yes. But vengeance, justice, that is right," she whispered into the open space of the warehouse. "I owe it to Cavanaugh. To Chance," she entreated.

I trust you.

I love you.

You've done nothing wrong.

Defeated, Raleigh put the safety back into place and looked around the room, blindly seeking an alternative. She couldn't kill him yet because she had to have answers. How had he survived the blast? Why had he turned against the ISA? Why had he betrayed his wife and best friend? *I will keep him alive long enough to get the truth,* she told herself. Then she would keep her vow to Cavanaugh, to her father.

And even if Adam's voice played in her head and her body retained the memory of their endless night together, she'd survive.

And even if her heart cried out for Adam's love and rebelled against the inevitable, she'd survive. She had before. She would again.

Over in the corner, an empty dolly leaned against the wall. She retrieved the dolly and, with great effort, stretched Phillip out on the base. Then she gathered the papers, the blueprints, and the laptop and shoved them into her satchel.

Upstairs, the first guard stirred, waking from the fumes. She circled around the prone entry guard and pushed Phillip to the clearing. After she dumped his body into the backseat with effort, she handcuffed him, removed her mask, and got behind the wheel.

Raleigh drove to the edge of the marketplace, where Scimitar had gunned Cavanaugh down. She'd take him to the cavern to interrogate him. Then she would determine his fate.

"What the hell?" Phillip asked groggily as the drugs wore off.

Raleigh ignored him as she maneuvered the car between the abandoned carts and stalls.

"Who are you?" he demanded.

Raleigh turned off the ignition and slung her satchel across her shoulder.

"I want an answer!" he shouted.

"Shut up," she said mildly. She climbed out of the front seat and opened the door to take hold of his shoulders. "Hello, Phillip," she offered in mock greeting.

His eyes widened. "Chimera?" Phillip stared at her in disbelief. "What are you doing? Why are you here?"

Phillip recognized her, which could only mean that he'd seen her on the trip with Cavanaugh. "You mean, why aren't I dead like Cavanaugh?"

"What are you talking about? No," he said. "I thought you and Adam were out gathering supplies."

"So, you *are* the traitor?"

Phillip furrowed his brow, confused by the accusation. "I'm the inside man, yes."

"You bastard," spat Raleigh. "No polite denials? You just admit that you betrayed us all?" she said with incredulity.

"Betrayed? I've risked my life the past few days to make sure you two won the contract. That doesn't count as betrayal."

"What about Cavanaugh? Did he get in your way or something? Why did you have him killed?"

Phillip shook his head in denial, his voice awash with confusion. "I didn't kill him," he said. "Cavanaugh's alive."

She reached inside the backseat to drag him out of the car. "What?" she asked when she propped him against the side of the car. "Cavanaugh's dead."

"No, he's not.." He squinted in the harsh glare of the sun. "Unless Zeben found him out yesterday. You know he's Zeben's silent partner, right?"

Raleigh's vision blurred as his words punched her like a fist to the gut. "You've seen him?"

"Of course. The night I rigged the tournament for you. He told me you and Adam would be there, so I fixed the game. But you didn't need my help." Phillip shrugged his shoulders. "I also switched your scroll for the scavenger hunt. You found the diamond and the blueprints, just as we'd planned. But I don't understand why you're here. Zeben said you two were out buying supplies."

Too shaken to answer immediately, Raleigh held up a hand for silence. *Think, Chimera, think. Cavanaugh wouldn't double-cross you like this. It must be a part of Phillip's game. Just get him to the cave and then interrogate him.* She pulled out Adam's gun and aimed it at him with one hand. With the other, she rolled a large stone away and unearthed a knotted rope. She tossed the rope over the cliff; its other end was secured to the ground. The rope was dirty, almost undetectable.

"Move," she instructed, guiding Phillip to the lip of the cliff. "When I unlock your handcuffs, grab the rope and slide down to the next ledge. Wait for me—and don't try to escape."

"Where would I go?" he grumbled. She removed the cuffs, and Phillip lowered himself using the knotted rope.

"Step away from the rope and keep your hands where I can see them." Raleigh scrambled down the rope and landed lightly on the ledge. She tucked the rope into a crevice on the hillside. Once at the cavern, she shoved brush and scrub away from the entrance. "Inside." Following Phillip, she flicked on a suspended lantern and illuminated the space. An air mattress, an empty cooler, and a radio unit dotted the floor inside the cavern.

She set her satchel on the ground near the lantern and reached for the neon bag she'd left behind a few weeks before. A canteen landed at Phillip's feet. "Drink," she said, "or you'll get nauseous again."

Phillip unscrewed the cap and took a swig. Confusion and distrust flitted across his strong features. "Why did you bring me here?"

"For answers." *Something isn't right here,* she thought. *I've got the pieces, but they don't fit.* Phillip had come with her way too easily. No fight, no struggle. Plus, he volunteered information as though she had a right to know.

He hadn't looked like a man caught in the act. He exuded honesty. This was the man Adam idolized. She and Phillip had only met twice before, and neither had said much, but she'd been impressed even then by his sincerity. All she knew of Phillip Turman came from Cavanaugh and Adam. Neither of them told stories that would prepare one for betrayal. But the alternative was much, much worse.

She rubbed at her brow, soothing the beginnings of a headache. Questions jumbled in her head, with no obvious explanations. Why would Cavanaugh fake his own death? Why would Phillip help them if he wanted them dead? Could she believe Phillip and not Cavanaugh? Did Atlas know about Cavanaugh?

Hold on, she ordered herself. *One step at a time. First, ask Phillip for his story. Then contact Atlas. Then make your decision.*

Raleigh fixed Phillip with a stony glare as she refitted his handcuffs. "Take a seat on the mattress," she ordered.

Phillip caught himself as he lost his balance and sat awkwardly. Raleigh did nothing to assist him. He righted himself and jangled the chains on the cuffs. "Are these necessary? I'm not going anywhere. I haven't tried to run, despite the less-than-hospitable greeting." He took a deep breath and exhaled in a slow stream. "How did you drug me, anyway?" His tone was quizzical, not accusatory.

His easy acceptance of her treatment bothered her, but she repressed her natural concern. "How I got you isn't important," she stated coldly as she sat cross-legged on the ground in front of him. "And the cuffs remain on until I have the truth."

"And then?"

She shrugged negligently, her gaze boring into his. "Then I decide if you live or die."

Phillip blinked at her response. Then he took a second, deep breath and said, "What do you want to know?"

She ticked off the list on her fingers. "Why are you in Jafir instead of in Washington? Why would you let your best friend believe you died three years ago? What do Cavanaugh and Atlas have to do with any of this?" Each question fell from her lips, a separate barb of acid and accusation.

Phillip did not flinch, did not react at all. He looked at her steadily, and she could see his mind working. "All right." Phillip nodded in understanding.

"Start at the beginning."

"Atlas recruited Adam and me at a bar in Boston," he began in a storyteller's voice.

"Not that far back," Raleigh interrupted, not amused.

"I've got to start there if you want to have the whole picture."

"Go ahead."

"In college, I majored in computer science. When I got to Harvard, I met Adam. Not only were we best friends, but he also became my boss. I worked part-time for his company, CompuSecure. Then, right before graduation, Atlas approached us and invited us to join the ISA. I had already accepted a position with the Justice Department. They needed a man on the inside, to keep the organization informed."

"So the betrayals began with your nation," Raleigh taunted.

Phillip stiffened and frowned disapprovingly. "I didn't give away government secrets, Chimera. I ran interference between U.S. agencies and the ISA. I never compromised national security," he stubbornly asserted.

She dismissed his explanation and decided to focus on the issue at hand. Besides, she certainly could not sit in moral judgment of a fellow agent's tactics, no matter how dubious. "How did Praxis come into play?" she asked.

"When Adam told me about Praxis, he said he needed Cavanaugh and me to run a background check. Everyone came out clean, except Darrick Josephs. Cavanaugh and I decided to go to Atlas before we reported to Adam."

"He'd already been recruited by the ISA?"

"Yes. Atlas told us that we were to clear him. He worked for Domestic Espionage."

Raleigh leaned forward, angling her head to examine Phillip with critical eyes. "And you agreed? You placed a spy inside your best friend's company?"

"We placed an operative inside a multinational corporation doing immense amounts of federal research. Including the construction of a potentially world-altering device," he defended. "Adam was vice president and responsible for research and development. He had to know that there would be someone watching him. He intimated as much to me."

"But did he know you put the man there?"

"No." Phillip lifted his captive hands, palms facing upward. "I had a duty not to tell him. Cavanaugh and I both agreed to remain silent."

"Darrick Josephs, a green recruit, gets a plum position at GCI. He monitors the development of Praxis and reports back to the ISA. Have I got it right so far, Sphinx?"

With a short nod, Phillip continued his story. "A few months later, Adam was assigned to infiltrate Scimitar. By then, I'd been elected to Congress. My jobs with the ISA were becoming more and more infrequent. Plus, I was placed in the Foreign Affairs committee, the African subcommittee."

"Convenient," Raleigh said caustically.

"ISA," he corrected. "Discussions about environmental degradation had started in earnest. The West wanted international treaties banning certain forms of air pollution. Of course, third-world nations could never meet the standards, and they'd lose funds. Like any good congressman, I started looking for solutions."

"And you remembered Praxis."

"Praxis was the key! I asked Adam about securing more federal funds for the project, but he balked at the idea. Federal funding meant greater oversight and control. He felt the same way as I did about its development, but he didn't want to use U.S. money."

Raleigh heard the resignation in Phillip's words. He hadn't been happy with Adam's decision. "So, you decided to steal the technology from him?"

"No. I decided to feel out a few of my fellow Congress people. I thought we might be able to siphon off funds for the project, without a great deal of publicity."

"Were you successful?"

"Almost. But they wanted assurances about the nature of the project and its impact. The implications for terrorism are tremendous. If a rogue organization, like Scimitar, got its hands on Praxis, the results would be deadly. I negotiated a compromise with Atlas' help. We would test the technology in a neutral state."

Raleigh easily supplied the name. "Jafir."

"I was to meet with Adam and the president of Jafir. If they could quash Scimitar, with the ISA's assistance, then they would be the first to access Praxis. Depending on the outcome, they would gain exclusive rights to deploy Praxis in neighboring states, as the nations joined the African-Arab Alliance the president envisioned."

"Did Adam know about the deal?"

"I couldn't tell him until everything was in place. Congressional orders."

She understood those kinds of orders. "What went wrong?"

"I met with President Robertsi as planned. And you and Adam did your part to get Adam inside Scimitar. It would be maybe six more months before Scimitar fell, and a couple of years before Praxis was complete. Jafir would have time to broker the alliance and GCI could complete Praxis. We'd have constant updates because Darrick would report to the ISA and to me."

"Where did Cavanaugh fit into all of this?"

"Cavanaugh was Atlas' secondary on the deal. He was working with me to secure Jafir's agreement."

"But he left weeks before you arrived?"

"One of Zeben's demands was the Kholari diamond. He believed in the legendary powers of the stone. Cavanaugh was dispatched to recover it from a thief in Prague."

"Cavanaugh said he never recovered it."

"Cavanaugh lied. He told me Atlas decided to hide the diamond from everyone, including you and Adam. He wanted to keep it as insurance."

"For what?"

"In case Adam failed. It would be another way to control Zeben. Atlas intended to tell Adam, after the first transaction was finished."

Raleigh stood and walked to the mouth of the cave, staring at the lamplight. "Let's get back to that. The night of the ambush. Adam was supposed to be with you, and he came to see me in the warehouse. They attacked your satellite hut and us. Why?"

"I didn't know it at the time, but the Jafirian government had gotten wind of your activities. But they didn't know you were with the ISA. When they sent soldiers to the satellite hut, one of the men recognized me and took me into custody." Phillip shifted on the mattress, and Raleigh turned at the noise.

Images of her fight with the commandos played in her head. She'd fought hard, but they'd overpowered her in a matter of seconds. "Scimitar soldiers captured me. Not Jafirians."

He explained slowly, "Scimitar was tipped off about the raid. But no one other than Cavanaugh and I knew who you two really were. And I couldn't help because the government didn't believe my story. I couldn't tell them about you two without destroying the mission. And I didn't know who the traitor was, so I kept silent. They locked me up for almost two years."

"Did you escape?"

"I made a deal. I got to Robertsi and told him part of the story. I agreed to infiltrate Scimitar for them, if they'd allow me to do so."

"And you couldn't let the ISA know? We had dozens of agents on the island."

"None of whom knew me. And I didn't know them. They could have sold out to Scimitar or anyone else."

"So you went renegade and decided to bring Scimitar down by yourself?" Raleigh scoffed at the notion. "I thought the maverick behavior was more Merlin's style than yours."

"It was. It is. Last year, I was contacted by Cavanaugh and reactivated. He told me to work out a deal with the Jafirian government and get inside Scimitar."

"Robertsi trusted you that much?"

"He had nothing to lose. By then, I'd been missing for almost two years." His eyes darkened with pain and regret. "My country thought I was dead, and an ISA agent made the deal for me. Cavanaugh has a lot of friends here. With Cavanaugh as Zeben's silent partner, I made some headway with Scimitar and rose through the ranks. Robertsi was ready to form the alliance, and we were running out of time. News of Praxis had already started to leak. Zeben promised to reward anyone who could bring it to him."

"Where does the Kholari fit in?"

"Zeben needed funding, and Cavanaugh knew where the diamond was. He brought it here a few months ago."

"Six weeks," Raleigh mumbled. Six weeks ago, when she'd thought that she caused his death.

"Yes. We met at the warehouse. He brought the schematics for Praxis and the diamond. I was to begin construction."

She remembered the day perfectly. A messenger slipped her a note telling her to come to the marketplace for information on Praxis. She was told to come alone. When she returned to the hotel, Sashu had been waiting for her to tell her about the attack.

"What happened next?"

"I told Cavanaugh I couldn't do this without help. Adam is the only one in our world who can. A few days later, Cavanaugh told me about the tournament. He said that you and Adam had signed up. I offered to rig it for the two of you. He told me to go ahead."

Phillip struggled to his feet. "I wanted to finish this. I want to go home. I miss my life. My friends."

"If you cared so much about friendship, why couldn't you figure out a way to get in touch with Adam? Your 'death' almost destroyed him!"

"I told you, I couldn't at first! Then, when I made contact with Cavanaugh, he instructed me to remain silent."

"Why?"

"Because Adam wasn't with the ISA any longer. You know the rules, Chimera."

Yes, these damned 'Rules of Engagement.' "Have you had contact with Atlas?"

"Only through Cavanaugh." Phillip paused and held up his wrists. "Now, why don't you tell *me* what's going on?"

Raleigh stood in front of Phillip, numbed by the truth. Cavanaugh. Her mentor. Her surrogate father. He'd betrayed her. The rocks in the cave seemed to echo with the news. *I trusted him,* she thought vaguely. *I loved him. Why would he do this to me?* She could feel herself breaking apart. *No, no. It's not true. Maybe Atlas did tell him to hide the diamond. Maybe Civelli lied about the contract. Maybe Phillip is the partner, and he's just trying to confuse me.*

Before Phillip's startled eyes, Raleigh knelt on the cold, damp ground of the cave, her head buried in hands that shook with rage and sorrow. Phillip levered himself up and approached her, as though she might bolt.

"Chimera?" he said softly. "What's going on?"

"Cavanaugh," she whispered, the words ripping through her. "He's the one. The one who ordered the hit on the warehouse and the satellite hut. The one who hired Civelli to kill Adam and me. He stole the Kholari. Atlas just found out you were alive. But we thought you were the traitor." Her voice, a raw, harsh sob, broke over the last words. "Cavanaugh did this. To all of us."

Sixteen

With more questions and answers than she could process and her mind begging for silence, Raleigh opened the hotel room door and stumbled inside. She needed a few minutes to understand. Layers of half truths and falsehoods shadowed her, demanded that she doubt friendships and confidences.

He'd lied to her. Cavanaugh had lied to her.

And the one man who'd been honest with her she'd used to accomplish Atlas' ends—and her own. She was no better than Atlas or Cavanaugh. *And maybe even worse,* her heart cried out.

Raleigh squared her shoulders and dismissed the sting of shame. Right now, her wounded heart and pride would have to wait. If Cavanaugh planned to use her to help him, or if Atlas had suspected the truth, it didn't matter now. What mattered was Praxis and stopping Zeben.

The room was dim, the shutters drawn. *At least I made it back before Adam returned from his meeting with our suppliers,* she thought dully. Perhaps she would have time to decide what to tell him. He had a right to know. But how could she explain her role without losing his trust? The obvious, inevitable answer was that she couldn't. Telling him anything meant telling him all. And that meant the end of whatever had grown between them.

The end of love.

Bone-weary, she set her satchel by the door and reached for the lights.

"Don't bother, Chimera. I'm not certain I want to see your face," Adam said from the recesses of the living room.

She lowered her hand and gathered her defenses. "Of course, I didn't beat you," she said with grim resignation. "Of course not." In defiance, she flicked on the switch, flooding the room with light. Adam stood by the window.

He'd changed clothes. He wore a muted, gold silk tie and tailored black slacks. His jacket was slung across the back of the sofa. His face was impassive. "Going somewhere?" she asked.

"Where were you?" he countered, his tone as forbidding as his expression.

"Out." With careful movements, she made her way across the room and took a seat on the arm of the sofa. She'd already been condemned, but he didn't know the half of her crimes. "You're back early."

"I thought you weren't feeling well." Adam raked her with his somber gaze. "I thought I'd hurt you somehow, last night. I came back to check on you." He pointed to the jacket lying beside her. "To take you out to dinner."

She didn't react to the censure, in spite of the blanket of shame. "That was sweet of you." *Forgive me.*

"But you were gone," he said. He lifted a tumbler from the table and took a deliberate swallow. "Marie said you never returned."

"I changed my mind." *I'm sorry. So sorry.*

Adam continued, as though she hadn't spoken. "I got dressed and waited for you. Then, after a few hours, I started to worry. I thought maybe Zeben and his men had you. Like the last time."

She reached for him then, the movement involuntary and quickly checked. "No, I wasn't with Zeben." *I had no choice. There was no other way.*

"I went to the marketplace. Sashu told me he didn't know where you were. But he was certain Scimitar didn't have you." Adam rolled the tumbler between his hands. "I asked him how he could be so sure."

He stopped speaking and the silence lengthened. Hopeless eyes probed his face for yielding. She saw a vacant hope for an explanation he could trust. She saw the yearning but could offer him nothing but the damning truth. They would play this out, as it had been written. *I won't crumble,* she vowed. *When he takes everything from me, I will survive.* With a negligent shrug and an imperturbable expression, Raleigh asked the question she knew Adam was waiting for and prepared herself for the end. "What did he say?"

Cool. Reserved. Aloof. Adam stared at Raleigh, searching for some hint of the fire he thought he'd seen before. Had the emotion been an act? Was there a real woman beneath the veneer of nonchalance? Last night, he would have sworn there was. But now, as she looked at him with dispassionate eyes, he couldn't be sure. He'd rushed from his meeting to check on her, only to find her gone. With effort, he banked the fury that seethed within. "He told me you had a meeting."

"Yes."

Her breathtaking eyes held his, and not a hint of remorse shone in their chilly, golden depths. So beautiful. So treacherous.

"You took my gun."

"Yes."

The indifferent response spiked his temper and the rage and concern of the past few hours bubbled over. "He said that you'd gone off to avenge Cavanaugh's death. Alone!" He slammed the tumbler to the table, and brandy sloshed over the side. "You lied to me." He made a move toward her, then stopped himself. If he touched her now, he wasn't sure what damage he'd do. "You know who the traitor is. You've known all along. When we found the diamond and the specs, you knew the truth."

"Yes and no."

"Which is it?"

"Yes, I know who the traitor is, but I didn't know until this afternoon." She took a deep breath, still coming to grips with the truth. "Adam, I have something to tell you."

He cut her off with a fist pounded into the table top.

"Why did you bring me here, to Jafir? You and Atlas didn't need me. You had your suspects. And Atlas had you, Chimera, to do his dirty work for him. Why the hell would you bring me back here, make me relive all of this? For fun? For revenge? To pay me back for leaving you here?"

"No," she protested. Unable to remain silent, she walked over to stand before him. "It had to be." She placed a hand on his arm.

Adam flung the offending hand away and took a step back. "Don't touch me," he ordered furiously. "You used me. I want to know why."

Raleigh responded with the bitter truth. "I couldn't have gotten into the tournament without Caine Simons. With Cavanaugh gone, you were our last chance. We needed your help." Pride hardened her expression. "I had to get back inside."

"Why the charade? Couldn't you just tell me what was going on? If you had a suspect, why didn't you tell me who it was?" He stepped closer, hoping to see an answer he could accept. What he saw in her face was icy resolve and an arrogant pride. And maybe a flicker of guilt he could hold on to. A spark of concern he could be convinced was for him.

"I wasn't allowed to."

"Why not?"

"Because you may not have agreed to do it."

"That doesn't make sense. I quit, but I would never let a guilty man go free. If Darrick Josephs was the suspect, I would have taken him down."

Raleigh faced him, the decision made. "And if the suspect was Phillip Turman? What then?"

He flinched as though she'd struck him, and he stumbled into the table.

"Adam?" she said anxiously and extended an arm to catch him. But one look from his steely, murderous eyes halted her. Then the expression evaporated, and Adam Grayson was gone.

Phillip, alive? In an instant, the world tilted on its axis. Then it simply stopped. His hands balled into fists, and he thrust them into his pockets to prevent unforgivable violence. He almost reached for her, to right himself, but he thought her faithless skin would likely burn his soul. Instead, he leaned heavily against the table, dragging in breaths that seemed to scorch his lungs.

"Adam?" Raleigh said gently, frightened by his collapse. "Adam, listen to me."

"Is he alive?" Adam whispered, and he covered his face with his hands. "Is Phillip really alive?" The words were harsh, hopeful, torn from him.

Raleigh closed her eyes, and tears crowded her throat. "Yes. He's alive." She bowed her head, then looked at him squarely. "He's here, in Jafir." She went to her satchel and took out the book. Handing it to him, she explained, "This is the American fable Zeben mentioned. Phillip is the one who's been helping us."

Adam held her look, his eyes a desolate wasteland. "Phillip's alive. How long have you known?"

She wanted desperately to turn away but did not. "Since the day Cavanaugh died." Even now, she couldn't bring herself to speak the awful truth aloud again.

"Liar," he shot back at her, refusing to believe. "How long have you known?" he shouted.

Raleigh winced. "Cavanaugh told me right before he died. I swear I didn't know before."

"So, you knew that night, in the garden?"

"Yes."

"When we made love?"

"Yes. But I couldn't tell you."

"Why not? Was it retaliation for my leaving you? Because the Scimitar soldiers captured you? Was it payback?"

"It was never about revenge against you, Adam."

"What was it then, Raleigh? It had to have been extremely important for you to torment me. What was it?"

Through the acrimony, she heard his plea for an

explanation she couldn't give him. She would keep that last betrayal to herself. "I had my reasons."

"Reasons? What reasons?" Then it struck him, the full absurdity of her reasons. "Orders. You had orders not to tell me. You let me believe my best friend was dead and that I was responsible, all to abide by your precious rules of engagement."

She said nothing.

"Defend yourself, damn you! Tell me it wasn't Atlas' injunction."

Raleigh carefully blanked her expression, revealing no hint of her turmoil. He wanted reasons? *Honor. Duty.* Hollow, empty words now. She had abandoned honor when she plotted to kill his best friend for a man who lied to her. She'd forsaken her duty when she violated Atlas' order to keep Phillip's status a secret. He wanted reasons? Any explanation would only prove her to be both a coward and a fraud because she couldn't finish the deed or abide by the mandate. So, she said nothing.

Adam refused to accept her silence. There had to be a better justification than her blind adherence to regulations. Determined to ferret out the truth, he got to his feet. He approached her and cupped her face in his hands.

He leaned in, inspecting her features intently. There was innocence in the glow of her eyes, courage in the tilt of her chin. He could almost believe in their reality.

But he'd learned, too late, not to believe. She'd taught him well. Yet, his heart refused to accept that it had all been an invention of his mind, a trick of moonlight. If he could only get inside, he would have his reasons. She had hurt him as no woman ever had, and he needed to know why—why she would hurt him, not out of malice, but out of the complete lack of feeling. Temper he could understand, forgive. But her act had been cold, passionless, mean. He had to know.

Compelled by mordant anger and a depraved, unquenchable desire, he covered her soft mouth with his own. Perhaps this, this fire between them, this alone had been real. Insistent, demanding, he moved his lips over hers, seeking entrance. He kept his eyes open to read her reaction.

Desire and longing bloomed inside Raleigh. One last taste, a salve for the lonely nights that stretched before her. On the brink of capitulation, she stared into his eyes. In their ebony depths, she saw expectation. Needs she could never fulfill—commitment, loyalty, reliability.

Phillip's tale proved she didn't engender those feelings in others or possess them herself. She didn't trust other people, and they didn't trust her. The evidence was piling up. Alex, her best friend, didn't know her. Then there was Atlas, with his smoke and mirrors, pitting them against each other. She'd followed blindly and did not think to protect Adam. And Cavanaugh, the man who'd been a father to her, had lied to her. Used her.

When had she ever known love, learned its secrets enough to return it? What she'd learned, what she knew, was betrayal and lies and half-shadowed stories. She couldn't trust, couldn't give. Not even to the man who thought he loved her.

The awareness crushed her, banished any hope. She did not respond but returned his gaze steadily. Breaking the kiss, she hunted for the cold and ice that sustained her, gave her distance from her heart's demise. With deliberate, precise calm, she said coldly, "I had my orders." If her heart broke or her knees quaked, she would not show it.

One long-fingered hand closed around the thin column of her throat. "Last night, when I told you how much I loved you—trusted you—you lay in my arms and let me believe I was holding something worth having. You petty, soulless coward."

Anguish clawed at her, but she refused to yield to the pain. "I am the same woman I always was."

"That's what I'm afraid of." Repulsed, Adam released her. "Where is Phillip?"

She managed to remain upright when he took his touch away. If he stripped pieces of her soul away, she would bear it. "I'll take you to him."

"I don't want anything from you." He stalked over to the door. "I'll find him myself."

Raleigh took a shallow breath, trying to calm the inner tumult. Adam still didn't know the full story.

"Before we go, there's more."

"You've got nothing else to tell me, Chimera," he spat out. "I wouldn't believe a word you said."

"Cavanaugh is Zeben's silent partner. He hired Civelli to kill you. He bombed the warehouse. He's been using Phillip to get Praxis built."

"How do you know?"

"Phillip." She reached for the hotel key she'd laid by the door. "Let's go." She walked over to him and grabbed her satchel. "Come on."

In silence, they headed down to the lobby. Adam spoke to Marie briefly and seconds later had the keys to a car. The black Mercedes purred as he started the car.

"Why don't I drive?" Raleigh asked. "I know where we're going. I promise I'll take you to him." She took his gun from her bag and offered it to him. She doubted he'd allow her to take the wheel without some assurance that he would remain in control. Tenderness and thoughtfulness had been replaced with hatred and mistrust. And that it was justified simply strengthened her resolve to see this end quickly. "If it makes you feel better, you can keep this trained on me the whole time."

Adam glanced at the gun and gave a short laugh, without humor. His next words confirmed her suspicions and her own thoughts. "The only reason I haven't killed you with my bare hands is because I need you to finish this. But don't tempt me."

"Head to the plateau," she said quietly, shaken by his threat. "Stop at the abandoned stalls."

They rode the rest of the way in silence, Adam heading unerringly to the clearing. They soon reached the place Raleigh indicated. Adam got out of the car and waited impatiently for Raleigh to join him. She led him to the cliff's edge and revealed the rope. "Wait for me on the ledge," she told him.

Raleigh followed him down. Midway down the rocky cliff face, her fingers missed a knot and she lost her grip.

She screamed as she fell into space, unable to regain her grip on the rope.

Adam heard her scream and turned in time to see her falling. In seconds, she would hit the ledge and fall into the ocean. He leaped into action and snatched her out of the air. "Thank God," he muttered as he braced them both against the wall, his arms banded tight around her waist, her face tucked into his shoulder. "Are you okay?" he said into her hair, the tiny curls tickling his chin.

Raleigh savored his hold, her hands flattened against his chest. "I'm fine," she said and reluctantly pushed away from him. "Thank you." She briskly uncovered the entrance.

Adam brushed past her and walked into the cave. Dimly lit, the room contained a few items and a lone figure sitting on a mattress. Adam remained at the cave's entrance, obscured by the shadows, afraid to be convinced, to believe.

Then the figure spoke. "Adam?" Phillip rose and stared in disbelief. Then he rushed over to Adam, arms extended in greeting. "My God, Adam, it's you."

"Phillip," Adam said the name carefully, still afraid it was a dream. When Phillip came to a halt in front of him, he embraced him, brother to brother. His best friend was alive and well. Three years of torture ended in a single moment. Then, without a word, he hit Phillip with a hard right across the jaw, the crack of his fist reverberating throughout the cavern. Phillip dropped like a stone to the ground.

"What the hell was that for?" he complained, cradling his mouth. In his joy at seeing Adam, he missed the gleam of anger. Phillip recognized he had a great deal of explaining to do. But first things first. Let Adam expend his deserved rage, then they'd talk. Cautiously, he tried to stand, although his head reeled from the blow. Adam had always packed quite a solid right jab.

"That was for letting me believe you were dead," Adam said as he lifted him to his feet. He steadied Phillip. "But I assume you had a good reason."

"Yes, I can explain." Phillip rubbed his jaw and looked at Adam, just in time to see a left hook flying toward his face. He went down a second time, the echo now ringing in his head. "Come on, Adam!" he grumbled. "That wasn't fair."

"That was for sticking a mole inside GCI." Adam squatted beside him. "Is there anything else?"

"No!" Phillip exclaimed and held his hands up in self-defense. "Didn't Chimera tell you what happened? I did everything but send up flares to let you know what was going on. I rigged the scavenger hunt to give you the diamond and the clue about the riddle. Cavanaugh and Sphinx. I'm disappointed, Adam."

Adam lifted Phillip to his feet. "Why don't *you* tell me?" He spared a derisive glance for Raleigh. "Don't leave anything out." Adam clasped his shoulder. "I've missed you, man."

While Phillip recounted his story to Adam, Raleigh moved to the rear of the cave. The murmur of male voices told its own tale. Occasionally, there was a bark of laughter or a growl of disbelief, but nothing akin to the wooden silence that hovered over Raleigh and Adam. *Adam will forgive Phillip,* she thought without rancor. They had a lifetime of friendship between them to soothe the hostility and soften the deception.

But she and Adam only had two months in a make-believe world, where they hadn't even known each other's real names. And three weeks lived out under the shadow of lies. The first lie had been hers, a lie of omission when she kept Phillip from him. And the final lie was hers also, when he asked her if she loved him, and she had said no.

It was too late to tell him of her feelings, way too late. He wouldn't believe her, anyway. His anger, his hatred would not let him trust the words—no matter what they were.

The saddest part was that she couldn't blame him. Trust was the currency of fools in their world, and he'd gambled on her and lost. She'd lied to him, deceived him, and exploited his sentiment for her own ends.

Besides, she'd never truly trusted him either. Or so she wished. Because that would make the end bearable. If she thought about the secrets she shared with him under the cover of darkness, she'd be lost. It didn't matter that she told him about Cavanaugh and Chance, stories that not even Liz and Alex knew.

Not only did she love Adam Grayson, but she also relied upon him. She had, with her confession, entrusted him with her life, her heart. For once, she trusted another person as much as herself. For a brief time, she was not alone. In those precious moments—in his arms, in his heart—she'd been safe and whole.

Yet, lies had been told and discovered. Lies that would ensure she remained alone. That she could accept. But one deception wasn't hers. Atlas had lied to them both.

Raleigh put her personal feelings on hold. It was time they contacted Atlas and unwound the tangled mess that recovering Praxis had become. *He has a lot to answer for,* she fumed. He was the master who'd moved them around—pawns in a bloodthirsty chess match. They all deserved to hear his reasons for his actions. And she needed to believe that Cavanaugh was innocent.

She set up the video communicator and established a connection.

An ocean away in Washington, Atlas turned on his viewer. "Atlas," he barked.

"Chimera."

Adam and Phillip heard her speak and came to join her. She held a hand up for silence.

Atlas relaxed in his executive chair and munched on a doughnut. "Report."

"Have acquired target. Sphinx in custody at Eagle Point."

"Good work, Chimera." Atlas sat up, a broad smile wreathing his face. "Where is he?"

"Right here, Atlas," Phillip said.

So, Raleigh found him and got him to the cave, Atlas thought. *Alive.* He'd hoped for that, but he hadn't fully expected that Phillip would survive the encounter. But it was a chance he'd had to take. "Good. Good. And Merlin? Does he know about Sphinx?"

"I do now, you conniving son of a bitch." Adam crouched in front of the communicator, his fury now directed at the man on the other side. Phillip's story made sense, especially the double duty Atlas had assigned to Raleigh and Phillip. Forgiving Phillip had been easy, almost unnecessary. Phillip understood how imperative Praxis was. Adam couldn't fault him for protecting it. But Raleigh's betrayal was an entirely different circumstance. No one held her captive, except her rigid code of conduct. "You picked the right woman to set me up, Atlas. She did an excellent job."

Atlas sat up in his chair and dropped the doughnut in his lap. Powdered sugar fell everywhere. As he brushed the offending substance from his slacks, he fumed. He should have known the girl would go and do something like this. "Cat's out of the bag, it would seem. How much do y'all know?"

"The better question is what do *you* know, Atlas," Raleigh challenged. "Is Cavanaugh dead?"

Atlas froze. "You told me he was."

"But you didn't believe me, did you? I never verified his death," Raleigh snapped at him. "You didn't just send me to find Phillip. You sent Adam to find Cavanaugh."

Adam looked at Raleigh in disbelief. "Is that true, Atlas?"

Atlas sounded old and weary when he spoke. "He was the closest thing I've ever had to a best friend. Cavanaugh and me. I didn't want to believe it, but I had to know for sure."

"Why did you suspect Cavanaugh?" Phillip asked.

"There was a message sent to Zeben about a diamond. I knew it was the Kholari. Cavanaugh told me he couldn't find it"—Atlas coughed, interrupting his story—"I had to know for sure."

Raleigh spoke again, without sympathy. "Did you ever think it was Phillip?"

"It was possible." Atlas shook his head. "Didn't know he was innocent. That's why I picked you."

Raleigh ignored his latter comment and held on to her righteous indignation. "You sent me in to do your dirty work? Either turn on Cavanaugh or Phillip?"

"I sent you in to find out the truth. I knew you would. You've got a gift for playing by the rules, Chimera. If Cavanaugh was the mole or if Phillip was, you'd have found out first, acted later. And you'd do your duty. Adam is too headstrong, and Phillip is too cautious. I needed you to solve the puzzle. And you did."

"You manipulated me!"

Atlas' voice frosted over, the Texas drawl thick and lethal. "I'm supposed to, young lady. I'm your boss, and you're my agent. Hell, the three of you are operatives. And you operate at my discretion. That's what you do."

"That doesn't give you the right to use my feelings against me. My emotions are my business. Neither you nor anyone else has a right to make me feel what I don't want to feel!"

"Now, Chimera—"

"Shut up," she raged, on her feet now. She would say this, expunge the demons. "First my father with his cards. He realized I'd take care of us, and I did. Then Cavanaugh. Yes, he gave me a choice, taught me this life. But he had no right to use me! He turned on me and let me believe that he was dead and that I killed him. Because of greed!" She poked an irate finger at the radio, as though Atlas could see her. "And you! You overbearing, sadistic, meddlesome moron. What I feel is *mine.* Not yours. And if you ever try to use me like this again, I quit. And I mean it."

Spinning around, she pinned Phillip. "You could have made contact with Atlas. Me. Verified Cavanaugh's story. Adam grieved for you for three years." Guilt and shame made Phillip lower his head. "Praxis is important, I agree. But so is love. You don't deserve it if you won't take care of it."

She turned back to the radio and encountered Adam's quizzical gaze.

"Nothing for me?" he taunted.

Drained, she said quietly, "No. I'm finished."

"Glad to hear it," Atlas boomed over the speakers. "Don't get too big for your britches, girlie. I am still in charge here." His voice grew hard. "Praxis is more important than any of you, and saving it is my responsibility. You all knew that when you signed on. Don't pretend you didn't. Be as angry with me as you'd like, but remember what we all are. Trained liars and thieves paid to do a job. Usually for the good guys. In the end, that's all that matters."

Phillip decided to break the tension. "Now that we have all the facts, don't you think it's time we captured Zeben and Cavanaugh and got Praxis out of their hands?"

"The delegations arrive tomorrow. Chimera and I are supposed to begin construction in the morning. According to Sphinx, he's the third member of the team. The prototype will take about two days to complete," Adam filled in. "So, we have to act fast."

Atlas heard the message. "So, they go down tomorrow."

"I'll head out today on the ISA Concorde prototype. I'll meet you at the warehouse tomorrow night."

"Agreed."

Seventeen

Raleigh assembled wires, accelerant, and a nitric compound onto a makeshift table in the cavern. She listened to Phillip describe the mansion's layout to Adam but remained isolated by her task.

Adam had not looked at her once since they ended their discussion with Atlas. He'd spoken, but only with caustic commentary or blatant jibes at her expense. Even without the remarks, she could feel the waves of disgust emanating from him whenever she spoke. Was it her impromptu tirade? Or the duplicity of her admonitions to Atlas and Phillip? Perhaps he thought, as she did, that she had little cause to blame them for an act that she, too, was guilty of committing. Treason of the heart.

"Will that give you enough time, Chimera?"

She returned to the conversation, dismayed by her lack of attention. The only way to eliminte Zeben and Cavanaugh and any threat of Praxis falling into his hands would be a simultaneous attack. Phillip explained how far he'd gotten in construction before he'd needed Adam's help. It was imperative that the warehouse that contained Praxis be destroyed. He also told them about a storehouse of weaponry behind the warehouse. Most of the Scimitar guards were stationed at the mansion, with a few men assigned to each post.

Raleigh would rig the warehouse and the storehouse to detonate at the same time. Meanwhile, Adam and Phillip would break into the mansion and apprehend Zeben. Atlas had called in reinforcements, but Adam and Phillip had to capture Zeben first.

The timing of the attacks was crucial, yet she'd missed a substantial portion of the discussion. Such a lapse was inexcusable.

"Enough time?"

"Pay attention, Chimera," Adam snapped at her. "This is no time for daydreams. If you can't handle this, let us know now."

Raleigh stared angrily at Adam, bristling under the harsh charge. He could question her loyalty, but not her work ethic. "I was distracted for a moment. It won't happen again," she responded in clipped tones, her features a cold mask of disdain. Then, with a lightning change, she turned a brilliant, apologetic smile on Phillip. "Could you repeat the question, Sphinx?"

Phillip had been watching Adam watch Raleigh—and vice versa. It didn't take a genius to sense the undercurrents. He suppressed a chuckle and answered, "I said Merlin and I would head into the mansion at seven. If you get the warehouses set up by dusk, we'll have an hour to locate Cavanaugh and Zeben."

"We'll stop construction at five," she added. "During the day, I'll gather the remaining equipment that I'll need. Yes, I should be ready by seven."

"Merlin will radio you once we're in position outside the mansion. But we have to terminate contact when we get inside. Zeben has beefed up his internal monitors. He'll track down any radio communication instantly."

"Will an hour be enough for the two of you?"

"It should be. If he follows his routine, Zeben will be in his study, playing with the Kholari. There are seven guards surrounding his office and twenty who monitor the compound. Luckily, he'll invite us in, so we won't have to subdue those guys."

"You should take my dart gun. At close range, you'll have no problem with deployment."

"Is that what you used on me yesterday?" Phillip asked with a rogue's interest. "Excellent tool. I never knew what hit me."

Raleigh basked in his praise, a welcome balm to Adam's cutting remarks. "I designed it myself," she said almost shyly. "Would you like to see it?"

Phillip walked over to her eagerly. "Of course."

Raleigh reached for her satchel and removed the weapon. "I used a new chemical compound that explodes the casing. The fumes permeate the body immediately."

Phillip sat beside her, leaning forward. "Amazing." Their heads pressed together as they examined the gun. Raleigh's face brightened as she described her invention.

Anger, strong and fierce, flooded Adam. If it resembled jealousy, he didn't acknowledge it. Dark thoughts burned at the base of his skull. How dare she flirt with Phillip? Did she have any scruples at all? One minute, she was orchestrating his death, the next minute, they were old friends.

He thought he knew her, had figured out the mystery of Chimera. Innocent, vulnerable, brave, and capable. He would have sworn he'd seen that and more in her. But like her namesake, the woman he loved was an illusion. Scheming, conniving, duplicitous, and cold. That was the real Raleigh Foster.

He looked over at the two of them. Phillip was measuring the base of the weapon along his hand.

"Does it have a strong recoil?"

Raleigh took his hand to show him the trigger mechanism. "No, because the projectiles are so light. When the trigger is released—"

"Can we get back to work here?" Adam broke in sharply. "We can play show-and-tell later, Sphinx." No, it wasn't jealousy. It was disgust. Soon, she'd enthrall Phillip—just as she had him. And Phillip wouldn't know until too late that the warmth wasn't real. "We're running out of time, and some of us actually care about what we're doing."

With a conciliatory smile for Raleigh, Phillip returned to the crude map he'd drawn of the mansion. "We'll use Chimera's brilliant weapon and render our foes unconscious. Then, we grab Zeben and Cavanaugh and the diamond. The mansion has a series of hidden tunnels." He pointed to one on the map. "We'll take Zeben and Cavanaugh out through here and to the car. By then, the cavalry should arrive and take care of the remaining Scimitar soldiers."

"After they are in custody, the organization falls apart," Raleigh said to Phillip.

He concurred. "Zeben is fiercely intelligent and imaginative, but paranoid. When Zeben is gone, Scimitar is a snake without a head. Crushing the rest of the body won't pose a great problem. The African-Arab Alliance can make it their first order of business."

"What about Cavanaugh?" Adam wondered aloud.

"My guess is that he's in it for the money. He's

never struck me as a zealot. Scimitar certainly won't follow him, if that's your concern," Phillip answered. "Right, Chimera?"

Raleigh nodded her head in mute agreement. Phillip cringed at her expression. "I'm sorry. I forgot."

"It doesn't matter. He brought this on himself."

"Never let loyalty get in the way of self-interest, right, Chimera?" Adam scoffed. "No mercy from you?"

Raleigh didn't respond but instead returned to her work. Phillip punched Adam in the shoulder. "Leave her alone, man."

He said to Raleigh, "We'll finish up, and then Praxis comes on line and Jafir becomes the test site." At her somber expression, he intoned in a mock Texan drawl, "And the world remains safe for democracy." Pleased by Raleigh's responsive laughter, he continued, "All in a day's work, ma'am."

Adam flinched at the sound of her husky laugh, and Phillip smiled to himself. Whatever had gone wrong between them, a spark obviously remained alive. He'd never seen Adam react to anyone the way he reacted to Raleigh. Three years ago, every conversation had been about Chimera. And now, again and again, Adam would start to speak, only to abort the words when he realized they were for Raleigh's benefit. He'd been gone for three long years, but Phillip Turman still knew Adam Grayson. And Grayson was in love. He'd lost three years of his life, and Adam had lost the same time with Raleigh. He would see to it that neither would remain alone because of Scimitar's machinations.

"Adam, will you walk outside with me for a moment?" Phillip rolled up the map and went outside, without waiting for Adam's answer.

After a moment, Adam rose and followed him. "What's up?"

"That's what I wanted to ask you." Phillip took a deep breath. "I needed the fresh air to combat the tension in there." He indicated the cave with his thumb. "What the hell happened between you two?"

Adam stiffened. "Nothing," he said tautly. "Is that all?"

"I've been gone for three years, Adam, but I've known you a lot longer. You were in love with her then and you love her now. Why the animosity?"

Staring at Phillip incredulously, Adam mocked, "Why the animosity? She lied to me, Phillip. About you, about this mission. You don't think that warrants a bit of anger?"

"Sure," Phillip placated, "but Atlas explained her reasons. She had orders to keep silent. Plus, she planned to kill me. She couldn't exactly share that with you."

"You think it's okay that she planned to kill you? Maybe you've been working with Zeben and Cavanaugh a bit too long."

Phillip shrugged good-naturedly. "It's the way our world works. I'd have done the same thing. I can't fault her for it."

"I can," Adam replied stubbornly.

"And me? Do you hate me as well?"

"Of course not! You were trying to help me. Without Scimitar's help and then Atlas', you'd never have gotten Praxis into Jafir. Or Zeben and Cavanaugh out of it."

"Why is my crime so different from Raleigh's? We both deceived you about the same thing. I did it to protect Praxis. She did it to protect you."

Adam took a step back. "What do you mean? She

wasn't looking out for me. At best, she was making up for other imagined crimes."

"If she'd told you that I was alive and was the traitor, what would you have done?" Phillip asked.

"I would have exonerated you."

"And if I *had* been the traitor?"

Adam didn't speak for a long moment. "I don't know."

"Neither did she. So, she didn't make you decide."

"You don't know that's what she was thinking."

"And you don't know it wasn't."

Adam turned away from Phillip to look out over the ocean. "I've fallen in love with her twice, Phillip. I don't think I can do it again."

They stood on the ledge for a while longer, and then Phillip patted Adam's shoulder and reentered the cave. Raleigh lay on the air mattress, her eyes closed. She was a beauty, Phillip thought to himself, despite the lines of strain on her face. Adam would be a fool to lose her. He knelt in front of her to wake her.

Sensing someone's presence, Raleigh sat up abruptly. Ducking her head, she muttered, "I'm sorry. I was resting for a minute."

Phillip stood and turned away. "It's fine," he said. "You had a long day yesterday. And a very busy morning."

The embarrassment grew stronger at Phillip's innocent reminder of how she'd spent the night before. "I've got everything I need," she told him. "We can go whenever you're ready."

"Let's head back up." Phillip briefly squeezed Raleigh's shoulder and went to retrieve the map. "I'll go to the top first and hide in the car. You two can follow in a minute or so. Drop me off at the warehouse."

"How will you explain your disappearance?" Adam questioned. "Two guards were wounded, and you've been missing for almost eight hours."

"Three guards," Phillip corrected. "Chimera had to take out one on the upper level."

"Three."

"I'll tell them that some disgruntled competitors thought to kidnap me. Might as well blame it on Civelli."

"He'll buy it?"

"No reason not to."

One by one, they ascended the cliff face. They arranged to rendezvous at the warehouse in the morning, after their meeting with Zeben. At the hotel, Marie met them in the lobby.

"I hope you enjoyed your sightseeing, Mr. Simons," Marie purred with a speculative gleam in her eyes.

"It was very . . . enlightening," Adam said.

Raleigh stood at his side, waiting passively. *We are still supposed to be lovers,* she reminded herself. *Even if he can't bear to touch me.*

"I'm tired, Caine," she murmured. "It's time for bed." Raleigh curled her fingers around his forearm and tugged him toward the elevator. "Good night, Marie."

"Bon nuit," Marie replied.

Once inside the room, Raleigh headed for the bedroom to check the scrambler. Adam inspected the one in the living room, then went to the bedroom. Raleigh was gathering her toiletries.

"Going to bed so soon?" he taunted.

Raleigh ignored him and closed the bathroom

door. She quickly showered and changed. As she walked into the room, a cloud of steam followed.

Adam inhaled the scent—Raleigh's scent. She folded her clothes and then pulled a blanket and sheet from the bed. Moving to the door, Adam cut her off and caught hold of her arm. "Where are you going?"

She yanked at her arm once. Unable to jerk it free, she subsided. "I'm going to the sitting room. To sleep."

"The bed is in here," he pointed out. "You sleep here."

"You *can't* be serious," she protested.

Adam ran an insulting finger down the center of her throat. "Deadly serious, Andrea."

Her temper flared at the use of her alias. She tossed her head back, summoning the ice she needed to coat her words. "The game is over. There is nothing in here for me."

Fury, ripe and vicious, bloomed in midnight-black eyes. Raleigh knew he was enraged, hurt. But she hadn't known his emotions were so dark, so intense. Fear and desire crept along her spine, and she prepared to bolt. "Let me go."

"Not yet," he whispered as he slid his hands up to frame her face. He could feel the rage, eating him alive. He could feel the love, tearing him apart. He gave in to both. "You can't run away from me, Raleigh. I won't let you." He lowered his mouth to hers. For measureless moments, they clung to each other, mouth to mouth, heart to heart.

Enthralled by the dark promise in his kiss, Raleigh offered a last protest. "You don't want me. You can't."

"I can," he said as he pulled the strap of her gown down her arm. "I do."

She leaned away from him, searching his eyes. This last time could not be about revenge. If it was, she would walk away. "Is this punishment? Or forgiveness?"

"Yes," he answered, reaching for her lips.

It will be enough, she decided, meeting his kiss.

In the quiet shadows of the room, he drew her into his embrace. Tonight, he would cherish her. No speed, no urgency. He would tell her with his body what his mind would not allow him to say. Where her throat curved into her shoulders, he traced light circles of heat. Where her breasts rose into deep brown peaks, he gently kissed the proud crests. With restraint, he uncovered the silken planes of her body, the beautiful curves. Slowly, tenderly, he loved her as only he could in the darkness.

Raleigh tasted the tenderness, confused. She felt the care, uncertain. Gone was the fire, the insistence of the night before. No matter how she touched him, stroked his naked flesh, he still lingered at the soft line of her waist. If she tugged at his head, he refused to quicken the pace of his kiss. Flames smoldered between them, their fire banked by patience.

Gently, he protected them and readied her, their bodies fitted as though they were one. Softly, he entered her, their hearts beating in unison. Easily, they slipped over the edge, their souls united for that time.

Later, in the darkness, Raleigh moaned restlessly. "I couldn't do it. I'm sorry. No more blood," she pleaded to an invisible audience.

Adam woke at the first cry and quickly gathered Raleigh to his side. Her breathing was erratic as she thrashed on the mattress. "Raleigh, wake up. Darling, it's only a nightmare."

She moaned again, oblivious to Adam's entreaty.

"Cavanaugh, I'm sorry. I couldn't hurt Adam again. Not even for you."

Adam stared at her, her confession piercing his bitter heart. "Raleigh, darling, come on. Wake up."

Suddenly, her eyes flew open, and she gripped his shirt. "Chance? Cavanaugh? I can't do it again. No more blood."

"Raleigh, it's me. Adam." One hand stroked her hair, and the other covered her hands clinging to his shirt. "It's okay. It was just a dream."

The dregs of her nightmare faded, leaving Raleigh agitated and confused. "Adam?"

He caressed her cheek softly, soothingly. "You were having a nightmare. Everything is okay."

"Okay," she repeated, sinking into his warmth.

Adam remained awake, stroking her hair. Sleep never came.

Throughout the morning, Raleigh, Phillip, and Adam worked side by side. Adam's suppliers had come through. Zeben accepted Phillip's tale of ambush and introduced the three partners to one another. Adam dismantled Praxis, jamming its circuits and disassembling the pods, trying to look busy. While he worked, Phillip began routing Scimitar's funds to other accounts. By the end of the night, Scimitar would have empty coffers, no weapons, and a deposed leader. Sooner than they expected, the sun began to set. Phillip made arrangements for a guard to escort them to the mansion, leaving only two guards in the warehouse.

She'd spent the day fashioning a remote controlled explosive that she could detonate from the warehouse. All that remained was to get into the storehouse to plant the small box. She'd set the first explosive, return to the warehouse, and touch off both explosions. The warehouse would go up in stages, with three medium-sized charges set around the ground floor and one upstairs. She needed to be at the warehouse to make sure the Praxis prototype was obliterated.

As she walked them to the door, Phillip took her hand. "Thank you," he said quietly.

"For what?"

"For trusting Adam's judgment and not killing me when you had the chance." He smiled at her, man to woman, compelled to soothe the tension in her eyes. "He'll learn his lesson. He can't afford to lose you."

Adam approached from behind Phillip, and Raleigh stepped away, her hand still in his. Her answering smile was heartbreakingly sad. "He's learned his lesson. He can't afford to love me." She released his hand. "Take care of him."

"Everything is set," Adam said as he reached them. "We need to get going."

"One hour." Phillip read his watch. "Synchronize timepieces," he quipped.

Adam didn't smile. He didn't want to leave Raleigh here alone, but it would take two of them to get into the mansion. "We meet back at the hotel, okay?"

"I'll be fine." Raleigh nodded to both of them. "Go on. This is what I do."

The two men left the room, and Raleigh headed back to the table. Behind her, a hand clutched her arm and spun her around. A hot, hard kiss engulfed her, and she held on to Adam with stunning desperation.

"Be careful," he instructed. Then he walked away. He slid into the car beside Phillip, and they drove to Zeben's compound.

The wrought-iron gates swung open at the guard's command. Phillip circled the house and guided the car to the side carport. The tunnel would end at the rear of the house, and they would carry Zeben to the car.

"Mr. Frame. Mr. Simons," Marie greeted them as they entered the house. "Where is Ms. DeSalle?"

"At the warehouse. She's quite conscientious about her work," Phillip replied.

Adam looked around the foyer. Three guards. He smiled at Marie and bent to kiss her cheek. Moving away, he asked, "Is Zeben in?"

"In his study, I believe. He is quite anxious to hear how the work is proceeding."

"Then, by all means, let us report." Adam accepted the hand she extended. She led them down the hallway to the west wing, where two more men stood watch. Zeben protected his home better than his weapons, Adam noticed. At the entrance, Marie stepped back. "He would like to see you in private."

A uniformed guard opened the door and motioned them into the anteroom that led to Zeben's study. Phillip had been right about the number of guards protecting him. Adam and Phillip approached the study door and knocked. The door swung open.

"Mr. Frame and Mr. Simons. It is good to see you again," Zeben greeted them. He sipped at a glass of white wine and dabbed his mouth with his handkerchief. "Please sit."

"This isn't a social call, Zeben," Adam said as Phillip circled around from the opposite side. "Where is Cavanaugh?"

"Who?" Zeben asked, setting the glass on the bar. "I do not know a man named Cavanaugh."

"What about Ethen Rhodes? Do you know him?"

"Mr. Rhodes and I are acquainted, yes. What matter is it of yours?"

"Where is he?" Adam demanded. The room, the conversation, didn't feel right. Zeben was too hesitant, as if waiting for a signal.

"He is inspecting your work now, I believe. I sent him to the warehouse." Zeben smiled contemptuously. "That is, I believe, where the fair Ms. DeSalle is now."

"No," Adam whispered before Zeben spoke again.

"My men should have her now. Ethan explained his dilemma. It is a shame you three will not be here to witness the greatest triumph of Scimitar. Or that you, Mr. Simons, will never see your masterpiece in operation." With that, he pressed a button by the bar. "Such a shame."

"Not quite," Adam muttered as he charged the older man. Phillip moved to the panel leading to the tunnels. The door to the room flung open, and guards streamed in.

Adam detonated the miniature smoke bomb Raleigh had given them and shoved Zeben toward the tunnel. Shots fired above their heads. "Move, Phillip, move!"

Raleigh trekked across the rocky ground leading back to the warehouse. Planting the bomb had been simple. A diversionary light show gave her ample time to put the box in place. She patted the remote in her pocket. She'd retrieve the blueprints from the warehouse, then set off the fireworks.

She readjusted the strap on her satchel and was reaching for the warehouse door when she noticed a Range Rover sitting off to the side. As she prepared to flee, a heavy hand covered her mouth. She kicked at her assailant, but other hands grabbed her hands and legs. They carried her into the warehouse and dumped her at Cavanaugh's feet.

Gallantly, he reached down to help her stand. "Raleigh." Cavanaugh brushed a hand down her hair. "Why didn't you do as you were supposed to?"

Raleigh shifted, and his hand fell away. "What was that, Cavanaugh?" she asked blandly, deciding to save her struggles for later as she tamped down the anger boiling in her veins.

"Tell Atlas about Phillip and stay out of this! I've worked hard to keep you clean, Raleigh." He looked at her, then fumbled for a cigarette. "Why couldn't you just stay away?"

"Because you taught me better," she said quietly. "You taught me loyalty and sacrifice. I came back to avenge you." She twisted her lips into a mirthless smile. "I wanted to make up for deserting you. Isn't that ironic?"

"Deserting me?" Cavanaugh lit the tip and watched the red ember glow. "What are you talking about?"

"That day, when I snuck off to meet a contact," she explained, slipping back into their familiar pattern. "I left you to face Scimitar alone."

Cavanaugh dragged his free hand through his hair. "I set you up, Raleigh. I sent the message for you to leave. You weren't supposed to follow me."

"Sashu thought you were in danger. He told me

where to find you." *Can a heart break if it's already broken?* she wondered. "You were dying."

"The soldiers you killed, they were from the Jaffirian secret police. Not Scimitar."

"No." Her lips trembled, and she raised a hand to her mouth. "You let me kill innocent men?"

"You weren't supposed to be there," he protested. "I tried to save you. You must believe me."

Raleigh felt herself crumbling, pity and love and loyalty binding her to him. "Why did you do it, Cavanaugh? Was it money? Power?"

"Two hundred million for Praxis and Grayson," he answered simply. "Twenty-eight years of this Raleigh. Of bad versus evil, of gray versus gray. There are no lines, no right and wrong. And we're the worst of them all. We pretend to help when all we do is prop up a regime or destroy a fledging revolution. For what? To do it again tomorrow?"

"We save lives. We stop wars."

"We take lives. We start wars. And for what? We can't have families, we can't have friends. What did I ever have with the ISA?"

A strangled sob caught in her throat. "I thought you had me."

"Raleigh," Cavanaugh began, reaching for her.

"Don't touch me!" she shouted as she backed away. "What about the prison, Cavanaugh? Were you a part of that?"

His face flooded with crimson shame. "They made me tell them where you were when I didn't turn over the diamond. The explosions were a warning. You had time to leave." Blue eyes dropped away from her own. "I got you out as soon as I could."

"Will you let me go now?" Fear still skidded along her spine, but it didn't matter. She knew his answer.

"I can't. Zeben won't let me." He crushed out the cigarette stub. "He won't pay me until I deliver you and the men."

"I never knew you were so weak. So pathetic." Sweat beaded his brow as he lit another cigarette. "I won't help you kill them."

Impotent with rage and embarrassment, he shouted, "You will tell me what I want to know!" He slammed his fist into the table and gestured for the guards. Four men surrounded her, guns drawn. "Where are Grayson and Turman? I must know!"

"I won't tell you," she retorted calmly.

"Don't make me hurt you! If you don't tell me, you will die," he said, almost apologetically.

Raleigh smiled then, a cold, dangerous smile. "And you will join me." She stared at the stranger who had once been her mentor. "I've set the building to explode. On my command. You try to kill me, and I'll detonate it before I die. Or we can walk out of here together."

"You're bluffing," Cavanaugh scoffed, but his eyes darted around the room, nervously.

Raleigh held her gaze steady. "You know me, Cavanaugh. You know I don't joke about my bombs." She folded her hands in her lap, within reach of the remote. "You decide."

"I don't believe you," Cavanaugh announced.

Raleigh pressed the first button and said, "Detonate one." The voice activation was a bluff, but the explosion wasn't. The first charge blew off the sidewall.

Cavanaugh stared at her in disbelief, then lunged. Reading his intent, Raleigh rolled out of his path, and he fell into the chair. She scrambled to her feet in time to confront one of the guards.

Cavanaugh roared at the astonished guards, "Kill her."

The man drew his gun. Raleigh slashed down with her arm, sending the gun flying.

With a loud boom behind them, the warehouse door crashed open. Police officers filled the room, with Adam, Phillip and Atlas leading the charge.

Cavanaugh ran for the door leading to the second floor. Raleigh sprinted after him. She tackled him at the door. Straddling him with his arms pinned to his sides, she closed her fingers around his throat. "How could you?" she demanded. Cavanaugh gasped for air and tried to buck her off. "I trusted you!" she sobbed.

"Raleigh," said Adam, gently.

Raleigh's head whipped around at the sound of his voice. "Go away," she panted. "Leave me alone."

At that moment, Cavanaugh flipped her over and pulled his gun. Before he could fire a single shot, Adam fired first. Cavanaugh collapsed on Raleigh, stunned.

"I'm sorry, Raleigh. I tried to save you," he gasped. Red bloomed on his chest as his life seeped away. Phillip and Adam rolled the body away. Phillip quickly checked for a pulse. "He's gone."

Adam gathered a frozen Raleigh into his arms and held her against him, impossibly close.

"Why?" she cried into his shirt. "Why?"

"It wasn't your fault, baby," Adam whispered into her hair. "You didn't do this. He did."

Raleigh remained cradled in Adam's arms. Below them, Atlas directed the teams to confiscate Praxis and take the Scimitar soldiers into custody.

After the storm of grief subsided, Raleigh unwound her arms from Adam's waist and moved away from him. Nothing had changed. She summoned her most professional voice. "So, now what?"

Phillip answered with a comforting hand on her shoulder. "Zeben will rot in a Jafirian jail for several lifetimes, and Praxis will come home with us." Phillip shook his head in wonderment. "I'm going home. *Home.*"

Raleigh covered his hand with her own and gave him a tremulous smile. "Yes, I guess it *is* time to go home."

She looked at Adam. She hesitated, waiting for a sign that last night had not been a good-bye. But he said nothing. "Atlas will want my report. Then I'll make flight arrangements when we get to the hotel."

"I'm going to head out of here tonight," Adam said quietly. "You two are welcome to come with me."

Raleigh shook her head. A clean break was better. "I need to stay here and wrap up."

Adam didn't try to persuade her. "Phillip?" he asked.

"I'm not staying here a moment longer than necessary."

"I'll arrange the charter." Adam looked over Raleigh's head, unable to make eye contact. "I'll get my things from the room."

Was it possible to lose everything all at once? "Whatever."

An officer approached them, speaking in accented English. "Ms. DeSalle?"

"Yes," Raleigh said.

"Will you come with me?"

"Of course." Raleigh gave Phillip a brief, hard hug and walked away.

Phillip thumped Adam on the shoulder. "Don't be a fool, Adam."

"This can't work, Phillip. I can't do this."

"It was your world once."

"Then I met her, and I lost everything. I don't know how to trust her."

"Liar," Phillip snorted. "Don't do this, Adam. To either one of you. Go to her."

He walked up to her, just as she finished with the officer. "Raleigh, what do you want?"

"I don't know, Adam."

Remembering Phillip's words in the cave and their time together the previous night, Adam cupped her face in his hands. He would offer himself one more time and trust that she wouldn't betray him. "I love you, Raleigh. Do you love me?"

The truth trembled on her tongue, but fear kept her silent. Fear of disappointing him, of hurting him. What did she know of love? She opened her mouth to speak, then closed it again.

Adam pressed a gentle kiss to her mouth to silence the words that never came. "Good-bye, Raleigh. For a moment, I'd forgotten what a brave and loyal coward you were. I thought you didn't trust me enough to love me. But it's not me. You don't trust yourself. I do love you, Raleigh, but I won't beg for you." Then, he turned and walked away, out of the warehouse.

Eighteen

Washington in the fall was awash with bustling students, harried politicians, and residents struggling to survive from day to day. Raleigh watched the passersby at evening time, her mind numb. She'd been this way for four weeks, since her return from Jafir. Atlas had accepted her request for a leave of absence without argument. Obviously, he knew that anything he said would only push her further away. As any wounded animal did, she'd retreated to lick her wounds. But the nights grew longer, and the pain rarely eased.

A knock sounded at the door, the bang insistent, pervasive. She contemplated not opening it, certain of what awaited her.

"You look like hell, Raleigh," Alex announced as she sailed past her into the living room. Her friend's tall frame was thin to the point of gaunt. Dark shadows dulled her amber eyes, but the look gave her an air of romantic misery. "Of course, you looked like hell last week, too."

"Good to know I can always count on you for support, Alex," Raleigh muttered as she shut the door. She was not in the mood for company, particularly Alex's brand of effervescence. The woman had an endless supply of energy.

"You can." Alex replied. "For exactly four weeks. Today is the beginning of week five." Alex headed to the kitchen for a Coke. Raleigh trailed behind her.

"What are you talking about?"

"Your depression over Adam Grayson. It ends today." Alex opened a cupboard. "Raleigh, you have no food here. What am I supposed to eat?"

"The food at your place, maybe?" Raleigh rudely closed the cabinet, hoping Alex would take the hint.

Alex shrugged and returned to the refrigerator. A box of leftover Chinese food beckoned. She snagged the carton and sat at the table. "Can you hand me a fork?"

Exasperated, Raleigh retrieved a fork and gave it to her. "That was supposed to be my dinner tonight."

"Nope. Tonight you're dining out." Alex dumped her purse's contents onto the table. A slender envelope finally emerged. "These are your plane tickets. Your flight leaves at seven."

"I'm not going anywhere, Alex. Definitely not tonight." Raleigh pushed the tickets back to Alex without looking at them.

"These babies are nonrefundable. And, because I am a starving artist, you know I can't afford to lose the money," Alex cajoled over a mouthful of lo mein. She shoved them back at Raleigh.

Raleigh shot her a fulminating glare. All she wanted was to mourn in peace. "First of all, you're always eating my food, so you can't be starving. And you have a trust fund, Alex. You could buy the airline."

"I'm on a budget this month." Alex finished the noodles and drained the rest of her Coke. She propped her elbows on the table. "I never took you for a coward, Raleigh."

Alex's accusation echoed Adam's parting shot. "Prudence and cowardice are not the same things." She picked up the empty carton and threw it into the trash.

"You're afraid, honey. That's why you've been sitting in this apartment alone for almost a month." Alex took a slim hand into hers. "What are you so afraid of?"

"That I can't do it," Raleigh whispered shakily. "That I don't know how to love."

"Bull," Alex snapped.

"You've told me yourself what a horrible friend I am. I don't share. I don't try."

Alex shook her head. "I was angry. You're a wonderful friend with a secret life. A life he can be a part of."

"He won't. Alex, I don't know how to love him."

"Did you even try?" Alex asked.

Raleigh sat in silence. "Why does it matter?" she asked finally.

"Because you love him, and it's tearing you apart," Alex said fiercely. "I bet he doesn't even know how you feel."

Raleigh shrugged. "There was no reason to tell him."

"There was every reason. But, you probably didn't trust him enough."

"I trust him!" Raleigh protested. "He knows that!"

Alex scoffed. "How? Telepathy?"

"Don't make jokes, Alex."

"I'm not kidding. You don't talk to people, Raleigh. You won't tell us how you feel, what you want. And if some brave heart dares to ask, more than likely, you'll lie. But, as one such intrepid soul, I know that this is worth it. You're worth it."

Raleigh smiled, then shook her head. "But what if it doesn't work? What if I let him down?"

"Shouldn't he get to decide? And what if he lets you down? Love is a partnership, Raleigh."

"I know that—"

"Do you? Then, why are you here while he's in Atlanta?" Alex picked up the tickets and pressed them into her hand. "You love him. Trust yourself enough to believe in him."

Raleigh took a deep breath and stared at the tickets. "What if he doesn't love me any more?"

"Then he's a fool who doesn't deserve you, anyway," Alex said firmly. "Now go pack a bag and come on. My car is double-parked."

"I'm fine, Mom. Just tired." Adam rubbed at the headache that had taken up residence at the base of his skull. For more than a month now, it had laid in wait, ready to pounce whenever he thought of her.

"You've missed family dinner twice now, Adam. That's not like you." Carolyn Grayson pushed a little harder, certain that the truth behind her son's absence would come flying out. "Is it the business? Praxis?"

One more bitter reminder. "No. Everything is under control. Jafir did the first demonstration test a couple of days ago. The results were spectacular. And the alliance seems to be holding." Phillip had been there to witness their triumph. Even Atlas made an appearance. Only Raleigh was missing.

Carolyn tried a more direct tack. "If it's not the business, then it must be personal."

"I missed dinner. I won't do it again," Adam conceded, purposely ignoring her meaning.

"If it is something personal, you know you can still talk to us."

"Yes, I know, Mom. But there's nothing you can do about this." The headache was sticking pointy claws into the back of his head now.

"I can listen," Carolyn said quietly.

Adam settled deeper into the couch. Maybe he just needed to talk it out, and then she'd lose her hold on him. "Essentially, I'm in love with this woman, and she doesn't love me."

"Impossible," Carolyn countered with maternal loyalty.

Adam chuckled despite his melancholy. "It is quite possible, Mom. She walked away from me and hasn't looked back."

"Did you two fight?"

"Always."

"Was that the problem?"

"No. The problem was trust. I trusted her. She didn't trust me. Of course, I didn't *always* trust her, but I had good reason."

"Did she have reason not to trust you?" Carolyn loved her son, but she also knew him. He was honest and good and a bit too quick to condemn. He'd never really learned to see shades of gray.

"I did nothing to make her doubt me."

"But you could doubt her?"

"It's not the same thing."

Carolyn smiled into the phone but kept her voice level. "When it comes to being in love, it's always the same thing. If you can't accept all of her, you don't want her."

"She didn't even give me a chance to find out," Adam argued.

"Did she disappear?"

"Well, no."

"Then what's your excuse?"

Adam conceded defeat. "I don't have one. You know, the business world lost a lot when you retired, Mom."

"But now I can dedicate all of my time to my silly children. Go get Raleigh, son."

"How'd you know her name?"

"I'm your mother. I know all. You can have the jet fueled and ready in an hour."

"I'll think about it."

"Don't wait too long. You just might lose her for good."

"I love you, Mom."

"I love you, too."

Adam hung up the phone and turned on the stereo. Then, the doorbell rang. He opened the door—and came face to face with Raleigh.

Raleigh. Here. Was he dreaming? "What are you doing here?" he asked, his mind wiped clean.

She stood stiffly in the doorway, as beautiful and distant as ever. "May I come in?" Without waiting for his answer, she moved past him into the apartment. "I got here as soon as I could."

"You came as soon as you could?" he repeated dumbly. He clenched his hands by his sides, to stop himself from touching her. But he wanted to touch her. Instead, he asked, "What are you talking about?"

Could his voice be any colder? she wondered. "I'm talking about us," she explained tersely. "Sit down, please." Maybe he'd listen to her, hear her. She kept her expression impassive, the better to shield herself when the rejection came.

Adam started to sit, then stopped. He stood up again, ramrod straight, and glared at Raleigh. She had a lot to answer for. Four weeks with no word. And if she was here to tell him good-bye again, he'd rather hear it on his feet. "No. Say what you came to say."

Her heart lurched as she read the forbidding expression on his face. She twisted her fingers together behind her back, knotting them tight. This wouldn't be easy, but it would be right. "I had to make sure you understood, Adam," she began.

He knew it was a trap, but he dove right in. "Understood what, Raleigh?"

"Why I lied to you."

She's here to explain, Adam thought. Not to tell him she loved him. Not to come back to him. He stared over her head at a painting on the wall, seeing nothing. She needed closure, and his was the next name on her list. Disappointment enveloped him. "There's nothing to explain. You thought you were doing your job." He walked to the door, grasped the knob. "Thank you, anyway."

Raleigh watched him open the door, her mouth a mutinous line. *The last time I walked away, I thought nothing could ever hurt as much,* she thought. But watching him prepare to send her away, she knew she'd been wrong. She froze in his low settee, unable to move as the pain of loss ripped through her once more.

Adam saw only the shadows he attributed to lack of sleep or a hard case. "Go away, Raleigh. Please. You have nothing new to tell me."

Raleigh squared her shoulders. She would finish it.

Even if he rejected her, she would know that she tried. "Maybe I do. Maybe I didn't say everything the last time."

Was this about Cavanaugh? Adam had searched for guilt about what he'd done, but he knew that if Raleigh's life were in danger, he'd do it again. "I'm sorry Cavanaugh betrayed you. He fooled us all. But, I can't apologize for shooting him," he said defensively. "He would have killed you without a second thought."

"This isn't about him," Raleigh replied softly, her eyes shuttered.

She can't bear to look at me. "Is there anything else?" Adam asked as he turned away to pour himself a drink. It didn't matter. He couldn't stand to see the condemnation in her eyes.

She couldn't look at him, lest he see the love in her eyes. But, as she peered up at him, she saw the flicker of doubt. Raleigh went to him then, taking his hands. If she went down, it would be in glorious flames. "And if I want to tell you that I love you? What then? Or that I need you? Will you still make me leave?"

"Is that all you want to tell me?" His heart knocked against his ribs, but he was afraid to believe.

"What more do you want?"

Adam swallowed his hope. She said nothing about trust. "The one thing you can never give me."

"What else do you want, Adam?" She gripped his arms, forcing him to face her. "Before you make me leave, tell me what you want. Give me that much, at least."

"I want your trust!" He broke away from her, turning to the window. "You don't trust me, Raleigh.

You never have. It wasn't simply the secret about Phillip. It was why you didn't tell me."

"I had my orders," she started, then stopped. She'd come to give him the truth. All of it. "No, the truth was that I wanted my revenge. And I couldn't trust you to stay out of the way."

Adam sighed, acknowledging defeat. "Thank you for that much at least."

"Is that all you want from me?" she asked, her voice trembling.

He heard the quaver. She was worth one last chance. They were. But he couldn't let her disappoint him again. "No, that's not all. I love you, Raleigh. Four times now, I've told you how I feel. Have you ever trusted me enough to give me anything to hold on to? With you, even 'I love you' is a question. There are no rules of engagement for love, Raleigh. It's all up to you." Adam turned back to her then, a mute appeal in his eyes. *Say something, anything, to make this real.*

Somewhere deep in her heart, she heard his plea. This time, the risk would be hers. Could she take the chance? She took a deep breath, "I do trust you. And you were right. It's *me* I don't trust. Look at my past, Adam. I'm no good at this, loving people. It doesn't work. But I want it to. With you." She cupped his face in her hands, her fingers shaking. "I love you, Adam Grayson. And I trust you with my heart. With my life. I always have. I always will. I love you, Adam."

He held her then, searching for hesitation. "Do you love me enough to marry me?"

"I do."

"To share your life with me?"

"Yes."

"I love you, Raleigh Foster."

With gentle hands, she drew his mouth down to cover hers. Against his lips, she whispered her vow. "And I love you, Adam Grayson. Forever. Always."

Dear Readers,

For my first novel, I wanted to combine two of my favorite plot elements: intrigue and romance. Raleigh Foster is the woman I wanted to be when I was fifteen—a brilliant spy with an air of mystery and nerves of steel. Adam Grayson is the man I wanted to fall in love with when I was eighteen—a smart, sexy man with ambition, sensitivity, and a dangerous streak. Ten years later, having not been recruited by the CIA, I decided that if I could not live a double life, I could write it. The ISA was an invention of my espionage fantasies of youth. My chemist friend Darrick Williams and my own work in environmental justice gave me the idea for Praxis, and Rules of Engagement was born.

However, writing the romance of Raleigh and Adam was a bit of a special operation itself. Her dark past, his deep suspicions, and the lies between them were lethal pitfalls when the target was love. So, I plotted my strategy—rekindling an old flame—and used the secret weapons of humor and partnership and trust. The result, I am happy to report, is mission accomplished!

I would love to hear what you think of *Rules of Engagement*. Please e-mail me at selena_montgomery@hotmail.com or write to me at P.O. Box 77771, Atlanta, GA 30357-1771, and I will be happy to reply.

For my next assignment, I am looking for the right man for Raleigh's best friend, Alex Walton. I will keep you posted on my progress.

Yours,

Selena Montgomery

COMING IN JUNE 2001 FROM ARABESQUE ROMANCES

__THROUGH THE FIRE
by Donna Hill 1-58314-130-8 $5.99US/$7.99CAN
After a devastating tragedy left her convinced she'd never love again, successful songwriter Rae Lindsay took refuge in the only thing that still brought her comfort: her music. But when Quinten Parker walked into her life, Rae suddenly found her peaceful solitude threatened—along with her heart.

__UNDENIABLY YOURS
by Jacquelin Thomas 1-58314-131-6 $5.99US/$7.99CAN
For two long years after the devastating plane crash, undercover agent Matthew St. Charles mourned the loss of his beautiful Kaitlin—and the searing passion he could never get enough of. But just as he finally decided to start living again, he discovered that she was alive and living in Mexico with his bitterest enemy.

__THREE TIMES A LADY
by Niobia Bryant 1-58314-165-0 $5.99US/$7.99CAN
A single father with five children, Jordan Banks doesn't have time for a personal life. Yet when his kids plot to pair him with the new next-door neighbor, Mia Gordon, it doesn't take long for Jordan to discover what he's been missing. Now all he has to do is convince Mia to take on a new venture—one that includes a ready-made family and a man who loves her.

__LOVE AT LAST
by Rochunda Lee 1-58314-211-8 $5.99US/$7.99CAN
Casey James decides she can make a difference in a child's life by volunteering in the Big Brothers and Sisters of America. Although she is committed to helping nine-year-old Christie, she still has an empty place in her heart. Can Albert, Christie's divorced father, be exactly what Casey has been missing?

Call toll free **1-888-345-BOOK** to order by phone or use this coupon to order by mail. ALL BOOKS AVAILABLE JUNE 1, 2001.
Name ____________________
Address ____________________
City ____________ State ________ Zip ________
Please send me the books I have checked above.
I am enclosing $________
Plus postage and handling* $________
Sales tax (in NY, TN, and DC) $________
Total amount enclosed $________
*Add $2.50 for the first book and $.50 for each additional book.
Send check or money order (no cash or CODs) to: **Arabesque Romances, Dept. C.O., 850 Third Avenue, 16th Floor, New York, NY 10022**
Prices and numbers subject to change without notice. Valid only in the U.S.
All orders subject to availability. **NO ADVANCE ORDERS.**
Visit our website at **www.arabesquebooks.com.**